Spears could... stayed wherever the hell that was but another, more twisted part of her wanted to end this once and for all. The only way to do that was to face him again.

Jess sipped her room-temperature wine as she recalled a line from an old Clint Eastwood movie. "Go ahead, Spears, make my day."

Poor Mrs. Simmons. She had actually prayed for Jess's help. Bless her heart. She had no idea. Jess was no hero. Far from it.

Pounding on the front door made her jump. She dropped her plastic cup in the tub.

She felt on the floor next to the tub for her Glock, her heart racing a hundred miles per hour, and snatched it up. Who the hell would be at her door at this hour?

So much for her Dirty Harry attitude.

Weapon in hand, she stood, grabbed a towel, and wrapped it around her. One dripping foot hit the floor, then the other. She flipped on the light and eased the bathroom door open...

Praise for the Novels of Debra Webb

"*Impulse* solidly establishes the Faces of Evil as the 'must read' thriller series of the year! The characters you loved in *Obsession* are back in a chilling story that could only come from the inventive mind of Debra Webb."

—Peggy Webb, author of *The Tender Mercy of Roses* (as Anna Michaels)

"Compelling main characters and chilling villains elevate Debra Webb's Faces of Evil series into the realm of high-intensity thrillers that readers won't be able to resist."

—CJ Lyons, *New York Times* bestselling author

"Just when you think Debra Webb can't get any better, she does. *Obsession* is her best work yet. This gritty, edge of your seat, white knuckle thriller is peopled with tough, credible characters and a brilliant plot that will keep you guessing until the very end. Move over Jack Reacher—Jess Harris is comin' to town."

—Cindy Gerard, *New York Times* bestselling author

"Debra Webb has done it again with *Obsession*—which may well be her best book yet—a top-notch thriller that will keep you riveted to the page and wanting more. Webb is a writer's writer, who delivers the kinds of books we all wish we had written."

—Robert Browne, author of *Trial Junkies*

Also by Debra Webb

The Faces of Evil Series

Obsession

Impulse

POWER

FACES OF EVIL

DEBRA WEBB

FOREVER

NEW YORK   BOSTON

Forever
Hachette Book Group
237 Park Avenue
New York, NY 10017

www.HachetteBookGroup.com

Printed in the United States of America

First Edition: March 2013
10 9 8 7 6 5 4 3 2 1
OPM

Forever is an imprint of Grand Central Publishing.
The Forever name and logo are trademarks of Hachette Book Group, Inc.

The Hachette Speakers Bureau provides a wide range of authors for speaking events. To find out more, go to www.hachettespeakersbureau.com or call (866) 376-6591.

The publisher is not responsible for websites (or their content) that are not owned by the publisher.

A huge thank-you to true friends and talented authors
Regan Black, Kathy Carmichael, Cindy Gerard,
Vicki Hinze, CJ Lyons, Toni Magee-Causey,
Peggy Webb, and Robert Browne. You gave me
the strength and the courage to persevere.

Acknowledgments

I would like to acknowledge and thank Dr. Michael Stone, forensics psychiatrist, whose research and analysis of evil inspired me to focus more closely on motive and the real person behind the evil when creating the villains in this series.

I will forever be grateful to the city of Birmingham for many reasons. My father was born and raised in Birmingham. His determination and kindness helped to mold me into the person I am today. Birmingham's prestigious Children's Hospital saved the life of my older daughter, giving us a priceless gift. Birmingham truly is the Magic City.

Power tends to corrupt and absolute power corrupts absolutely.

—John Emerich Edward Dalberg-Acton

POWER

Prologue

It was so cold. The chill crept deeper and deeper into her body, like a snake slithering through her veins.

How could she be so cold? Summer was in full force in Birmingham. The one thing she shouldn't be was cold.

Yet she was so damned *cold*. Her body twitched, then stilled, probably because of the strange chill.

What in the world was wrong with her?

Darcy Chandler stared up at the glittering chandelier far, far overhead. Hung high above the winding staircase that flowed upward from the grand marble foyer, the lights twinkled, sending jeweled patterns over the vivid blue walls.

She told herself to move. To get up and see that the rehearsals were on track after lunch. But she couldn't move. *Strange.* All she seemed able to do was lie there as the cold overtook her completely. It was the most peculiar sensation.

Maybe she should call out for help. Surely someone would hear her and explain why she was so very cold and why she couldn't move.

Andrea! Girls!

Her mind screamed but her lips wouldn't form the words. Her tongue felt glued to the roof of her mouth. A foul, coppery taste swelled around her tongue, threatening to spill past her lips.

This was completely ridiculous. She had to get up...to tell someone...*to do something.*

There was such silence around her...inside her...as if her very heart had stopped beating.

What a silly thought.

Something warm brushed her ear.

Someone was beside her!

Thank God. Maybe they would know why it was so cold and why she couldn't seem to move.

Darcy tried to turn her head but her body simply would not obey the command.

Wait! She could hear something!

Words...someone was whispering in her ear.

Help me! She tried to shout, but again her voice failed her.

She struggled to focus on the words but everything was changing...swirling somehow and growing dimmer and dimmer until the darkness swallowed her. She suddenly remembered the story she'd learned in Bible school about Jonah and the whale. What a thing to recall just now. She hadn't thought of Bible school in decades.

Oh, she was so very cold.

Why had the lights gone out? Why couldn't she see?

More whispered words, the sound so faint, echoed in her brain.

"Dead ballerinas don't get to dance."

I need an estimate on time of death as soon as possible."

The young doctor who Jess suspected was new to Jefferson County's coroner's office shot her a look from his kneeling position next to the victim. "Chief Harris, I just got here. There's an order to the steps I'm required to take."

Definitely new. Once he'd played his part at enough crime scenes he would understand that there was nothing orderly about murder.

Jess rearranged her lips into a smile that was as far from patient as the harried expression on the inexperienced ME's face. "I'm well aware of those steps, Doctor, but"—she glanced down the long center hall to ensure herself that Sergeant Harper was successfully keeping the potential witnesses away from the French doors and windows that overlooked the mansion's palatial gardens—"I have six little girls out back who are in various stages of hysteria and their mothers are chomping at the bit to take them home. I need time of death so I can question them with some reasonable grasp on the timeline we're dealing with here."

Before their mothers got any antsier and decided to lawyer up, Jess kept to herself.

The fact was she had heard enough rumors about the typical dance mom mentality to understand that once the shock of this tragedy wore off, things would change. Not only would lawyers be called in but the ladies would close ranks to protect whatever secrets they felt compelled to keep, particularly if those secrets carried any ramifications whatsoever on their daughters' placement on the food chain of this exclusive dance studio.

Technically, Jess was supposed to ask if they wanted to have their attorneys present during questioning, but mere technicalities had never hampered her before. With the level of panic among the girls as well as their mothers when Jess first arrived, who would be surprised if she failed to ask if one or more wanted their attorney present?

Unmoved by Jess's explanation, Doctor What's-his-name shifted his attention back to the victim sprawled in an unnatural manner on the unforgiving marble floor. "Like I said, there are steps. I'll get to that one momentarily."

Jess pressed her lips together to prevent saying something she would regret. What was it about this younger generation that prompted such flagrant disrespect? She hitched her bag higher on her shoulder. When she was his age, early thirties she guessed, Jess would never have sassed her elders. She wouldn't do that now, for pity's sake. The notion that she was nearly a decade older than the ME was considerably depressing, but it was a reality she'd learned to deal with since whizzing past the dreaded *forty* milestone.

Whoever said that sixty was the new thirty was so very full of crap. Forty wasn't even the new thirty.

Well—she pushed her glasses up the bridge of her nose—there wasn't a thing she could do about getting older. The insolence, however, she refused to stand for. Just because the still-wet-behind-the-ears ME was cute didn't mean she intended to ignore his attitude. "Excuse me..." He gazed up at her with egregious reluctance. She lifted her eyebrows in question. "Doctor...?"

"Schrader. Dr. Harlan Schrader."

"Well, Dr. Schrader, I understand you have steps, but if you would kindly just get your little thermometer out of your nifty bag and give me an approximate time of death I promise I'll be out of your way." She propped her lips into a smile she hoped wasn't too blatantly forged and added the perfunctory magic word, "Please."

"Okay." He held up his gloved hands in a show of dramatic surrender. "I'll do that right now."

"Thank you, Dr. Schrader."

Jess stepped to the door and surveyed the activity beyond the official vehicles cluttering the cobblestoned drive that encircled the massive fountain in front of the house. The historic mansion sat in the middle of seven elegant and rare acres. With any luck the towering oak and pecan trees with their low-slung branches prevented street traffic from identifying the official vehicles ominously gathered. At the street, BPD uniforms guarded the gated entrance to the property in an effort to keep the

curious and the newshounds at bay once word hit the airwaves. Having the press show up in droves, and in this
posh neighborhood they definitely would, complicated
any investigation. Frankly, she was surprised the impressive residence didn't come with its own private security
team. Oddly, there was no security, not even at the ornate,
towering entry gate, and no housekeeping staff—at least
not today.

The crime scene techs had already documented the
scene with photographs and video. Prints and trace mate-
rials were being collected now in hopes of discovering
some sort of usable evidence. Sergeant Harper had gotten the call from BPD's finest at one forty-eight. He and
Lieutenant Prescott had rushed over without mentioning
that as of today they were no longer assigned to Crimes
Against Persons. Suited Jess just fine. Sitting on her lau-
rels until a case was assigned to her new SPU, Special
Problems Unit, wasn't how she'd wanted to start off her
first week in the department.

Then again, foul play had not been established in this
case as of yet. Jess considered the position of the body
in the foyer next to the grand staircase. It appeared the
victim, Darcy Chandler, had fallen over the upstairs railing to her death. Or she'd jumped. Either way, her death
was, to their knowledge thus far, unaccompanied and
obviously of a violent nature. An investigation was standard protocol.

When she first arrived Jess had followed the techs up
the stairs and checked the landing. Her attention wandered there now. The hardwood floor was clear of debris
and substances that might have posed a trip hazard or
made it slippery. The railing didn't meet the height cri-

teria for current building codes, but with historic homes, and this one dated back to the mid-1800s, features like the railing were grandfathered in. A good thing for those who appreciated history, not so good for Ms. Chandler.

The only odd aspect of the scene Jess had noted so far was that Ms. Chandler's very expensive fuchsia-colored Gucci pumps, which exactly matched the elegant sheath she wore, sat next to the railing on the second floor. The careful placement gave the appearance that she had removed the shoes and positioned them just so as if she feared scarring her favorite pair of designer shoes while taking her fatal dive. Judging by the meticulous organization of her closets as well as the pristine condition of the house in general, the victim was unquestionably a perfectionist to some degree. That could very well explain the decision to remove and set aside her shoes. Maybe. But in Jess's opinion the shoes merited a closer look.

"I would estimate time of death," Dr. Schrader announced, drawing Jess's attention back to him as he checked his wristwatch, "at between twelve noon and one."

Less than two hours before the arrival of the BPD. "Thank you, Dr. Schrader."

The glance he cast her way advised that her gratitude was not appreciated any more than her pushy approach had been. She'd have to find a way to get back in his good graces another time. Maybe a gift certificate from one of the trendy shops in the Galleria would do the trick since the polo, sports jacket, and stone-washed jeans he wore could have been stripped right off the mannequins adorning the storefronts of said shops.

Right now, however, a woman was dead and that was

Jess's top priority. She could make nice with Dr. I'm-Too-Sexy-for-Manners later.

Armed with the vital piece of information she needed, she headed for the French doors at the end of the long hall that cut through the center of one of Birmingham's oldest and grandest homes. She squared her shoulders, cleared her throat, and exited to the terrace that flowed out into the gardens designed by some master gardener who hailed from England. And who, according to a bronze plaque that boasted the bragging rights, descended from the gardener of *the* royal family.

Only the rich and self-proclaimed fabulous would display the pedigree of the guy who cut the grass and watered the roses. Where Jess lived she was lucky if the guys who wielded the lawn mowers and weed whackers spoke English much less shared their pedigrees. That information would likely get them deported. Not that Jess minded one way or the other as long as the job was done properly. Considering she spent the better part of her formative years in a carousel of foster homes, she wasn't one to judge.

Sergeant Chet Harper met Jess just outside the grand doors. "I don't know how much longer Lieutenant Prescott can keep the girls calm and their mothers compliant. One's already demanded to know if they're suspects."

Jess resisted the urge to groan. "Thank you, Sergeant."

Prescott, the girls, and their mothers were seated in the butterfly garden. As soon as Harper had called, Jess had instructed him to see that the girls did not discuss the incident among themselves or with anyone else. Not an easy task. Particularly once the mothers had started to arrive and to demand to see their children. The girls all had cell phones and had called their mothers while the assistant teacher called 911.

Guess who showed up first? Not the police or EMS. Which guaranteed the scene had been contaminated repeatedly by little fingers and feet as well as curious and horrified mothers.

God, she didn't want to think about it. Whether a murder had occurred or not, the scene should be handled with the same vigilant protocol.

"FYI," Harper added with a knowing glance above his stylish Ray-Bans, "Andrea insisted on calling the chief."

Jess did groan this time. Andrea Denton, Chief of Police Daniel Burnett's stepdaughter from his last failed marriage and a survivor from the first case Jess had worked with the Birmingham Police Department scarcely two weeks ago. Funny, this was the third case Jess had supported since returning to her hometown and Andrea had been a part of all three. The poor girl apparently had a knack for being in the wrong place at the wrong time.

"I suppose he's coming," Jess commented, trying valiantly not to show her disappointment. There was nothing like having the boss watching over her shoulder on her first official case as a deputy chief. Even if the boss was Dan—a man with whom she had a difficult-to-define off-duty relationship. Leaving the bureau and returning to her hometown was supposed to have uncomplicated her life. *Not*.

Clearly she had been delusional to believe for one second that she could exist in the same city, much less department, with Dan and avoid complications.

"He is."

Marvelous. "Any luck locating the husband?" Darcy

Chandler, the one and only daughter of one of the city's most noteworthy families, was married to some apparently equally famous Russian dancer, now retired and teaching ballet classes to the children of Birmingham's who's who. "What's his name again?"

"Alexander Mayakovsky," Harper reminded her. "Haven't located him yet. His cell still goes straight to voice mail."

"Since this is where he works, he's obviously not at work." Frustration and impatience creased Jess's brow. She consciously forced the lines away. She had enough wrinkles, all of which had taken up residence in all the wrong places on her face. *Not that there was a right place,* she amended. What she didn't have was the vic's husband. The worst part of working an unattended death, whether accidental, suicide, or homicide, was informing the next of kin.

"Go to the vic's parents. Maybe they'll have some idea where he is. Get as much information as you can before you give them the bad news." As coldhearted as that tactic sounded, it was the only way to glean coherent information in a timely manner. And when a person died some way other than by natural causes, he or she deserved a timely investigation. Since Darcy's parents hadn't shown up, there was reason to believe unofficial word hadn't reached them yet.

That would change very soon.

"Yes, ma'am."

Harper went on his way and Jess steeled herself for entering foreign territory. "You can do this," she murmured.

As she approached the mothers, their prepubescent daughters clinging to their bosoms, all six women started talking at once.

Jess had interviewed every manner of witness and person of interest, including more than her share of sociopaths and a handful of psychopaths, but she'd never dreaded conducting interviews more than she did at this very moment.

Children absolutely, completely, and utterly unnerved her. Give her a run-of-the-mill serial killer any day of the week.

2

It was true. Though Jess loved her niece and nephew, she had no children of her own and there was a good reason for that. She lacked patience and all those other soft and earthy motherly skills. And at forty-something-or-other she had no desire to deal with the issue.

As if the good Lord wanted to remind her that going against the natural scheme of things made Him less than happy, the children all started whining at once.

Simultaneously, only in louder voices, the mothers wanted to know why they were being detained like suspects. Did they need to provide their fingerprints? Where was Alex, Darcy's husband?

Jess wouldn't mind knowing the answer to that last question herself.

"I know this is difficult," she said above their escalating demands. "But it's imperative that we all stay as calm as possible." Thankfully the whole frazzled entourage fell silent. "My name is Deputy Chief Jess Harris. At this time it won't be necessary to take any fingerprints, but I will be interviewing each of you, along with your daughters."

Evidently finding her announcement utterly disagreeable or somehow debatable, the women launched more questions.

"As I said," Jess cut them off firmly, "I know this is very difficult, but I need your patience and your cooperation. Ms. Chandler is counting on us to do this right."

The suggestion seemed to calm the mothers. Unfortunately it had a different effect on the daughters. A fresh wave of tears commenced. Jess cringed inwardly at the idea that she'd made the little girls cry again. She really was no good at this.

"Lieutenant Prescott, if you would keep these ladies comfortable while they wait for their turns, we'll get this done."

"Whatever you say, *Chief.*"

Prescott's tone was pleasant enough but the irritation simmering in her gaze didn't quite rise to the challenge. She was not any happier now than she'd been a week ago when word that Jess had gotten the position of deputy chief had flowed along the BPD grapevine like a bad Chianti.

Prescott's subsequent assignment to Jess's unit just seemed like bad karma for them both. Case in point, Prescott had wanted to start the interviews with the daughters before Jess even arrived at the scene.

No, the woman was not happy.

Jess shifted her attention to Andrea, the chief's step-daughter and the assistant teacher at this ballet school while she was home from college for the summer. "Andrea, if you would come with me to the conservatory, please."

Relieved to escape the mayhem that would no doubt descend as soon as she was out of hearing range, Jess marched toward the conservatory. Andrea followed, still dressed in her black leotard and dance slippers.

The conservatory was a massive addition to the back of the house that had likely been used at one time as a sunroom and a place for entertaining. For the past thirty or so years it had served as a dance studio. First by Darcy Chandler's nationally celebrated grandmother, then, more recently, by her and her famous husband whose name Jess still couldn't pronounce properly no matter that Harper had repeated it to her three times.

When the door was closed, Jess took a moment to survey the space. Gleaming wood floors had replaced what had likely once been tile or stone. A soaring ceiling was surrounded by towering glass walls that allowed sunlight to fill the room. The view of the gardens was nothing short of spectacular. Talk about living like royalty.

With a gesture toward the one table surrounded by chairs near the garden entrance, Jess asked, "Why don't we sit here?"

Visibly shaken, Andrea wilted into a chair. The nineteen-year-old dragged in a halting breath. "I can't believe Ms. Darcy is dead." She shook her head. "Every time I try to get on with my life something else happens."

Jess had to give her that. The poor girl had been abducted by a couple who'd gone around the bend. Then, only last week, a serial killer had used her to get at Dan in an attempt to bait Jess. Now this. She imagined Andrea was ready to put this summer behind her. Returning to college for her sophomore year was likely looking better every day.

"I can certainly understand how you would feel that way." Jess sat down on the opposite side of the table so she could keep an eye on the garden and any new arrivals. "Why don't you tell me what happened here this morning? Start with when you arrived and go from there."

Andrea moistened her lips and visibly braced herself. "I came at ten this morning and worked with the competition team. Then at noon we broke for lunch." She glanced beyond the glass walls of the conservatory toward the French doors that led from the terrace into the main house. "That's when Ms. Darcy went inside to make some calls."

Jess fished for her pad and pencil to make a few notes. "How long have you known Darcy?"

"Her grandmother was my ballet teacher until I was ten. By then Ms. Darcy and her husband, Alex, had taken over the school. I was on the competition team until I left for college. Ms. Darcy offered me a position as assistant teacher when I came home in May for the summer."

"Is Darcy's grandmother still involved with the studio?" The Chandlers were one of Birmingham's most prominent families, but between college and working for the Federal Bureau of Investigation at Quantico, Jess had lived away for the past two decades. She'd never been very good at keeping up with the city's elite anyway. But you couldn't grow up in Birmingham and not know who the Chandlers were.

"She lives at Southern Plantation. Even at eighty she attends all the local competitions."

Jess knew the place. High-end, exclusive senior living for those with the proper bank balance and no desire to be troubled with overseeing a grand home. "Was the vic— Darcy—with you and the students most of the morning?"

Andrea nodded. "Except for going in the house to make phone calls, but she came back out a few minutes after that."

"The six girls waiting on the terrace have been here since ten as well?"

She nodded again. "There were eight others but they left at lunch." Andrea shifted her gaze back to Jess then. "There are fourteen girls on the Alabama Belles competition team. The ones still here compete as the international team. They stay for lunch and then we rehearse until three when their mothers pick them up."

"There was no one else here?"

"I didn't see anyone. But I didn't go back in the house until...Katrina found her...like that."

"So Darcy served lunch to you and the girls after the others were gone?" At some point the vic was separated from her students for the last time. For how long? With whom, if anyone? Those were the answers Jess needed. Seemed simple enough, but getting straight answers from the witnesses after a tragedy like this was more often than not painstaking and complicated.

"We had a picnic," Andrea explained. "We do that a couple of times a week. Usually on Mondays and Fridays. The mothers take turns bringing the food. Today it was Ms. Dresher's turn. She dropped off the food just before noon. The girls and I brought everything outside for the picnic while Ms. Darcy saw her out."

Jess jotted down the Dresher name and the fact that she'd delivered lunch. "Did Darcy join your picnic after seeing Ms. Dresher to the door?"

"She stayed in the house." Andrea looked around the room as if maintaining eye contact was too uncomfortable. "She was still busy with phone calls. We had lunch and then came back in here to begin rehearsal."

"What time did you become aware that there had been an accident?" The call had come into 911 about one fifteen. Judging by the ME's estimation of time of death, Chandler may not have been dead very long when her body was discovered.

"We were about to start rehearsal but we needed the boas for our routine and I sent Katrina inside to get them," Andrea explained, sadness clouding her face. "The girls had been playing upstairs earlier, before rehearsals began this morning, and two of them had left their boas up there. Some of the moms have appointments or whatever and drop their girls off a little early. Ms. Darcy lets them play in the upstairs den." She chewed her lower lip a moment or two before continuing. "A few minutes after going for the boas Katrina came rushing back. She was in tears and shouting that something was wrong with Ms. Darcy."

"When you say a few minutes, do you mean ten or fifteen? Five?"

Andrea shrugged. "I don't know. The other girls and I were doing warm-ups and talking. I really didn't pay attention."

That was as good as Jess was going to get on the timing. "So you didn't see Darcy alive again after she went inside the house with Ms. Dresher?"

"The next time I saw her she was . . . dead."

Jess surveyed the girls waiting somberly with their mothers. All six wore hot pink leotards. Four had their boas hanging around their shoulders. Her interest lingered on the Dresher woman and her daughter Katrina. Harper had given Jess a who's who rundown.

"Did anything out of the ordinary happen this morning?" Jess asked, focusing on Andrea once more. "Did Darcy seem upset about anything?"

Andrea shrugged again. "No more than usual." She twisted her fingers together. "She and Mr. Alex are separated and things have been awkward."

Instincts on point, Jess rephrased a pivotal question. "Did you see Alex today?"

"Not today. He..." Andrea fell silent.

Jess leaned forward a fraction. "It's very important that we know as many details as possible if we're going to understand what happened."

"Ms. Darcy filed for divorce. They've been fighting for weeks." Her slender shoulders slumped with defeat and disloyalty. "The rumor is he's cheating on her with one of the moms."

The image of Darcy Chandler lying on that cold marble floor, her skull likely shattered along with untold other internal injuries, filled Jess's mind. The shoes removed and set carefully aside filtered in next. That part just didn't fit, unless they were already there before Chandler's fall. Maybe forgotten for some reason. But then where were the shoes she had been wearing at the time of death? Had to be those Gucci pumps. They matched her dress. A dress that she would have had to hike up in order to throw a leg over that upstairs railing. That, Jess would come back to. For now, she needed info on Chandler's husband, the Russian.

"Do you have reason to suspect that rumor is true?" This was a small, elite dance studio. The likelihood of any secret staying secret for long was somewhere in the vicinity of zero.

Andrea scrunched her face as if it pained her to speak

on the subject. "That's what everybody thinks but I can't say for sure it's true."

"Any idea which mother the others thought was the troublemaker?" Beyond Andrea, six of the mothers waited—all wealthy, all gorgeous, whether by nature or by design. Could be any one of them.

Andrea gave another shake of her head, her eyes carefully averted. She suspected someone but she wasn't saying. Jess could push for that when and if the time came.

"Andrea, would you say you know Darcy as well as any of the other assistant teachers or students, or moms, for that matter?"

Hesitation slowed her response but she nodded with conviction.

"I know you're upset," Jess hedged, "but I want you to answer the next question without analyzing your answer first. I'll ask the question and you say exactly what comes to mind in that instant. Okay?"

"O . . . kay."

Jess reached across the table and patted her hand. "Thank you, Andrea. I know this is just an awful time for you, but you're helping more than you know."

Tears shimmered in her eyes as she nodded, her lips pressed tightly together.

"Here we go. Do you believe"—Jess watched Andrea's face closely for the coming reaction—"Darcy was capable of taking her own life?"

"No!" Her eyebrows drew together as she underscored her answer with an adamant shake of her head. "No way. She would never do that!"

"Not even with her husband cheating and divorce looming?" Jess had no evidence that indicated one manner of death over the other at this time. Still, a nasty divorce slanted the already odd circumstances in a more disturbing direction. Were there financial problems to boot? Not from the looks of things, but looks could be deceiving.

"That's impossible," Andrea stated firmly, her eyes reflecting that certainty. "I heard her talking to him just before she went into the house to see Ms. Dresher out. She wanted to make him pay for his infidelity."

"Did he stop by?" A few moments ago Andrea had said she'd seen no one other than the dancers and Chandler. Then she remembered Dresher. Cutting Andrea some slack, extreme anxiety often caused confusion. But if the Russian was here anywhere near the time of death, Jess needed to know.

"She got a call from him on her cell. At least I think it was him. Ms. Darcy told whoever it was that she was going to make them pay one way or the other. Then she had to go because Ms. Dresher showed up with lunch." Andrea flattened her palms on the table and stared directly into Jess's eyes. "She was really angry. If you knew Ms. Darcy you would know she's not the kind of person who would admit defeat and just kill herself. She would fight." Tears spilled past her lashes. "No way did she do this on purpose."

Jess nodded. "Thank you, Andrea. Anything else you think of, you call me immediately."

The door opened and Chief of Police Daniel Burnett walked in. As if it hadn't been only yesterday when Jess had last seen him, naked and sprawled in her bed, her entire being went on alert like a GPS locking in on a destination.

He looked damned good for a guy who'd been beaten

and stabbed less than a week ago. Her throat tightened at the memory of those long hours they'd spent entwined in each other's arms on Saturday night…and Sunday morning.

"Jess." He nodded to her, a flash of remembered heat in those blue eyes, before shifting his focus to Andrea. "You okay, sweetie?"

The girl burst into tears as she jumped out of her chair and ran into his arms.

That was Jess's cue to move on. "I'll give you two some privacy. I have interviews to conduct."

In view of the time and the emotional state of the girls and their mothers, not to mention Prescott's scowl, Jess opted to share the load. She usually preferred to question potential witnesses herself but that didn't make sense in this situation.

With a BPD uniform keeping the remaining daughters and mothers company, Prescott took one of the girls and her mother to another venue in the garden while Jess interviewed Corrine Dresher and her daughter, Katrina, in yet another. No wonder they'd needed such a fancy gardener. This place was like a maze, with dozens of lovely little seating areas created from nothing more than nature's glory.

"When you entered the house to get the two missing boas," Jess asked the girl when they were settled, "did you hear anything at all? A door? A phone? Footsteps?"

Katrina's face pinched with visible effort as she thought hard on the question before answering. "It was quiet. I could hear the grandfather clock ticking. Then I saw Ms. Darcy on the floor."

"Did Ms. Darcy say anything or move at all?"

Katrina shook her head. "I thought she was asleep, but her eyes were open."

"Did you try to wake her up?"

The girl's eyes widened as she nodded. "I shook her and called her name but she didn't say anything." Katrina touched her ear, then her lips. "There was blood. So I ran to get Andrea." Big tears rolled down her cheeks. "Did I do something wrong when I tried to wake her up?" She turned to her mother. "I didn't mean to do anything wrong. I really didn't!"

"Can't you see how upset she is?" Ms. Dresher demanded. "You've held these girls here for more than an hour and we just want to go home. This has been horrifying for us all."

Jess reached for patience. This mother was, as far as they knew, the last person to see Darcy Chandler alive. The daughter was the one to find her body. Anything either of them remembered could make all the difference. "I understand, ma'am. I have just a few more questions and I promise you can go home then."

Ms. Dresher dabbed at her eyes. "I can't believe you're doing this to these girls. Haven't they been through enough?" She huffed an exasperated sound. "Just do what you must so we can go home and mourn this terrible, terrible tragedy."

"All righty then." Jess focused her attention back on the daughter. "Katrina, I like your boa. Is it the only one that's white?" The other girls had black boas, at least the ones who were wearing theirs. Jess made a mental note to check upstairs for the two that were missing.

Katrina's stricken expression brightened. "I'm the best. Whoever performs the best the previous week gets to wear the white boa. Mr. Alex picks the superior performance each Saturday. This time he picked me. I get special privileges all week, like being Andrea's helper."

"Did you see Mr. Alex today?"

She wagged her head. "Ms. Darcy said he won't be our teacher anymore."

The split between Chandler and her husband appeared to be common knowledge as Andrea had indicated.

The girl peered up at her mother. "Who'll be our teacher now?"

Both erupted in tears.

Jess managed to get a few answers out of the mother. She'd brought the lunch, veggie pizzas and vitamin water, as Andrea stated. Chandler had seemed fine when she'd walked Dresher to the door on her way out. She had gotten a call on her cell but Dresher could not speculate as to the identity of the caller. The two women had hardly exchanged a dozen words during her brief visit. Darcy Chandler was alive and well and ranting at her caller, Dresher insisted, when she departed the premises. Some minutes later, Dresher couldn't say how many, though she willingly showed Jess the call list on her cell, she received a call from her daughter who was hysterical and who had just gone into the house and found the body. That call had come from Katrina's cell phone at one-oh-two, which narrowed time of death considerably.

Darcy Chandler had fallen between twelve fifteen and one o'clock. And based on what they had so far, she had been alone in the house...just Darcy and those damned shoes.

Even though the ME had taken the body away, Jess suggested that Ms. Dresher and her daughter not exit through the house. The child didn't need any further trauma, and no one needed access to the house until Jess had another look around.

The rest of the interviews went the same. No one saw or heard anything. Darcy Chandler seemed distracted but otherwise fine. No one admitted to knowing any additional details about the divorce but all appeared upset at the idea that the teaching team had been torn apart. And all showed more concern about who would take over the girls' dance instruction than the fact that a woman was dead. Extending the benefit of the doubt, Jess supposed the lack of compassion could be chalked up to shock.

By the time the interviews were completed and Jess returned to the conservatory, Annette Denton had arrived to take her daughter, Andrea, home.

Jess composed a smile for the woman who was Dan's most recent ex-wife. That part might not have bothered Jess so much were the woman not totally gorgeous and entirely elegant. Everything about her was perfect.

"Annette."

The other woman gifted Jess with a forlorn glance. "This is just devastating." To Dan she said, "I can't believe she would fall like that. She's been a dancer her whole life. Balance is everything."

"You knew her well?" Jess inquired.

"Darcy and Annette have been friends since elementary school," Dan answered for her. "They attended Brighton Academy together."

Jess wanted to remind him that she was speaking to Annette but she opted to ignore him instead. However, she did make a mental note of the fact that Annette had attended the same fancy school as Dan, which meant they had known each other most of their lives. News to Jess, who had gone to public school and hadn't met Dan until she was seventeen. Just one more indication of how different her world and Dan's had been. She hadn't known any of his rich-kid friends back then...only him and that crazy wild passion that burned between them.

"If she didn't lose her balance and fall," Jess countered, "that would mean she jumped." Which was a strange way to commit suicide since, at that height, the odds of survival with horrifying consequences were far too great. "Do you have reason to believe Ms. Chandler had sufficient motive to want to end her life?"

The woman's marriage was on the rocks, but would that have been enough to push her over the edge, figuratively and literally? Not according to Andrea and the others. If Annette was a close friend of Darcy's, she might be privy to inside knowledge that the kids couldn't know or comprehend.

A number of emotions played across Annette's face, not the least of which was confusion. "Are you suggesting suicide?" She shook her head. "I don't believe that. Darcy would never do that to herself, much less her parents or her students. She loved life—her life—far too much."

"Would her husband want her out of the way?" The home and dance studio were Chandler's, obviously. What did he stand to lose in this divorce?

"Alexander?" Annette laughed but quickly pressed her fingers to her lips and adopted a properly shamed countenance. "I'm sorry, but he's absolutely not that desperate. And he loved Darcy. He just didn't have it in him to remain faithful. She knew that about him. She'd simply had enough this time. A divorce was inevitable from the day they said 'I do.'"

"Do you know how we can contact him?"

Annette's hand went to her chest. "Are you saying he doesn't know?"

"We haven't been able to locate him."

Dan stepped away to take a call on his cell.

"He has a loft in Five Points." Annette frowned. "He's not answering his cell?"

"Unfortunately not, and his voice-mail box is full," Jess elaborated.

"The husband is downtown," Dan announced as he rejoined their friendly little huddle. "BPD picked him up a few minutes ago at the Botanical Gardens. He was meditating. Chief Black is interviewing him."

Jess's jaw dropped, but not because they'd found the missing husband meditating at a local point of interest. "Why is Black interviewing him?" This was her case. Her detectives had been the first on the scene. Her first real day on the job and already the good old boys' network had reared its ugly head.

"I should take Andrea home." Annette gave Dan a hug, then smiled briefly for Jess. "Let me know if there is anything else I can do."

When Andrea had gotten in another hug, the strikingly beautiful mother and her equally stunning offspring departed the premises.

Jess waited until she had Dan's attention. "Why," she demanded, "is Deputy Chief Black interviewing the husband?"

"Crimes Against Persons does homicide, Jess," he reminded her unnecessarily. "*If* this is a homicide, Black isn't too happy that you tried to hijack his case."

"I didn't try to hijack anything. My detectives got the

call. They were the first on the scene. I was under the impression that murder fell within the scope of my unit as well." So this was the way it was going to be. No surprise. The Chandler case would be a high-profile one whatever the cause of death turned out to be. Black didn't want Jess horning in on his territory under the circumstances.

"We can iron this out downtown."

"Fine." Jess grabbed her bag. "As long as everyone involved understands that this is my case, we're good."

Dan took her by the arm, waylaying her departure. She mentally kicked herself for shivering at his touch. Damn it. She was old enough to have better control than that. Apparently age had nothing to do with chemistry or one's ability to contain it. A textbook illustration was the idea that she was ridiculously jealous of Annette Denton. That was just wrong.

"As good as you are at the job, Jess," Dan said, his tone and his gaze uncomfortably direct, sobering her instantly, "there will be no playing favorites. We talked at length on the subject this weekend. You said, and I agreed, that on the job there can be no perception of favoritism. We follow the chain of command. This case belongs to Crimes Against Persons. Are we clear?"

"Clear as a bell." She withdrew her arm from his hold and walked away.

Why would she want this case anyway? Let Black deal with the tutus and the overbearing dance moms.

"You missed your appointment this morning," Dan called after her. "I rescheduled for the same time tomorrow morning. Do not miss that one."

Jess hesitated at the door. Here they were, trying to pretend the weekend hadn't changed anything between them.

She didn't know how she wanted to feel about that. The woman in her wanted to be incensed at his all-business attitude. But this was what she'd wanted. No. Not wanted. Demanded. She had made the rules. Off duty they could explore this thing that still burned between them after twenty-odd years. But on the job, he was the chief of police and she was just another of his deputy chiefs.

Funny, she had liked the concept so much better in theory.

Determined to play by the very rules she had laid down as law, she turned and gave him a big smile before saying what needed to be said. "You're the boss."

3

Dan Burnett understood there would be hell to pay with Jess for the decision he'd made on the Chandler case, but there was no way around it. Keeping the peace in the department and ensuring the smooth operation of all divisions was his job.

The job was rarely easy, and at moments like this he wondered why he had ever agreed to accept the position. Years of counseling likely wouldn't uncover all the reasons he'd felt it necessary to attain the highest law enforcement position in the city. Then there were the marriages and divorces...and Jess. His and Jess's relationship would provide enough fodder for a multivolume boxed set of couples therapy journals.

Nothing was ever simple or routine between the two of them.

Now was a perfect example. Jess stood before his desk, arms crossed over her chest as daggers flew at him from those furious brown eyes. Her blond hair and the sleek-fitting rose-colored dress with the matching sexy high heels could not camouflage what was on her mind. But they went a hell of a long way in distracting him from what he knew had to be done.

Oh yes. There was hell to pay, and he had the decidedly unpleasant task of doing the paying.

"My detectives and I were on the scene first. Territorial issues aside, answering the call from the initial officers on the scene should account for something. The least Chief Black could do is acknowledge my assessment and consider my suggestions for interviewing the family."

"Have a seat and we'll go over this once more if that'll make you happy," Dan offered.

As difficult as squaring off with her like this was, their future working relationship depended upon the standard he set now. Today. On this case. With their shared history common knowledge and considering the position he had created specifically for her, the whole department was watching their every move. Jess had reminded him of that point repeatedly over the past week. The problem this morning was that she wanted the Chandler case and Deputy Chief Black was claiming dibs. An unaccompanied death with violent circumstances could logically fall under the scope of either Jess's new unit or Black's division. Admittedly there was some gray area here, but Dan could not afford even the suggestion of favoritism. The buck stopped here, and this was the first necessary step in proving to the entire department that their shared history carried no impact on his and Jess's ability to do the job.

Even if finding the zipper on that dress and getting

it off her this instant was the prevalent image moving through his mind. It had been a long day. He was weak.

Her eyes narrowed, warning that his high-handedness was duly noted and absolutely not appreciated. Or maybe she'd read his mind. "Darcy Chandler's husband has not one witness who can confirm his alibi between eleven this morning and one this afternoon." She made a face that indicated just how unbelievable she found his alibi. "He was driving around and then meditating at the Botanical Gardens?" She spread her arms wide apart and turned her palms upward in disbelief. "*Really?* We're just going to take his word for that and give him a pat on the back and say how sorry we are for his loss?"

"Chief Black was showing respect for the deceased and the husband who, so far, we have no reason to suspect of wrongdoing other than his inability to remain faithful, and that's hearsay," Dan pointed out. "Down here in the South, if you think back, I'm sure you'll recall, respect and compassion are SOP, especially at times like this."

Jess dropped her head back and made an exasperated sound.

Her assessments were valid. There was no denying that. Mayakovsky had stated that he'd spent a good deal of the morning driving around arguing with his wife by phone and attempting to make sense of what came next in their marriage. That part of his statement, at least the calls, was corroborated by the victim's cell phone call list. During the interview Mayakovsky had broken down in tears at the idea that his final interaction with his wife was such a fierce battle. She had made up her mind to proceed with the dissolution of their union and he'd been beside himself. He'd said things he now regretted, but he hadn't harmed her. He swore over and over that the last time he saw his wife she was alive and well.

Dan understood a little something about the end of a relationship and the dreaded journey through divorce. A man didn't always show the depth of pain he experienced, but the inability to convey those emotions in no way diminished his pain. In Dan's estimation Mayakovsky was sincere when he lamented the agony of having his wife kick him out of their home, and then just this past Saturday she further informed him that he would no longer be a part of the renowned dance school in any capacity. Those statements were substantiated by the interviews Jess and Prescott had conducted. Mayakovsky seemed genuinely shocked and devastated that his wife was dead.

"Chief Black is working with the cell carrier to confirm exactly where Mayakovsky was while he made those calls to his wife," Dan added, no matter that Jess was fully aware of the steps. "We'll know in a day or two whether or not he's telling the truth."

Jess harrumphed her discontent and her arms went back over her chest. "Like it'll matter in a day or two. The first words out of the victim's father's mouth when he heard the news was a demand to know what the hell his son-in-law had done. That tells us something about the relationship between Chandler and her husband. And Black just lets him go his merry way? A well-traveled man of means with a valid passport? By the time Black's finished checking out his alibi, Maya-whatever-his-name-is could be back in the motherland. Do we have an extradition agreement with Russia?"

She was not making this easy. "The husband is under

surveillance. If he attempts to flee we will intervene. Since, at this time, we have no evidence indicating he's guilty of any crime, he has the right to mourn his wife. In fact, we don't even know if her death was anything more than a tragic accident." He paused, dialed back the frustration and impatience that had been ramping up the decibel level of his voice. "There's this little"—he held his thumb and forefinger close together—"thing called the law that determines in large degree our actions on this case and all others. Until we have proof this was no accident and that there is guilt on his part, we can't hold or charge Mayakovsky."

Completely unmoved by his logic or his authority, it seemed, Jess popped her chin up even higher in barefaced defiance. "It wasn't an accident, Dan."

At least she'd called him by his first name. Maybe there was hope she would get over being mad as blazes at him. Why that continued to matter more than whether she paid the proper respect to his position defied all reason.

"The shoes alone aren't sufficient evidence, Jess. That said"—he held up his hands stop-sign fashion when she would have interrupted—"you don't know Chief Black or the others here like I do. I can assure you that he will give this case due diligence. He's meeting with Chandler's attorney right now to see if he'll share any thoughts on his client's frame of mind or any suggestions of violence she may have shared relevant to her husband."

"Good luck with that," Jess grumbled. "Zacharias Whitman didn't get to be Birmingham's most notorious attorney by advocating the team spirit. He's not going to give up anything unless there's something to be gained and if the victim's parents tell him to keep his mouth shut, he will. Money talks and"—she flashed Dan a bogus smile—"you know the rest."

"I will remind Chief Black that you are anxious to support his efforts in whatever capacity he needs."

She laughed in that rich earthy quality that made him think of the other primal sounds he'd plied from her this weekend. "I won't hold my breath," she let him know. "I spent all morning searching for briefings because no one invited me to their party. And since SPU doesn't have any cases, Prescott, Harper, and I ran out of things to talk about fifteen minutes into ours."

"I'm certain none of the briefings were relocated or canceled because of you, Jess." As frustrated as she made him, there were the moments like this when she confessed to feeling left out and misunderstood and he wanted to hug the hell out of her and promise her it wouldn't happen again. How she went from livid to vulnerable in three beats he would never know. "Maybe when you completed the SPU briefing you should have gone to that appointment with Dr. Oden. I got my appointment out of the way first thing this morning."

"I told you it slipped my mind. Then I got the call about Chandler and I had more important things to think about. Like how a woman with perfect balance falls over a railing in her own home. And why the shoes she was wearing ended up set aside just so before the fall."

Same old Jess. As much as he wanted to be at his wit's end with her methods, he never ceased to be amazed by her view of the cases, the victims, and life in general. Unorthodox didn't begin to describe her blunt, overbearing tactics. She bemoaned her lack of friends and the idea that the others guarded their territory with rabid ferocity around her, when the truth was that those who knew her respected her immensely. Those who didn't were terrified of landing on her radar.

"I can call you tomorrow morning and remind you about the appointment."

She retrieved her cell phone so she could wave it at him. "I set a reminder. I'll be there."

"And"—he leaned forward and picked up the folder on his desk—"I have a case for SPU."

She sank into the chair in front of his desk, equal measures of surprise and suspicion vying for top billing as her petulance faded. "What kind of case? Why didn't you tell me that already instead of badgering me about Black and respect?" As she dug for her reading glasses, her attention settled on the red folder in his hand.

Badgering? He wasn't even going there. "DeShawn Simmons. Nineteen. African American. Volunteer of the year with Hands on Birmingham. He's supposed to start Jeff State next month. The first ever in his family to achieve that goal. The bad news is he left home for work on Friday afternoon and no one has seen him since."

Jess accepted the folder and opened it to view the contents. "No one reported him missing until today?"

"When he wasn't home by Saturday morning his grandmother filed a report but, considering his age and the lack of any suggestion of vulnerability or foul play, was told there was nothing the police could do at that point."

"No criminal record?"

"None." Dan wished he could turn back time forty-eight hours and get a do-over on this one. It shouldn't have happened. Closer consideration had been warranted.

"Graduated valedictorian from Parker High School. He had to be doing something right, until recently anyway." Jess closed the folder. "Were his cell phone records ordered? His friends and coworkers interviewed? Anything?"

"The case just made its way here. Some preliminary groundwork was started this morning but nothing to speak of. You have all we know so far right there."

Her eyebrows lifted in blatant incredulity. "Which isn't much." She tapped the folder. "The address is in the Druid Hills area. Are the crime statistics still having a negative impact on the neighborhood?"

The area had long suffered economic and social issues, drawing the urban criminal element like flies to a rotting carcass. No matter that the city, with Mayor Pratt serving as a primary catalyst, had put forth considerable effort to draw opportunities into the neighborhood, it wasn't happening. Little had changed that painfully repetitive cycle of despair in recent decades.

"There's been some revitalization, but lately the gang activity has been on the increase. Our Gang Task Force is headed up by Captain Ted Allen. Black has already run the kid's name by Allen and he's not on any of their watch lists. Considering this case represents the kind that all too often falls between the cracks of the system, Chief Black and I believe this might be a good jumping off point for SPU."

"Doesn't hurt that I'm familiar with the neighborhood."

"Christ, I hadn't thought of that." Damn it. How could he forget something like that? "Is that a problem, Jess?" Her parents had been killed in an automobile accident when she was ten. An aunt she and her sister had scarcely known had taken them in. One year and four drug and prostitution busts later, Jess and her sister had been removed from the aunt's home in Druid Hills and placed in foster care.

"It's not a problem." Jess gave a shake of her head. "I have no idea if my aunt's still alive, much less where she lives."

No matter, he felt like an ass for not remembering. "If you're certain you're okay with this, we need you on it. This is going to be a hot-button issue."

"I guess that explains the spiffy red folder."

"Starting now we're giving this case priority." He'd scarcely gotten back to his office from the Chandler home when the mayor had called. His office had been fielding questions and complaints all morning. Mayor Pratt wanted this taken care of ASAP.

Dan had a long list of differences with the mayor, but on this one he was right.

Jess's dark brown eyes narrowed again. "It's a missing persons case. He's not underage and there appears to be no indication of foul play or vulnerability, according to what you have here. What's the hot-button issue beyond determining whether he left of his own free will?"

"This may turn into a race issue."

"This is Birmingham, Alabama. That's not a hot-button issue; it's a way of life. And it'll stay that way until we stop seeing color and social class and start seeing people. Why is this young man's disappearance any different from that of the other four or five thousand folks who went missing across this country in the last forty-eight hours?"

The media would be blowing this out of proportion the next few days. There was no point in pretending it was going away without a public outcry. BPD had dropped the ball on this one in their eyes. Jess knew it as surely as he did, but she intended to make him say it.

"You're well aware that two weeks ago we pulled out all the stops for five missing girls, all age nineteen, all Caucasian. This family wants equal attention. No one can blame them. Their grandson is missing and they're terrified. When they didn't get the initial response hoped for, they sought out other avenues."

"The press has already called you or the mayor," she surmised.

"Friends of the family are holding a rally at nine tonight. The press is going to be all over it." Dan turned his hands up. "The officer who took the report followed the rules. BPD has made no true missteps legally speaking, but we can't afford the bad press those kinds of accusations bring. Frankly, as long as we have the manpower, the extra effort should be made in every missing persons case. At the very least I want to see the cases treated individually. I'd like that change to happen now."

"We both know that's hardly feasible with budgets shrinking every year."

"Maybe with SPU we can do more," he pressed. This was a prime example of how badly they needed Jess's extraordinary ability for seeing what no one else did. "That was the catalyst for forming a new unit. No family should have to wonder where their child, two or twenty, is when he or she doesn't show up as expected. Particularly a young man like Simmons who has no history of trouble and who is on his way to a bright future."

"You're right." She looked at the folder she held, then glanced back at him. "SPU can make a difference with cases like this. We'll get right on it."

"Take Harper with you to visit the family. The sooner the better." There was another aspect to this case that he'd have to explain eventually but not today. He needed her on this and he needed her completely focused.

"If he's available we can go now."

"Make him available, Jess. I don't want you making house calls in that neighborhood alone. Keep in mind that time is of the essence. We need to find this young man and prove to our citizens that things aren't the same as they were in the sixties."

"You sure about that? As the saying goes, you can put lipstick on a pig but...it's still a pig. Would we still be having this conversation if racial and social lines had really changed? The case involving Andrea and the other girls got immediate attention because they're white and nearly all are from a family high enough up the social ladder to generate real noise and to call in favors." She tapped his desk with the red folder for emphasis. "Feel free to correct me if I'm wrong."

The lady had always been disarmingly blunt. "You made your point. SPU was created to close that gap. To ensure *no one* gets overlooked. We're making the effort, Jess. Starting right now."

She stood. "Then maybe you need to have an all-hands staff meeting and let the folks over in the other precincts know that things have changed. When a nineteen-year-old with absolutely no criminal record and everything going for him goes missing, we don't need to give the bad guys a forty-eight-hour head start."

He pushed to his feet. No one else on this planet could rile his indignation quicker and still be right on the matter. "Already on the schedule. Monday morning, nine sharp. You're the guest speaker." She would be, at any rate, as soon as he scheduled the meeting. By tomorrow noon it would be on the agenda of every division chief in the department. Contrary to the statement he'd just made, maybe he hadn't thought of it first, but he would make it happen.

"They may not like what I have to say," Jess warned.

"Why change strategies now?"

"I'm right about the Chandler case," she stated again, for the record apparently. "If Black isn't careful his killer will get away. It happens all the time. Remember the Susan Powell case? Mother goes missing. Husband is sent home and a mountain of evidence and motive are overlooked. And look what it cost? Her children are dead, too, because her crazy husband got away the first go-around. Funny how easy it is to overlook the obvious sometimes."

"Jess," he offered patiently, "trust me when I say that we were investigating cases like this and doing a pretty damned good job before you showed up. If your instincts are on target, Black will reach those same conclusions and he will get the job done. You're just angry because it's not your case. That's not a good foundation for the relationships you're building here. If you want the others to accept you and invite you to play, you have to accept them and show some trust and respect for their abilities as well."

That was more than he'd intended to say but she'd pushed all the right buttons. Jess was very good at pushing his buttons. In and out of bed.

"You're right, of course," she announced as she reached for that huge black leather bag she carried. "I'll work on that. As soon as I find this missing young man."

She gave him her back and marched toward the door. For about two seconds he got a little caught up in watching the sway of her hips. Kicking his mind out of the sack, he called after her, "Don't go without Harper."

"Yes, sir." She slammed the door behind her.

He focused on lowering his frustration level and tried to relax in hopes that enough deep breaths would reverse the hard-on sparring with her had aroused. Even when she was cutting him off *above* the knees he wanted to spread hers and burrow between them.

The intercom buzzed, followed by his secretary's voice. "Chief, Mrs. Burnett is on line two for you."

No need for deep breaths after all. A call from his mother did the trick instantly. He grabbed the receiver and pressed the necessary button. "Hey, Mom. Everything okay?"

"Is there any news on Darcy?"

She'd called twice already. "Not yet. Chief Black may have news for the family by tomorrow."

"I just can't believe she's gone. You have to get to the bottom of this, Son. We're all depending on you."

"We'll know more when we have the preliminary autopsy results," he told her. The Chandlers were friends of his mother's and whenever a case involved part of her social network she made sure he didn't forget.

"What about Jess? Is she working on the case, too?"

Since he was seventeen there had been one absolute certainty in his life. His mother did not like Jess. That she asked about her in connection with the case was surprising to say the least. "Jess is working on a missing persons case. Deputy Chief Black and Crimes Against Persons is handling the Chandler case."

His mother hummed a note of surprise, or maybe it was disappointment. "In any event, you'll keep me informed, I'm sure. Darcy's family is just devastated. Daniel, they need answers to this tragedy."

With a few more assurances she finally let him go. For the second time today he hoped he'd made the right decision. The rules or Jess's instincts?

Black had nearly thirty years in the department. He and his detectives knew how to investigate a case. Still, Jess had drilled her point about the shoes deep into Dan's skull. He'd invited her to watch the interview with the husband since, as she'd pointed out at least a dozen times, she was the first on the scene and had interviewed the dancers and their mothers. Chandler's family and friends were being interviewed even now. Maybe he should have suggested that she and Black work as a team on this one.

But she was needed on the Simmons case. His department had made a mistake on that one and he hoped like hell it wasn't too late to make it right.

As much as Dan respected every member of his department, he knew in his gut that if anyone could find Simmons it was Jess.

He relegated Jess and her warnings to the back of his priority list for the time being and focused on clearing his desk. The autopsy report and evidence analysis would provide better insight on the Chandler case. Most of the assessments at this point were speculation. It was difficult to comfort a family when so few facts had been established. They needed the facts, not speculation.

Who was he trying to convince? Dan shook his head and chuckled at his own self-doubts. Even twenty years later Jess still possessed the power to make him second-guess his every move and decision. She had always held that power over him. Almost always bested him.

His cell vibrated against his desk. He shuffled through the files and papers to find it. Surely Jess and Harper hadn't run into trouble already.

Annette calling.

He exhaled a heavy breath. He hoped things were better with Andrea. She'd been a mess since the kidnapping. After today, she may have fallen apart again.

If Andrea needed him, he was there.

A rap on his door prevented him from accepting the call.

The door opened and his secretary poked her head inside. "Chief Burnett, Mayor Pratt is here to see you."

He'd known this was coming. He just hadn't expected a face-to-face visit. "Send him in, Sheila."

Five seconds later the door opened again and Birmingham's esteemed mayor strode into the room. Sheila closed the door behind him. Taller than Dan, Joseph Pratt had maintained his lean build well into his sixties. He came from old money and enjoyed the power of holding public office without care as to the modest salary.

"Dan, I'm certain your time is limited, so I'll get right to the point."

"I'm caught up at the moment, Joe. Have a seat." Dan had to wonder why the mayor would bother coming over for a discussion so brief that surely it could have been handled by phone just as their discussion about the Simmons case had been earlier today.

Pratt settled into a chair, his posture as well as his expression far from relaxed. "I'm here to urge you to ensure a speedy resolution to the Chandler case."

The woman had scarcely been dead half a dozen hours. "I'm aware that your families are close," Dan offered. The Chandlers and Pratts shared a passion for everything from the Historic Preservation Society to the Arts Council. Both families went back several generations and continued to represent the wealthiest of Birmingham's residents. "I'm certain you understand that we will do all we can as quickly as we can."

The urgency on Pratt's face signaled he was far from satisfied with that response. "Darcy and Alexander have been frequent companions of my son Jarrod and his wife, Cynthia, for a number of years now. We do not want to see this drawn out in the media. The swifter the action by this department, the less time for the media to sensationalize this tragedy. There are those who thrive on gossip and innuendoes when it comes to families like the Chandlers."

"That is an unfortunate reality," Dan agreed. "I can assure you that we will work as quickly as possible on this case, just as we will on the Simmons case." He felt confident that the mayor hadn't forgotten his earlier request already.

"Chief Black assures me he is handling the Chandler case," Pratt noted.

Dan shouldn't be surprised that the man had spoken to Black already. Yet somehow he was. "That is correct."

"Good." Pratt nodded. "Chief Harris would bring undue media attention to the case, and the family simply doesn't need that sort of added nuisance."

Oh, Dan got it now. This wasn't about a speedy closure for the Chandler family. This was about keeping the connection between the Pratts and the Chandlers off the media's radar. "Of course. With Jarrod running for the senate, we wouldn't want him connected to any sort of scandal." And considering Darcy Chandler's husband's numerous affairs, a scandal was likely.

"I knew you'd understand." Pratt stood. "Those of us in positions of community oversight must always consider the greater good." He straightened his elegant suit jacket. "I'll be expecting regular updates on the progress of your investigation."

With that final order on the table, Pratt departed as quickly as he'd arrived.

Dan had a feeling Jess was right about this one. And no one, particularly not the mayor, was going to like the way it played out.

His cell vibrated, dragging him from the troubling thoughts.

Annette calling.

Again.

4

Druid Hills, 7:20 p.m.

As a kid Jess had lived just two streets over from this one. The neighborhood looked pretty much the same now. Sadly neglected; unnervingly hopeless. The major difference she saw today was the obvious signs of gang tagging. Thirty years ago the only gangs in the area were local ruffians with an itch to intimidate and a dime bag to sell.

Things had changed dramatically. Not just because of the symbols and threats spray-painted on the abandoned homes but because of the increasing lack of concern for one's neighbor. Turning a blind eye was as rampant as drugs even here in the heart of the good old South.

"Several residents have reported gang activities in the neighborhood," Harper mentioned as he drove through the cluttered streets, the yards and curbs lined with vehicles in various stages of disrepair. "That abandoned house"—he indicated a run-down ranch coming up on the right—"is one of many that pop up in police reports on a regular basis."

Gang activities were increasing across the country, particularly in the financially devastated, chronically neglected neighborhoods of larger cities. It wasn't enough that the United States had its share of homegrown gangs; there were increasing numbers of imports. And like the car business where the imports worked extra hard to outsell those manufactured domestically, the imported gangs were ruthless in their attempts to gain control of a given territory.

"How efficient is our Gang Task Force?" Jess had reviewed the divisions but there hadn't been an opportunity for her to do in-depth research on any one in particular. She would need to familiarize herself with all the BPD's divisions and various units. To do that she needed time. Two weeks wasn't nearly long enough in light of the fact that those fourteen days included dealing with multiple abductions and her own personal stalker, a serial murderer called the Player.

"Word is Captain Allen is good," Harper said. "He has twenty years under his belt and he's organized an outstanding group of cops on his task force. They're on top of this for sure, but they need all the help they can get." Harper slowed for the turn onto Fifteenth Avenue. "This is the kind of support that typically falls to an SPU if a department is lucky enough to have one." He sent her a quick smile. "Lowering the incidence of violent crimes is a number one priority of any Special Problems Unit."

He was preaching to the choir. "At least we have a case now and can actually work toward that goal. Since the one we were accused of hijacking was taken from us." She was obsessing about Darcy Chandler. Not attractive no matter how it was accessorized.

"I guess we did. Hijack the case, I mean." Harper chuckled. "I knew when I took the call that the case didn't fall within the purview of our mission statement."

"Our unit didn't even exist until one week ago. You're saying we have a mission statement and a *purview* that's written down somewhere?" News to her.

"We do. There's a copy in the folder you received from HR."

"There's something in that folder from Human Resources besides tax and insurance forms?" If she'd bothered to look this morning, she might have noticed that, but she'd had other business. Like finding the briefings she hadn't been invited to. So much for team spirit. Cutting the department some slack, she was fresh from not-so-pleasant business with the bureau. Maybe she was a little defensive. And a lot sensitive. And Burnett was right. She was the new kid on the block. If she wanted to be invited to the parties, she had to take the first steps and make nice.

God, she hated all that dancing around. Why couldn't people just do and say what they meant? Who needed all the social expectations and principles of etiquette? Work hard. Get the job done. What else mattered?

"You should read it," Harper suggested. "Sheriff Griggs and Chief Burnett came up with quite an interesting philosophy for our mission. Reads like they had considerable input from other divisions."

There was a warning in there somewhere. Harper had worked with Chief Black for several years and probably felt some level of loyalty still, so he didn't name names. Sheriff Roy Griggs, Deputy Chief Harold Black, and Chief of Police Daniel Burnett were members of the same team—the good old boys. Harper wasn't exactly a nonmember, but he liked and respected Jess and so did Detective Lori Wells. As much as she appreciated their support, Jess was still going to have to earn the trust and respect of every other member of the BPD. To do that meant playing by all the rules. Which also meant she had no choice but to go to that needless, utter waste of time psychological evaluation appointment Burnett kept bugging her about.

She wondered if Lori had gotten hers out of the way. Jess had missed the call from the shrink on Friday morning, hardly more than twenty-four hours after the shooting. The investigation into her actions during last week's showdown with a serial killer had already begun. There really was no point pretending she could disregard that reality.

Didn't keep her from trying.

Maybe she'd drop by tonight and check on Lori. See how her appointment, if she'd had it already, had gone. Get a feel for the department shrink. Better the devil she knew. And she'd like to see for herself how Lori was doing.

"How's Lori?" she asked Harper.

"She's good. Yesterday she moved back to her place." He laughed. "It was either that or blow a gasket with the way her mother was hovering over her."

Lori loved her mom and sister but she, like Jess, was fiercely independent. Jess was surprised she'd suffered the hovering this long.

"I'm glad she's feeling up to getting back into her normal routine." Jess didn't have to ask if Harper had seen her. The two had a thing. Both would deny it, but Jess knew. She also knew that they were all damned lucky to have escaped the Player and his sadistic accomplice with scarcely more than a few bruises and scratches. The same couldn't be said for the two federal agents who had lost their lives. That familiar combination of pain and rage twisted in her belly. One day soon she hoped she got the opportunity to stop that bastard once and for all.

"She wants to come back to work."

Jess banished the ghost that plagued her like a persistent rash. "Not until she's well enough physically and has the dreaded psych eval."

"You had yours yet?"

"Are you spying on me for Burnett?"

Harper kept his attention straight ahead despite no doubt sensing her staring a hole through his profile.

"He might have mentioned something about reminding you."

If Daniel Burnett intended to play by the book, he couldn't have it both ways. No checking up on her through her subordinates.

Harper slowed and parked at the curb in front of their destination.

The home was another modest ranch-style house, like most of the others along this street. Unlike the others, the yard was well maintained as was the exterior of the home. A ray of hope in the bleakness.

"Shall we see what kind of reception we get, Sergeant?"

"Yes, ma'am."

By the time Jess completed her visual assessment and released her seat belt, Harper was at her door, opening it like the good Southern gentleman he was. Like her, he had already slipped into secure mode, attuning to their surroundings and monitoring all senses intently.

Jess was grateful to have Harper on her team. Lori Wells, too. They were top-notch detectives. Officer Cook, who would be reporting for duty on Friday, had earned his spot in Jess's unit when he jumped at the opportunity to spend his off-duty time following up on her lead in the case that had brought Jess back to Birmingham. Lieutenant Prescott had started today. Despite the promotion she felt had belonged to her, so far she hadn't asked to be transferred back to Crimes Against Persons. Jess doubted that meant the lieutenant liked her. The more probable scenario was that Prescott intended to hang close and wait for Jess to screw up or drop dead.

One day when the dust had settled Jess would invite her out for drinks. Not the girlie martini types but the ones with balls, like bourbon straight up or scotch neat. With good stiff drinks in their guts they could hash this out woman-to-woman.

There she went, getting distracted with frustrations that were completely irrelevant to the moment. This was not the time or the place.

Thankfully the neighborhood was fairly quiet, which made for hearing trouble well in advance of it coming into view. A pit bull at the neighbor's house got to his feet, stretched, and then sniffed the air. As she and Harper headed up the drive to the front door, the dog barked and growled, then launched toward them. His chain snapped tight, holding him at the property line. Jess wished there was a law against having dogs chained up like that.

The front porch of the Simmonses' home was really nothing more than a small stoop. Jess fanned herself. It was just too damned hot for a house with no porch. Two concrete steps, flanked by potted plants that somehow managed to survive in this heat, led to the door. A security storm door had been installed, as had iron bars over the windows. Nothing said welcome like iron bars. For those inside, the attempt at deterrence made them feel a little safer. In Jess's experience if a bad guy wanted in badly enough, he was getting in.

Harper rapped on the steel door.

Inside, the high-pitched yap of a small dog erupted, easily outdoing the drone of the television.

Another series of raps on the door. The television volume was lowered and the dog, Chi-Chi, was shushed by a firm male voice. In Jess's opinion the yappy dog was a far more reliable deterrent than the bars.

Locks clicked and the door opened. A man, late sixties or so, gray hair and bifocals, scrutinized first Harper, then Jess. "You Jehovah's Witnesses or cops?" he challenged, his voice gruff. "If you're Witnesses, we belong to the Baptist church over on Sixteenth Street, so don't waste your time. If you're cops, you damned sure took your time."

Jess displayed her credentials, as did Harper. "Mr. Simmons, I'm Deputy Chief Harris and this is Sergeant Harper from the Birmingham PD. May we come inside and speak with you about your grandson?"

Without a word, the man unlatched the security door. Sergeant Harper pulled it open and waited for Jess to go in before him. The home smelled of fried okra, fresh sweet corn, and hot corn bread, reminding Jess of the way her mother's kitchen had smelled when she was a child. Her stomach rumbled. She pressed her hand there and hoped no one noticed.

The living room was homey. Worn comfortable sofa

and chairs. Tables cluttered with framed photos, most of which were of the grandson. The man who'd answered the door along with a woman who looked to be around his age stood on either side of the boy at his high school graduation, diploma proudly displayed. Chi-Chi, a tiny Chihuahua with a yap ten times her size, danced around Jess's feet.

"Well, hello, you itty-bitty puppy." Jess reached down and the dog snarled in warning. Guess Chi-Chi wasn't as friendly as she looked.

"Helen, the police are here," Mr. Simmons called down the hall that in all probability led to the bedrooms. He turned back to his company. "Go on and sit down. She'll be here directly. She's getting ready for the prayer vigil."

Prayer vigil? Burnett had said a rally. Not the same thing at all. Jess took a seat on the sofa. Harper joined her. Chi-Chi stayed under the coffee table, eyeing them suspiciously. "Mr. Simmons, we wanted to ask you a few questions about your grandson's disappearance."

He collapsed in the recliner that held a key position in front of the television, then settled his attention on Jess. "Did you find his body?"

Surprised by his question, Jess answered it with one of her own. "Do you believe your grandson is dead, sir?"

Simmons pulled the lever that lifted the footrest and removed his glasses before meeting her expectant gaze. "That boy ain't never been late getting home. Not once in his life. He made near straight A's in school. Got a full scholarship to Jeff State, which he had to put off for a year to stay here and help his grandmamma with me." He patted his chest. "I've had three heart surgeries this past year and my wife just couldn't do all that needed to be done." He waved his arm as if dismissing his health concerns. "DeShawn stayed right here. Took care of me until I was strong enough to take care of myself. Then he got a job over at the Captain D's until school starts. He's a shift supervisor. Now." Mr. Simmons looked from Jess to Harper and back. "I'm telling you that if that boy was alive, he would've come home or called by now."

"You keep telling that tale and they won't never look for him!"

Harper stood as the woman from the photographs, Mrs. Simmons, Jess presumed, entered the room and took the chair next to her husband. She was dressed in her Sunday best. It was glaringly obvious why the otherwise healthy-looking woman was unable to attend to her ailing husband's needs. Her right arm hung useless and withered at her side.

She looked straight at Jess and nodded once, a spark lighting in her eyes. "I know you. You're the one was all over the TV when those girls were missing."

Jess offered a smile. "Yes, ma'am. But don't believe everything you hear."

Mrs. Simmons shook her head. "Never do. But I know what you did. You found those girls. I've been praying the Lord would send you to find my boy. When I filed the report I asked for you by name. I told 'em to send Jessie Lee Harris to see me." The lady clasped her hands together and smiled, her lips trembling with emotion. "Praise the Lord. I was beginning to think you weren't coming."

Well, that explained why she'd been taken off the Chandler case. The poop was about to hit the fan in the media and Jess was going to be the star yet again.

Thank you, Burnett.

"Well." Jess took a breath. "I'm here now. I want you to tell me everything there is to know about this fine grandson of yours and then I want you to tell me about Friday from the moment you got out of bed until you filed the report the next morning."

Helen took the lead, regaling Jess with stories about how DeShawn had come to live with them when he was only three. His mother, their only child, had died of a drug overdose and they'd never known his father. DeShawn was studious and kind and completely committed to his grandparents. Within a month of taking a minimum-wage job with Captain D's he had been asked to join their management team. He took the bus to work since gas had gotten so expensive. He dated occasionally but his main focus was on his future. He saved most of what he earned. He went to church every Sunday with his grandmother. According to his grandparents, DeShawn set the pattern that all other grandchildren should follow.

Jess waited for the other shoe to drop. There was almost always, no matter how wonderful the son or daughter, some little thing no one expected. A new friend, activity, or contact unknown to the parents. Some deviation from the norm. Though it was certainly possible, if he had not disappeared of his own accord, that DeShawn had been the victim of random violence, far more likely he was the victim of a wrong choice.

"You forgot to mention that girl who's been calling him," Mr. Simmons put in.

"That girl is not his girlfriend," Mrs. Simmons argued. "She's just a friend he helped out by getting her a job."

"Who is this girl he helped out?" Jess inquired, searching both faces for that telltale flare of knowledge that could prove far more important than either one understood. Anticipation spurred a little burst of adrenaline. This could be the element of DeShawn's background that might provide some insight as to why he'd gone missing.

"She's Mexican," Mr. Simmons said with obvious disdain. "Her name's Nina something. She was all mixed up with one of them thirteen gangbangers. And our boy was doing a lot more than helping her get a job. He was helping her hide."

"We don't know any such thing for sure," his wife argued. "Whatever she was involved in, DeShawn would not have gotten mixed up in that gang mess. He said she was hiding. He didn't say he was helping her hide."

That burst of adrenaline became a full-fledged flood. "Mr. Simmons, are you referring to *MS-13*?"

"That's it! DeShawn said her ex-boyfriend—or whatever he was—was some kind of leader of that trash. He was scared they might hurt her if they found out where she was hiding."

On a scale of one to ten, with ten being bad, this was a twelve. "Do you recall her last name?"

Mr. and Mrs. Simmons exchanged a look. Both shook their heads.

"Where was she hiding when DeShawn was helping her?"

"In that empty house down the block on the corner. DeShawn took her a blanket and a pillow and food. He was worried about her safety but she refused to go to the police. Then she just disappeared. Poof!" He made an abrupt gesture with his hands. "Next thing we knew

DeShawn was gone, too." His voice trembled on the last. "They've done something bad to our boy. I know it."

"We don't know that," Mrs. Simmons argued again. "DeShawn was just being nice. He didn't do anything wrong."

Jess knew exactly the house Mr. Simmons meant. The one with all the gang tags. She also understood that Mrs. Simmons was in deep denial. If this young man had crossed someone in the MS-13 in any capacity, his grandfather was correct. They would do or had done something bad to him. "When did Nina go missing?"

"On Wednesday," Helen answered as she dabbed at her eyes. "DeShawn was very upset that she didn't answer the door when it was time to go to work Wednesday afternoon. He went inside that old house and she was gone. I tried to tell him that she probably just took off. With girls like that you can't never tell."

Jess made a note to check the house. "Did he notice signs of a struggle?"

Helen shook her head. "She was just gone and he was worried sick. Two days later he was gone, too."

"Did you tell this to the police when you filed the missing persons report?"

Helen exchanged another look with her husband. "I didn't. I was afraid you wouldn't look for him if you knew about that part. I knew the police would try to say he was involved with that mess. But I can promise you right now he didn't run off to join no gang, not for that girl or anything else. They took him. That's all there is to it."

Jess dug for her pad and pencil. "I need as much information about the girl as you can give me." She turned to a new page in her notepad. "Don't leave anything out," she warned. "I can't help you or your grandson unless I know *everything*."

8:45 p.m.

Jess promised Mr. and Mrs. Simmons she would find their grandson. The department's sketch artist was scheduled to meet with the Simmonses tomorrow morning to work on a rendering of this unidentified person of interest called Nina. Jess suspected she was the key to DeShawn's troubles.

Harper exited the premises first and scanned the street in both directions as they walked toward his SUV.

The sun had gone down, leaving that dusky-not-quite-dark time of the evening when folks ushered their kids inside and streetlights began to flicker to life. As she walked along the driveway the pit bull made another dive that snapped his chain tight.

"Stop wasting the effort," she told him. "You won't be able to break that log chain."

She hoped Harper was far enough away that he'd missed her giving advice to the dog. She needed the distraction. Anything to get her mind off the last hour. This was an undeniably bad situation. The chances that DeShawn Simmons was alive were minimal, and that was the good news.

She didn't want to think about the bad news.

Not much had changed in this neighborhood at all since that year she'd spent here as a kid. She wondered if her aunt was still alive and living around here someplace.

The woman had chosen her drugs and her johns over

Jess and her sister. She surely couldn't have expected them to keep in touch. The truth was, Jess hadn't thought of her in decades. Why start now?

Jess cut across the lawn and was halfway to Harper's SUV when she heard a sound that made her blood go cold.

Tha-thwack.

An engine roared to life. A vehicle rocketed from between two parked cars. Up the block on her right.

Harper lunged toward her. They hit the ground, his body shielding hers before the first bullets exploded from at least one pump shotgun and numerous other automatic weapons.

They were in the open.

No cover.

There was nothing they could do except ride it out.

The squeal of tires and growl of the engine diminished in the distance before the echo of the final shots faded.

Just as suddenly as it had begun, it was over.

Before she could make a move to get up, Harper was on his feet and reaching for her. "You okay, ma'am?"

Jess got to her knees and retrieved her bag. Thankfully the contents hadn't flown in a dozen directions. "Pretty damned good, considering." She accepted his hand and levered to her feet, then wheeled around to see if the Simmonses' house had suffered any damage that might have endangered the people inside.

"Get backup over here," she said to Harper as she fished out her Glock. "I'm going in to check on Mr. and Mrs. Simmons."

Before the order was fully out of her mouth, the front door burst open and the elderly couple bounded out of the house with far more agility and speed than Jess would have expected.

"Get back in the house," she shouted. There was no way to know what the shooters would do next. Stay gone, most likely, but there were no guarantees.

The couple stared at her a moment, then at the gun in her right hand, before obeying her command. The shattered security door slammed behind them, safety glass showering the stoop.

Harper had dispatch on the horn and was relaying the situation. Jess surveyed the neighborhood. Folks on both sides of the street had started to wander out into their yards.

She motioned with her free hand and shouted, "Birmingham PD! Go back in your homes until we give the all clear."

By the time Harper closed his phone, sirens were wailing in the distance and the curiosity seekers were going back inside.

For the first time since the initial pump of that shotgun, Jess hauled in a decent breath. Her gaze stalled on Harper and his slight limp. The knees of his khaki trousers were stained by the dive into the grass, but it was the darker stain on his left thigh just above his knee that worried her, made her own knees go weak.

"You're hit." She moved toward him to get a closer look.

"It's just a flesh wound." He showed her where the bullet had entered and exited his trouser leg. "I'll live."

"Is EMS on the way, too?"

He nodded. "Captain Allen as well. I figured GTF needed in on this."

"You figured right, Sergeant," Jess acknowledged. Damn it all to hell. "Let's get you inside and off that leg."

"Backup is almost here, ma'am. I should wait for their arrival. But it would be best if you waited inside."

Like hell. Jess tightened her grip on her Glock. "I think I'll take my chances with you, Sergeant."

5

How long you think we'll be safe here?"

DeShawn Simmons paced the worn carpet. This motel was too close to his neighborhood. He didn't care that it was a dump, but wouldn't the trouble they were trying to escape be turning this side of town upside down? And what about DeShawn's grandparents? This was too close to them. He didn't want them pulled into this whacked-out situation.

This was too close. Too close, and still he couldn't let them know he was here. They would be worried. His grandfather didn't need this kind of stress.

Nina ignored him as if he hadn't said a word. She just kept staring out the dingy motel window. She'd acted funny ever since they made the decision to leave their lives and Birmingham behind.

The whole thing had been her idea. He hadn't wanted to go. His grandparents needed him. She just kept saying they were doing okay and he had to grow up and be a man.

That was what he was trying to do now and she wasn't listening. They hadn't run anywhere. What was she waiting for?

How was he supposed to protect her from those low-life gangbangers if she wouldn't listen?

"Didn't you hear me?" DeShawn strode to the window and glared down at her. She made him so angry. He wanted to shake her. But she'd already suffered enough. The bruises from her last beating were only now fading.

She looked up at him and his chest ached. Man, he loved her so much. He wished he could take back the words. He didn't want to hurt her, but he was scared to death and his grandparents would be freaking out by now.

"Nina, you—"

"Baby." She took his hands in hers and smiled, her big brown eyes hopeful. "You have to trust me. This is the only way. If he finds us, we're dead." She pulled away from him, hugged her arms around herself. "I shouldn't've dragged you into this. I'll never be rid of him. I should've stayed and let him kill me. Then it would be over."

DeShawn reached for her, pulled her against him. It was the only time he felt right, with her next to him. "Don't say that, baby girl. We'll figure this out." He stroked her long silky hair. "I just wish I could let my grandparents know I'm okay. They worry about me."

She hugged him hard, the sound of her voice vibrating against his chest as she spoke. "If you told them anything and he found out, he would do terrible things to them." Her gaze moved up to DeShawn's once more. "Believe me, I've seen what he can do when he wants to hurt someone."

"We can't hide like this forever." He was supposed

to start Jeff State next month. His grandparents were depending on him. As much as he loved Nina, he didn't want to let them down. His grandmother would tell him that this was a fine time to think about that. He'd made his bed hard and now he would have to lie in it.

Nina grabbed his hands and pulled him down to the floor. "Let's pray, Shawney. Our heavenly Father will help us make the right decisions." She reached up and stroked his cheek. "He's gotten us this far and we're still alive."

DeShawn closed his eyes and tried to focus on her words. As hard as he tried to pay attention, in his mind, where she wouldn't hear, he said a prayer of his own.

Dear Father, please keep my grandparents safe. Watch after them if I don't make it through this.

He opened his eyes and watched as Nina fervently begged for God's guidance and protection. She wanted so bad to be away from the gang life. DeShawn wanted just as bad to help her. To keep her safe for the rest of her life.

And, Father, he prayed, *forgive me for loving this girl so much that I had to keep secrets from my grandparents. Help us, Father, we're in bad trouble.*

Rubber screamed against the cracked concrete outside their room. The screeching echoed right through the paper-thin walls.

Nina's head jerked up, her eyes wide with fear.

DeShawn's heart rammed against his rib cage. "Get under the bed," he told her. "I'll run. While they're chasing me you can get away." His voice shook with his own fear. He had to be strong. Had to be brave.

She held on tight to his hands and shook her head. "No. If we die, we'll die together."

6

Howard Johnson Inn, 11:50 p.m.

The hot water relaxed her muscles and seeped deep into her bones. Jess exhaled a chestful of tension and eased lower into the water. It might not be a jetted tub or even one with bubbles, but filled with hot, steamy water this old motel tub did the trick. And as long as she kept her eyes closed she could imagine that she was surrounded by sleek travertine and glistening fixtures. The fragrance of vanilla bean drifted from the candle she'd picked up at Walmart and parked on the toilet tank.

Cracking one eye open she reached for the plastic cup of wine perched on the toilet lid. The sweet white pleasure was room temperature, but after three generous cups she was well on her way to not caring. The flickering flame of the candle gave the dark, cramped room a hint of ambiance.

She cleared her mind of work—especially those damned shoes Darcy Chandler should have been wearing as she took that fatal plunge. Not her case. Finding

DeShawn Simmons and analyzing the Druid Hills gang problem was the only case on her agenda. Captain Ted Allen from the Gang Task Force had provided an on-the-spot and comprehensive briefing into his investigation of the gang activities in Birmingham. Based on what Harper had told her, Allen had done an outstanding job, but the problem was out of control. He needed help. He needed SPU.

And DeShawn Simmons needed to be found. Allen couldn't connect Simmons with any gang members or activities on his radar. Ordinarily that might prove fortunate, but since Jess was better than ninety percent certain his disappearance was gang related, the lack of available information was rather unfortunate. Jess told Allen as much. If he monitored this territory as thoroughly as he claimed, why wasn't he aware of Simmons and some gang leader's ex-girlfriend named Nina? Allen had no answer for her.

After the drive-by situation was wrapped up at the Simmons home, Jess had dropped by the ER to ensure that Harper was patched up and had a way home since she was driving his SUV—which, incredibly, had survived with less damage than if he'd driven through an unexpected hailstorm. She'd requested a security detail for the Simmons home for the next couple of days. Though she suspected the intent of the shooters had been to send a message to the cops, if the intent had been to show the cops who was boss by taking one or more out, then tonight's shooters were scandalously bad shots. With her and Harper out in the open like that, even a half-assed shot should have been able to do better than grazing a thigh.

For Jess, the message was loud and clear. DeShawn Simmons crossed the wrong person and had paid the price. If his grandparents insisted on pursuing the matter, there would be trouble. But what those thugs needed to bear in mind was that their problem was Jess, not the grandparents.

If, as she suspected, Simmons's disappearance was related to MS-13, that reality added a whole new layer of ugliness to the situation. MS-13, Mara Salvatrucha, represented a growing and mobile threat in most communities. They were fearless and used the most violent tactics. As recruiters they were relentless, as enemies ruthless. Their range of criminal activities was broad and varied. Drugs, murder, prostitution, robbery, you name it. There was little they wouldn't do and violence was always the overwhelming theme. Their members were either immensely loyal or stone-cold dead.

She and Harper were damned lucky that, for whatever reasons, this evening's warning had been decidedly non-lethal. It didn't quite fit unless that was only the preview before the main event.

To her surprise Burnett hadn't shown up at the scene or at the hospital. Usually he was Johnny-on-the-spot to do the protector thing. Which would have provided the opportunity for her to demand why he'd kept Helen Simmons's request from her. Why not just tell her that she couldn't stay on the Chandler case because she had been requested by the family of a possible victim in another case?

Helen Simmons had prayed for Jess's help after watching the news. Had she missed the part about how badly Jess had screwed up the Player case?

Evidently so.

Jess squeezed her eyes shut and forced images of Eric Spears and Matthew Reed from her head. Spears, the Player, had gotten away. A serial killer with dozens of murders on his score sheet, and he had slipped through their fingers.

Through her fingers. Not once but twice.

His protégé, Matthew Reed, hadn't been so lucky. He was dead. The sound of the bullet exploding from her Glock echoed in her brain. She'd had no choice. She'd do it again if necessary. Reed had killed Special Agent Nora Miller and he'd very nearly done the same to Realtor Belinda Howard just last week. The bureau had since learned that Reed had killed his own parents and planted them in the backyard of their West Coast home. Those three murders were documented. There was no way to know how many others he'd murdered. As much as she believed in and respected the justice system, there were those who didn't deserve a trial...who didn't deserve even the most remote opportunity to repeat their heinous acts.

Matthew Reed had been one of those people.

Didn't matter to the powers that be that she had used that single bullet fired from her weapon on a twisted killer who would have kept on killing as long as he had breath in him. She still had to deal with the consequences. The internal review into her actions was ongoing, and that included a psych eval.

"Whoop-de-do." Who didn't want some shrink crawling around inside their head? She had a degree in psychology, for heaven's sake. Another human being was dead because of her. Yes, she understood that. She had committed the ultimate violent act against a living being. Got it. But it was either kill him or allow him to keep killing innocent people at the bidding of an even more evil man. She had made the right decision. The only decision.

Given the chance, she would put a bullet between Spears's eyes as well. A smart man would never allow himself to get that close to her again. But maybe even the most brilliant of evil men had temptations they couldn't resist. If she needed to test that theory, all she had to do was consider that Spears still contacted her when the right occasion presented itself.

He'd had the audacity to text her before boarding a commercial airliner to flee the country just five days ago. The bureau had lost him and Jess hadn't heard from him since. But she had a feeling that he wasn't finished playing his games with her just yet.

Until next time.

"That's right, Spears. I'll get you next time."

If Burnett found out the peace lily plant sent to the hospital when he was recovering from last week's stabbing had come from Spears, he would be fit to be tied. Spears had apparently placed the order before boarding that flight out of JFK. He could be anywhere now. Part of her hoped he stayed wherever the hell that was, but another, more twisted part of her wanted to end this once and for all. Wanted to ensure he never killed again. Burnett, on the other hand, would prefer that Spears never got anywhere near her again. The problem with that scenario was that letting him close might just be the only way to get a killer like Spears. Dangle the bait and wait. That was precisely the reason she couldn't tell Burnett about any contact with the bastard. As long as Spears had some sort of twisted attraction to her there was a chance she might find herself face-to-face with him again.

Jess sipped her room-temperature wine as she recalled a line from on old Clint Eastwood movie. "Go ahead, Spears, make my day."

Just further proof that she actually did need that psych eval. Poor Mrs. Simmons. She had prayed for Jess's help. Bless her heart.

Pounding on the door made her jump. She dropped her plastic cup in the tub. "Shit."

She felt on the floor next to the tub for her Glock, her heart racing a hundred miles per hour, and snatched it up. Who the hell would be at her door at this hour?

So much for her Dirty Harry attitude.

Weapon in hand, she stood, grabbed a towel, and wrapped it around her. One dripping foot hit the floor, then the other. She eased the bathroom door open and listened. Besides the candle, the dim glow from the table lamp by the bed was the only other illumination in the motel room that currently served as her home.

She mentally ran down the list of people who knew her temporary address. Wouldn't be Harper. He would call first. Lori, maybe? Jess doubted she would show up without calling first either.

Another round of pounding followed by, "Jess! You in there?"

She rolled her eyes. *Burnett.*

"Hold your horses!"

Where was her robe? *Closet.* After placing her weapon on the counter, she swabbed her damp skin with the towel, then tossed it aside and grabbed her robe.

"Coming!"

At the door, she drew in a deep breath and wished she had taken the time to comb her hair. The wild mess was pinned haphazardly on top of her head. Unfortunately she wasn't one of those women who could pull off the freshly-risen-from-tousled-sheets look.

Be that as it may, she unlocked and opened the door. "I was trying to relax in the tub. What's up?" *Why didn't you call?* she didn't bother tacking on.

If she had her guess, he was here to scold her about not being better prepared in a neighborhood like Druid Hills. Or for making that comment to Captain Allen about his Gang Task Force having completely missed the Simmons connection. Oddly enough, Allen had taken her dressing down pretty well.

One look at Burnett's grim expression and she decided that maybe Allen hadn't taken it so well after all.

She'd built her reputation on crossing lines. Why was Burnett or anyone else surprised at her tactics? Actually, he should be here checking on her well-being. Not to mention her top detective's.

"What happened tonight?" Burnett demanded.

"It's almost midnight. Are you just now getting the news?" He was the chief of police. Didn't someone inform him when there were bullets fired at one of his deputy chiefs? And what was with the two cups of Dunkin' Donuts coffee? He towered in her doorway, a cup in each hand. A peace offering? Chocolate would have been a better choice.

Or more wine.

For two weeks she had fussed at him about checking up on her and worrying about every little thing she did and doing the protector thing. Oddly, after being shot at, she was a little miffed at not getting *any* of that.

She mentally added wishy-washiness to her list of reasons the psych eval was a good thing.

Those blue eyes that she quite often felt could see through brick walls and definitely could see through her big fat lies searched her face before skimming her robe-clad body. "Are you all right?"

She relented and backed up. "Get in here before my neighbors mistake you for a drug connection or a pimp."

"After this weekend I suspect it's too late to avoid all sorts of conclusions." He came inside and closed the door. "I wouldn't lose any sleep over what the regulars in this neighborhood thought."

The heat that swept through her like a flash fire whenever she thought about this past weekend scorched her now. Frustrated the hell out of her. Twenty-some years ago they had been madly in love and then he'd given up on *them* and walked away. Before a couple weeks ago she hadn't even seen him in ten years. Another annoying flash fire roared through her at the memory of them running into each other in a Publix supermarket that Christmas over a decade ago. They'd ended up in bed together that time too.

What did it say about her that she kept repeating that particular mistake?

"Don't start again with where I live." This motel was only temporary. She had to sell her house in Stafford before she could consider buying one here. Unlike the Dentons and the Burnetts of the world, she couldn't afford to own two houses at the same time and drive luxury vehicles to boot. Besides, she might not even opt to buy another house. She was rarely home. Why not just get an apartment or condo? Who needed all the lawn maintenance responsibility? She kind of liked knowing that stuff was taken care of. This secret would go to her grave with her, but she had grown somewhat attached to having a maid as well. Not that the one here was that great, but not having to worry about vacuuming or making the bed was a serious perk.

All those years she had castigated Katherine Burnett for being too lazy to clean her own house. Well, now she knew.

He held up the coffee. "You're right. No more low-rent-district jabs." He offered her one of the cups. "I know it's late. I brought coffee. Thought we could catch up on what happened this evening."

That he still wore the charcoal suit he'd been wearing at work today told her he hadn't been home yet. He worked too hard. But the fine lines all that responsibility had etched into his handsome face just made him look distinguished. Unlike her, he pulled off the rumpled look as if he'd taken lessons from George Clooney.

"I don't want any coffee. Are you just leaving the office?"

The instantaneous and complete lockdown that closed his expression gave her the answer before he opened his mouth to offer whatever excuse he was clearly scrambling to dredge up.

It was too late to take back the question. Mortified, she suppressed a groan. That they had shared the bed only a few feet behind her for most of Saturday and Sunday didn't give either of them controlling stock in the other's business. They had rules about that. Sort of.

"I had dinner with Annette at Bottega's. We needed to talk about Andrea." He shrugged, the gesture too quick and blatantly stilted. "She's having a tough time and after today it's only going to get worse. I didn't realize my cell was on silent until I was headed home."

Wow. He had dinner with his most recent ex-wife and had his cell on silent? He didn't even do that when they had sex. Far more suspicious was the idea that it was almost midnight and he was just leaving Annette.

Jess stiffened her spine. She absolutely refused to show the nasty green jealousy currently coursing through her veins. "What does Brandon have to say about all this?" Brandon was Andrea's father and Annette's current husband who used to be her ex. Jess did a mental shake of her head. These people were the ones who needed a psych eval.

"Brandon's out of town on business."

Do tell. "With her husband out of town," Jess offered, "she had nowhere else to turn, I'm sure. It's a good thing you could be there for her." *Gag.*

Avoiding eye contact now, Burnett crossed the dinky room and placed the cups of coffee on the counter next to her Glock. Turning back to her he did a double take and studied the open bathroom door an extra second or two. Oops. He'd spotted the bottle of wine on the bathroom floor. Damn. She should have closed that door.

He gave her one of those looks that came from the chief of police, not the man. "Wine and a hot bath? That's a dangerous combination for a woman alone in a motel room. Don't you watch the news?"

Way to change the subject from his ex-wife and her out-of-town husband. "That tub is hardly deep enough for me to slip under the water on purpose much less by accident." She would never in a million years admit that he had a valid point.

Another survey of the room and then his attention settled firmly on her. "Nine tomorrow morning. Dr. Pricilla Oden. You have her address on Nineteenth Street. Don't forget."

He'd already given her that instruction. He'd even had Harper checking up on her. Now he comes to her after dinner with his ex at one of Birmingham's finest Italian restaurants wagging coffee to remind her that she needed to see the department shrink. "Thanks for the reminder, Chief. Now"—she gestured to the door—"I'd like to get back to my bath. And, FYI, Sergeant Harper was shot but it was only a flesh wound and he'll be fine."

For a long moment Burnett didn't move. Just stared at her as if there were many things he wanted to say but somehow he couldn't find the words. And, standing this close, she was nearly certain she could smell Annette's perfume clinging to his jacket. Of course that could be explained by a mere hug. Everyone hugged in the South. It was some sort of unspoken rule or irresistible compulsion.

Jess had never been a hugger. Maybe it had something to do with multiple foster homes and nearly two decades in the bureau. Annette, on the other hand, was a hugger. She and her daughter often gave and accepted hugs twice in a row.

"I spoke to Harper a few minutes ago. He called to let me know what happened. No one else felt inclined to do so."

He was blaming that on her? "And if I had called, how would you have known since your cell was on silent and you were otherwise occupied? After ten o'clock the work side of my brain retires for the evening."

"You're disappointed about the Chandler case. I get

that," he said finally, apparently opting to blame her attitude on work rather than his nightlife. "But I have to play by the rules, Jess. If you recall, we talked about rules on Saturday."

Her face flushed and he noticed. The rules he referred to had been about their personal relationship, or more precisely their physical relationship. That she couldn't control an outward reaction to the memory or to his pointing out the fact flustered her.

"That's right," she granted. "We've had that conversation already." She wasn't having it again unless he changed his mind about bending the work rules from time to time. Like allowing her to be involved in the Chandler investigation. That wasn't going to happen unless Black begged for assistance. And *that* definitely wasn't going to happen.

The position she had accepted at the BPD had looked a whole lot better when she was unemployed and her future, personal and professional, was up in the air. Now, in the harsh light of reality and the fact that all the best cases might get hogged up by Black, she was, frankly, having second thoughts. If that made her selfish or arrogant, then so be it. Wine did that to her sometimes.

Besides, these days she felt more comfortable about working murder cases. It was hard to do additional damage to a victim who was already dead...but finding one who might still be alive before it was too late was a whole different game.

For seventeen years she had profiled evil and investigated cases with the bureau and never once doubted her ability. Eric Spears had taken that away from her.

The department shrink would have a field day with that revelation. Except Jess wasn't telling.

"I don't know all the details on what went down this evening," Burnett said instead of leaving, "but you could have been killed. Harper could have been killed. I assigned the Simmons case to you and that makes me responsible. I'm the chief of police; ultimately I'm always responsible."

Now he wanted to play protector again. And guess what? That ticked her off, too. Maybe there was no neutral place in their relationship unless it was between the sheets. "We had that conversation, too. I don't need you trying to protect me from my work. If Chief Black had been in my position would you be dropping by to see him with coffee at this hour? I don't think so."

That his attention remained on her lips a beat or two too long made it difficult for her to capture a decent breath.

"It's late," she announced in hopes of breaking the tension. "We both have big days tomorrow." Hers wasn't so much big as it was dreaded.

He blinked as if her words had just penetrated his brain. "I guess I'll see you *after* your appointment." He started backing toward the door.

"I guess you will."

At the door he didn't immediately reach to open it or even turn away from her for that matter. He just stared at her as if he wanted her to invite him to stay. Or maybe he wanted to explain that what happened in this room on Saturday and then again on Sunday couldn't ever happen again. Whatever he wanted to say, he looked way too tempting for her to continue to ignore the hum of desire now vibrating stronger and stronger through her.

"The truth is," he admitted, sounding as breathless as

she felt, "I assigned the Simmons case to you because they need you, Jess. As tragic as Darcy Chandler's death is, she's gone. There might be hope for the Simmons kid. His family needs you. They deserve the same advantage Andrea and the others got. They deserve to have you on the case."

"You didn't tell me the grandmother asked for me. You didn't tell me any of this." His heartfelt admission would have made accepting the decision about the Chandler case a whole lot more palatable.

"I should have but I didn't because I needed you to accept my decision because it was my decision."

"Oh. I see." Guess she'd crossed the line again. Failed to respect the chain of command, and all the other deputy chiefs were watching to see if she got away with it. Okay, she got it. It was late and she didn't want to think anymore. The fight drained out of her in one sudden whoosh. "You're right. I shouldn't have questioned your decision."

For a long time they just stood there watching each other. She imagined he was wondering the same thing she was. What now?

Might as well put them both out of their misery. "Night, Burnett."

He reached behind him for the door and muttered, "Night, Jess."

Then he was gone.

Jess locked the door behind him and collapsed against it.

Somehow they had to find their balance in this relationship. He couldn't be her boss and play the part of personal protector at the same time. He damned sure couldn't be her lover and show up armed with coffee in the middle of the night with the scent of another woman on his clothes.

She certainly couldn't take note of his absence like she

had after the shooting this evening and then be pissed that he showed up to check on her—with coffee no less.

That was a discussion they apparently needed to have at some point. Where work was concerned, she had been investigating crime too long for him to be checking behind her as if she were a rookie. She needed to stop with the waffling back and forth on the matter and get a grip on her professionalism. If she was completely honest with herself she would admit that the past few weeks had turned her life upside down and she was still reeling.

Any lingering frustration she felt fizzled.

He'd left without even giving her a good-night hug.

So much for Southern traditions or her professionalism. From the moment she had arrived back in Birmingham, Alabama, nearly two decades of expertise and experience had flown out the window.

7

Nineteenth Street, Tuesday, July 27, 9:45 a.m.

Have you been sleeping well, Chief Harris?"

"Like a rock." Jess smoothed a hand over the hem of her skirt, mostly to avoid eye contact—a maneuver the shrink would likely recognize. How well was she supposed to sleep when her job was to find and stop evil?

But she wasn't about to delve into that can of worms with the doctor who possessed the power to remove her from duty. Presenting a calm, rational, nonviolent facade was key. All she needed now was for a Nobel Peace Prize nomination to suddenly appear in her personnel jacket so they could be done with this charade. She and the nice Dr. Oden had been dancing around the events of last Wednesday for nearly an hour. The woman should get to the point, but Jess doubted that would happen in this session.

Shrinks were like lawyers—they billed by the hour.

"What about your dreams? Anything unusual since the shooting?"

"Nothing at all." Jess folded her hands together in her lap to conquer the urge to reach for her cell. It was driving her nuts not to know what was going on this morning. Had Harper learned anything on the Simmons case? How was the sketch artist doing with getting a likeness of Nina on paper? Had the ME's office given any preliminary results on Chandler's death?

She wouldn't know because she was stuck here. Not that the latter was any of her business.

Speaking of the Simmons case, Jess wondered how long it would be before the good doctor learned about the drive-by shooting and added that to the pile of reasons Jess couldn't possibly be stable.

While Oden made more notes and decided on her next question, Jess wondered if the doctor had chosen the decor in her office. The plaid upholstery on the chairs clashed annoyingly with the striped drapes, and there was enough brown and tan in the room to depress a mud turtle. It wasn't normal to be this neutral and drab. Oden really needed a color intervention.

"How are things at work? Any problems fitting in? Sometimes it takes a while to feel like you belong when an abrupt career change occurs later in life."

Later in life? Now there was an uplifting thought.

"None at all," Jess said with a smile. Except for Lieutenant Prescott wanting to scratch her eyes out and Chief Black stealing back the case Jess had stolen from him. Gangbangers shooting at her and, oh yes, Burnett getting up close and personal with his ex at a private dinner for two and then showing up to play the boss for Jess. Things were downright dandy.

"Your former relationship with Chief Burnett hasn't

made you feel awkward in your new position at the BPD?"

Apparently the doc could read minds. Either that or Jess's new boss had given a little more info than necessary when writing up his evaluation. Or maybe he'd spilled his guts during his own psych eval. The annoyance and impatience needling at Jess turned to something far less polite. This session was about her shooting and ending the life of Matthew Reed, not who she'd had sex with last.

"My *former relationship* with Chief Burnett, having taken place more than twenty years ago, is absolutely irrelevant to these proceedings, Dr. Oden. Nothing related to our shared past makes me feel the slightest bit awkward about anything at all, then or now."

There were enough lies in those two sentences to guarantee her a seat on the train to hell.

"I see." Oden jotted a few notes.

"I see" was code for "I think I'm onto something." Jess had news for the nice doctor: she was done. She grabbed her bag and eased to the edge of her chair in preparation for making her exit before Oden could zero in on just how right she was.

"Here's what I see, Dr. Oden. I shot and killed Matthew Reed, a sociopath who murdered at least three people. The shooting was justified since at the time he had two hostages, both of whom were mere moments from certain death. Yes, one was my former lover and current boss, but the other was a detective I'd known only a few days. So let's not make anything of the idea that Burnett was even in the room. I did my job and I have no regrets. No bad dreams. No inability to sleep. No loss of sex drive and no problem getting along with others."

Maybe that last part was a stretch.

"You believe you don't need these sessions." Oden studied her with open skepticism. "That this is a waste of your time. Is that a fair assessment?"

That was a trick question. "I think you're doing your job, Doctor. That's what I believe." Jess stood. "Now, if you'll excuse me, I need to do mine."

"You may suffer later for ignoring your mental health, Chief Harris. You're aware of the consequences, just as I am. Why add that kind of easily avoidable regret to your already complicated life?"

Jess hesitated at the door. She told herself to keep her cool but she'd suddenly catapulted past any possibility of doing that. She turned back to the well-meaning shrink. "My only regret, Doctor, is that I didn't find and kill that monster before he mutilated and murdered a federal agent who was a wife and mother. That's a regret I'll have to live with the rest of my life. Unfortunately there isn't a thing I can do or you can say that will fix that. But thank you very much for giving it the old college try."

Before Oden could organize a response, Jess was out the door. She didn't wait for the elevator. It was only two flights of stairs and there was no worry about snapping a heel or twisting her ankle. Not in these generic old flats she had worn to show her practical side. Thank goodness she had her blue pumps in the car. She hadn't ever been vain, not really. She dressed her best for the job because it was expected. People, strangers, colleagues, whoever, responded better to you when you were well dressed. The shoes, now that was a whole different ball game. The shoes were her one true vanity. And the bag. She loved it. She'd paid a killing for the Coach Bleecker tote bag on her fortieth birthday.

A little voice nagged at her for lying to herself. The M&Ms were a close second to the shoes. The bag was a definite third when set against the chocolate. Still, if that was her worst sin, she wasn't doing so badly.

At least she wasn't having dinner and hugs with her ex.

Then again, she and Wesley didn't have children. Andrea might only be a former stepdaughter, but she and Dan had grown quite close during his and Annette's brief marriage.

Jess escaped the stairwell and hit the lobby determined to erase Burnett and his ex, as well as the psych eval, which she might very well have just flunked, from her head.

Outside she took a moment to get her bearings, then headed in the direction of the parking garage a couple of blocks away. The streets were already jammed with medical district traffic. Birmingham physicians and facilities were tops in the nation. The streets were always crowded in this area. Parking was at a premium.

"Jess!"

She stalled in front of Starbucks and zeroed in on the voice that had called her name. Lori Wells. A smile slid across Jess's lips and she hurried to accept a hug from the detective. Jess had rolled back into her hometown husbandless, almost jobless, and definitely friendless. In a mere two weeks two-thirds of that sad state had changed.

Drawing back, she assessed her friend's recovery after being abducted by Matthew Reed. Lori's eye was still swollen a little but looked far better than a few days ago. The bruises on her cheek and throat had turned that ugly yellowy-purple color. Otherwise she was her usual tall, thin, gorgeous self. Long dark hair and rich green eyes.

Dressed in dark green slacks and a mint-colored blouse, she looked damn good for a woman who had escaped the worst kind of evil. God, Jess was glad to see her.

"You have a follow-up appointment with your doctor?" Jess couldn't imagine anyone tackling this traffic unless necessary. Lori had a couple of fractured ribs in addition to the more obvious signs of the beating she had taken. Like the mental trauma, the damaged ribs weren't visible to the naked eye. Sometimes what couldn't be seen was far worse than the readily apparent. As much as Jess wanted to ignore Oden's warning, the shrink was right. That kind of damage didn't just go away easily.

"No follow-ups today." Lori held up her iced coffee. "Unless you're in a hurry, let's find a quiet corner and catch up."

"I have some time." She could rendezvous with Harper and Prescott before lunch. Both were working the Simmons case. A few minutes with Lori would be good.

Inside the coffee shop Jess grabbed an iced coffee of her own while Lori laid claim to one of the comfy seating areas as far away from the counter as possible. Jess curled up in one of the big chairs. She hadn't had a break like this in decades. Not having cases stacked to the ceiling in her office was just another aspect of why she felt a little off balance.

Balance is everything. That was what Annette Denton had said about Darcy Chandler. How did a woman who had been a professional ballerina lose her balance and fall over a railing?

Not your case, Jess. Finding DeShawn Simmons had to be her singular goal.

"I'm here to see the department shrink," Lori stated

with about as much enthusiasm as a woman about to undress for her annual gynecological examination.

"Just left her office," Jess admitted.

Lori made a face. "Is she tough? Weird?"

Jess dismissed the unkind remarks that came immediately to mind. Oden was doing her job. Dislike of the system should have no bearing on her conclusions about the woman. "She's thorough and she's blunt."

"I suppose those are good traits in a shrink." Lori cradled her coffee in her hands and gave a little shrug. "My appointment's not until ten thirty." She laughed, the sound a little weary and a lot dry. "My mom was determined to stop by and make breakfast for me. She calls me every half hour if I'm out of her sight. I told her my appointment was at eight thirty just to get away from her hovering."

"You've been here for almost two hours?"

Lori toed her bag, pointing out the iPad stowed there. "Caught up on a little reading. Cruised Facebook. Sent a couple of tweets. Believe me, it was a relief to escape. I swear my poor mother is never going to treat me like a grown-up again."

"In time," Jess promised. Lori was the youngest detective at BPD. Quite an accomplishment, especially for a woman. But last week had taken its toll on her and her family. As *normal* as she sounded, there was a new guardedness in her eyes. Something that hadn't been there a week ago.

"I'm not really so worried about Oden," she confessed. "This isn't my first time going through a required psych eval. I had the honor after the shoot-out Harper and I survived six months ago," she reminded Jess. "This is a different doctor, but when you get down to the nitty-gritty, they're all the same, I guess." She sighed. "The real problem is, I think I need a shrink this time. It's not like before."

Jess understood completely. "When you took that bullet all those months ago, your actions were by choice. For all intents and purposes you were in control. When you were taken hostage, Reed stole all control from you. Both situations were deadly, but you're right, it's very different." She went for a lighthearted laugh but the effort fell a little flat. "People are terrified of flying because there might be a plane crash when, statistically speaking, they're far more likely to die in a car crash. But being on a plane takes away all the control. That helplessness fuels the fear. Makes the possibility more terrifying no matter that it's far less likely."

"Exactly," Lori agreed. "While I was with that psycho, I felt utterly helpless. I hadn't felt that way since I almost drowned as a kid. That whack job scared me. Scared the hell out of me."

"That was his goal."

Lori smiled, the real deal this time, and the shadows clouding her eyes faded just a little. "But he got his in the end."

"Yes, he did."

They tapped their cups together and toasted the victory. "Too bad the other sicko got away."

"One of these days he'll get his." Every instinct Jess possessed warned that Spears would be back. She would be ready.

"You check out any more real estate listings?" Lori relaxed into her chair. "Now's the time to buy. I'm even thinking of picking up something. A town house or condo. I love the location of my apartment, but why pay rent when interest rates and housing prices are this low?"

"I'll get around to it." Jess had barely gotten settled at the HoJo's. Why was everyone in such an all-fired hurry to get her moved into something permanent? Her sister, Lily, had e-mailed her at least a dozen listings since Friday.

"I need to come back to work."

If Jess didn't know better she'd swear Lori set up this unplanned meeting just to broach that subject. "If your physician gives you a release—"

"Already have it."

"And," Jess pointed out, "if you complete your psych eval and get a release from Oden as well, I'd love to have you back." That was an understatement.

"I'm hoping to have that about an hour from now."

Jess leaned forward and set her coffee on the ergonomic little table. Lori's confidence was admirable but Jess wasn't so sure. She doubted anyone would ever know exactly what went on during all those hours that Reed held Lori prisoner. "Are you absolutely certain you're ready to deal with work again so soon?"

"You sound like Harper." Lori exhaled a frustrated breath. "And my mother and Chief Burnett. They all think I need a couple more weeks at home."

Jess could relate. "You're going crazy, huh?"

Lori nodded. "Absolutely rip-my-skin-off insane."

"Let me know what Oden recommends." Jess caved. "If for some reason she believes you need more time off, there's nothing I can do about that, but there's no rule that says we can't get together and talk shop after hours. Your insights are always valuable."

"Deal." Lori smiled, and this time it reached all the way to her eyes.

"I guess Harper told you about our close call in Druid Hills last night." Jess felt confident he had. "We were extremely lucky."

Lori looked confused. "He didn't mention any close call. What happened?"

Uh-oh. Seemed she and Burnett weren't the only ones keeping secrets from each other.

Jess gave her the condensed version. "I'm sure he just didn't want you to worry."

"Wow." Lori was rattled. "I'm glad you two are okay."

"Last night was a warning for us to back off."

"Harper's doing follow-up today?"

She was worried. The uncertainty in her expression belied the nonchalance of her question. Understandable. "He's getting what he can from Captain Allen in GTF. Checking on interviews with DeShawn's family and friends. We've got some major catching up to do. This kid is a popular guy."

Jess's cell clanged that old-fashioned ringtone. "Sorry." She rummaged in her bag. "I need to...get this." She studied the screen of her cell. No name, just a local number she didn't recognize. With a dubious look in Lori's direction she accepted the call. "Jess Harris."

"Chief Harris, this is Dr. Harlan Schrader. We need to have a conversation. Face-to-face. There are things about the Chandler case you need to know...Can you meet me this evening?"

As much as she wanted to hear anything the ME had on the Chandler case, Burnett had gotten his point across. She had to at least make an effort at following the rules.

"It might be better if you called Deputy Chief Black about this. The Chandler case belongs to him."

Jess held her breath. Told herself she'd done the right thing and still she wanted to bite off her tongue.

"I'm calling you, Chief Harris. Do you want to hear what I have to say or not?"

She'd tried. Really she had. She even had a witness. Lori was sitting right in front of her and heard her plainly tell her caller that he should talk to Black.

Her day was already booked with legwork that needed to be accomplished on the Simmons case. "Name the time, as long as it's after six, and the place," Jess agreed. "I'll be there."

Finley Boulevard, Captain D's, 10:50 a.m.

"Mr. Davis, I appreciate your assistance in this matter." Jess surveyed the prep personnel from her seat next to the manager's desk at the back of the kitchen area. Harper was out front interviewing the servers who knew DeShawn. The store opened in just ten minutes but no one had complained about taking the time to answer questions. The smell of fish and hush puppies frying had already filled the air.

"Whatever I can do," Mr. Davis assured her. "DeShawn is an outstanding young man. He is sorely missed here, I can tell you." He glanced back at the crew working to prepare for opening. "I can't believe the police haven't spoken to Jerome Frazier already or that he hasn't come forward to assist in whatever way he can. He and DeShawn are the best of friends. Have been since elementary school."

Mrs. Simmons had mentioned Jerome Frazier as well. But Harper hadn't been able to catch him at home or here, at work, until now. "Mr. Davis, I really would like to speak with Jerome but I'll need some privacy. Can you spare him for a few minutes? We'll be right outside."

"Of course. I'll have someone take care of his station. You do what needs to be done, Chief Harris. We all want DeShawn found safe and sound."

The manager would have risen from his chair but Jess waylaid him with a question. "What can you tell me about DeShawn's other friend, Nina? The young woman you gave a job?"

Not once had Davis mentioned her. Even now he turned away from Jess's gaze. This was a subject he did not want to discuss.

"In thirty years of food service," he began, his tone defeated, "I have never broken the rules. But, for DeShawn, I did. He was desperate to help this young girl and I went along with it. I paid her cash for cleaning up after hours. Sometimes my night crew doesn't get everything done. I didn't ask any questions. I just did as DeShawn asked. I didn't want to let him down."

There wasn't anything they could do about that now. "This morning one of our sketch artists drew a picture of this Nina based on the description DeShawn's grandparents gave. Would you mind having a look to see if you can add anything?"

"Certainly."

Jess showed him the image she had received via e-mail scarcely twenty minutes ago.

Davis nodded. "That's her." He looked away again. "She has a tattoo on her left shoulder. I saw it one night when she was wearing just a"—he motioned across the upper area of his chest with both hands—"tube-like top."

There were numerous tattoos associated with MS-13 and other gangs. New, unique symbols popped up all the time. "Can you describe it to me?"

"It was the number thirteen inside butterfly wings. I might not have noticed except that one of the other employees mentioned it to me. She was worried that Nina might be associated with the MS-13. DeShawn insisted that wasn't the case, but I asked Nina about it myself. As much as I wanted to help them, I'm responsible for the safety of the folks who work here." He rubbed the bridge of his nose beneath the glasses he wore. "She told me she was born into that life but her mother stole her away when she was just an infant. When she was thirteen, her mother had the tattoo put on her shoulder as a symbol of her freedom."

"Did she give you any idea of where she'd come from? Did she grow up here? Is her mother still alive?" Jess needed to identify this young woman as quickly as possible.

Davis moved his head side to side. "She was very secretive. I was surprised she gave me that much information."

Jess had a feeling she knew why. "When did you confront her about the tattoo?"

"Last Tuesday. One week ago today." As if he'd just realized the same thing Jess was thinking, he frowned. "She never came back to work after that."

Because she disappeared. Then less than seventy-two hours later DeShawn vanished as well.

Jess thanked Mr. Davis and prepared to question Jerome Frazier.

Frazier wasn't too crazy about the idea of talking to Jess and Harper in the small storage building in the rear parking lot. Other than sitting in Harper's SUV, that was the only privacy they could hope for.

Standing amid the stacks of paper products required to run the seafood restaurant and still wearing his apron, Jerome folded his arms over his chest and remained silent.

"Do you understand the rights Detective Harper has just explained to you?" Jess asked. The Miranda rights weren't really necessary just now but she wanted him worried.

"I got nothing to say."

"Yes or no, Jerome?" Jess said more firmly.

The silent treatment continued.

"It might be best if we took him downtown, ma'am," Harper suggested.

Jess exhaled an impatient sigh. "I guess we have no choice."

Jerome visibly stiffened. "No way. I didn't do anything wrong and I don't know anything that can help DeShawn."

"Do you have any idea what happened to him?" Jess demanded.

"That ho he was messing with is part of that crazy-ass posse always chopping heads off and shit. I don't care what DeShawn thought—she was just using him."

"By ho, do you mean Nina?"

He gave Jess an incredulous look. "Who else? DeShawn's on a path. He's gonna be somebody. Until he met that Nina bitch, he didn't let no girl alter his focus. That girl messed with his head. He's gonna get himself dead trying to help her—if he's not dead already."

"How was DeShawn trying to help Nina?"

"She said she loved him. They could have a life together. All they had to do was get away."

"You think there's a possibility they've left Birmingham?" BPD uniforms had gotten a good deal of legwork done yesterday. If the couple had left the city, they hadn't done so in a taxi, on a bus, train, or plane. "What sort of transportation do they have?" DeShawn Simmons's eleven-year-old Buick was still at his grandparents' house.

Jerome shrugged. "Maybe Nina knows people. None of DeShawn's friends would help him make this kind of mistake. No way."

"I don't suppose he's tried to contact you?"

Nineteen-year-old Jerome shook his head but he made one mistake. He lied. Until then Jess had sensed he was telling the truth, but the way he averted his gaze and that little tick that started in his jaw gave him away.

"Thank you, Jerome. If you hear anything," Jess said, handing him a card, "call me immediately. Your friend's life depends on our finding him fast."

"Wait."

Jess turned back to Frazier.

"This says you're a fed." His gaze narrowed with suspicion.

"Sorry about that. I just started this job and I haven't had time to get new business cards made. Just ignore the fed part."

Jerome still wasn't convinced, but that was irrelevant as far as Jess was concerned. When she and Harper reached his SUV, she hesitated before getting inside. "We need Officer Cook today. Now. I want someone tailing Frazier. He either knows where DeShawn Simmons is or he's heard from him since his disappearance."

The parking lot had begun to fill with the early lunch crowd. The morning was gone and the afternoon would fly just as fast. Jess had a list of DeShawn's friends as long as her arm that she wanted to interview. Sheriff Griggs along with the deputy chiefs of both Patrol and Support had met first thing this morning to form additional search teams. The media attention DeShawn's case was getting had lit a fire under the BPD.

DeShawn Simmons was now the poster boy for a better awareness of social and economic equality. The mayor and all the others in charge of this city had better listen up. Jess had a feeling this was not going away.

"I'll put in a call to Deputy Chief Hogan in Patrol and see if we can make that happen ASAP," Harper said as he reached for his cell. "Frazier'll be on shift here until two thirty. We should be able to have Cook in place by then."

Before Jess could thank him or open the passenger-side door of his SUV, a van whipped into the parking lot and stalled behind them, blocking any possibility of backing out of the parking slot.

Channel 6.

After a nod from Jess, Harper walked away from the vehicle to complete his call. She turned to face the nuisance.

Gina Coleman.

Birmingham's most beloved reporter.

This made the moment truly perfect. Beautiful, talented, former lover of the chief of police, Gina strode determinedly toward Jess, her cameraman hot on her heels.

Jess was several inches shorter than both Gina and Annette. She walked with the purpose of a man and she had wrestled numerous criminals. She'd even shot a few.

No matter the designer label she wore or the time she took to apply makeup or style her hair, there was no way she would ever look like these women. Both far outclassed her in the beauty and style departments.

Just one more reason she didn't fit in Dan Burnett's world.

Her stomach knotted in protest.

"Chief Harris, is it true you were removed from the Darcy Chandler murder investigation?"

Apparently Jess's shrink wasn't the only one who could toss out trick questions.

"Any questions you have about the Chandler case," Jess said calmly, "you'll need to take up with Deputy Chief Black."

Jess reached for the door handle.

"So you were removed from the case?"

Jess produced a smile. "Since my full attention is required on the Simmons case, I am not involved with the Chandler case. That's true." To say she had been removed carried a negative connotation. Coleman wasn't getting that sound bite from her.

This time she actually got the door open before the next question was hurled at her.

"Were you assigned the Simmons case because of your past connection to his neighborhood? Have you spoken to your aunt since returning to Birmingham? Did you know she still lives in the same house?"

Fury whiplashed Jess. She slammed the door and got in Coleman's face. "Do you understand what you've just done?" The woman had just mentioned that Jess had family in the neighborhood where some of the worst gang activity in the city played out.

Coleman held up a perfectly manicured hand and her cameraman backed off. "I'll edit out that last part."

Jess wanted to like this woman. She really did. She doubted the feeling was mutual since she'd left Coleman holding the bag on a so-called exclusive story last week. But this was going too far.

"What do you want, Coleman?" Besides a pound of flesh.

"I want to know if Darcy Chandler was murdered."

"Like I said, you'll have to ask Chief Black."

"I'm asking you."

What was up with these people? First the ME and now Coleman? The ME could cite his age. Coleman was as old as Jess for sure. She'd just opted for Botox so it didn't show. In her line of work she could likely use it as a tax deduction.

"You owe me, Harris," Coleman reminded.

"Off the record," Jess made clear, "there are inconsistencies, but nothing substantial. Talk to Black. Ask him about Chandler's shoes."

Coleman nodded. "I will. Thanks. Do you have an update on DeShawn Simmons?"

Jess hadn't released the rendering of Simmons's mysterious female friend to the press. Maybe this would earn her some points with Coleman. She dug out her cell and forwarded the image to the number she had for Coleman. "We believe this young woman knows something about DeShawn's disappearance. If anyone recognizes her they should call the tip line."

Coleman checked her cell. Clearly surprised to get any kind of heads-up, she passed Jess a business card. "Let me know if I can be of assistance to your investigation."

As the reporter and her cameraman loaded up their van and drove away, Jess considered that she and Coleman didn't have to be friends as long as they were working toward the same goal.

Funny, as hard as Jess tried to keep the Chandler case off her mental plate, folks just kept shoving another serving her way.

Galleria Mall, 8:15 p.m.

Jess couldn't claim to have participated in any real covert investigations. A few times she'd ended up in the middle of an outburst and wound up in a struggle, but most of her professional battles had taken place over a desk or in a training facility. Her work as a profiler with the bureau had been conducted in formal interviews where those present understood the legal ramifications of any and all exchanges. She observed and analyzed. Before and after the interviews, she researched. The persons of interest, where they lived and worked, were extremely important to her final assessments of any case. Knowing how each individual involved acted and reacted in their daily lives was almost as telling as any physical evidence found at a crime scene.

Each act was motivated by an emotional reaction or lack thereof to stimuli. If the motive was unearthed, all the rest fell into place. It was that simple and, at the same time, vastly complicated.

The circus music accompanying the spinning of the mall's carousel dragged her from her musings. Where the devil was Schrader? He'd said eight o'clock. Near the food court at the carousel.

Jess had done her research on the cocky Dr. Harlan Schrader. He was in the final days of a forensic pathology fellowship program with the Jefferson County Coroner's Office. He was a short-timer, which meant he had little to lose if he decided to spill about something he'd seen or heard. Hotshot Dr. Schrader was on his way to the Mayo Clinic in just a couple of weeks. He either wanted to have a little revenge against a colleague who had rubbed him the wrong way or he genuinely felt compelled to reveal whatever information he intended to pass along.

If he ever got here.

Another check of the time on her cell showed it was five minutes later than the last time she checked. After hours of interviewing friends of DeShawn Simmons and sitting in on an update with the search team commander, she was pretty much exhausted.

She scanned the crowded mall. Who dragged their kids around in a public place at this hour? There were enough small children and bright colors to prompt flashbacks to Munchkin Land of the Wizard of Oz fame.

Her attention landed on a black tee and jeans on the other side of one of the play areas. Dr. Too-Sexy-to-Be-Punctual leaned down and kissed a young woman. Surprised, Jess watched as he ruffled the hair of a small boy before heading in her direction.

So the hotshot had a baby and the requisite baby-mama. Maybe he had a little more at stake than she'd gauged by his attitude and bio.

He surveyed the crowd in both directions with just about every step he took. By the time he reached her he would likely be suffering from neck strain. The doctor was a wee bit nervous. How big could his news be?

"Let's sit so we're less conspicuous." He motioned to a bench that had just been vacated a few feet away.

That he didn't wait for her to sit first was no surprise. "What has you so upset, Dr. Schrader?"

He stared at her as if she'd asked him to produce documentation that he was an actual American citizen. "I'm not upset. Who said I was upset?"

Jess kept her lips bent into a smile. "I'm sorry. You just seem a little out of sorts, that's all. And you mentioned on the phone that you were taking a risk. I just assumed that meant you were upset."

"I'm not upset," he argued, still scanning the crowd. "I'm frustrated and offended."

"I see. Why don't you explain the situation and perhaps I can help?"

"He's going to rule her death accidental."

The decision reached by Dr. Leeds, Jefferson County coroner, was not a total surprise. Since a complete autopsy wouldn't be necessary in a case where no foul play was evident, the coroner's decision would rely solely on the circumstances at the scene and the less invasive preliminary examination of the body, and, of course, a full toxicology screen. Considering the suspected cause of death, those procedures were sufficient to reveal the injuries consistent with a fall and any indications of a struggle that might have occurred prior to the fall. If the victim used one or more drugs that might have contributed to an impulsive act or the lack of balance in a woman with particularly good balance, those secrets would be discovered in a comprehensive toxicology report.

"Her injuries were consistent with a fall from that height," Jess guessed. "No signs of a struggle."

He performed another survey of the crowd. "Nothing irregular in toxicology. No drugs at all. Darcy Chandler was a very healthy thirty-eight-year-old female. The official cause of death is traumatic brain injury. The extent of the injury precluded any possibility of survival. She may have been conscious for moments or a minute, but death was imminent and inevitable. However, there were two inconsistencies in my opinion relative to the manner of death, and that's where my concerns lie."

"Did you bring these inconsistencies to Dr. Leeds's attention?"

"Of course." He swung his attention from the crowd long enough to glare at her. "He insisted those anomalies were not sufficient to warrant deeming her death anything other than accidental."

And Jess would just bet that given Chandler's standing in the community and the lack of any good-bye note, suicide was off the table. "Why don't you tell me about the inconsistencies that disturbed you?" The routine never changed. Someone came forward with information and inevitably she had to extract it.

"There was a first-degree contusion on the outside of the lower left leg. This mild bruising was not consistent with the impact of falling fifteen feet or with any other object in her path as she fell. It would have been far more severe had it occurred in the final impact of the fall."

"Maybe she bumped into something that morning." Unless he had more than this she would tend to agree with Leeds.

"The injury was very recent, minutes before death," he insisted. "And it was exactly the width of the upstairs handrail."

Now he had her attention. "You confirmed the width of the upstairs handrail?"

He cut her a look that warned he suspected she knew the answer to that question. "I measured. The bruising is exactly the right width. As if she fell over the rail from an elevated position, striking her lower left leg as she pitched over."

"Like someone threw her over," Jess offered.

"But she wasn't expecting the move, so she didn't have time to react. There was no indication of a struggle with another person or an attempt to catch herself. Her fall was totally unforeseen and unprepared for, in my opinion."

Jess conjured the scene in her head. "She might have stumbled as she started to climb over the railing if suicide was her intent." That one seemed highly unlikely.

"Darcy Chandler was right-side dominant," Schrader explained. "Her instinct would have been to put her right leg over first. And either way, there is no scenario where she would have bumped the top of the railing with the outside of her leg by lifting it from a normal standing position and going over the rail."

"Obviously you've considered the scenario at length."

"I went back to the house and proved my theory."

"How did you get back in the house?" Had one of Black's detectives escorted Schrader on a second review of the scene? Seemed the only feasible possibility.

"Mrs. Chandler asked me to take a closer look."

Was he kidding? "Mrs. Chandler, as in the victim's mother?"

He shook his head. "Her grandmother. She and my grandmother are close friends. She's convinced that Darcy was the victim of foul play."

And there it was. The proverbial hornet's nest. No way was Jess kicking that one. "Dr. Schrader, you really need to share your thoughts with Chief Black. This is his case and he will decide what direction this investigation needs to take."

She was not getting dragged into this emotion-driven war.

"I thought you would get it." He shook his head. "I read up on you. I expected more." He stood. "I guess I wasted your time and mine."

"Wait." Not that she was going to change her mind, but he had said there were two things. "You didn't tell me about the other anomaly." They were both here, smack-dab in the middle of Munchkin Land. She might as well get the whole story.

"There were traces of a material trapped between the fingers of her right hand."

Fabric from her assailant's clothing? Not hair or he would have said as much. "What kind of material?"

"Marabou. White in color."

"Marabou?" She didn't have a clue. Given a few seconds she could Google it using her phone.

The cocky expression reappeared on the handsome doctor's face. "Small, soft, white turkey feathers. Commonly used in feather boas. Since the victim wasn't wearing one, makes you wonder how she got her fingers entwined with one."

Jess knew exactly how.

8

Five Points, 9:45 p.m.

Lori waited until her cell started to ring before answering the door.

She opened it and Chet Harper looked up in surprise, his cell phone pressed to his ear as he listened to hers ring.

"I figured you were out." He lowered the phone, tucked it into the leather carrier at his waist.

His hands were broad, long fingered, and skilled at bringing pleasure. He was damned good at what he did, on and off the job. The lean waist, the broad shoulders, the handsome face, the entire package was loaded with sensuality. Even the way he said her name turned her on.

As long and hard as she had fought getting involved with him, she had lost the battle. After last week, she had no fight left in her to even stage a half-assed protest. She needed Chet Harper no matter that he so totally threatened her independence.

That sick bastard Reed had stolen something from Lori

during the forty-eight or so hours he had held her. The part of her that felt strong and assured was now weak and uncertain. She wasn't sure if she would ever get that confidence back.

"Why would I be out at this hour?" She stood in front of him, wearing short shorts and a skimpy tee, hands bracketing her hips. "Did you think maybe I had a date?"

He was slow to answer, primarily because he was busy inventorying how many of her assets were on display in her skimpy outfit. Good. She wanted him distracted. She wanted to remind him what he would be missing if he played games with her. This relationship, and she used the term in its loosest definition, would not survive distrust. Every aspect of their lives had to be on the table. Complete honesty.

And she needed him to know that he was as weak as she was...that she posed an equal threat to his autonomy.

Otherwise she feared she would become her mother. As much as she loved and respected her mother, her entire life had revolved around her husband. He had been the breadwinner, the decision maker, the strong, solid, sole head of the household. When he died, her mother had been at a total loss. It had taken her years to become a whole person.

Lori would not let that happen to her. She would be an equal in all aspects of any relationship.

"Well?" she pressed. "Is that what you thought?"

The shrug that lifted his shoulders was noncommittal, as if he feared giving the wrong answer.

Good.

"I thought maybe you had gone to your mother's or maybe to a movie with your sister."

He sounded so exhausted and sincere she should be

ashamed of herself for making him suffer like this, but he'd kept a damned big secret from her. That was not acceptable. He'd been injured in the line of duty and he hadn't mentioned it when they talked last night.

She turned and strode over to the sofa and plopped down on it. He waited just on the other side of the threshold for a moment before coming inside, closing and securing the door. He removed his jacket and hung it on the doorknob the way he always did.

"If you want a beer or something, check the fridge."

Rather than going for a beer he joined her on the sofa. "How was your appointment this morning? I tried to call."

He had called four times. She had ignored each one. "She thinks I need another week or so off duty."

"What do you think?"

"I think if I don't get back to work I might just explode. So I made a deal with her. She lets me come back to work on Monday and I see her once a week for two months."

"Great." He loosened his tie. "We have our hands full with the Simmons case. Lieutenant Prescott has been moved over to the GTF for now. That happened this afternoon. Chief Harris is on fire to solve the Simmons case, but she's a little distracted with the Chandler case." He dragged the tie from around his neck. "We're still finding our footing with this new unit, but we'll get there." He turned his face to hers and sent her a smile. "It'll be good to have you back."

How sweet.

"Why don't you let me get you a beer?" She laid her hand on his leg, right about where there was no doubt a bandage over his healing gunshot wound. The one he'd gotten last night and failed to mention.

He flinched.

"When were you going to tell me?"

The weariness in his eyes gave way to regret. "I knew you had that appointment today. I didn't want you stressing about anything else."

"That's very thoughtful of you, Harper, but I'm a grown woman. I can handle bad news. Or maybe you think I'm too fragile. Is that it?"

He traced a path down her cheek with his fingertips. She shivered. "I couldn't protect you from that bastard. He hurt you. I want you well again. Back on the team. This was just another worry you didn't need."

"Is that all you want?"

He shook his head. "I want all of you."

She took his hand and held it to her cheek. "He hurt me here." She lowered his hand, palm down, to her throat. "Here." She dragged his hand downward, between her breasts to her rib cage. "And here." Misery darkened his eyes. "But he couldn't touch me here." She flattened his palm against her chest, over her heart. "Because I knew you would come for me. There was no doubt in my mind or in my heart that you and Jess would find me somehow. I trust you that much."

He cupped her cheek in his big, warm hand. "I would have traded places with you in a heartbeat."

"I know." She pushed his hands away. "But you kept what happened last night from me. You can't do that again."

He put his arm around her and pulled her close. "Never again. You have my word." He kissed her hair. "I swear."

"How's Jess handling losing the Chandler case? She didn't say much about it when I saw her today."

"There's some inconsistencies," Chet said. "She's right about that, but Chief Black isn't coming out with an acknowledgment of her analysis. Mostly, I think, to stand his ground."

"The truth should be priority, not his pride."

"You know Black. He'll get around to the truth, even if it proves him wrong. He's a good man. He just has his way and Jess has hers. The two don't go together so well."

"I guess she was pissed that Burnett made the call in Black's favor." Lori understood the transition was difficult for Jess. She had to find her place, and clashing with the long-standing regime was part of the process.

"A little bit, I think."

Lori laughed. "A little bit like a dam bursting and a little bit of water slipping through."

"I don't think she'll be inviting him in if he shows up at her door tonight."

"Do you think she and Burnett will end up together? You know, really together?"

"That's a tough call. They're both damned hardheaded."

"Set in their ways," Lori agreed.

"Neither one wants to give an inch."

"But I think they've loved each other since they were teenagers. Surely that makes a difference."

"Maybe."

She searched his face. "What about you and your ex-wife? Were you in love as teenagers?"

Chet grinned. "We met after college. No lifelong romance there."

"You have a son together. Doesn't that sometimes make you wish things could be the way they used to be between you?" Why on earth had she asked that question? They'd been skating around this relationship thing for months and not once had she let him see how much that aspect of his past troubled her.

She hadn't meant to now.

"I wish I could say there was a time when we were really good together. That somehow things had gone wrong. But the truth is we were never good together. We always had different visions of our life together. I couldn't live up to hers and she didn't care if she lived up to mine. I guess we each thought that having a child would change things somehow. Mesh our differences. But it didn't. Just made those differences more glaring."

"I don't think our visions for the future are so different," she offered. "But we have vastly different ideas on how we get there."

"We'll find our way." He kissed her nose. "As long as we don't lose sight of where we're going, it really doesn't matter how we get there."

How this man made her want him even when she wanted to be stronger, to hang solidly on to her independence. She stood and offered him her hand. He accepted and allowed her to lead him to the bed. Her studio had no walls separating the bedroom from the living room, so the journey was quick and easy.

He waited patiently as she took her time unbuttoning his shirt. She loved undressing him. Opening his shirt to glide her palms over all that ribbed muscle. Then pushing the crisp fabric over those wide, sculpted shoulders and down his muscled arms.

She loosened his belt and drew it from his trousers. With just a look she prompted him to take a seat on the end of the bed. Going on her knees, she removed his shoes and socks. He watched, excitement glittering more brightly in his eyes with every move she made. He liked that she took so much time with him.

Obeying her every subtle command, he stood while she dragged the trousers and briefs down his long, powerful legs. She kissed his left thigh near the bandage that protected his wound. The idea that it could have been so much worse tore at her heart.

For several seconds he visibly resisted his own desires so that she could admire his nude body. Lori loved how he fought so fiercely to please her that way. Then he took his turn. He loosened her snap and zipper and the short shorts dropped to the floor. She'd forgone underwear. This pleased him immensely. Then the tee was peeled off in one smooth move. His breath hitched as his palms glided over her bare breasts and down her rib cage. She moaned her pleasure, her body already burning for more of his touch.

By the time they fell onto the bed, they were tangled in each other's arms and frantic to be joined.

Tonight he made love to her slowly. Maybe because of his injury or maybe just because he felt the need to savor each moment. She certainly did.

Afterward they lay together and Lori acknowledged something she had denied for months now.

She belonged in his arms this way. Needed it.

That was the scariest part of this relationship thing.

For now, that immense need was as much real estate as she was willing to give up where her heart was concerned.

He already owned way too much.

9

DeShawn wasn't buying this.

These fools had scared the good sense out of him last night. He glared at the four men seated around the table, their complete attention focused on Nina. Anger twisted around in his gut. He didn't like the way they looked at her. He damned sure didn't like the way they had busted into the motel room and dragged them out like hostages in a bad drug movie.

DeShawn glanced around the room. He'd had a bag over his head, so he wasn't exactly sure where they were. An old run-down house with beat-up furnishings. He hadn't heard any traffic noise outside when they arrived, so he was guessing they were somewhere out of the city. After they'd been dragged into the van last night the ride was a long one. At least it had felt long.

Nina laughed and he watched her. The ten o'clock news was on and something had obviously captured their attention. She said these guys were her friends. But he wasn't so sure. More gangbangers. MS-13 for sure. Why did she call them friends if it was that life she was trying to get away from?

He could just imagine how scared his grandmother was. His grandfather, too. It made him sick to his stomach to think about it. But what could he do? If he tried to contact them, that could put them in danger. Besides, his cell phone had died two days ago.

He'd begged Nina to go to the police. But she kept saying the police couldn't protect them. The man who wanted her dead would stop at nothing.

How was he supposed to help her? If the police couldn't, how could he? He was just a fry cook at Captain D's who was supposed to go to college next month.

Why were they still in Birmingham? If she wanted to escape, why weren't they getting out of here? "What're we doing?" he said out loud. DeShawn didn't care what these fools thought.

After a pointed look from her, the four men, all Latinos, got up from the table and left the room. Nina settled her attention on DeShawn.

"Com'ere, baby, I got something I want you to see." She gestured for him to come sit with her.

As he moved toward her, she dragged a chair closer so they could sit side by side at the table. She hugged him tight and kissed him hard on the mouth.

"You gotta see this." She picked up the TV remote and hit the button to go back to the broadcast.

These guys might live in a dump but they had a serious electronic setup. This just got weirder and weirder. It wasn't right. He knew it wasn't. Deep in his belly he had a bad feeling.

Nina hit play and the Channel 6 reporter was giving an update on his case.

DeShawn's stomach twisted into more knots. He felt like he needed to hurl. His grandparents and friends were seeing this. The reporter was talking about how unlikely it was that he was even still alive.

He looked away. "I don't wanna see this."

"Wait." She tugged at his arm. "You're gonna miss the important part."

He didn't want to but he looked anyway. Just because she asked. A photo of a blond woman flashed on the screen. The woman was chief somebody. DeShawn had never seen her before. Wait...maybe he'd seen her on the news when all those white girls went missing a week or two back.

"See that?" Nina enthused. "They got Deputy Chief Jess Harris looking for you."

DeShawn shrugged. "So?" Right now the only thing he wanted to do was go home but he couldn't tell her that. Nina would think he was a coward.

"She's that FBI woman who found all those missing girls. She's really important." Nina tugged his face to hers and pressed her forehead against his. "She can help us. She can stop *him*."

"How can she help us?" Just because the cop was important didn't mean she would bother with their problems.

"You have to keep trusting me, Shawney. She can help us. Then we can have our lives back without running from him until the day we die."

He hitched his head toward the door. "Did those guys tell you that?"

Fury flashed in her eyes. "No one had to tell me anything," she snapped. "I know things. The only thing they're going to do is help us."

Now he'd made her mad. "Maybe you don't need me anymore." Maybe that was the problem. She had allies now. She was no longer by herself. Maybe she didn't need DeShawn Simmons to protect her or to love her.

She pulled his mouth to hers. Kissed him until he gasped for air.

"I need you more than I have ever needed anyone," she whispered against his panting lips. "I can't do this without you." She looked into his eyes. "Without you, I'll never be free."

She ripped open his jeans and went down on him right there with those other guys right outside. He groaned her name. Clawed at the table.

They were going to make it...together. Just like Nina promised.

10

The room was large enough to squeeze in a small conference table and a handful of desks. There was no private
office for Jess but she'd had one of those for years at the
bureau and knew firsthand that particular status symbol
was overrated.

Filing cabinets and a case board lined one wall. Jess's
desk sat in front of a large window that extended the entire
length of another wall. Having a good window was a perk
that would never be overrated. The other four desks stood
in pairs facing each other. She didn't know how her team
would feel about the arrangement but she had no problem
with reorganizing.

For the next few days it would be just her and Harper
and Cook since Hogan had agreed to release him. Cook
had assumed surveillance detail on Jerome Frazier yesterday afternoon. Lori would be back on duty on Monday. Lieutenant Prescott would be working with the GTF

until needed in SPU. The Simmons case continued to stir the community's outrage, adding another layer to the already escalating gang problems. The sooner DeShawn Simmons could be found and the case closed, the sooner things would settle down.

Jess studied the timeline and facts Harper had chronicled on the case board for the Simmons investigation.

DeShawn Simmons, nineteen, no criminal record, no trouble of any sort. According to Mr. Davis, his supervisor at Captain D's, and the Parker High School guidance counselor, Simmons was a fine young man whose only fault was in trying too hard to help others. His minister had gotten Jess's number from Mrs. Simmons and called to give his own recommendation in support of the young man. According to the minister, DeShawn was as good as it gets with young folks these days. He was the model for young black men on the rise to accomplishment in Birmingham's community.

DeShawn's caring nature and giving heart had landed him in serious trouble, Jess feared. Every minute that passed lessened the likelihood of finding him in one piece, much less alive. Like most organized gangs, MS-13 liked doing things big and loud when they had an example to set, so there was a good chance Simmons was still breathing at this point. When and where they dumped his body would make a very public statement about who ruled in this territory.

And, as Burnett predicted, the debate in the media was reaching a boiling point. The community wanted answers and they wanted action.

The question voiced most often by all the media outlets was whether DeShawn Simmons was getting the same treatment the missing white girls had gotten. Jess was determined he would.

Search teams worked day and night. Every division had someone focused on this case. Rewards for information regarding DeShawn and the still unidentified Latina called Nina had been offered.

"Still no idea who the girl he was helping is or what became of her?"

Harper paused and capped his Dry Erase marker. "I've had a couple of statements from those who live in the neighborhood suggesting she belonged to Salvadore Lopez, the *primera palabra*—the man in charge of the local MS-13 cliques."

If that intel was on target, Simmons was in bigger trouble than she'd thought.

"We didn't find anything useful at the house where she'd been hiding out," Harper advised. "The blanket, pillow, and remnants of food Simmons had brought her were there, but no evidence to indicate how long she'd been hiding out there or under what circumstances she left the property. A couple of crime-scene guys lifted prints but we have no matches yet." He tapped the list of family members and friends on the case board. "We got nothing new from all these interviews."

Jess was all too aware of that. Despite having only gotten this case about thirty-six hours ago, she'd conducted many of those interviews herself. "Tell me about this Lopez character." She leaned on the edge of her desk and considered the mug shot Harper had posted. "He has an interesting rap sheet?"

Harper nodded. "A long and colorful one. Age twenty-five." He tapped the photo. "He's second-generation MS-13.

He was arrested in California for murder but another man came forward and confessed. Since the evidence was shaky, Lopez walked. Word was that the guy who made the confession was his *segunda*, his second-in-command. Things were getting a little hot for Lopez in LA, two strikes, so he came south about eighteen months ago to put Birmingham on the map of their Mexico-to-New York corridor."

"What's Captain Allen's take on Lopez?" Jess couldn't see a good ending to this. There was nothing even remotely good about anyone involved with MS-13.

"Keep in mind that Allen won't lay this on Lopez without confirmation. His contacts are maintaining they know nothing about Simmons's disappearance. As for Lopez, Captain Allen called him ruthless," Harper confirmed. "Back in LA his father, Leonardo Lopez, is like the messiah. If the Mexican cartel or anyone else wants someone dead, they call Lopez senior. Assassinations, human trafficking, drugs, gunrunning. Daddy does it all. Junior's job is to live up to his father's expectations."

"How has he fared since coming south?"

"That's where things really get interesting," Harper promised. "Captain Allen says the crime rate here has gone up exponentially since Lopez arrived. Half the African American homicides in the city can be attributed to Lopez's people or their activities. Hangings, decapitations, the more grisly the killing the better they seem to like it." He viewed the data he had documented on the board, then turned to Jess. "With all due respect, ma'am, based on what I've learned so far, I'd have to say DeShawn Simmons is a goner."

"I can see how you would come to that conclusion, Sergeant." She pushed away from her desk and studied the case board. "The one variable is whether or not Lopez has the girl, too." Jess moved closer to study the mug shots of Salvadore Lopez. He might have been a reasonably attractive man if not for all the tattoos and the shaved head. But, like most gangbangers, being marked was a part of the life. A rite of passage. "If Lopez has the girl, why not kill Simmons right off the bat and leave him for us to find? Why keep him for two or three days with no public demonstration of his sovereignty?"

"If she's still missing, there's no chatter on the street."

Jess braced one arm across her waist, propped the elbow of the other there, and tapped her chin. "There wouldn't be. Only those closest to Lopez will know the truth. He can't control his woman. That's far too humiliating to be common knowledge. Makes him look weak. But time is his enemy. The longer it takes to get his house in order the more likely the rumor is to spread. When he has the situation under control, he'll flaunt his triumph. Until then he and all those around him will protect his ego at all costs. Part of the power is in manipulating the perception of others. They see what he wants them to see."

"You think the girl may have gotten word that Lopez was closing in so she went deeper into hiding without telling DeShawn? Maybe to protect him but her plan backfired?"

"Maybe. Maybe not. This girl may have just been using Simmons. But I'd wager that if we find this Nina whoever-she-is before Lopez does, we might be able to lure him into a trap and just maybe save Simmons's life—if he's still alive."

"We could put the word out that we're offering immunity as well as witness protection if she turns herself in."

"See if we can make that happen. I'd say it's a given she has major information on Lopez and his operation. The idea that no one has come forward about her tells me she's close to him. Close enough to hurt him. If that's the case, I'm guessing the investment would prove worthwhile to the feds." ATF as well as DEA loved to get their hands on scum like Lopez.

The artist's drawing of Nina was running full force with the media blitz on Simmons.

Someone out there knew where he was being held or, less likely, where he was hiding.

All they needed was one witness to man up and come forward.

A soft knock resonated through the room as the door opened. *Lori*. A smiled lifted Jess's lips in spite of the current subject matter. "Good morning, Detective Wells. Come on in."

"I know I'm not officially back on duty until Monday, but"—she shrugged—"I thought I'd stop by and have a look at our space."

Lori looked good this morning. All dressed up as if she were ready to get back to work right this minute. Jess wished that were the case. No one, except Lori herself, wanted that to happen more than Jess. She imagined Harper had mixed feelings. As long as Lori was off duty, she wasn't in danger.

"We're going over the Simmons case," Jess explained with a wave to the case board. "But I think we're due a break, wouldn't you say, Sergeant?"

"I'll get the coffee," Harper volunteered. "It's good to see you, Detective Wells."

Like this was the first time they'd seen each other since

Lori had been released from the hospital. Jess bit her lips together to hold back a grin. These two were as bad as she and Burnett. Though she hoped not quite as complicated.

"Thanks, Harper." Lori watched until he was out the door and it was closed behind him. Her attention swung back to Jess. "I have an offer for you."

Intrigued, Jess dragged a chair over to her desk. "Sit. I can't wait to hear." Lori glanced back at the door as if she feared their time alone was limited and she didn't want anyone else to know what she was about to say, maybe not even Harper.

"I've been thinking about the shoes and the dress."

"Aha." Darcy Chandler. Jess had told Lori about the discrepancies that nagged at her and the strange meeting with Schrader. She'd had the perfect excuse since Dr. Oden had called with an official release date for Lori to return to duty. Too bad she'd left Jess in the dark about her own evaluation.

"There is no reasonable explanation for the shoes she was wearing that day, as confirmed by witnesses, to have been set aside like that," Lori said. "There has to be something we don't see. Then there's the marabou—from the white boa that Katrina had in her possession—and Katrina is the one who found Chandler. I find that a little convenient and unquestionably in need of further investigation."

"Maybe Chandler was still alive when Katrina found her," Jess offered, "and somehow grabbed hold of the boa. Katrina probably knelt down to check on her and the boa she was wearing fell against Chandler. If she clutched at it, it probably scared the child to death. Katrina may have jerked the boa free and run for Andrea. That would certainly explain what Schrader found."

"But," Lori countered, "you said Katrina insisted Chandler didn't move or say anything."

"She also said repeatedly that she didn't do anything wrong. That may be a guilty conscience talking. In her thirteen-year-old mind she may have somehow made the situation worse by reacting the way she did and snatching the boa from her beloved teacher's hand."

"Maybe," Lori admitted. "But her mother was in the house shortly before that, too. She was actually the last one to see Darcy Chandler alive. That's some serious coincidence."

"The problem is we can't prove whether Chandler was dead or alive when Dresher left her. And without any compelling evidence of foul play Chief Black is not going to push for confirmation. He'll suggest that since Chandler was a dance teacher of boa-wearing ballerinas, the trace evidence of feathers is to be expected."

"That's where my offer comes in." Lori glanced over her shoulder at the door again. "Why not put someone on the two most likely suspects? Dig for dirt. For previous acts of violence. That kind of thing."

"Black is watching Chandler's husband, but I have no idea if he's looking at anyone else. To him, *if* this was a homicide, the husband is the most likely candidate."

"That's typically the case, but..."

"The shoes," Jess finished for her. "That part is so wrong. And the feathers."

"And yet there's no evidence to prove any of it is wrong."

"Evidence and shoes aside," Jess said, growing annoyed just thinking about how Black refused to listen to anything she had to say on the matter, "the only way to find the truth as to whether it was a homicide or a suicide or just a freak accident is to find the motive for Chandler's death. Money? The dance studio? Another woman? A wardrobe malfunction? What drove her or her killer to act? What did either hope to gain?"

"Let me check out Katrina and her mother. All the dance moms for that matter. Some of the statements suggested that he was having an affair with a dance mom. It's time to find out which one and how serious the relationship was. Off the record, of course. If Chief Black isn't in the sharing mode, I can probably pick up a little info here and there from colleagues I've worked cases with."

Lori wanted this bad. The anticipation in her eyes and voice was palpable. Jess understood the need to feel as if she were accomplishing something. Allowing her anywhere near the Simmons case was out of the question. The players and the circumstances were too unpredictable. "If Black or Burnett finds out, they're not going to take it well."

"They won't find out. I'm on my own time. No one will know."

"Know what?" Harper asked as he entered with three steaming cups of coffee from the department lounge.

She and Lori exchanged a look of hesitation. They were a team. Jess wanted the communication lines kept open at all times.

"Lori's going to do some off-the-record research into the dancers and their moms, particularly Katrina and Dresher. If it's true that the Russian was having an affair, maybe that's why Darcy Chandler's dead."

Harper passed around the coffee. "Black has someone on that."

"Following up on the rumored affair?" Jess wanted to

be surprised but she wasn't. Not really. Any cop worth his salt would look into the possibility even without the obvious presence of foul play.

"Mayakovsky swears he wasn't having an affair," Harper explained. "He says he hasn't had one in almost two years."

"Give the guy a star," Jess grumbled. "How do you hear all this and I don't hear jack?"

Harper rolled over a chair and parked it next to Lori's. "You don't really want to know the answer to that, ma'am."

"How long, Sergeant, will I continue to be considered an outsider?"

A smile toyed with the corners of his mouth. "I'd say not more than a couple years. How long do you think, Wells?"

Lori laughed, shared a secret look with Harper. "Depends on if she keeps pissing people off."

Jess threw up her hands. "Forget I asked. So," she said to Lori, "you'll see what you can come up with on the dance moms and their talented offspring." She turned to Harper. "You and I will keep beating the bushes in hopes of scrounging up a lead on Simmons."

"Works for me." Harper stood, but before getting back on task, he turned to Lori. "You should pick out which desk you want, Wells. I've already staked my claim."

While the two debated who got the preferred placement of backs to the wall, Jess's cell rang. She stood, reached across her desk to nab it. The local number was one she didn't recognize.

She answered with her usual greeting. "Jess Harris."

"Good morning, Jess, this is Katherine Burnett."

Jess sank back into her chair. "Hello...Katherine. What can I do for you this morning?" Why would Dan's mother call her? Did Katherine intend to warn her to stay away from Dan? Annette was suddenly calling him about Andrea all the time. Maybe Katherine wanted Annette back as a daughter-in-law. Of course she'd have to get rid of the current husband first.

Whatever Katherine wanted, Jess would be only too happy to let the queen know that Dan came to her after hours of his own free will. She hadn't dragged him into her life or her bed. *Calm down. You have no idea why this woman is calling.*

"Since Dan senior and I were away when you returned to Birmingham, I missed the opportunity to give you a proper welcome."

Jess struggled to ungrit her teeth. Katherine had that Old South accent. Jess was convinced the woman had watched *Gone with the Wind* as a young girl and had latched onto Scarlett's persona.

"We've both been quite busy," Jess responded, breaking the awkward lapse of silence. "At this very moment I'm in a briefing with the members of my new unit. The one the chief of police and the Jefferson County sheriff designed specifically for me to head."

Mortification had Jess slapping her hand over her mouth. Twenty-plus years. A master's degree in psychology and numerous career achievements later and she still felt compelled to compete with Dan's mother.

"I won't keep you then. I thought we'd have lunch. Say twelve thirty at Chez Fonfon? It's on Eleventh. See you there."

The distinct tone announcing that the call had ended

sounded before Jess could tell the woman *hell no*! Not that she would have actually said that but she would have made up an excuse. A good excuse like maybe she had a root canal scheduled at that time.

Jess tossed her cell aside and considered the ramifications of simply not showing up.

But that would be like admitting that Katherine was the winner. At what, Jess couldn't name, but this competition dated back twenty-five years.

She stared down at her ivory pencil skirt and matching shell and high heels. Conservative yet sophisticated. The outfit was one of her favorites. Thank God she'd worn it today or she would have had to make a HoJo's run before lunch.

She reached for her phone again so she could Google the place and check out the lunch menu. Knowing what to order before she sat across the table from Queen Katherine would make those first moments far less uncomfortable.

What was she saying?

Every second she spent in that woman's presence would be intensely awkward and inordinately unpleasant.

Jess tossed her phone aside. It didn't matter what they served at Chez Froufrou or Fonfon or whatever it was.

There was absolutely zero possibility she could eat seated across the table from Katherine Burnett.

Chez Fonfon, 12:38 p.m.

Before the hostess could utter her greeting, Jess spotted Katherine. It wasn't difficult; the restaurant was very cozy. A little hint, *little* being the operative word, of Paris right here in Birmingham. Jess flashed the hostess a smile and pointed to the table where her own private hell waited.

Katherine had already ordered two glasses of white wine. She glanced up as Jess approached and displayed the kind of smile years of practice and tens of thousands of dollars of cosmetic dentistry had perfected.

"Jess, you're right on schedule."

Actually she was eight minutes late—not as a result of being unable to find the place but because she'd driven past it four times before parking.

"Katherine." A smile pasted into place, Jess settled into the only other chair at the intimate table. "How are you? You look fabulous, as always."

"Thank you, dear. As do you. Have you lost weight?"

A tick started in Jess's cheek at the effort required to maintain that damned fake smile. "I beg your pardon?"

Katherine shook her head. "Oh, silly me. It was your sister, Lily, who was the chubby one. How is she, by the way?"

Lily had ballooned up to a whopping size ten in high school. Jess supposed not every woman could maintain a size four like Katherine. Deep breath. "She's doing great. Her son is in college and her daughter's—"

"Drink your wine, dear," Katherine ordered before downing the remainder of hers. She placed her glass on the table and immediately did one of those little waves to attract the waiter's attention.

Jess was going to need considerably more than a glass of wine to get through this.

When Katherine's glass had been refilled, she turned her attention back to Jess. "Have you found a house yet?"

"I really haven't had time to look." Jess sipped her

wine. Wished it were bourbon. "I'll get around to it eventually. For now, HoJo's works just fine."

The little flinch Katherine experienced at the mention of Jess's low-rent motel proved immensely cathartic. It wasn't that Katherine cared where Jess lived. To the contrary. The thing that bothered her was the idea that she was dining with someone who lived at a Howard Johnson. Worse, that her only son was cavorting with a resident of said motel.

"Commitment is sometimes difficult. I suppose as long as you don't put down roots you can still return to Virginia or perhaps to California. Isn't that where your husband lives?"

As far as Jess was concerned, the fun was over. She downed her wine and stared straight into the other woman's eyes. "Ex-husband. My ex-husband lives in California. And I won't be changing my mind. I'm here to stay." She smiled, loving that her words were having such an ill effect on the woman. "I have Dan to thank for that. He's just determined to keep me here."

The look that passed between them was fierce. Jess recognized exactly where she stood with the woman—the same place she'd always stood, two steps behind. Katherine would never see Jess as anything other than not good enough for her son. Well, Jess had news for her, *tough*.

Katherine made a sound in her throat as if to clear away the shock that had lodged there. "I suppose you're wondering why I asked you to lunch."

Jess laughed a soft, dry sound. "Actually I thought you just wanted to talk about old times. No, wait. You said something about a proper welcome." She lifted her glass as if to toast. "Aren't you just the sweetest thing? I guess it's true that we mellow with age."

Fury glistened in those icy-blue eyes. They might be the same color as her son's but there was no warmth there. "Perhaps we should order."

Jess settled her glass on the table and made her decision. "I really don't have time for lunch, Katherine. Why don't you just say whatever it is you have to say and we'll both get on with our lives?"

Katherine lowered her gaze and fussed with her place setting for a moment. What was up with this woman? Who was dying? Not Dan senior, Jess hoped.

"I suppose I owe you an apology," Katherine said quietly when at last her gaze met Jess's once more.

"For what? Making me feel like a lesser life-form or for calling my sister fat?" The woman had some nerve, and Jess was finished playing games with her.

"I called you here under false pretenses," Katherine announced, totally ignoring Jess's comments.

The urge to get up and walk away wasn't nearly strong enough to override the train-wreck syndrome. Jess just couldn't stop staring at the catastrophe and waiting to see what would happen next.

"Dorothy Chandler, Darcy's grandmother, is a dear friend of mine," Katherine explained. "She and my older sister were best friends my sister's entire life. Dorothy was a tremendous support to me when my sister passed away."

Jess wasn't aware that Katherine's sister had died. "I'm sorry for your loss. I had no idea."

"This was years after you moved away," she explained. "In any event, the Chandler family is one of Birmingham's most giving families. Dorothy has literally given away a small fortune to help the underprivileged in this city."

The Chandler family had a long history of giving back; that was true. Jess had done some research, despite not being on the case. Even Darcy and her husband had spent enormous amounts of time teaching dance to children with special needs and those who might never have had the opportunity otherwise.

As true as all that was, it didn't explain why Katherine had asked for this meeting.

"Dorothy is convinced that Darcy's death was not an accident."

"Ready to order, ladies?"

Since her wineglass was still half full, Katherine waved off the waiter.

"Many times when tragedy strikes, the loss is more than we can bear and we create diversions to ease the pain," Jess suggested.

"Darcy had perfect balance," Katherine said. "There is no possibility that she lost her footing and fell. None whatsoever."

"Who would want to kill Darcy? I understand there was a prenuptial agreement that provided considerable compensation to the husband, so he had little to gain unless there was a sizable life insurance policy we haven't heard about yet." Jess had little new information.

"We feel certain it was Alex but we don't believe it was about money."

That was always easy to say when you had plenty. "If that's the case, why did he want his wife dead?"

Katherine braced her palms flat against the table. "We've had our differences, Jess. I recognize there is no love lost between us."

There were many things Jess could say given that

opening but she opted for the high road. "I never bring my personal feelings to the table when it comes to solving cases. Performing my duties to the best of my ability has nothing to do with the two of us, past, present, or future."

Visibly taken aback, Katherine acknowledged Jess's pointed summation with a single curt nod. "Very well, then. What I'm about to tell you is highly sensitive and the family wishes it to remain undisclosed. Particularly considering the memorial service is on Friday."

As much as Jess wanted inside info on the case, as desperately as she would love to prove she was right about the shoes, there were certain things that simply could not remain undisclosed in a possible homicide case.

"Before you say anything else," Jess advised, "understand that I cannot make any such promises. If you divulge information that might solve a case, I am compelled to pass that information along. The fact is, the Chandler case is Deputy Chief Black's. It's him that you should be talking to."

"Point taken. In any event," Katherine continued, "we fear Darcy was murdered because of an ongoing affair."

"Her husband stated he had not participated in an extramarital affair in nearly two years. Do you have proof he was lying? Or that his most recent affair was different from all the others?" They needed a motive. One they could prove.

"The issue that may have resulted in a fatal confrontation wasn't *his* affair, but that's all I'm at liberty to say. The rest will require your expert investigative skills."

Holy smokes. She hadn't been expecting that one. "You're saying Darcy was the one having an affair?"

Katherine gave one succinct nod.

"But you can't say with whom." Jess considered the only probable answer. "The other party is someone high up in social and/or political circles."

Picking up her menu, Katherine said, "The grilled asparagus is incredible."

Jess reached across the table and tugged the menu down so that Katherine would have no choice but to make eye contact. "What kind of family puts saving face above solving their own daughter's possible homicide? Don't you people realize that cops are like doctors—they can't help you if you don't tell them the whole truth?"

"Perhaps one day you'll understand that with position and power comes a different set of rules. Life is no longer just black and white. There are sacrifices that have to be made to maintain the necessary perception. It's that understanding and those sacrifices that determine where the power remains, Jessie Lee. Dan will tell you. He makes sacrifices with his every decision as chief of police. He has learned how very important perception is. Those who rise to the top are the ones who learned that lesson best and at an early age."

Jess didn't need her to spell it out. Dan had made certain choices. He wanted to be a part of the powers that be in Birmingham. To make that journey, there were certain expectations. The right public perception, the right home, the proper wife.

A strange combination of anger, disappointment, and sadness churned in Jess's belly. "What do you want from me, Katherine?" Jess had a case. A real case where normal people were depending on her.

"The Chandlers and I want you to find Darcy's killer."

"It's not my case." Why she didn't get up and walk out

she would never understand. Maybe she needed Dr. Oden more than she knew.

"We're aware of the protocol in the department and we realize you can't change that. It would mean a great deal if you could run a parallel case. Off the record."

"Does that mean you expect me to keep this from Dan?"

Silence thickened between them for several pounds of Jess's heart.

"Yes. My son cannot know. He can't be put in that position. This is strictly between you and me, Jess. I'm counting on *you*."

1:42 p.m.

Sweat beaded on Jess's forehead no matter that she'd started the Audi and set the AC to cold and the fan to high.

She needed a new car. Or at least enough work done on this ancient thing to have the necessary functions running properly, which would likely cost an arm and a leg that she didn't have to spare at this time.

Or maybe she just needed a good bicycle. With the price of gas soaring, maybe the whole world needed to start walking or biking again.

Katherine Burnett had placed Jess in a no-win situation. The Chandler case was not hers to investigate. If she went with her gut and with the Chandlers' wishes, she could start a tug-of-war with Chief Black and every other division head in the Birmingham PD. Respect was a serious issue, as well it should be.

"Hell's bells." Jess powered the window down and struggled to draw in the humid air.

But how did she walk away from what her instincts were screaming at her? If the Chandlers wanted her insight, that meant full access to the house, to any and all information available.

As appealing as the idea was, how could she even think about doing this without telling Dan?

Why was it that someone always dragged her into a thorny patch? Did she have *dissident* stamped on her forehead? It had never been her intent to go up against the rules. Events played out the way they played out and she ended up looking like the troublemaker.

Her fingers tightened on the steering wheel.

But, God, she wanted to find the answers that Darcy Chandler deserved. If she was murdered, her killer was out there getting away with it.

"Not your case, Jess." The right thing to do was to call Dan and turn the information over to him. He and Black could sort it out.

Her cell vibrated. Jess jumped, hoped it wasn't Dan. The man had always been able to sense when something was up with her. She snatched the cell off the console and checked the screen. Another local number she didn't recognize. Did everyone in town have her number? She almost didn't answer. But the curiosity that had always gotten her into trouble would not be suppressed.

"Harris."

"Jess, this is Andrea."

A new worry elbowed its way past all the others. "Andrea, is everything all right?"

"I need to talk to you." Her voice sounded muffled as if she were using her hand to prevent someone from overhearing her conversation. "It's really important."

Dan had mentioned that Andrea was having problems. Maybe she needed to talk to someone who wasn't her gorgeous mom or her doting stepfather, the chief of police. Jess had asked her to call if she remembered anything from the day Chandler died.

"Okay." Jess powered the window back up and reached for her seat belt. "Where and when would you like to meet?"

"Can we meet now? At your place? I don't want anyone ... to know about this."

Wow. Okay. "Now as in *right* now?"

"Please, Jess, I really need to show this to someone."

"All right." Jess gave her the directions. "I'll see you in a few. If you get there before me, stay in the car and keep the doors locked."

Jess was perfectly happy with her accommodations but it wasn't exactly the kind of place a young girl should be hanging out alone, even in broad daylight.

The thought gave Jess pause. Just a basic human reaction. Not a motherly instinct. She didn't have any of those.

The drive to the Howard Johnson's way, way on the other side of town far from Chez Fonfon, took about twenty minutes in the thin after-lunch traffic. Jess kept fighting the impulse to call Dan the entire drive. Would he be angry that she had agreed to meet privately with Andrea? Why would his own mother share Chandler family secrets with Jess and not Dan?

She feared the motive wasn't as cut-and-dried or as pure as Katherine wanted it to appear. If Jess blew this case wide open in the press, she would face the fallout. It was a mother's nature to want to protect her children but this was ridiculous. Dan was the chief of police. He had an obligation to pursue truth and justice.

If Jess had ever experienced a single doubt as to what Katherine's true feelings toward her were, she had none now.

As much as Jess wanted to believe this request was about her skill as an investigator, she didn't trust Katherine's motives one little bit.

Jess felt confident that Katherine was not so happy to have her back in Birmingham, enticing her son toward the tawdry and forbidden. Maybe this was her way of killing two birds with one stone: protecting her son from the necessary battle that the Chandler case was stacking up to be and giving Jess a firm push toward the city limits.

"Better folks have tried," Jess muttered.

Andrea and her sassy little convertible were waiting when Jess chugged into the parking lot. As soon as Annette and Brandon had Andrea home again after her kidnapping, the little economical Ford Fusion she'd driven had been history and a BMW 128i convertible had taken its place.

Jess removed her sunglasses and gave Andrea a big smile as she rounded the hood of her ancient Audi. "You been to dance rehearsal today?" A gym bag hung over Andrea's shoulder. The idea surprised Jess since their teacher was still on a slab at the coroner's office.

The stilted nod gave away the degree of Andrea's uneasiness. "Ms. Dorothy has taken over classes for now. She believes it's important to maintain some sense of normalcy for the girls. She said it's what Ms. Darcy would want. Today she cut the afternoon session short."

"The show must go on, I guess." Jess motioned for Andrea to follow. "Let's get out of this heat."

She led the way through a side gate that required her

keycard but the scanner was broken, so it stayed open. Another of those things Dan liked to point out. Her room faced the pool—the only perk to living here. The downside was that at this time of the day the sun heated the concrete and turned the area into a shadeless sauna.

Some of the regulars who appeared to live here full-time lounged by the pool. At least two of the five were hookers. They were all friendly and not inclined to get into anyone else's business. Neighbors like that were difficult to find in any neighborhood.

A quick swipe of her keycard and Jess slipped into the cool darkness of her room. She flipped on a light. "You want a Pepsi or water?" A dorm-size fridge had turned out to be a necessity. That and a small microwave.

"No, thank you."

Jess dropped her bag by the table that served as her desk and pulled out a chair. "Have a seat and tell me what's on your mind."

"I want you to see this video clip from one of last year's competitions." Andrea sat in the only other chair, her gym bag in her lap. She dug through it and produced a portable DVD player. Jess cleared a place for her to set it up.

Focused on getting the DVD set to play, Andrea explained, "I was watching some of them when I was looking for good clips to make a tribute DVD for Ms. Darcy and I spotted this." She turned it more fully toward Jess. "Okay, so watch for the couple at stage left."

For three or four minutes all Jess saw was the girls onstage. Most of them appeared to be the same Alabama Belles on the team this year. Wherever they were, there was a large crowd. The cameraman panned back, widening the view onstage as the girls spread out.

"Right there." Andrea tapped the screen.

A man and a woman were barely in the picture, but it was obvious from their body language that they were arguing vehemently. Some of their movements slipped out of the camera's view from time to time. The man was Alexander Mayakovsky. The woman...Jess wasn't so sure. She squinted and leaned closer to the small screen. The woman glanced toward the dancers onstage and Jess got a good look at her face then. Corrine Dresher. Katrina's mother. Jess studied the scene until the cameraman zoomed in on the dance team and the couple was no longer in the picture.

Jess started to ask Andrea if she recalled what the argument was about, but she hesitated as she considered the faces of the girls onstage. "Where's Katrina? Was she not in this dance?"

"Katrina was an alternate last year. It was her first year at the studio. She only moved up to a permanent spot on the team this year."

"Do you know what Corrine and Alexander were arguing about?"

Andrea shook her head. "I know Ms. Dresher complained a lot back then about Katrina being an alternate." Andrea shrugged. "But all the mothers complain when their daughters don't get what they think they should."

"There wasn't room on the team for Katrina?" Jess needed to understand the dynamics of how this worked. She hadn't had dance lessons as a kid. Or any other kind of lessons for that matter. She was lucky to have had a roof over her head and food in her belly.

"There wasn't a place for her, but..." Andrea seemed reluctant to say the rest.

"You can tell me whatever you feel, Andrea. This is just between the two of us. I don't have to pass along your personal feelings."

"Katrina really sucks," she blurted. "I don't know why they didn't find someone besides Katrina. If they win anything this upcoming dance season, it'll be a miracle. I think Ms. Darcy and Mr. Alex argued a lot about that."

And if Corrine Dresher knew about the difference of opinion, that would make her no fan of Darcy Chandler's.

"If she's not very good"—Jess opted not to go with sucked—"then why would she be allowed on one of the top teams in the South?" According to Jess's minimal research, the Alabama Belles were among the most celebrated teams in the nation and were quickly becoming tops in international competitions as well.

"Mr. Alex insisted. Ms. Darcy was not happy. She said Katrina could rehearse with the team until they found a suitable replacement. But she did not want her competing. Ms. Dresher was mad. She always went straight to Mr. Alex even though Ms. Darcy told her a couple of times that it was her studio and her decision."

Oh yes. That certainly put a different spin on the idea that Dresher was the last person to see Darcy Chandler alive. And that the kid who Darcy wanted off the team was the one to find her body was just flat-out suspicious.

"What happened to the other dancer?" Jess asked. "The one Katrina replaced? Did she move away?"

Andrea's expression turned sad. "She was in an accident and died over the Christmas holidays. It was very sad. The team had just come back from the final international competition."

"What kind of accident?" Jess backtracked the DVD

to watch the interchange between Alexander and Corrine again. Definitely some ugly chemistry there.

"She was hit by a car," Andrea explained. "It was—"

Jess's cell clanged. She'd taken it off vibrate after getting the call from Andrea. "Excuse me for just a sec." She dug for her cell while Andrea paused the DVD.

"Hey, Lori, what's up?" Had she found something already? Jess couldn't wait to tell her about the video.

"Are you near a television?" Lori asked.

Jess frowned. "What? Yes. I'm at my place."

"Turn it on," Lori urged, her voice grim. "Channel Six."

"Hold on." Jess hurried to the bedside table and grabbed the remote. It took a moment for the TV screen to flicker to life. Since local news was all she had time to watch, it was already set to Channel 6.

Gina Coleman, the Magic City's most celebrated reporter, looking as striking as ever, was sharing breaking news.

"For those of you just tuning in, we have shocking news on the Darcy Chandler case. An insider at the Birmingham Police Department says that Ms. Chandler's death will likely be ruled a homicide and her husband, internationally renowned dancer Alexander Mayakovsky, is the prime suspect of the investigation."

Oh damn. "When did this happen?"

Jess didn't realize she'd spoken aloud until Lori answered. "The news flash you just watched is the second one. The first aired about twenty minutes ago. Harper just called me."

Why hadn't anyone called Jess?

The beep indicating she had another call sounded

in her ear. She checked the screen. Harper. "Lori, that's Harper calling now."

"Brace yourself, Jess. According to Harper, the rumor is that *you* are the insider."

Me? Jess stared at the phone as the call ended and Harper's voice came through the line.

"Ma'am, you there?"

"Yeah, Harper, I'm here."

"We have a problem. Chief Burnett is looking for you. He wants you in his office five minutes ago."

The events of the day whirled and attempted to coalesce in her brain. She hadn't spoken to anyone about the Chandler case except Andrea, who now stood next to Jess staring at the television screen, and, well, Katherine Burnett maybe half an hour or so ago.

The first aired about twenty minutes ago.

Katherine had set her up.

That was the only explanation. Suddenly it was almost like twenty-some years ago all over again with Katherine doing all within her power to make Jess look bad to Dan. Except this was about manipulating the BPD without making her son look bad and her son was going to be livid.

Jess's phone beeped again with an incoming call.

Dan calling.

11

BPD, 3:00 p.m.

That's all you have to say?" Dan asked the question once more despite knowing he would get the same answer.

Good reporters never revealed their sources.

Gina Coleman had listened to his demands quite calmly. She'd made no excuses when he'd asked to see her ASAP. Half an hour later the top celebrity in local news had arrived at his office. Dressed in a killer lavender dress and mile-high stilettos, she'd listened quietly and respectfully to his speech about the importance of preserving the integrity of an ongoing investigation.

"I cannot divulge my source." She shook her head, that lush mane of black hair bouncing around her slender shoulders.

As anticipated, that was exactly what she'd said three times already.

"You and Deputy Chief Harris have made quite a team." If he hadn't been so pissed off, he would have recognized the envy in that statement before he stupidly uttered it.

The abrupt change in Gina's expression made it worth the damage to his ego. "You think Jess Harris is my source?" She laughed. "Like I would take her word for anything after she used me to announce her fake resignation."

The move had been a brilliant one. Jess had wanted the Player to believe she was on her way out with the BPD. The ploy had worked. Obviously Gina was still unhappy that Jess had left her holding the bag, so to speak.

"What you did last week," he confessed, "contributed to saving at least two lives." His was one of them. His side ached with the memory of the Player's knife sliding deep and then twisting.

"Glad I could be of service to the Birmingham PD by looking like a fool." Gina stood. "I am glad you're okay. Really. Even if you didn't bother calling so I wouldn't have to read it on my teleprompter." She squared her shoulders, accentuating the way the dress molded to her body. "Nice to see you, Chief."

He stood but before he could pull together a proper way to smooth over the incident she executed an about-face and walked out of his office.

Until about two weeks ago he and Gina had enjoyed a good relationship. A nice, mutually gratifying arrangement with no strings and no frustration.

What the hell had happened?

Jess.

Every aspect of his life had been tilted out of control since her return to Birmingham.

You needed her.

Yeah. He had needed her. He'd called and she'd come. Then he'd made sure she had every imaginable reason to stay.

A smart man would admit when he'd made a mistake. Dan chuckled under his breath. Maybe he just wasn't a smart man. Because he simply couldn't consider any aspect of Jess staying a mistake.

Speak of the devil, she opened the door and walked in. There was no way Jess and Gina could have missed each other in the lobby. What he would give to have been a fly on the wall.

"I don't know what you said to Coleman"—Jess hitched her thumb toward the door—"but she's not happy right now. She didn't even say hello."

What *he* said to her? "Did you ponder the idea that maybe her attitude has something to do with your faux resignation last week?"

An *oh* expression claimed Jess's face; then she shrugged. "I guess some folks like holding grudges."

"Sit," Dan directed.

Her eyebrows shot up. "Excuse me?"

"Please." Jesus Christ. He really needed to get his frustration level under control. Personal feelings had no place in this office. "Have a seat." He gestured to the chair Gina had vacated a couple minutes ago.

Jess sat. The ivory skirt she wore slid up her thighs as she crossed her legs. She hadn't mentioned having taken up running but he couldn't remember her legs looking that amazing even back in high school.

She cleared her throat.

Dan snapped his gaze up to hers. Which didn't help a whole hell of a lot since all that gorgeous, thick blond hair framing her face made him think of how it felt slipping over his skin when they made love.

Resuming his own seat, he gave himself a quick mental kick in the ass. What the devil was wrong with him? He was mad as hell about this damned leak and yet he couldn't keep his head on straight.

"Whoever is responsible for this leak is jeopardizing the just and speedy closure of this case."

"Unless Ms. Coleman had getting even on her mind, she surely told you I had nothing to do with that. I've been a little busy with gangs and a missing young man."

"This leak has turned the entire investigation on its ear." Dan intended to say his piece before letting her off the hook. "Chief Black is exploring every aspect of the Chandler case. He has found no evidence whatsoever to indicate Darcy's death was anything other than a tragic accident. This sort of buzz in the news doesn't help solve the case; it only hurts the family."

Jess folded her arms over her chest. "He's ignoring the bruise on her leg? The one that could only have been made by the second-floor handrail as she was tossed over the side?"

His distraction with her hair and those gorgeous legs vanished as his frustration amped back up. "Funny you mention that. Somehow my mother obtained knowledge of the ME's preliminary examination of Chandler's body. I can't imagine how that happened. Though she might have mentioned having lunch with you."

Jess held up her hands. "Your mother invited me to lunch and I accepted. As weird as that sounds, you cannot possibly believe I shared sensitive information with her." She scoffed or maybe coughed to prevent choking at the mere idea of sharing anything with his mother. "Whatever problems you're having with the women in your life, Chief, have nothing to do with me."

He didn't doubt her word but something was up where his mother was concerned. She'd asked about Jess and the case and suddenly there's a leak. Chief Black had already warned him that the Chandler family was not happy with the way he was leaning but no one wanted a public scandal.

This was exactly why chief of police was as close to politics as Dan ever intended to get.

"When did you discuss the preliminary results of a case that isn't yours with someone in the coroner's office?" Jess wasn't Gina's source; of that he was certain. And, as she pointed out, the odds that she had given his mother anything other than a hard time were slim to none. Yet she wasn't being completely straight with him. He knew her too well.

"That question is irrelevant. Why were her shoes set aside? What about the way she had to hike up the skirt of her dress? Feels like a lot of prep work for accidentally falling over the railing. And the bruise she got near the time of death matches the width and pattern of the handrail. So unless she climbed on something before jumping and then that something somehow got moved before we arrived, there is no way she jumped. Why aren't those questions being asked?"

Oh yeah. She had spoken to Schrader. That was the only way she could know about the bruise. He and Black had had a lengthy discussion about each of the inconsistencies she'd named. Dan was well aware of how the situation looked. But charges could not be levied unless they had evidence and motive. Speculation would not win a case in court.

"We're a team, Jess. All of us. You, Black, me...the whole department. I understand you reached certain preliminary conclusions about this case but the case is Black's. If you have assessments or gained knowledge that would be of use, then by all means, share that knowledge with Black. But don't walk around with this you-against-Black or you-against-me chip on your shoulder. That won't help us get the job done."

"I think maybe you need to have this conversation with Chief Black. I have my doubts as to whether he's interested in hearing anything I have to say. And, frankly, it sounds like the case is already closed."

Dan held up his hands in surrender. She was more right than she knew. *Keep the peace*, he reminded himself. "Maybe you're right. Maybe Black doesn't care what your assessments are, but I do." He settled his hands on his desk. "Give me your latest thoughts on the Chandler case. I'm listening."

She stared at him for a moment as if assessing whether he was merely patronizing her or not. "What's the motive? Evidence alone isn't enough. We both know that. And when there's no evidence, motive is everything."

"Since we don't have any evidence," Dan argued, "and no clear motive, we don't exactly have a case for anything other than accidental death."

She cocked an eyebrow. "Well, now, Chief, that depends on your definition of evidence and motive."

"Touché," he capitulated. "There are obvious inconsistencies that may or may not fall under the usual evidence categories, but those haven't led us anywhere. As far as motive, Chief Black has dug deeply into all those close to the victim. There's a sizable insurance policy the husband is set to gain, but he has an alibi that is confirmed by his cell phone records. He was, as he stated in the initial interview, at the Botanical Gardens when he and Darcy spoke last and during the time frame of her death."

"He could have paid someone to do the deed," she countered.

"Chief Black found no evidence to indicate that was the case."

"What time did that final call end?"

He picked up the file on his desk and reviewed the list of calls made from Mayakovsky's cell. "The last call ended at twelve thirty-one."

During the hesitation that followed, Dan could almost see the wheels turning in her head. She was calculating the time it took to drive from the Botanical Gardens to the Chandler home.

"Fourteen minutes," he said, relieving her of having to deal with the math. Chief Black had provided a Google map of the most direct route from the gardens to Chandler's home. "Sufficient time for him to have removed the battery from his phone so that it didn't reach out to any towers—or just leave it at the meditation garden until he returned—drive to Cotton Avenue, throw Darcy Chandler over the railing, and drive back without being seen."

"But you don't believe that," Jess challenged.

"I do not." Like Jess, Dan had some pretty good instincts of his own. Mayakovsky might be lying about a lot of things, but he was telling the truth when it came to how much he loved his wife. That, of course, didn't mean he hadn't flipped out and committed an impulsive act, but proving that would be almost impossible without some sort of evidence.

"What about the affair she was having? Was that avenue pursued?"

How the hell could she know about that? "What affair are you referring to?"

She shrugged. "It's probably just a rumor. I heard she was having an affair this go-around instead of the husband. Maybe the Russian didn't like having the tables turned on him. Maybe that insurance policy started to look better and better. Or maybe the guy involved in the affair rubbed him the wrong way."

"As I said, Chief Black has investigated all areas of both Mayakovsky's and Darcy's personal and professional lives. If Mayakovsky was having an affair, we found no one who could corroborate those rumors. And, just so you know, the prenuptial agreement provided for a settlement that's equivalent to the insurance payout, so money is not a viable motive."

"What about the dance moms? There are those who would do most anything to ensure their daughter's position on the competition team. Corrine Dresher certainly seems the type to go to great lengths to get what she wants. And her daughter was the one who found Darcy *and* the one wearing the white boa."

"Chief Black is on top of it, Jess. He has given due consideration to anyone at all close to the victim. Darcy Chandler spent a lot of hours with her dancers that morning, including Katrina and her white boa. You need to trust him and me on this."

"I'm really trying, but—"

The intercom on his desk buzzed. Damn it. This was

not the time for an interruption. He'd asked his secretary to hold his calls.

"Are we done here?" Jess stood. "I have work to do on the Simmons case. And that might be important." She nodded toward the phone on his desk.

"That can wait. I need to know we're on the same—"

The damned intercom buzzed again.

"We can finish this another time." She turned and strode toward the door.

"Jess, wait."

Ignoring him as she so often did, she opened the door and came face-to-face with Annette.

His secretary, Sheila, tried to peek beyond the two women. "Chief, I—"

Instead of moving aside, Annette and Jess started talking at once. Sheila shook her head and walked away.

"I'm sorry for the interruption," Annette was saying.

"We were finished anyway," Jess tossed back.

He'd spoken to Andrea not two hours ago and she'd seemed fine. Had something else happened that Annette felt couldn't wait?

The door had scarcely closed behind Jess and Annette was already around his desk and in his arms, tears streaming down her cheeks.

"What happened?" His impatience and frustration wilted.

She burrowed her face in his jacket and murmured, "Brandon is leaving me and I don't know what to do. I need you, Dan."

12

If Jess were really lucky she would escape the building without running into any more trouble. Being called before the boss once a day was plenty. Running into his ex-wife in his office was just icing on the cake.

Things felt strange between her and Burnett since he'd showed up at her motel room way after hours with Annette's perfume on his jacket. Maybe the whole strange thing was her imagination running away with her. Or his way of keeping the necessary distance on the job. But it felt like something more complex than simply being discreet.

Annette just kept showing up in the mix. Jess didn't want to be jealous of her. If Annette needed Burnett's help with Andrea, Jess certainly understood. But it hadn't felt like Andrea was having real problems related to her abduction when she and Jess met earlier to view the video. Sure, the kid had reason to be all screwed up, but she'd seemed more determined than anything else. A little sad, yes, but mostly determined to help solve the mystery around her dance teacher's death.

Maybe Annette had decided she wanted Burnett back. A massive knot immediately formed in Jess's gut. Annette and Brandon could be falling apart again. It had happened before.

Jess couldn't slow down to consider the concept or why she felt as if she'd swallowed a bag of rocks one by one. She needed off this floor and out of this building. Fact was, she didn't want to analyze those confusing and abrupt feelings she suffered way too often of late. Burnett's love life was no more her business than Annette's was. Jess had made it clear with her rules that her relationship and Burnett's was more like an adult version of friends with benefits.

God, had she just thought that?

It was true. She wasn't supposed to get all hung up on the emotional issues.

Get your mind on work, girl. The work rarely let her down. Just that once. With the Player.

The next item on her agenda was checking in with Harper to see if he had ferreted out any more leads on this Nina woman and getting an update from the search team commander. Then she needed to pay a visit to the high-and-mighty Katherine Burnett. She owed Jess an explanation. Not that she actually expected to get one, much less an apology, but she did not intend to simply let it slide.

"Now it's my move."

At the elevator she decided the stairs would work to her advantage. Burn off a little adrenaline and avoid being anyone's captive audience.

Once inside the stairwell with the door closed between her and the fourth floor, she paused to catch her breath. She checked her cell for calls and set the ringtone from silent to that wonky clang she preferred—only because it was impossible to miss no matter the chaos surrounding her. She stared longingly at the steps that would take her down and out of the building. Away from any possibility of running into that trouble she wanted to avoid. The longer she was in Burnett's presence the more likely he was to pick up on the idea that she was up to something. Yet part of her wanted to go back to his office and boot Annette Denton out of the way so she could come clean with him.

How mad could he get at his own mother? He already knew about the ME's concerns, so there was no need to spill on Schrader. The part that she really felt guilt over not sharing was the video Andrea had shown her. That he needed to know about. Jess had called Lori on the way over and given her the update.

She really should tell Burnett but since he was otherwise occupied, she could drop by Black's office and tell him. Would that put more pressure on Andrea? Would it have the slightest impact on Black's final decision?

Probably not. One documented argument that was a whole year old did not a motive for murder make. Except that the woman in the video was the last person to see Chandler alive, to their knowledge. And her daughter was the one to find the body and she'd been wearing that white boa.

Black needed this information to properly assess his case.

The door burst open behind Jess, and Deputy Chief Black joined her in the stairwell.

Well, here was her chance.

"Chief Black, I was just about to come by your office."

"That's good, Chief Harris. Saves me the trouble of dropping by yours."

Great.

Jess's office was on the third floor in the only available space large enough to accommodate SPU. Black's office, on the other hand, was just the other side of Burnett's.

He opened the stairwell door she had just exited. "After you."

Jess couldn't help wondering as she passed Burnett's office if Annette was still in there.

One would think with a degree in psychology that she could head off those foolish and immature emotions. That she would have some extra insight that explained away those feelings of uncertainty that went along with her career as well as her personal life. But that wasn't the case.

Sometimes it just didn't matter what you knew. The heart had a mind of its own.

Just now, she had a feeling her heart was not the part of her that was in jeopardy.

"Please, sit down, Harris. Let me get organized and we'll get this done."

Jess perched on the edge of one of the chairs in front of his desk. Her desk was exactly like Black's. Big, rose-wood or mahogany. She never could tell the difference between the two. Her team members had the midlevel management desks. Faux wood and metal. They also had the more generic chairs. Like Black, Jess had the high-back, leather-tufted executive chair. The one glaring difference between their offices was the file cabinets. The ones lining the wall in her office were beige metal beasts. Black's file cabinets were an exact match to the rich wood of his desk.

But her window was bigger. She'd take that over wood file cabinets any day.

"Chief Burnett assured me that you were not the source of the leak at Channel Six."

Startled to attention, a moment was required for Jess to formulate a response. "That's right." Burnett had told Black she wasn't the leak?

"You can understand," Black suggested as he took his seat, "how I might have arrived at that conclusion."

Wait a minute. Her head was still spinning from his announcement about Burnett. "When did you speak to the chief?" As far as she knew, he was still in his office with Annette.

"I was in his office when the news first aired." Black adjusted his glasses. "I admit that you were the first person to come to mind. I was certain you were responsible but the chief assured me that was not possible."

Jess blinked, stunned just a little. "Is that why you wanted to talk?" She owed Burnett an apology or maybe he owed her one. Why had he made her feel as if he suspected her when he'd obviously defended her before they'd even discussed the situation?

More of those confusing signals.

"There's more," Black assured her. "Why don't we get comfortable and do this right, Chief Harris? I think it's time we found our common ground."

Oh Lord. She'd heard about Black's *let's-get-comfortable* briefings. "I'm all ears, Chief."

"You were not pleased about the Chandler case coming back to my division."

Old news. "I got over it." Did every step have to be rehashed repeatedly?

"Whether you realize it or not I have taken into consideration your thoughts on the shoes and the bruising on the victim's leg. We've diligently attempted to address those issues, but there simply doesn't appear to be any relevancy. Those two points, together or separately, do not change my final assessment of the tragedy that occurred."

Jess wasn't really surprised. More disappointed than anything. Oddly, Burnett hadn't talked as if the decision was a done deal. He'd assured her that Black was still weighing the case. "I hope you're right, but my instinct says you're not." It was just the two of them. Might as well say what was on her mind.

"We found no evidence of suicide or homicide. No glaring motive for the husband to want his wife out of the way." Black turned his hands up. "I can only assume that Ms. Chandler dropped something or reached for something we could not find and fell in the process."

Jess had considered that theory. She had gotten down on her hands and knees and inspected the wooden ledge beyond the railing. She'd searched for an earring back. A ring. Anything. She'd found nothing.

"So you're going with accidental and calling it a day." Now she really was disappointed.

"The coroner has already signed the death certificate. He just called a few minutes ago. I was about to pass that news along to Chief Burnett but he's busy at the moment. Unfortunately, this false leak to the press precluded my official public announcement. We'll get to that in the morning, I suppose."

"Was the family notified?"

"Of course." He shook his head. "That's actually the part I find so troubling. This groundless leak does nothing but hurt the family."

Jess felt confident that Burnett's mother wasn't the only

one behind the leak to the media. Dorothy Chandler, the grandmother, had most likely spearheaded the maneuver in an effort to head off Black's public announcement. Ballsy lady. Was the woman so determined to find the truth that she'd hoped to force the BPD's hand?

Couldn't blame her for that.

"So that's it? Doesn't matter that the husband had one affair after the other or that Darcy Chandler was having one of her own? The problems between the husband and Corrine Dresher? The white boa feathers between her fingers? None of that matters?"

Black's gaze narrowed in suspicion. "Who said Darcy Chandler was having an affair?"

Oops. "It may have been one of the dance moms." That was a flat-out lie but it didn't really matter now, it seemed. Funny how he honed in more on the affair than anything else Jess noted.

"I don't recall reading that in your interview reports."

"Really? I was sure I made note of the possibility of an affair on her part."

"Let me be clear. We are closing this case, Chief Harris. There is nothing more to be gained from keeping it open. With a high-profile family like this, dragging our feet in closing the case allows for exactly what happened today. Gossip and innuendos. For the family's sake, we're settling this business so that they may get on with their lives. No one wants to prolong the pain of their loss."

Evidently he was trying to tell her something, but the victim's family was telling her something different. "Shouldn't justice be our prevailing motive? Families like the Chandlers know the less pleasant aspects that come with their positions in society. Their every move, good, bad, or otherwise, is picked apart by the media. Why would we be swayed by that one way or the other?"

"The case is closed. We will not be pursuing the Chandler investigation further unless new evidence comes to light."

"Burnett has given his seal of approval?" She was pushing here and she knew it, but this felt wrong. Particularly since she hadn't gotten that impression from Burnett.

"The final decision came down from a higher office, Jess," Black warned, using her first name for emphasis. "Let it go."

The affair. That had to be the motive for a speedy closure.

What trumped a Chandler? Jess had been gone from Birmingham too long. She would need Lori's help there.

"Are we clear? Do you need me to have Chief Burnett confirm where the department stands on the matter after he and I have spoken?"

Jess focused on the man staring at her expectantly. "That won't be necessary, Chief Black. I think we're more than clear here."

Black reclined in his chair and studied her a moment. "I worry that somehow we are not where we need to be, Chief Harris. I feel some amount of animosity or resentment festering between us. I don't need to remind you that we are on the same team."

She should let it go. She really should. Burnett had urged her to play nice so she would eventually fit in and be accepted, sooner rather than later. But she'd never been very good at holding back when it came to what she believed in.

"As long as I stay clear of your territory, is that right?" No use pretending that wasn't the true issue.

"You believe that our differences stem from my not acknowledging and respecting your position as a deputy chief. Is that right?"

Jess smiled. If only it were that easy. "I suppose you could boil it down to terms as simple as that. You question all my decisions and rarely agree with my conclusions. And this isn't the first time. Should I think differently?"

He did not smile. "Shall I speak frankly, Harris?"

"Absolutely." She braced for battle.

"I find your tactics questionable more often than not. Your lack of respect for the chain of command, particularly Chief Burnett, appalling. And your absolute certainty that you can do the job better than anyone else, regardless of rank or experience, utterly unacceptable." He turned his hands up. "Other than that, I recognize that your investigative skills are exemplary."

Wow. Harper was wrong. It would take far longer than two years to earn this man's respect. "I see. Well. It appears we have a ways to go before that whole team concept really sets for us."

He clasped his hands in front of him, steepled his fingers. "I hope that doesn't prove the case. Time is rarely an asset we have to spare in our line of work."

Jess struggled not to let his opinion get to her, but it did. Didn't matter that she had suspected as much. Hearing it this way wasn't so easy to swallow. "I appreciate your candor." She reached for her bag. "We'll have to do this again sometime." Like maybe in ten or so years. Or never.

"Just so you understand," Black said, stalling her preparations for a quick exit, "my feelings are based entirely on my concerns for this department and for Dan. I've known him since he was just a rookie. He's worked hard to gain the position he holds. I don't want the actions of anyone else to detract from his achievements. He wants you here. I hope you won't force him to regret that decision."

Jess couldn't breathe. Her eyes burned. Had Dan shared his misgivings about her with Black?

That clunky clang called out from her bag. She forced the painful thoughts away. "Sorry." She reached for her cell, immensely grateful for the reprieve.

Lily calling.

Her sister.

But Black didn't know that.

"Excuse me, Chief, I have to take this." Jess stood and turned her back to him. Blinking to hold back the tears she refused to shed, she accepted the call. "Jess Harris."

"I found the perfect house!" Lily squealed.

"What's the address?" Jess went for a business tone in hopes of leading Black to believe it was Harper.

"Right across the street from me!" Another delighted squeal.

Oh God.

"Thank you for keeping me up to speed. I'll get right on that."

"If you want to see it, I'll have to call the Realtor. Do you want me to call?"

"I can handle it. Thank you." Jess ended the call and turned back to Chief Black. "I have to get out to Druid Hills. I'm glad we had this chat, Chief."

Her sister was probably still staring at her phone, aghast that Jess had basically hung up on her.

"Good, solid communications are always best. We—" The intercom on Black's desk buzzed, cutting him off. He looked from Jess to the phone and back.

"Take care of that," she suggested as she backed toward the door. "I can see myself out."

Before he could argue, his secretary's voice reverberated from the speaker. "Sir, I'm sorry to interrupt but Detective Roark is on the line. He's at the Chandler home. There's been a new development and he needs to speak with you immediately."

Jess stalled. Her gaze locked with Black's. What now?

Breathless, the secretary rushed to add, "Alexander Mayakovsky has just confessed to killing his wife."

The Russian was lying.

Jess didn't need to be in the same room with him. Having a sense of the rhythm of his breathing might have been a bonus but wasn't really necessary in this case. She watched his every move through the viewing room's two-way mirror. Listened to his voice as he spoke, noting his pauses as he struggled to find just the right words... the tremble in his voice whenever he said his wife's name.

He was lying.

"Walk me through this once more," Black said quietly. "This time we'll make sure the tape recorder works right."

Detective Roark fumbled with the handheld recorder and placed it back in the center of the table. The malfunctioning recorder was a ruse. Video and audio was at that very moment capturing every image and sound and digi-

tally storing it for use in a court of law just as it had been
for the last three-quarters of an hour.

Chief Black sat with his back to the viewing mirror,
allowing Jess and Burnett an unobstructed view of Darcy
Chandler's husband as he confessed to killing her—
accidentally, of course—in a moment of overpowering
angst and frustration. Detective Roark slouched at one end
of the small table. A suspect always felt more intimidated
with two cops in the room. The attorney, Isaac Matheson,
occupied the chair at the remaining end of the table.

Matheson—not quite the powerhouse his colleague
Zacharias Whitman, the Chandler family attorney, was
but a big name around these parts nonetheless—had
advised his client not to make this statement but the Russian was determined to spill his guts.

Problem was, his statements up to now were so far off
the mark that he couldn't possibly be telling the truth. Not
in Jess's opinion anyway. But this wasn't her case and her
opinion didn't carry much weight. If she'd had any doubts,
she now knew for a certainty.

"Talking on the phone wasn't working. So I came to the
house. I only wanted her to listen," Alexander repeated.
"She refused. I followed her up the stairs..."

Right there was where Jess would have asked why they
had gone up the stairs. "Why doesn't Black ask the obvious question?" she muttered, her exasperation kicking up
a notch.

"Give him time." Burnett glanced at her, gave her that
knowing look of unqualified confidence that men in positions of power and experience so loved to toss around.
"He's done this before."

Jess reminded herself that she was lucky to even be

watching this interview. With that hammered into her brain once more, she scraped up whatever patience hadn't fled or expired in the last forty-five minutes and focused on the interview.

"Why did your wife go upstairs?" Black asked.

No way was she meeting the gaze now fixed on her. Just because Burnett was right about Black getting around to the question didn't make him right about anything else.

"What'd I tell you?" he remarked.

"Shhh." She wanted to hear the answer to that long-awaited question.

The Russian shook his head. "I don't know. She went. I followed. I needed to make her hear me. To destroy our marriage was one thing, but to destroy the studio—which would be nothing without me—was absurd. She needed to be reasonable."

That last part sounded heartfelt...sincere.

"Was there anyone else in the house?"

Jess groaned. "He already said no to that! Rephrase the question!"

"Wait," Black said before the suspect could answer his last inquiry, "did you say Ms. Dresher was still on the property delivering lunch for the dancers in rehearsal when you arrived?"

"Hmm. Interesting alternate approach," Burnett commented just to get on her nerves.

"Fine. Fine. That works."

Burnett chuckled. "You just can't stand the idea that anyone else can do this as well as you."

She was not going there with him just now. Her feelings were still stinging from Black's comments. Was it possible that Dan regretted having offered her this position? The bottom line was that Black was right about her actions directly affecting Dan. But she couldn't think about that right now.

"Ask him about the shoes," she suggested, knowing Black could not hear her but determined to ensure Burnett knew exactly how she would handle every step of this interview.

The Russian shook his handsome head. "There was no one else in the house. No one."

He scrubbed his hands over his face, then through his long blond hair. It was no wonder Chandler was ready to be rid of her husband. He looked exactly like the kind of guy whose destiny it was to be unfaithful. Too handsome. Lean, muscular body that looked as good in jeans as it did in tights. An eastern European accent that would make most any woman swoon. A man accustomed to being showered with attention from all who orbited his universe. Like Annette said, the union was likely doomed from the beginning.

"Might someone have heard the two of you before you went upstairs?" Black ventured. "That marble floor in the entry hall of your home has a tendency to echo, especially the way a lady's high heels click-click-click."

"Uh-huh." Burnett folded his arms over his chest. "And the shoes are on the table."

"Yeah, yeah." Black wasn't doing a bad job. Too bad his suspect was lying like a rug. His every mannerism, facial expression, the subtle nuances of each word signaled extreme distress and an urgency to provide an answer that made him look guilty enough. Not good signs in a murder confession.

The husband shrugged. "I don't remember hearing any sounds like that... There was no one else in the house... to hear us. I'm certain of that."

How was he certain? Half a dozen little girls were with Andrea in the conservatory. Unless he checked every room of the massive house, he couldn't sit there and say with such conviction that there was no one else in the house.

"So when you got upstairs," Roark spoke up, "you saw your chance and you tossed your unsuspecting wife over the railing. Bam!" He banged the table. "Just like that!"

Even Jess jumped at the abrupt display. "That was a little over the top."

"What is the meaning of this?" Matheson railed. "Don't say another word, Alexander. This has gone too far already."

Chief Black scolded his detective, though Jess felt confident the moment was staged, then ordered him out of the room. Talk about old-school.

When the door had closed behind Roark, Black righted the overturned tape recorder and held up his hands in a show of dismay. "I apologize. As you can imagine, we're all a little tense. The pressure is on for us to get this right. Please, gentlemen, let's continue."

The Russian blinked a couple of times and glanced at his attorney who shook his head. To Jess's surprise, he kept going despite his attorney's advice. Why the hell would a guy with so much to gain, a seven-figure insurance payout and the freedom to set up a new studio wherever he chose, confess to killing his wife when the police had no, N-O, evidence a homicide had even occurred?

Didn't make sense.

"Once we were in the upstairs hall," Alexander went on, "the disagreement escalated into something more physical."

Jess leaned as close to the glass as possible and tried

to see his pale blue eyes. "The truth this time," she whispered.

"She slapped me. I grabbed her by the arms and shook her. She tried to pull away and..." He dropped his face into his hands. "She went over the railing. I couldn't reach her quickly enough. I couldn't save her."

Shook her? Jess wanted to go in there and shake him all right. She wanted to shake some sense into the guy. If he had grabbed Darcy Chandler and shaken her that way, why weren't there bruises on her arms? And what about the damned shoes?

After a lengthy stretch of silence, Black prompted, "What happened then, sir?"

"I rushed down the stairs and tried to help her." He flattened his palms against the table and visibly fought for composure. "She was dead. There was nothing I could do."

"It couldn't have happened that way," Jess commented. She kept expecting Burnett to say something along those lines. The ME had diligently scanned the body for signs of a struggle. None existed. The only mark on the body that did not appear consistent with Chandler's crash landing was the first-degree bruise on her lower left leg.

"Did you notice that your wife wasn't wearing shoes?"

The Russian looked up, his face red and damp from crying. "Shoes?"

"Yes." Chief Black glanced at the open file in front of him. "Her shoes were set aside upstairs near the area where you stated your struggle took place. Did you set them there? Had she been wearing her shoes when she fell, they would have landed somewhere below, perhaps near her body."

The husband shook his head. "I don't remember her shoes. When I realized she was dead, I"—he made a keening sound deep in his throat—"ran away...I was in shock."

"Without bothering to call for help," Jess mumbled, "in case you were wrong about her being dead." Calling for help was a basic human reaction, shock or no. The man was absolutely not being truthful about all or most of his story.

The same man who spoke his wife's name so reverently, who could scarcely speak of her without breaking down, just takes off, leaving her on the floor, without calling for help? A man with no criminal record? If the events had happened as he'd just stated, her death was an accident. Why flee the scene and risk having it look any other way? What was he hiding?

"Let's go back to those final moments before she fell," Black suggested. "Do you remember when you were shaking your wife if you pulled her toward you? Perhaps lifted her up to your eye level to get her attention?"

Jess recognized where he was going with this. He'd taken a different route than she would have but he did appear to be getting to the proper destination. Although she couldn't believe Matheson wasn't screaming that his client was being led by the phrasing of the question.

"Why don't you just write him a script?" Matheson demanded. He threw his hands up. "This is so far beyond ridiculous."

Better late than never, Jess supposed. It was like watching the Grammy Awards with that five-second delay in case of unexpected wardrobe malfunctions or colorful language.

The husband considered the query a moment. "Yes." He nodded. "Yes, I did. I wanted her to look me in the eyes. She"—his voice quivered—"was so much smaller than me. I lifted her like a tiny doll."

"You see," Burnett offered. "There's the answer to the bruise on her leg."

But it didn't explain the lack of bruising on her upper arms. To grab her, shake her, and lift her up, he had to be gripping her tightly. No matter that the Russian considered his wife small, she had been about Jess's height and weight. A firm grip would have been necessary to lift her up to his eye level.

And it still didn't explain the shoes.

"One last question, Mr. Mayakovsky."

Jess couldn't wait to hear this one.

"What made you decide to come forward now?"

The husband took a moment to compose himself. His chest swelled with a big breath, then fell with the audible release. "I saw the news. I knew it was only a matter of time before you discovered what I had done. The announcement gave me the necessary courage to come forward with the truth." He dropped his head and shook it, then lifted his gaze to Black. "I swear to God I did not mean to harm her."

Chief Black nodded. "Thank you, sir. That's all the questions I have for now." He pushed a notepad and paper across the table. "We like to get all statements in writing. You take your time and I'll find you and Mr. Matheson some fresh coffee."

"And he nails it," Burnett announced. "See, I told you Black had this under control."

Jess faked a smile. "It seems he does." Except for the big glaring fact that the Russian was lying through his perfect white teeth.

"Black and his people have this wrapped up. What do you say we catch an early dinner? We can hash out any misgivings you still have. You can bring me up to speed on the Simmons case."

Standing here now in this semidark booth with him not two feet away, she felt the distance widening between them.

Had last week's intensity prompted feelings that were only temporary? Maybe their shared past combined with the extreme emotions related to the missing girls and then the Player case had created an illusion of a connection that wasn't real. Was this the new normal between them? Or was this the regret Black had suggested Burnett might begin to feel?

"There's a place over on Twenty-Ninth, Cappy's," Burnett continued. "Has the best burgers, wings, and ribs in town, according to just about everybody in the department. Something like forty kinds of beer. We can talk shop or we can just relax and forget about work."

The last time they had forgotten about work, they had spent about twenty-four hours in her bed. This was certainly a drastic turnaround. Chitchat at a cop hangout.

Yes. Things had definitely changed.

"As long as you're buying."

Relief washed over his face. "You're on."

Cappy's Corner Grill, Twenty-Ninth Street, 6:05 p.m.

Jess showed up a few minutes after Burnett. She'd used the excuse that she needed to stop by her office and make a couple of calls. Taking her own car rather than riding with him was the real reason. Escaping was a lot less trouble that way.

The pub was wall-to-wall cops. Every table, every booth, and all the stools lining the long bar were occupied by law enforcement personnel. She didn't have to know the faces or the names. Spotting a cop was easy. The seemingly relaxed but subtly braced posture. The deft and frequent surveys of their surroundings.

As a matter of fact, cops and criminals had those two innate traits in common. Neither wanted to get caught off guard.

The music was a little loud but no one seemed to mind. Their conversations added a kind of background harmony that rose with their boisterous laughter and fell with their quieter, more intimate exchanges.

Jess spotted Prescott in the lineup at the bar. She and another female appeared to be in deep conversation. Prescott was probably complaining that some outsider had gotten her promotion. But that was nothing new. That kind of talk had followed Jess throughout her career, usually coming from those who either didn't like her personally or resented her professional accomplishments.

She was dedicated. Getting the job done was her top priority. Personal relationships and kids and all that other stuff had always taken a backseat to work and the risks required to rise above mediocrity. Yes, she had climbed high and accomplished much but there had been sacrifices. No one ever pointed those out. Not even her.

Who wanted to dwell on all that?

Burnett popped up from a booth about midway across the crowded space and waved to her.

As she wove her way toward him, his attention roved

down her body, lingered on her legs before making a slow path back up to her face. The simple act of a male checking out the assets of a member of the opposite sex shouldn't have set her pulse aflutter but it did. *He* did. The suit coat and tie were gone; the top two buttons of his shirt were undone. Her heart skipped a couple of beats and her throat parched just a little. How had she kept thoughts of him at a distance for all those years only to be so totally incapable of doing so now?

What happened to the rules she had introduced just the other day?

Apparently she was having more trouble sticking to them than Burnett was.

She'd had the same trouble after that little run-in at the Publix ten years ago.

"I ordered you a Miller Lite."

The chilled, frosty mug waited on the table for her. "Thanks."

She pushed her bag deeper into the booth as she slid across the faux leather. Burnett reclaimed his seat opposite her and waited until she had sipped her beer before asking, "You want to see a menu?"

"A burger sounds good." She'd skipped lunch. Well, most of it anyway. She had managed to get down a piece of artisan bread served on a tiny cutting board. Sitting across the table from Katherine Burnett and her appetite were mutually exclusive under the best of circumstances.

He snagged a waitress and placed their order, somehow remembering that she hated onions and wanted extra pickles.

When the waitress had moved on to the next table, Jess started the first round of personal interrogations before he could. "How's Andrea?"

He stared at his beer. "She's getting through this better than I expected." He nodded. "She's a strong kid."

Considering she was putting together a tribute for Darcy Chandler and had brought that video to Jess, she would say so. The young woman was handling the loss quite admirably. "And Annette?" Jess dared. "She's handling things reasonably well?"

He took a long pull from his beer, to buy time in her opinion. His cell lay on the table and he glanced at it before answering as if he feared it would interrupt at any second. "She's good. Overly concerned about Andrea, I think. But otherwise, good."

He did not want to talk about Annette and that said it all.

"How do you feel it went with Dr. Oden this morning?" he asked, changing the subject.

Like he didn't know. "She didn't e-mail you a report as soon as I left her office?"

Burnett braced his forearms on the table and leaned toward her. Jess somehow misplaced the ability to breathe. "Actually it was about half an hour after you left her office and she said you had no desire to complete the evaluation."

"Perceptive lady." Jess kicked aside the foolish tangle of emotions that had twisted around her for a second and stared right back into those deep blue eyes. "I think she gets me."

Burnett nodded. "She says you're arrogant, stubborn, and a possible loose cannon." He laughed. "Of course, she had all these big words that basically meant narcissistic traits. Not to worry, though, I told her you'd been that way since you were seventeen and I had realized over the years there was no way to change you. She relented and gave you a pass."

Few humans were lacking in the narcissism department. Everyone got at least a small dose. Maybe Jess had her share and someone else's, too. She had no problem with a frank analysis. She was pushy, certain no one could do the job as well as she could, and demanding of those around her. But every iota of that arrogance and stubbornness was directed at finding the truth...at ferreting out and stopping evil.

"Good thing you set her straight." Jess lifted her mug. "I guess I owe you one." Maybe she owed Oden one for the pass. She could have dragged out the sessions just to torture Jess. God forbid that Chief Black ever got his hands on that evaluation. He already had Jess pegged a little too well.

He tapped his glass to hers. "She also said"—Burnett's tone went all serious then—"that because you ignore all boundaries, you were among the category of cops most likely to die young. I told her I knew that, too."

"Wow. I'm flattered the two of you see me that way."

He leaned close again. "Don't try your best to prove her right, Jess. That's an order."

She melted a little at the concern that tinged his voice. "Yes, sir."

The smile that twitched his lips did strange things to her heart. Maybe things weren't so off this week after all.

"Remember when we used to sneak out to the Sloss Furnaces back in the day?" He grinned, that sexy, boyish one that totally mesmerized her. "We'd climb up that rusty old ladder and sit high above all the ghostly tunnels and ruins below."

God, she hadn't thought of that in ages. She was glad

they hadn't torn down the old blast furnace. The whole place was now a national landmark. "It's a miracle we didn't break our necks."

"But we didn't because we had each other's backs."

He was right, and looking into his eyes at that moment she understood with complete certainty that aspect of their relationship hadn't changed. He had her back. He'd covered her with Black and the media leak. He'd covered her when it came to the psych eval with Oden.

She took a deep breath and did what had to be done. "It was your mother."

That was something else she and Burnett had always shared. The ability to anticipate each other's needs. He needed the truth from her and she owed it to him. "Why am I not surprised?" He laughed. "Of course. She's been all over me about the Chandler case."

"The grandmother, Dorothy, is probably the reason. She's convinced that Darcy's death was not an accident. Your mother was only trying to help her friend. She asked me to look into the case. I'm certain she or Dorothy tipped off Coleman."

He glanced around as if measuring the risk of talking further on the subject in their current setting. "Here's the thing"—he leaned in close again—"we got nothing. You know this. The first time the husband was interviewed I would have bet my house that he was telling the truth. That bogus leak hits the news and suddenly we have a confession from him. If he's telling the truth this time, which I have my doubts, the leak probably saved the department a lot of grief. I hate to think how embarrassed we would have been if Black had made the official announcement he'd been intending before Mayakovsky's confession."

"Bless your mother's heart." Jess flashed a fake smile. "Especially since Black, as you say, was ready to announce Chandler's death was accidental despite several inconsistencies of which he was well aware."

"The damned coroner ruled her death accidental, Jess." Burnett cleared his throat and glanced around again. "There's more to this than we know even now. But we got no place to go with our hunches."

"Your mother isn't the only one who came to me," Jess admitted.

His eyebrows reared up in expectation. "How did I not know all this?"

"Both instances happened this afternoon. There hasn't exactly been time to tell you."

"When I confronted you in my office about the leak, you didn't feel compelled to share then?" There was no hiding the frustration in his tone.

"I didn't want to out your mother. She hates me already."

He frowned. "She doesn't hate you."

"She called my sister fat."

"What?"

The look on his face did her in. Jess laughed. "She did. I swear."

He shook his head. "I apologize on her behalf. Sometimes she shocks even me."

Jess relished a long swallow of her beer. Finally, *they* felt normal again. Or was her relief just wishful thinking? When she swiped her lips with the back of her hand, he was watching her. "What?"

"You said my mother wasn't the only one who came to you about the Chandler case."

"Andrea."

His confusion was back. "Andrea talked to you about the case?"

"She brought a video she wanted me to see. It was shot at a competition last fall. In the background you can see the Russian and the Dresher woman arguing."

"Does Andrea know why they were arguing?"

"She thinks it was about Katrina. Apparently no one wanted Katrina on the competition team because, as Andrea put it, she sucks. But then, she also admitted that most of the mothers complain whenever they think their daughters aren't getting the proper attention. What bothered Andrea was the fact that Dresher was the last one to see Darcy Chandler alive and her daughter found the body. So when she spotted the argument while working on a tribute to Chandler, she wanted me to know about it."

"She should have taken this to Black."

Jess held up her hands. "That's exactly what I said to her and to your mother. But keep in mind that Andrea is still mostly a kid. She wanted to tell someone she knew. As for Black, the only reason I didn't tell him about any of this was because the Russian decided to confess before I had the opportunity. I was already in Black's office to do just that."

Burnett downed another swig of beer. "I guess we'll just have to see how this plays out."

"Also bear in mind that if the Russian had grabbed Chandler, there would have been bruises on her arms. This might be over, but it's far from right." Now seemed as good a time as any to broach the other question on fire in her brain. "Black said the demand for a speedy closure of the case came from *above*. What's that all about?"

Burnett's expression shut down like rush-hour traffic

on I-65. "The Chandlers are a powerful family. The longer this drags on, the more the media will hound all those involved. Like the leak today."

"Today's leak got you a confession," Jess reminded him. "If the husband stands by his confession, there'll be no need for a trial. It doesn't get any better than that if you're on the winning team."

So much for having each other's back. This was one secret he didn't care to share.

"That would seem to be the case."

"Except," Jess pushed, "I have my doubts as to whether any part of the Russian's statement is true. He's covering for someone. Maybe for the lover he claims he doesn't have but everyone else seems to think exists. Could be true love. Or just maybe the real killer has something on him and is forcing him to confess. There are worse things than going to prison." Jess made an oh-my-God face. "Then again, Darcy Chandler's affair with some Birmingham who's who could be the motive for murder. Whatever the case, we'll never know because we're shutting down the investigation to protect some Magic City muckety-muck."

Expression still closed, he insisted, "You know better than that."

"Really? I spent the last hour trying to figure out who in this city trumps a Chandler, and you know the only name that keeps coming to mind is Pratt. The mayor does have that one son who threw his hat into the senate race this year. I imagine an affair coming to light with the victim of a possible homicide would not be a good thing for the married father of two who happens to be a major force in his church and at the top of the polls in the senate race. Has anyone interviewed the would-be senator?"

The regret in Burnett's eyes gave her the answer before he spoke. "Let it go, Jess. Black will handle this the right way. You can count on that."

"Not a problem." She grabbed her bag. "Thanks for the beer."

As she scooted from the booth, he stood. "Jess, wait. You have my word that I looked into that particular situation personally. Don't leave like this. Stay. Eat. Let me explain."

She started to tell him that she'd lost her appetite but his cell interrupted. Jess glanced at the table where it lay shimmying and shuddering, and even without her glasses she could see the image of Annette Denton flashing on the screen.

"Looks like you already have a full agenda for the evening."

And with that parting shot, she left. Angry at him and angrier at herself for not having better control of those damned emotions she wanted so desperately to hide.

Jess drove away from Twenty-Ninth without looking back. She wished it were dark so no one could see her flee the scene. She had been back in Birmingham just over two weeks and already she was screwing things up. It had taken her nearly eighteen years to destroy her career at the bureau. Was she on the fast track now that she had a little experience in the art of self-destruction?

She had allowed the Player case to get to her. With every fiber of her being she had been convinced that Eric Spears was the serial killer known as the Player. But she hadn't been able to prove it. So she'd broken the rules in an attempt to get the job done. Oh, she'd had a reputation for stepping on toes and pushing hot buttons, but she'd never crossed the line.

Until Spears.

And she had failed. He'd gotten away, with no telling how many murders to his credit, not once but twice.

She turned onto Druid Hills Drive, not realizing until she made the turn that the Simmonses' neighborhood was her destination. Jess slowed to a stop. She'd lived here for a year. Gone to school just a few streets over.

Jess made two more turns as dusk slowly sank around her, compressing the humidity and heat against her chest and making it harder to breathe. She parked across the street from the small square box that according to Gina Coleman was still her aunt's house. The house had been white at one time. Now it was a dingy gray. The red shutters Jess remembered were gone. Probably lost to neglect and disrepair. The lawn needed a mowing. The ancient Toyota in the drive looked at least a couple of decades older than Jess's Audi.

She'd hated this place. How could her parents die and leave her and Lily to live in this dump? At night back then Jess had lain in the bed she and Lily shared and asked herself that question over and over while her aunt entertained in the next room. Her stomach roiled even now at the memories.

She and Lily had lost everything. Their parents, their lives as they knew them. That fragile yet loving innocence good parents wove carefully around their children had been ripped apart. Something changed deep inside Jess during that horrifying year. For her, failure could not be an option. She had to succeed and she worked harder than her peers to ensure that happened. Meeting and falling in love with Dan in high school hadn't been on her agenda. But she'd soon bought into the dream. Maybe she could have it all and him, too.

Until he'd had enough and then he'd returned to Birmingham, leaving her alone and fractured. But she had survived and she'd accomplished every single career goal she'd set out to attain.

She stared at the run-down shack her aunt called home. Oh yes, Jess had refused to stop until she had reached her goals. And then somehow things had gone wrong. One failure shouldn't have screwed up everything, and yet it felt exactly as if it had. Now she was hell-bent on proving she couldn't fail again. She had to prove Deputy Chief Black was wrong about the Darcy Chandler case. She needed him to be wrong; otherwise she might never trust her instincts again.

She wanted desperately to find DeShawn Simmons alive despite recognizing there was very little chance that would happen. She was setting herself up for another failure rather than simply investigating the case to the best of her ability.

Lights came on in the front room of the house. Her aunt would be sixty now. How was she surviving? Had she finally gotten married again? Her first husband had been killed in a military training accident. Apparently she'd never gotten over the tragedy. Instead she'd turned to a life of drugs.

What the hell was she doing here? She and Lily had stopped considering Wanda Newsom family the day the police had taken them away from this place.

Maybe Jess was like her aunt Wanda. Stuck in a rut of self-destruction, destined to repeat the same mistakes over and over because of some defective gene.

Jess faced forward and reached for the gearshift. She wasn't her aunt and she wasn't looking back.

Something slammed down on the roof of her car at the same instant that a face pressed against the glass of her driver's side window.

Her heart launched into her throat. Her right hand moved instinctively toward her bag where her Glock was stashed. But she couldn't take her eyes off the ones staring at her. At first all her brain registered was hoodie and African American. Then the familiar features of the face filtered through her apprehension.

Jerome Frazier.

Her fingers now tight around the Glock, Jess powered the window down a few inches. "Mr. Frazier, I was just going to drive by your home."

"Are you trying to get me killed?" he demanded, clearly angry.

Her cell rang. Jess wasn't about to let go of the Glock to grab the iPhone. This guy was pissed and she had no idea what he wanted just yet.

"We need to talk." He hustled around to the other side of the car and waited for her to hit the unlock button.

Was he out of his mind?

Another vehicle eased up next to her.

What now? The air inside her Audi thickened until she could no longer draw it in.

The passenger side window of the other car powered down.

"You see this shit!" Frazier banged on the roof of her car again. "This is what I'm talking about."

"Chief Harris, you okay?"

Officer Chad Cook stared expectantly at her from the

driver's seat of the other car. Before she could ask him
what the hell was going on, he added, "I ran your license
plate when Frazier approached your vehicle. I needed to
know who he was meeting."

Jerome Frazier's face appeared in the passenger window of her car. "Why you got this dude following my ass?
I ain't done nothing!"

"Mr. Frazier and I are going to talk," Jess told Cook.
"You can pull over and give us a few minutes."

Cook nodded. "Yes, ma'am."

Jess hit the unlock button and allowed Frazier into
her car.

She reached for calm once more. "What's on your
mind, Mr. Frazier?"

"Look, DeShawn, he's my friend. But I ain't dying for
him 'cause he was too stupid to listen."

"Is he in trouble?" More than she already knew.

Frazier shook his hooded head. "Not DeShawn.
That crazy Mexican bitch that has him under a spell or
something."

"Nina?"

Frazier nodded. "She's using DeShawn. She wants out
of the life and he's gonna get himself killed if he ain't
dead already."

"What else can you tell me about her? Do you know
her last name?"

"DeShawn said he had to keep her name a secret. Said
she was in big trouble."

"What kind of trouble?"

"The name Salvadore Lopez mean anything to you?"

Jess shook her head, feigning ignorance. "Should it?"

Frazier looked around as if fearing someone besides

Cook was watching him. "Look it up. You'll get my meaning then. And tell your boy to stop dogging my ass. I don't know where DeShawn is. Dead probably. But having five-oh hanging around me is gonna get me that way, too."

"If you need our help, Jerome," Jess offered, "we can help you."

His gaze held hers in the darkening gloom for a long moment. "Just help my buddy DeShawn and we'll be square."

When Frazier had disappeared between the rows of houses, Jess told Officer Cook to call it a night. Frazier had given her all he knew and he was likely right about surveillance getting him the wrong kind of attention.

Jess started to pull away from the curb but movement at the window of the little white shack across the street snagged her attention.

The curtain dropped back into place and Jess drove away. She'd had enough of memory lane for one night.

14

Jess adjusted her glasses and studied the latest updates to the case board as Harper finished the last entry beneath the official mug shot of one of Salvadore Lopez's known associates. She had called him immediately after her meeting with Frazier last night. Harper had done his homework.

"Jose Munoz. Twenty-five," Harper said when he'd snapped the top back on the marker and set it aside. "His criminal history began at age twelve and was highlighted by a manslaughter charge for which he did time in Mississippi. Released when he was twenty-one and headed west to find his calling, MS-13 under Lopez's father. Rumor has it Munoz heard stories in prison and decided the Mara Salvatrucha was the life for him. He came to Birmingham eighteen months ago with Salvadore Lopez and serves as his *segunda*."

"If Munoz is the second in command, he'll know all about his boss's activities." Made sense to Jess. If there was no way to get to Lopez, Munoz would be the next best thing.

"Captain Allen has Lopez, Munoz, and their whole entourage under surveillance. Since there's a joint task force between BPD, the FBI, ATF, and DEA as well, he's not going to want us getting too close for fear we'll screw up their plans." Harper gestured to Lopez's photo and then Munoz's. "These dudes are the worst kind of news. In light of Simmons having disappeared one week ago tomorrow, I'm thinking we're not likely to find him alive unless, as you pointed out, the girl is still MIA and is as important to Lopez as we suspect. That possibility might provide Simmons with a temporary stay of execution."

"You're suggesting that this multiagency task force will not allow the investigation into a missing person, dead or not, to jeopardize their ongoing investigation?" If she had a nickel for every time that technicality caused a stumbling block, she would be a very rich lady. No one appreciated another cop stumbling into their ongoing pet project.

Harper nodded. "That's what I got from all Allen's hedging this morning when I asked him about Lopez's clique. He's happy to give us a heads-up if he spots Simmons or learns intel on him, but otherwise, closing in on Lopez is not on the table at this time. Evidently there's something bigger coming and they need to wait for that. Simmons is irrelevant in the grand scheme of things as far as they're concerned."

Hadn't the ATF or anyone else learned their lesson yet? Murder trumped gunrunning and drugs. More than one federal agent had been murdered by the very weapons these agencies left on the street in hopes of making the bigger bust. Letting the bad guys get away with murder for the so-called greater good wasn't on Jess's agenda. If her missing young man was dead, someone was going to prison for murder—no matter who had bigger plans for him.

"I would think that if Allen has this entourage under surveillance"—Jess moved closer to the case board and considered the arrogant expression on Lopez's face—"that he would be aware of any rumblings within that tight-knit little group. If the girl is back with Lopez, Allen should know this. Anyone brought in or out should be listed on their surveillance log."

"That's where things get a little touchy."

Jess turned to Harper. "Touchy how, Sergeant? I understand territorial issues, but Captain Allen is one of ours and this op is taking place in Birmingham's jurisdiction. Anything the feds do is only because we allow it. Surely we can count on him, if no one else, for whatever information he can give." It was one thing for cops within a department to get a little territorial with each other, but the locals usually banded together when it came to the feds horning in.

Harper made a skeptical face. "He's been very forthcoming and helpful about his task force in general. But when it gets to specifics about Lopez's location and any comings and goings, he gives the impression of not being in the know or the chain of command."

"And you don't buy that?"

"No, ma'am. What I really think is that Allen has moving up the career ladder on his mind. If he can make the right impression, one of those three-letter federal agencies will welcome him on board. The pay is better and so are the benefits."

Harper was correct. Federal pay grades were typically

better than those in local law enforcement. God knew the federal insurance was better, for now anyway. And there was a certain prestige that went along with being a federal agent. But sometimes money and position weren't everything...sometimes a person had to step down or back to find her future.

"Can't blame a man for wanting to boost his career, but it won't be because he stepped over DeShawn Simmons's body." Jess walked over to her desk and sifted through the statements they had gathered in the case. "Since we still have no last name for this Nina, did you find anything in any of the missing persons databases?"

"Two hundred twelve with the first name Nina, forty who are Hispanic and in the right age group. But none that look like the drawing we have. In spite of that, I showed the photos to Mr. and Mrs. Simmons but didn't get a hit. This Nina they saw with their grandson wasn't a match to anyone in the database."

Jess glanced at her watch. She hadn't heard from Lori this morning. Not that she had a specific time for checking in. She was on leave after all. Certainly the detective was more than capable of taking care of herself in spite of recent circumstances. But any level of investigating, even simple remote surveillance, could turn dangerous.

"No credible tips on the hotline?"

The media blitz on DeShawn Simmons was ongoing. This would be the third day, but unless there was a better response this morning, they had nothing to speak of yet. Even with a sizable reward for information. Just went to show that few wanted to risk crossing the MS-13.

"Four sightings. I checked out two and Lieutenant Prescott checked out the other two. Dead ends."

Jess peered at the artist's rendering of the female on the case board. "If we can just find this Nina, she might be able to give us what we need to find DeShawn alive or to nail his killer."

"I got the impression that if we find this Nina, we're going to be in for a battle with Allen and his fed friends over who gets control of the leverage."

"That's an easy problem to solve. If we find her first, they can have her as soon as we get what we want and not one minute sooner." The feds were the ones who could offer Nina long-term protection. That was where she should end up. Jess had hoped they would agree to putting that word on the street but so far they hadn't responded to her request.

"If she's still alive," Harper qualified.

"Big fat if," Jess agreed.

The clang of her cell had her reaching for where she'd left it on her desk. She checked the screen. *Andrea?* Again?

"Jess Harris."

"Jess, this is Andrea. I know you're probably busy but I think there's something about what happened to Ms. Darcy you need to know."

"Andrea, didn't you watch the news last night?" Surely Annette had mentioned the latest turn of events since they were close with the Chandler family. "Darcy's husband confessed."

"I know..." Other voices vibrated in the background. "Can you come to the studio? Now? Please?"

She should say no. This was Chief Black's case and he had just closed it with a full confession. Not to mention he'd flat-out told her that her tactics were unappreciated.

He'd even suggested Burnett would come to regret his decision about bringing her on board. She should definitely decline.

"I'll be there in twenty minutes."

Andrea thanked her and at least two other high-pitched little voices echoed the same.

On some level, Jess couldn't resist interaction with Andrea merely because she was Annette's daughter and because Annette still interacted with Dan. She could admit that. She was only human, even if some would disagree. But the truth was she genuinely liked Andrea. And Jess was one hundred percent certain about the Chandler case. The Russian was lying. Worse, he was hiding something and Jess wanted to know what that something was.

"We have a problem we didn't already know about?" Harper asked.

They definitely had several. "That was Andrea Denton. She and some of the Alabama Belles need to talk to me."

"You know—"

"Chief Black won't like it. I do know that, Sergeant." Good grief. Harper was getting as bad as Burnett. "If they have anything relevant to pass along, I'll get word to Black. I'm only doing this because Andrea asked."

"I get it now." Harper gave a nod. "Those little girls like you. They don't want to talk to anyone else."

Jess snorted. "Must be my nurturing nature."

Harper checked his cell. "Just got another five possibly credible hits from the hotline."

"Damn." She grabbed her bag. "I'm going with you. The girls will just have to wait."

"Cook has phone duty at the task force headquarters.

She can go with me. You take care of those little ballerinas." He winked, then slipped on his Ray-Bans. "Could be good practice."

"Funny."

On the way to the parking garage for her Audi, Jess called Lori and asked the detective to meet her at the Chandler mansion. Lori reported that Dresher and her daughter were at the orthodontist's office, so the timing was good for her.

The idea that Katrina wasn't at the studio rehearsing with the other girls seemed odd to Jess. But then, what did she know about kids and their maintenance?

Cotton Avenue, noon

The massive, ornate entry gates stood wide open as Jess turned onto the long drive. The only vehicles parked in front of the Chandler home were Andrea's BMW and a vintage Rolls-Royce.

Had to be the grandmother. Birmingham's grande dame of the arts, Dorothy Chandler.

As she climbed out of her Audi, Jess surveyed the drive and the cobblestoned parking circle for Katherine Burnett's posh Mercedes. There was no sign of her or her car, thank God. Jess climbed the steps and raised her fist to knock on the opulently carved front door. It opened before she could make contact and an older version of Darcy Chandler appeared before Jess. If she'd ever met anyone with better posture, the recollection escaped her. Tall, slender, and undeniably beautiful, Dorothy Chandler wore her hair in the same meticulous French twist she'd worn when she was an internationally celebrated ballerina. The tailored sheath and matching high heels hadn't come from any store at which Jess had ever had the pleasure of shopping. Though the dress was unquestionably elegant, the soft gray color was just somber enough to announce the woman's state of mourning.

"Chief Harris."

"Ms. Chandler."

"Please come in." The graceful lady stepped back and opened the towering door wider in invitation.

Lori's sassy red Mustang roared up the drive and parked next to Jess's ancient Audi. "That's my colleague, Detective Wells."

Chandler nodded. "Show her in. We'll be waiting in the garden."

Dorothy Chandler turned and walked away, her steps precisely measured and as smooth as if she floated on air.

Lori bounded up the steps, any indication of the beatings she'd taken last week no longer visible in her movements.

"What've we got?"

Jess shrugged. "I don't know, but it's a command performance."

Lori's expression lit with anticipation. "Interesting."

"Maybe."

Inside, Jess led the way through the center entry hall. She couldn't help glancing at the place where Darcy Chandler had landed on the cold marble floor.

The French doors at the back of the grand home that led onto the terrace were open. Two of the dancers waited with Andrea and the elder Chandler in the butterfly garden. The colors and scents and fairylike figurines created a whimsical setting that lured butterflies and children like bees to honey.

"Wow," Lori murmured.

Jess's lips quirked. "Yeah. This is how the one percenters live."

When they reached the waiting group, Andrea jumped up and hugged Jess. "Thank you for coming."

She ushered Jess to the bench closest to Chandler. Lori joined her there.

The two girls Jess had heard in the background on the phone sat with Andrea on another limestone bench while Chandler sat, back ramrod straight, on the third.

When no one else kicked off the conversation, Jess said, "You are aware this case is closed."

"I am aware that your department believes so, yes." Eighty years old or not, the woman spoke with supreme confidence.

"And you're also aware that Deputy Chief Harold Black is in charge of this case."

"I am. But it's you I wish to speak with."

Jess sent Lori a you-are-my-witness glance before continuing. "Whatever the story is, ladies, please start at the beginning."

"Andrea, take Sylvia and Lauren into the house for refreshments."

"Yes, ma'am."

Andrea ushered the girls across the terrace and into the house. When the French doors were closed, Chandler began her story. "In January of last year Corrine Dresher and her daughter Katrina moved to Birmingham from Seattle, or so she claims."

Jess waited for her to continue.

"Since she isn't employed and has no husband, I can only assume she has a trust or some source of income. Even before she was settled in a permanent home, she enrolled her daughter in my Darcy's dance studio. Generally we have a process, including tryouts and an interview, but since Katrina had been accepted into Brighton Academy she was given priority status."

Brighton was another Birmingham institution. Sending a kid there was like paying college tuition the dozen or so years before college. It also guaranteed acceptance to most any college or university in the country. Still, the Alabama Belles Dance Studio was a private business. No one made Darcy Chandler enroll the child. "But your granddaughter accepted Katrina's enrollment at the studio."

Dorothy conceded with a nod. "She had no idea the mistake she was making."

Jess needed more than blunt, emotional statements. "I know this is difficult, but I need you to explain what you mean by that. What aspect of enrolling the child was a mistake?"

"Corrine became one of the pushiest mothers. She complained about everything. Her daughter's talent was far from this studio's usual standard, but Katrina was immediately moved into the position of competition team alternate. The entire chain of events was a fiasco."

"Why would Darcy make a decision like that?"

"It wasn't her decision. It was *his*. He allowed that horrid child and her evil mother to become an integral part of the team, as if they had always been here. The other girls had worked years to rise to the level they have achieved. Darcy was furious."

"Do you believe Alexander was having an affair with Corrine?"

The elder Chandler reflected on that question for a time. "Darcy insinuated there was something between the two, but whether Alexander was screwing the Dresher woman or not wasn't as relevant as it might have once been." She dabbed at her eyes.

"Meaning?" Jess prodded.

"Darcy was embroiled in an affair of her own."

"Was this affair with Jarrod Pratt?" Jess had a feeling that was why the mayor wanted the case closed quickly.

Dorothy Chandler looked away. Her hand shook as she covered her mouth for a moment to compose herself.

"Ms. Chandler, I'm sorry to have to ask these questions, but if you believe your granddaughter was murdered by someone besides Alexander, we have to know the answers to the hard questions."

She squared her shoulders and met Jess's gaze. "Not with Jarrod. With his wife, Cynthia."

Well, there was a twist Jess hadn't expected. Talk about a scandal. No wonder it was being kept on the down low. This was Alabama where being black, Hispanic, or queer was still only marginally acceptable and rarely discussed in public. "Were either of the husbands aware of this affair?"

Dorothy nodded. "There was quite a heated yet discreet battle taking place. Cynthia had agreed to wait until after the election to seek a divorce. Darcy was to get hers now." The matron of the Chandler family frowned. "But something changed two weeks ago, and Darcy decided she didn't want Alexander to have any part in the studio anymore. She refused to discuss it with anyone. Not even me. But it seemed to have something to do with that unpleasant child, Katrina, and her mother."

"I understand that you have reservations and the facts you've related to me are compelling, but what reason would Alexander have for confessing to a murder he didn't commit?" Jess wholeheartedly agreed that the Russian was likely lying. They needed to know why and to be able to prove it.

"He's covering for the real killer and I believe that person is Corrine Dresher," Chandler insisted. "Whatever power Corrine holds over him, it's enough to have him step forward to ensure the truth is never found. Alexander doesn't have the guts to commit murder. He's protecting someone—my granddaughter's killer."

"You haven't mentioned any of this previously. Why are you sharing this information now?" If she genuinely believed Dresher was involved in her granddaughter's death, why keep it to herself?

"Andrea showed me the video clip. While we were watching, Lauren and Sylvia came into the parlor. They were supposed to be rehearsing with the others. Andrea and I had let the time get away and everyone else was gone except those two. Sylvia was the first to speak up. She reminded Lauren about the way Katrina bullied Michelle."

"Michelle is?" Jess inquired.

"The child we lost just before Christmas last year."

Oh yes. Andrea had told her one of the dancers had died in an accident. Katrina had taken her place on the competition team. "Was there some question about Michelle's accident?" Andrea hadn't mentioned anything but then they had gotten interrupted by Jess's call from Burnett after the so-called BPD leak hit the news.

"She fell in front of a car on the main street that crosses in front of the school. It was a horrible tragedy. She lived for three days but she never regained consciousness."

Jess's instincts sat up and took notice. "But it was an accident, right?"

"That's what everyone said. Katrina and her mother were right beside her when it happened. They were supposed to ride to rehearsal together. The mothers rely on each other when there's an appointment or an illness. If you're not familiar with how things work at a studio, especially an intimate one like ours, the dancers and their mothers become like a family. That day Corrine was to pick up both Katrina and Michelle. But for some reason she'd forgotten her pickup line pass so she'd parked a block away from the school. It's quite an annoying rule, but like all rules it has its purpose. Corrine met the girls at the school's main entrance gate and the three walked along that busy street to her car. After the accident, they claimed Michelle had dropped her cell phone and stumbled into the street as she tried to retrieve it."

"You have some reason to believe it wasn't an accident?" Once again, they needed more than speculation. Although Jess did find it quite a coincidence that yet another person with extraordinary balance stumbled and fell. And Katrina and her mother were the only ones around at the time.

Dorothy met Jess's expectant gaze with fear in hers. "Sylvia and Lauren insist Katrina bullied Michelle unmercifully. She would tell Michelle that if she broke her leg she wouldn't be able to dance and Katrina would take her place. Every day it was something. Very cruel. It just seems strange to me that Corrine forgot her pass and decided not to bother going back home for it that particular day. Michelle died as a result of that decision. And now my Darcy is dead."

"But no one who witnessed the incident that took Michelle's life could say otherwise?"

Dorothy shook her head. "There were two eyewitnesses who came forward but none could say that Corrine's and Katrina's stories were false. It just happened too fast. Still, a few weeks later at a spend-the-night party Katrina was angry because the others were taunting her about her poor performance in rehearsal. They said something like they wished they had Michelle back. Katrina told them to shut up or they would be sorry just like Michelle." Dorothy pressed her fingers to her lips for a moment. "She warned them that her mother would make them sorry."

Dorothy Chandler was absolutely convinced that the Russian did not have the courage to kill Darcy. She was equally convinced that somehow Corrine Dresher was responsible not only for her death but also for Michelle's. Yesterday she had hired a private investigator to see what he could find on Dresher. Jess couldn't say she wouldn't have done the same thing. Unfortunately, without evidence or an immensely compelling motive, the hands of the police were tied in both cases.

While Lori questioned the two girls, Jess checked up on Andrea. Lori would also look into the story about Michelle Butler once they were finished here. There would be a case file on the Butler accident at the BPD. Perhaps the family would be willing to talk.

"You hanging in there, Andrea?" She certainly seemed to be in the thick of this painful situation.

"I'll be glad when this is over." She hugged her arms

around her middle. "I just want justice for Ms. Darcy and I want my mom to stop being sad."

Burnett had said that Annette and Darcy Chandler had been friends. But Jess hadn't gotten the impression that they were that close or that she was taking it quite so hard as Andrea seemed to think.

"We'll get this case settled and then you and your mom can move on."

"I don't think that'll fix things for my mom. She hangs on me whenever I'm home. Says she hates being alone. I can't even leave the house without her calling a hundred times like some stalker." Andrea released a big, burdened breath. "When she's not driving me crazy, she's calling Dan."

"If it's not the case, then what's going on with your mom?"

"It's my dad." Andrea shook her head. "He's an asshole. He's leaving again and Mom just can't deal with it."

The memory of smelling Annette's perfume on Burnett's jacket filled Jess's senses.

Well, now she knew.

Her cell clanged and Jess ditched her pity party and dug the phone from her bag. "Harris."

"I'm on my way to Pelham." Harper rattled off an address on Lee Street, just off 52. "We got four dead MS-13 members and one dead African American male."

An ache pierced Jess's chest. "Is it DeShawn Simmons?"

"No ID on any of the victims, but that's what the first officers on the scene believe."

"I'm on my way, Sergeant."

"We don't have a lot of time, ma'am. Officer Cook has just arrived on the scene. He called me instead of GTF. He can't wait much longer before notifying Captain Allen."

"I'm leaving now, Sergeant."

Jess assured Dorothy Chandler she would do what she could to determine if there was any merit to her suspicions. Lori stayed behind to finish up.

Jess had so hoped that DeShawn Simmons would be found alive.

Disgust and anger welled in her chest. The bastard responsible for this wasn't going to get away with murdering an innocent kid.

Not on her watch.

Lee Street, Pelham, 1:42 p.m.

The house was one of a few residential properties in a mostly light industrial area. A holdover from the days when this had been a neighborhood rather than an eclectic mix of low-rent businesses operating on shoestring budgets. Six of BPD's finest were on the scene. Crime Scene techs were en route as were two MEs from the coroner's office. Folks from the Donut Joe's down the street had gathered in the parking lot to watch the show. Employees from a nearby warehouse did the same. When a gang hit went down, silencers were rarely used. Discretion was not the goal. Sending messages in the loudest and clearest manner was the primary objective.

Two news vans had passed Jess as she'd exited Pelham Parkway and turned onto Highway 52. Thankfully, Lee Street had been blocked off from 52 to Old Tuscaloosa Road. For the next few hours only official vehicles would be allowed to pass. The longer this tragic event could be kept off the airwaves the better.

Jess stepped gingerly through the front room of the house that was posted as being for lease and supposedly vacant. From the strewn clothing and mattress on the floor, that was undeniably inaccurate. Empty food containers and other household garbage lay amid the human carnage.

The tattoos on four of the victims identified them as members of MS-13. Whatever tattoos a member chose, the number 13 or MS-13 was proudly displayed as a part of the design. Automatic weapons had left line after line of holes in the walls. Windows were shattered, as was the front door.

It was a bloody mess.

Jess zigzagged her way through the path of bullet-riddled and decapitated bodies to the one that really mattered to her. She crouched down next to the young black man on the floor.

"Oh God."

Jerome Frazier. He'd been shot twice in the chest but spared the beheading. His young face was unmarred, making identification a simple matter.

Jess turned away long enough to compose herself. Putting him under surveillance had been the right move. Had that decision cost him his life? Or was being DeShawn Simmons's friend the deciding factor? She hoped he hadn't attempted to find DeShawn on his own. Whatever the case, the young man was dead and Jess was no closer than before to knowing the whereabouts of DeShawn or the identity of Nina.

Fury roared inside her. There had to be a better way to stop this kind of evil. All the damned gang task forces created in city after city seemed to be getting nowhere.

Well, this was Birmingham, her hometown, and she

was back. One way or another she was going to make a difference here.

Jess blinked back the emotions stinging her eyes and looked across the room where Harper waited. They were done here. There were two things she could do for Jerome Frazier now. Notify his next of kin and find the bastard responsible for murdering him.

Jess didn't spend a lot of time praying. Seemed a waste of time. No matter. She sent a quick prayer heavenward for Jerome and his family. He hadn't deserved to die this way. Pushing to her feet, she said to the closest officer, "When the MEs get here, you see that this young man is taken care of first."

"Yes, ma'am."

This was the kind of message killers like Lopez liked to leave behind. Jerome's murder was a nuisance kill. He was dead because he annoyed the wrong person or got in the way. The others were decapitated because they were traitors. That the traitors had been killed along with Jerome meant something. Jess just needed to solve the hidden message.

The most probable scenario was that Jerome had thought he'd discovered a contact who could lead him to his friend. And Jess hadn't had anyone in place to give him backup. That was on her.

When she reached Harper, he said, "Officer Cook is on a guilt trip. I explained that he was following orders, but he's not taking it very well."

"I'll talk to him, but first I need to make a call to a source who might be able to help us."

"Someone local?" Chet looked surprised.

Jess shook her head. "Someone I know in the bureau.

He works with the Anti-Gang Initiatives and Partnerships on the West Coast. If Lopez's father is a who's who out there, my contact will know about him and his son."

"Allen won't be happy that you went around him."

"Good," Jess allowed, "because right now I am very unhappy."

She stamped outside, away from Officer Cook, who waited near his vehicle and looked ready to puke.

On second thought, she turned around. Might as well put him out of his misery first. Five more minutes before making the call wouldn't hurt.

"Officer Cook."

He looked up as Jess approached. "Yes, ma'am."

"You are in no way responsible for what happened here." She pointed to the house. "This is on me. I gave the order for surveillance on this kid and I gave the order for it to end. *This* is not your responsibility; it's mine. Are we clear?"

He nodded but didn't meet her gaze.

"The best thing we can do right now is to focus on finding DeShawn Simmons alive, and if we're lucky we'll nail the people responsible for this travesty in the process. But we can't do that if we get stuck on the things we can't control. Now let's get on with doing what we have to do."

He managed a jerky nod. "Yes, ma'am."

"I guess you'd better put in a call to Captain Allen."

Jess had a call of her own to make. She selected the name from her contact list and did the thing she'd sworn she would never again do.

Her ex-husband answered on the second ring.

Her heart stumbled and she moistened her lips. "Wesley, I need your help."

15

Dan stared at the file open on his desk. He'd read and then reread the coroner's report on Darcy Chandler's death. He'd even called Leeds and gone over the facts one by one. Page by page he had reviewed the witness interviews and the crime scene reports.

There was no indication whatsoever of a struggle. No marks on the victim's arms or hands, the most likely places when a struggle occurs. No scratching or bruising on her face. Nothing under her fingernails. Every single injury was related to the impact from her fall.

Except that small bruise on her lower left leg. Likewise, there had been no visible marks on the husband's face, hands, or arms at his initial interview only hours after Chandler's death.

If Mayakovsky had killed his wife, there was no evidence to support his claim. And the question of motive still remained unanswered. No financial motive, no evidence of squabbling over her affair, although his had clearly caused a rift between the couple. Why not just go through with the divorce?

Where was the motive for murder?

Motive is everything. Jess had hammered that into Dan's head so many times the past few weeks that he had to look long and hard at that now.

Any act of violence against another human is compelled by motive. That was Jess's motto, pure and simple.

If his motive wasn't related to money or jealousy, then Jess was right.

"He has to be covering for someone." Dan shuffled the reports back into a neat stack and closed the file Black had given him to review.

What if Darcy Chandler had decided to commit suicide and he was protecting her reputation...her memory?

But why would Chandler take her own life? Admittedly, the idea of the husband giving up everything to protect her honor was over the top.

Had Chandler opted to kill herself in hopes he would be accused as some sort of payback?

Where the hell was the motive in either scenario?

Dan stared at the phone on his desk and considered calling his mother and demanding to know her motives for going to Jess behind his back. If she had information about Chandler's death she was keeping from him, he wanted to know that, too.

Had she really called Jess's sister fat?

Maybe Jess was right. Maybe two-plus decades had changed nothing when it came to the way things were between the two of them. Whether or not she cared for Jess, his mother would never have set her up to look like the department leak. Obviously she felt strongly that Darcy's death was no accident. But why hadn't she said this to him?

That conversation with his mother was best carried out in person. Just the two of them without his father to run interference for the wife he had always allowed free rein.

His parents had recently celebrated their fiftieth anniversary. How had they managed to maintain their relationship for half a century? Dan sure as hell hadn't figured out the secret.

He pushed back his chair and walked over to the window that overlooked the Linn Park fountain. The last several days he'd felt restless. Off-kilter somehow. The extreme highs and lows of the past two-plus weeks had crashed into a more normal routine and he couldn't seem to find his footing. He and Jess weren't ensnared in a life-and-death investigation as a team. She was investigating her case and he was here, doing the job he'd worked so hard to attain.

He missed the fieldwork. When he and Roy Griggs had gone into that farmhouse and found Andrea...Dan couldn't find the proper words to adequately articulate that feeling. A week later having Jess come to his rescue—and save his life—in that warehouse had changed something deep inside him.

Nothing felt the same anymore.

The job he loved felt constraining, pointless.

What he wanted for the rest of his life was suddenly undefined. He felt uncertain and damned unsettled.

A soft rap at his door drew his attention there. His secretary was gone for the day but Tara, the receptionist, should be at her desk. Maybe it was Black. He was having the same doubts about Mayakovsky's confession as Dan, but Black would take them to his grave before sharing those feelings with Jess.

Somehow Dan had to help those two become friends, allies at the very least.

He crossed the room and opened the door. To his surprise Annette waited there.

"Your secretary wasn't at her desk."

"Is Andrea okay?" That seemed to be his stock question whenever Annette called or showed up. Her surprise announcement that Brandon was leaving her had done just that, surprised him. He and Annette had been friends for years before they became involved as a couple. He wanted to be there for her. But being a supportive friend was all he could offer.

She nodded. "She's fine. Assisting with tomorrow's memorial service for Darcy has been a big help to her. Andrea's been focused on being supportive of the family rather than what she's been through."

"That's great. Jess mentioned seeing her and said she looked and sounded well." Made him feel less like a jerk to interject Jess into the conversation. That was something he didn't exactly understand. It just was.

"Are you busy?"

"Not with anything that can't wait. Come in. Have a seat."

He really was having difficulty focusing this evening. In part because Annette's frequent calls and appearances were contributing to that off-balance feeling. Though they had been divorced for more than a year, there were still feelings he couldn't deny. He wanted Annette and Andrea safe and happy. He wanted both of them to feel comfortable turning to him.

He wanted to be friends.

But that was all he wanted.

The signals Annette was giving off made him believe she wanted more. Possibly he was overreacting. Whenever he got right with that conclusion she would make a move that changed his mind. The last time he'd narrowly avoided a kiss right on the mouth. Further proof was that dress she was wearing. Shorter and tighter than usual. The stilettos higher than the norm for her. He recognized her on-the-hunt attire. He'd admired it before.

When she'd settled into a chair in front of his desk, he returned to his—on the opposite side. She seemed too distracted to notice.

Annette didn't like the idea of being alone. He'd figured that out about her soon after they were married. She'd still been in love with Brandon, her first husband, and she'd only turned to Dan because she needed someone she could trust to hold on to during that tumultuous time. Six months later she had realized that undeniable fact, and she and Dan parted amiably. Brandon was Andrea's father and that detail had a great deal of bearing on Annette's decisions and actions.

Annette was a beautiful, intelligent woman. Her insecurities about standing on her own two feet without a husband were so very unnecessary. But Dan couldn't make her see that. She defined herself completely by the partner in her life. He hoped one day she would recognize how very wrong that was.

If she and Brandon were over again, Dan couldn't fill her dance card the way he had last time. At some point he would have to make that clear. For now, he had to tread carefully. The last thing he wanted to do was give her the wrong idea. Hopefully all she needed this afternoon was a compassionate ear and a strong shoulder.

"He's coming home next week," she said at last, "and he wants to start divorce proceedings immediately." She dropped her purse into the other chair and turned her hands up. "I don't understand why he can't give us a fighting chance. It's hardly been seven months. That's not long enough to rebuild what we once had: We need more time."

There were things Dan could say like the fact that Brandon was an ass of the highest order. The arrogant prick liked the idea of having a wife and a daughter but he didn't want to be burdened with either or both all the time. Dan would bet his next raise that Brandon was cheating. But he wasn't about to say that to Annette. If it was true, she would find out soon enough.

"If you feel you need more time," he suggested, "tell him. Don't just give in to his demands without laying out a few of your own."

"What's wrong with me, Dan?" The tears spilled past her lashes. "Why can't I be what he wants or needs?"

Damn. He kept his seat, as tough as that proved. He reached into the drawer where he kept a box of tissues and passed it across his desk to her. "This is his problem, Annette, not yours. It's Brandon who's lacking, not you. He doesn't deserve you. Can't you see that?"

She plucked tissues from the box, set it on the edge of his desk, and dabbed at her tears. "It feels like he finds fault with me on purpose. Like he's looking for a reason to go."

"Only you can give him that kind of control over your feelings. You know who you are. You don't need him to verify or prove anything. If he's so shallow that he doesn't see what he has right in front of him, let him go. It's his loss."

She shot to her feet and rounded his desk. He stiffened but she didn't come to him. She went to the window and stared out as he had moments ago. He felt like a fool just sitting there, but he knew what would happen if he moved to comfort her. She'd already shown she wanted more than his consoling embraces.

Jess elbowed her way into his head and he almost smiled. She would tell him to get a grip and man up.

He stood and took a position at the window next to Annette. "Don't let him have all the power, Annette. You can do better."

"I did better."

He dared to look at her then.

"And I screwed that up." She launched into his arms.

Holy hell.

His cell vibrated against his desktop. He owed somebody big for that reprieve. He unwrapped her arms from his waist and stepped back. "I have to get that."

She nodded and pressed a hand over her mouth as if she might burst into sobs.

"Burnett." He answered without even checking the screen. Whatever the interruption, he was thankful.

"Chief, this is Ted Allen. I think we have a major problem."

"What sort of problem, Captain?"

"You're aware we took over a former carpet warehouse positioned kitty-corner to where Center and Twenty-Second intersect."

"I am." Dan searched through the mental list of ongo-

ing activities in his jurisdiction but wasn't mentally landing on the details on the Center Street operation.

"We've been keeping surveillance on that Center Street
residence for six months now," Allen explained. "We're
within days of busting a major drug and gunrunning op."

Center Street was a joint venture between the BPD's
Gang Task Force, the ATF, FBI, and DEA. "I understand
you're saying this is a pivotal time in your operation, but
I'm unclear on what your immediate problem is and what
you need from me." The guy needed to get to the point. In
his experience, Allen wasn't generally one to beat around
the bush.

"The problem is Deputy Chief Harris and Sergeant
Harper just parked in front of the house we have under
surveillance. They're headed for the front door as we
speak and we're all scratching our balls and wondering
what the fuck."

Comprehension materialized and Dan's heart dropped
to his feet.

"Who's inside the house, Captain?"

"The worst of the worst. Salvadore Lopez and his
crew."

"Intervene, Allen. Now. Do not allow Harris to walk
into that situation."

"Chief, my hands are tied. We let the feds have lead
on this operation. There's nothing I can do unless shots
are fired. I'm just giving you a heads-up in case the shit
hits the fan and you end up with a dead deputy chief and
detective on your hands."

"I'm on my way. Have the agent in charge call me on
my cell." Dan ended the call and sent an apologetic look
in Annette's direction. Unless he sprouted wings, there

was no way Dan was going to get there in time to stop Jess.

He hoped like hell she knew what she was doing. She sure as hell hadn't shared her agenda with him.

Just something else that needed to change...assuming she didn't get herself killed first.

16

Chief Harris banged on the neglected front door of the house a contact of Chet's claimed served as Lopez's hangout. The house was an old craftsman, probably from the twenties or thirties. Not so run-down, just sadly in need of routine maintenance.

The locos inside wouldn't be interested in home maintenance.

Chet had done all within his power to prevent Harris from coming here, but she had refused to listen. Considering what her FBI contact out in Cali had told her, she was way pissed off. This girl, Nina, was not Lopez's girlfriend as they had thought. She was his seventeen-year-old sister. Their father had sent her here to stay with her brother for a while until things calmed down after her boyfriend's murder. If the girl was missing, Lopez was likely in hot water with his old man.

That information and the fact that a joint task force

operation was set up across the street with Lopez and his people under 24/7 surveillance were the only details in their favor. Whether that would prevent an all-out war from going down in the next few minutes, Chet couldn't say.

He had no desire to die today and he damn sure didn't intend for the chief to get herself killed. But she was one hardheaded woman.

Like Lori. Her image…her voice whispered through his mind.

More banging on the door dragged his head back to where it should be.

"Doesn't sound like anyone's home, ma'am." The dead silence inside provided some sense of relief. Maybe they would get through this alive. "Lopez and his people may have some other crash pad they use to avoid surveillance."

"I don't think so, Sergeant. This is the place." Harris rapped again, harder this time. "Why would Lopez avoid surveillance? He doesn't do the dirty work. People do that for him. As long as he's here, the cops are watching him and not his henchmen. That's why he's been here for eighteen months and hasn't been arrested. Allen knows he's responsible but he can't prove it." She glanced across the street. "Maybe he doesn't want to prove it."

Chet wasn't even going to try to analyze that last statement. "Maybe we need to rethink this strategy," he attempted once more. "Chief Burnett will not be happy."

"I gave you a direct order to wait in the vehicle, Sergeant. You've already committed insubordination. I wouldn't worry about what Burnett will and will not be happy about."

"I can't allow you to do this alone, ma'am." The woman

was being completely unreasonable. "If that makes me insubordinate, I apologize in advance." He might not have the opportunity later. He hated to think what would happen if someone did open that door. "Your safety is priority."

"Though I appreciate your concern, Sergeant, this won't take more than three or four minutes."

Harris was understandably upset about Frazier's murder. She clearly was not thinking rationally. Three minutes in a nest of vipers was an eternity.

In light of the fact that they were having this conversation on a porch that allegedly belonged to an MS-13 clique, he had to admit that maybe Harris wasn't the only one behaving irrationally.

She pounded on the door again. Loud enough to wake the dead. Damn but she was pissed.

Chet thought of his little boy and how he would feel if something happened to him. Harris swore she didn't have any nurturing instincts, but Chet was pretty sure she was wrong. She just didn't want to own a softer side.

The door opened and Jose Munoz looked them both over before leaning one shoulder against the door frame. "Whatever you're selling, we ain't interested and we damned sure ain't buying." He looked Harris up and down a second time and snorted. "Unless it's what's under that skirt and I don't usually pay for that."

Harper eased forward one step, his hand settling on his hip, drawing attention to his holstered weapon.

The chief showed her credentials. "I'm Deputy Chief Harris, Birmingham PD, and I'm here to see Salvadore Lopez."

Munoz laughed. "Who?"

"Your *jefe, pendejo*," Harper snarled.

"There's no one here by that name," Munoz popped back, clearly amused. "Maybe you got the wrong address."

"Tell your *jefe*," Harris said, "that we know about his sister, Nina."

"Let them in," a voice called from inside the house.

Munoz stepped back, drawing the door open wider.

Chet followed his boss inside. He would have preferred to go first, but she was pushy in addition to being hardheaded.

The place stank of cigarette smoke and booze. The shades were all drawn tight, leaving nothing but the beat-up lamps positioned around the room to drive away the darkness. Lopez was sprawled on the sofa. Six others, his security team, held positions around the room.

The front door slammed shut. Harper flinched in spite of knowing it was coming. It took every ounce of courage he owned not to look behind him.

No weapons were visible but they would be handy. Three dogs, one rottweiler and two pit bulls, stood at attention around the room. None of the three were restrained.

Great.

"Where is my sister?" Lopez demanded.

Chet braced for what Harris would say next. She was mad as hell.

"Why don't you tell me? The way I hear it, you're the one who lost her."

Rage tightened Lopez's face. "Is she under arrest?"

"Not yet," Harris said. "But that may change as we investigate the death of Jerome Frazier and the disappearance of DeShawn Simmons. She may be an accessory to more than one murder."

Lopez nodded to Munoz, who stepped forward and asked, "Are you wearing wires?"

"I am not." Jess held up her hands. "Feel free to check for yourself."

Chet gritted his teeth as the bastard put his hands on the chief. She didn't so much as cringe. Then it was his turn. He endured the bullshit only because it was what Harris wanted. What he wanted was to put a bullet in the head of every lowlife scumbag in the room.

"My sister had nothing to do with any murder. She's innocent," Lopez announced. "The Negro you're all worried about took her. But I'll find her. There might be a little collateral damage here and there, five-oh. You got you some evidence that marks me as your perpetrator? Maybe you need to arrest me now."

"I don't think that's necessary at all, Mr. Lopez. I think you'll be in enough trouble if you don't find her before your daddy finds out she's missing."

Lopez's gaze narrowed in a warning. "I will attend to my family problems, *Deputy Chief Harris.*"

"Well, now you have a new problem."

Chet tensed. What the hell was she trying to do, get them both killed?

Lopez shot to his feet like a panther and swaggered over to her.

Chet stepped slightly in front of her.

Lopez glared at him before turning his attention back to Harris. "And what kind of problem is that, *chiquita*?"

"I'm going to get so far up in your business that you'll think *I'm* part of the family."

Lopez laughed. His crew burst into laughter with him. The dogs grumbled at the racket. Then Lopez abruptly stopped and sneered at Harris with pure hatred. "What you think you can do that the fools across the street cannot?"

She smiled. "I'm not like the ones across the street, Mr. Lopez." She inclined her head. "You see, I don't care about taking you or any of your friends alive. Dead works just fine for me."

The silence thundered for three, four, then five seconds.

"Watch yourself, *chiquita*. My people might get the wrong impression. They already gave you one warning. Are you bucking for another?" He leaned closer, putting his face in hers. She didn't even flinch. "I know where you live. Now," he demanded, "where is my sister?"

"Here's the deal, Mr. Lopez. If you or any of your people harm DeShawn Simmons, I will see that you and your sister pay. And I will get you for the murder of Jerome Frazier; that's a given. I don't care about your connections or what you do or don't know. I just want to see justice done."

"Are you threatening me, bitch?" Lopez growled.

"Absolutely. I spent the entire time I was forced to explain to the Frazier family that their son had been murdered thinking of ways to make you pay. And if I have to deliver that same news to the Simmons family, your *padre* will be most unhappy. You see, I know people in LA. People who know your father well. I can have a personal message delivered to him anytime, day or night."

For reasons Chet could not begin to fathom, there were no sudden attacks and no gun blasts. Lopez and the chief just stood there for about ten seconds and stared at each other while sweat slid down Chet's back.

"Any other questions?" Harris asked.

Lopez glowered at her a moment longer but said nothing.

"Thank you for your time, gentlemen."

Harris turned her back and walked out. Chet stayed right behind her, though he didn't risk turning his back.

Once they were in his SUV, Harris faced him. "Thank you, Sergeant."

He nodded. "Yes, ma'am."

"Before we call it a day I'd like to drop by and give Mr. and Mrs. Simmons an update."

"Heading there now." Chet guided his SUV onto the street. "You must have one hell of a contact in LA."

Her contact had not only known that Nina was Salvadore Lopez's half sister, not his girlfriend as they'd suspected, but he had also known that the Lopez patriarch had sent Nina to Alabama to get her away from a young man in a rival gang. A young man he had personally executed. Just went to show that even gangbangers had routine family problems. Now she was missing, and as they'd suspected, Salvadore did not want his father to find out. Harris hadn't been worried about facing off with the guy, because she had his number. He was scared of his father. The last few minutes had just confirmed both theories.

"Let's just say he owed me one," she said in answer to his comment about her contact.

Chet spotted the tail in their rearview mirror. "We have company, ma'am."

His cell and Harris's rang at the same time.

"Just keep driving, Sergeant. If they want to talk to us, they'll follow."

17

Jess waited on the stoop of the Simmonses' home. The extra security door that had been here the last time she visited was gone. Those MS-13 thugs had shattered it just as completely as they had ended the life of Jerome Frazier.

Burnett's fancy Mercedes waited behind Harper's much more affordable Nissan. Behind Burnett were two other vehicles. She suspected the nondescript sedan belonged to one of the three-letter agencies. The other was probably Captain Ted Allen. They were all no doubt pissed and out for blood. But not one would dare make a scene at the home of a victim.

The front door of the Simmons home opened and DeShawn's grandfather looked from Jess to Harper and back. Chi-Chi peeked out but didn't bother with a yap.

His expression lapsed into one of misery and defeat.

"We haven't found DeShawn," Jess assured him, though at this point she wasn't so sure the news was reassuring. "But we do have information you need to be aware of."

"Come on in." He turned back into the house and shouted, "Helen, Chief Harris is here."

Jess followed Mr. Simmons into the living room. She sat down just as she had before on the worn, comfy sofa. Sergeant Harper did the same.

Helen hurried into the room. She hesitated behind her husband's recliner. Fear and denial scrolled across her face. "Did you find my boy?"

"Not yet." And that was the good news.

"Come on round here and sit down, Helen. Lord have mercy, woman, we got company. Don't just stand there asking questions."

Jess related the bad news about Jerome Frazier. The Simmonses were visibly shaken. Jess hoped that tragedy would help them to see the merit in her next suggestion. She drew in a breath and prepared for a fight. "The young woman with your grandson is Nina Lopez. She's the sister of Salvadore Lopez, who heads up MS-13 here in Birmingham."

Mrs. Simmons's hand went to her throat. "Has he already hurt my boy and you just don't want to tell me?"

"We haven't found DeShawn or Nina yet, but the good news is neither has her brother. I took a little chance and prompted the truth out of him. I'm convinced that he has no idea where his sister is. So wherever she and DeShawn are, there's reason to believe they're still safe."

"What happens now?" Mr. Simmons wanted to know.

"We keep searching and hope we find them." This was the tricky part. "But I need a favor from the two of you."

"Anything," Mrs. Simmons answered promptly.

"I want to be sure the two of you stay safe. We've had an officer watching your home but that might not be enough. Do you have friends or family you could stay with for a while? Maybe in a neighboring town? I'll keep you posted on everything that's going on, but if I don't have to worry about your safety it'll be so much easier for me to focus on finding your grandson."

Maybe the guilt factor would help her cause.

"We could stay with your cousin Gladys," Mr. Simmons suggested, "over in Tarrant. That wouldn't be so far away."

Mrs. Simmons shook her head. "I want to stay right here in case he calls me and I need to get to him."

"We'll have your landline forwarded to your cousin's home," Jess assured her. "I'm certain DeShawn would feel better if he knew the two of you were safe."

It took a few more minutes but Helen Simmons finally agreed. The officer currently assigned to surveillance would escort the couple to Tarrant.

When the good-bye hugs were exchanged, Jess was ready to face the ramifications of her actions.

Burnett and the entire joint Gang Task Force were no doubt furious with her.

Harper moved out onto the stoop first. Jess joined him and the door closed behind them.

"You ready for this, Chief?"

Jess laughed. "My aunt had a saying, Sergeant: They can kill us, but they can't eat us." She shook her head. She hadn't thought of her aunt in decades, and yet now that she was back home... "I always thought that was the stupidest saying."

"It's against the law," Harper said as he took the steps down to the sidewalk. "Eating humans, I mean. Therefore, they might very well kill us—in this case make us wish we were dead—for what we did, but they can't eat us. At least that's my theory."

"Well, there you go." Jess squared her shoulders. "I don't know about you but I feel a lot better."

Harper chuckled. "A whole lot better."

Burnett climbed out of his SUV as they approached the street. The other two vehicles had left already. Looked as if Burnett had won that pissing contest. He got first shot at her.

"Chief Harris, come with me," he ordered. "Sergeant Harper, be in my office at nine sharp tomorrow morning."

"Yes, sir." Harper nodded to Jess. "See you in the morning, ma'am."

"Assuming your theory is correct," she tossed at her detective.

Despite the fury and frustration emanating from Burnett's expression as well as his rigid posture, Harper smiled before walking away. The pit bull next door went through his usual routine, barking and snarling.

Jess strode over to Burnett's big, fancy SUV and climbed into the passenger seat. Whatever he said, she wasn't backing down. She had done the right thing. The GTF, FBI, ATF, and DEA could just get over it. Strange how she'd never considered how absolutely ridiculous all those acronyms were until now.

Burnett guided his Mercedes away from the curb and pointed it in the direction of downtown.

Jess focused on the traffic. It was quitting time for all the day shifters. Navigating the traffic would make the trip twice as long. She imagined Burnett would fill the time railing at her for overstepping her bounds and stomping on toes across multiagencies.

Let him have at it.

She was ready for whatever he threw at her. There were significant aspects of the law that were on her side. She and Harper had discussed them at length between paying that somber visit to the Frazier home and giving Lopez what for.

To her surprise Burnett said nothing.

By the time he reached First Avenue the silent treatment had gotten to her.

"Just so we're clear, I knew what I was doing."

No response. Not even a grunt. She dared to look at him. Oh, he was mad. Fire spitting, break something mad.

That square jaw looked as hard as the limestone bench she'd sat on in the Chandlers' impressive butterfly garden today.

He wouldn't look at her even when he stopped for a traffic light. Oh yeah. This was a pissed-off zone Daniel T. Burnett rarely crossed into. He was always Mr. Control. Rarely lost his cool. Always kept a level head.

Well, a nineteen-year-old boy was dead and another was missing because the authorities watching the monster responsible for both were waiting for the "big" bust. They could all just get right with it. She had done what she had to do in order to prompt a lead in her case. She now could assume with some level of certainty that DeShawn Simmons was still alive because Lopez had no freaking idea where his sister was. He had no idea that he had provided the answer to the question Jess most wanted answered.

Nina Lopez was running away from her brother *and* her father. And Salvadore would do anything to prevent Daddy from finding out.

Jess now had a fifty-fifty chance of finding DeShawn alive.

The thirteen minutes required to reach the downtown parking garage was just enough time for her to reach maximum overload on the frustration and wrath front. Burnett had made a serious error in judgment in waiting to have his say. She was way beyond playing nice now.

The instant he shifted into park she slid from the passenger seat and slammed the door. It was a Mercedes; it could take the abuse. Without waiting to see what he did next she stormed from the building, across the street, and all the way to the department's front entrance.

Flashing her badge, she didn't hesitate long enough for security to ask to see inside her bag. Since the guard, who knew her but had a job to do, didn't attempt to call her back, she assumed Burnett took care of any questions.

She bypassed the elevator. No way was she going up four floors in the elevator with him. She hit the stairwell. Hopping on first one foot and then the other, she removed her high heels and tucked them in her bag. Four flights of stairs weren't so bad, but in four-inch heels it bordered on masochism.

She had to stop on the third floor and pick up a little something in her office. Thanks to Harper, that little item covered her actions today.

This situation with Lopez was going to be a war. No question. Jurisdiction, geographically and legally, would be scrutinized. Whose case was more important? Did homicide trump drugs and guns?

Maybe not. After all, it was just one African American kid from a low-class neighborhood, and all those federal agencies were looking at the so-called *bigger* picture.

On the third floor she stopped to shift her bag to the other shoulder. Damn. She had to be out of her mind taking the stairs at the end of a physically and emotionally draining day like this. Knowing that making Burnett wait was only going to make him angrier, she made that quick run to her office.

By the time she reached the fourth floor, she was ready for a cold drink and something to dab the perspiration from her forehead and her armpits. Did they turn off the air in the stairwells at five o'clock?

Uncaring if she made him wait a few minutes more, she ducked into the ladies' room and splashed some cold water on her face. The paper towel dispenser didn't want to cooperate, so it took several tries to get a handful. Meanwhile the water had rolled down her blouse. She patted herself dry and fussed with her hair a few seconds. She looked exactly like a woman who'd inspected a homicide scene involving multiple victims and exchanged heated words with the head of a gang clique.

After a stop in the lounge where she grabbed a Pepsi, she made her way toward his office. In the corridor between Burnett's receptionist's desk and his door, Jess paused and mulled over the idea that she had tucked her shoes in her bag to facilitate taking the stairs. She could put them back on. Not. As much as she loved her high heels, there were just times where they proved a hindrance.

That was it. When she had something to do that made having on high heels problematic, she took them off. Either set them aside or stashed them in her bag. That was exactly what Darcy Chandler had done.

Oh my God! How ordinary was that?

Tomorrow she was going back to the Chandler house and have another look on that second-floor landing.

She had missed something.

After depositing her empty Pepsi can into the recycle bin next to Tara's desk, Jess put those last few steps behind her. She didn't have to knock at the door to Burnett's office since it stood wide open. She walked in. He looked up.

"Close the door."

She didn't see the point. Everyone was gone for the day. She hadn't passed a soul in the stairwell, on this floor or on the one below it. It was after five. It was Thursday. No one wanted to be here this late so close to the weekend.

She didn't want to be here.

The carpet felt good under her bare feet. If he noticed her shoes were MIA, he didn't let on and she didn't care. She parked in one of the chairs in front of his desk and settled her undivided attention on him. Then she waited.

He didn't sit down. His hands were planted at his waist. The suit jacket was gone, his tie was torn free of his throat, and at least one button of his perfectly pressed shirt had been released. She crossed her legs and relaxed more fully into her chair. Either he made the first move or they'd just spend some time looking at each other.

Her pay was the same either way.

"You crossed several lines this afternoon, Jess," he said quietly, calmly. "While you were in the Simmonses' home, I was working to calm down Captain Allen and his counterparts on the joint task force. They all want you off this case ASAP. But I told them that wasn't possible. The Simmons case is yours and you will see it through."

This was surreal. Where had the anger and frustration gone? Why wasn't he shouting at her?

"Salvadore Lopez and his crew," he continued in that same unruffled monotone, "are slated to go down day after tomorrow for a stack of federal crimes the likes of which you cannot imagine." He shook his head slowly from side to side, his expression growing more somber. "Your actions jeopardized that operation without regard to the resources that had been expended to finally take down a major player along the southeast drug-running corridor."

Jess stood. She approached his desk, flattened her hands on the cluttered surface, and looked him in the eyes. "He sent a whole slew of his followers to murder a nineteen-year-old kid who was guilty of nothing more than being the friend of DeShawn Simmons. In doing so he also murdered four unidentified Hispanic men who were probably former members or rogue members of his own clique. When did homicide stop being the priority, Burnett? If those other guys don't have enough evidence after expending all those resources to salvage their case, that's a real shame, but this is my case and I've got it covered. Besides, Lopez knows what Allen and his people are up to. He said as much. He's just sitting back and waiting for them to make their move."

Burnett cleared his throat but he couldn't keep his anger at bay this time. "However you rationalize your action, you took enormous risks with an ongoing operation for which you showed no regard."

Jess reached into her bag and retrieved the SPU handbook she'd grabbed from her office on the way up here. The handbook she hadn't read. Thankfully Harper had. She placed it on Burnett's desk. "Section four, paragraph two. SPU will operate fully and without hindrance in Jefferson County, Alabama, to include the city of Birmingham. All local law enforcement divisions will keep SPU apprised of ongoing operations."

She straightened, crossed her arms over her chest, and met his steady gaze. "You and Sheriff Griggs had this handbook drafted, and the powers that be signed off on it. If I unknowingly infringed on an ongoing operation, that's because Captain Allen failed to brief me in a proper and timely manner despite having had ample opportunity. He was well aware that I was investigating the Simmons case, and he also knew who Nina was all along. He left me out of the loop because he was protecting his own ass...his own case."

"I can assure you that Captain Allen now fully understands his own missteps in this unfortunate situation, as do I. I take full responsibility for that oversight. I should have ensured from day one that all division chiefs and team leaders understood the dynamics of SPU."

"I'm glad we got that cleared up." Jess grabbed her SPU handbook and stowed it. Maybe the thing hadn't been such a waste of trees after all. She was beat. She needed a bottle of wine and a long, hot bath. Maybe not in that order. "Anything else?"

She probably should thank him for sticking up for her with Allen and the feds. Maybe not. As chief of police, that was his job.

"Just one more thing," he said when she had about decided he was done.

"What's that?" He'd better make it fast or she was going to expire from sheer exhaustion and total starvation. She couldn't even remember if she had eaten today.

"If you ever walk into an unknown situation again the way you did this afternoon, I will put you on administrative leave."

A frown wiggled its way across her forehead. She

scrubbed at it with the back of her hand. The protector thing was back. What do you know? She wondered if he had conversations like this with Black or Hogan. "Would that be paid leave? Like a vacation?"

"I am dead serious, Jess," he growled. "If you don't care that you could have gotten yourself killed, what about your detective? I'm certain you're aware that Harper has a son."

"I had no intention of Harper going in there with me. But he insisted. In fact, he disobeyed a direct order." She shrugged. "Besides, I had a handle on the situation." She couldn't exactly tell him that one of Harper's contacts had told her about the ongoing operation across the street, which basically meant dozens of law enforcement personnel were watching and only yards away.

"How is it that you had such a good handle on the situation?" He folded his arms over his broad chest and waited for her answer. Judging by the expression on his face, whatever she said wasn't going to satisfy him.

"I have my resources. My LA contact told me Nina was Lopez's sister and that she was the father's princess. I knew then why the whole thing with Simmons had been kept on the down low on the street. Salvadore Lopez is terrified his father will find out little sister ran off with another guy. Big brother was supposed to be making sure that didn't happen again. He has no more idea where his sister and DeShawn are than we do. I needed verification of that and to make him understand what I would do if he hurt DeShawn."

Burnett shook his head, anger now glittering in his eyes. "And all that knowledge was your safety net? You took that kind of risk just to confirm that Simmons might still be alive?" He took a breath, probably in an attempt to regain that composure. "I want your word right now that it won't happen again. If I cannot trust you to make rational decisions about how to proceed in a dangerous situation, then maybe I made a mistake offering you this position."

Her belly clenched at that below-the-belt blow. There it was. That regret Black had suggested Burnett might eventually feel. "I can't give you my word on that and you know it." She did what she had to do and she would do it again.

"Why the hell not?" He threw his hands up in exasperation. "Why do you have to make this so damned difficult? The safety of every member of my staff is my responsibility. It feels like you left the relative safety of your position with the FBI and came here to see how fast you could get yourself killed." He scrubbed a hand over his face and lowered his voice a few decibels. "I need you to be more careful, Jess."

That last part came straight from Dan, not from the chief of police. He was worried about her. And she wasn't making his job easy. Every cop, all the way up the chain of command, was watching the dynamics of their relationship, and she understood this. Maybe she was punishing him somehow by refusing to conform to the expectations of others. Maybe it was her way of keeping some amount of emotional distance.

Wesley had sworn that was what she did to him. She married him and then did everything possible to push him away. He called her a coward—afraid of falling too far.

Why hadn't hearing his voice today evoked even one hint of what she felt just standing here being lectured by Burnett?

Even knowing how Burnett made her feel, she didn't trust herself or him...not the way she needed to. The idea that Annette and her husband were having trouble flashed through her mind. Was that the kind of woman he preferred? One who wouldn't give him so much grief? Or was Jess just looking for a way to stay out of the truly dangerous territory?

Maybe she had let her emotions and determination override her logic today. But that happened sometimes. The need to do the right thing outweighed the self-preservation instinct. That territory was familiar...it was *this* kind of territory that terrified her.

"This is what I can promise," she offered. "I will never walk into a situation like that without knowing what I'm up against and the odds of pulling it off without casualties. You have my word on that." Which was exactly what she had done today. A strategic move with a small measure of risk and the potential for a huge payoff.

He stared at her as if he expected more. Jesus Christ, what did the man want from her?

"Are we good now?" she ventured.

Suspicion clouded his eyes. "You never mentioned your contact in LA. That must be one hell of a contact to have all the information you needed just like that." He snapped his fingers.

Jess flinched. Her pulse fluttered at the rigid lines that now defined his face. "He's head of the bureau's West Coast gang initiative."

Burnett nodded. "Captain Allen mentioned the guy. A Supervisory Special Agent *Wesley* Duvall. Wait, I know that name. I think that's your ex-husband."

Jess boosted a smile into place. "It's a small world.

Seems like exes are bound to come back into our lives."
She gave him a little salute. "Good night, Burnett."

She absolutely would not stand here and justify calling
her ex for information on a case when *his* ex was crying
on his shoulder every time he turned around.

Walking out without another word carried far less
impact considering she was barefoot.

Just like Darcy Chandler when she flew over that banister.

18

Nina was drinking with those men. She even danced around the room and laughed when they leered at her and made remarks DeShawn didn't understand.

He didn't like this. It was wrong.

Watching this made him sick. What was wrong with her? Was she so afraid of her brother that she thought she needed these guys to protect them? DeShawn wanted to protect her. He wanted to take her far away from here where her scumbag brother would never find them.

As he looked away, something on the television caught his attention. He stared at the muted screen. For several seconds the images didn't make sense. Then Jerome's face appeared front and center.

DeShawn rushed to the table where the TV sat and grabbed the remote. He pumped up the volume. The reporter was talking about multiple homicides in Pelham.

This couldn't be right. Why would Salvadore kill Jerome? He didn't know anything. No one did.

DeShawn's heart slid down to his feet as he listened to the details of the gruesome gang killings. Jerome was dead. Murdered by a bunch of thugs. Four others were dead, decapitated. Their faces appeared on the screen. His heart nearly stopped altogether then. Those were the four men who had brought him and Nina here.

They'd left and hadn't come back. The six in the other room had filtered in throughout the day and evening. He didn't know any of them but Nina seemed to know them all.

Then that lady cop, Jess Harris, was on the screen again. A picture of DeShawn appeared next to her. Ms. Harris was working overtime to find him and his female companion, the reporter said. A drawing that looked a lot like Nina came on the screen next. There was a big reward for anyone with information on either of them.

Why didn't the news show anything about his grandparents? Were they okay? If Salvadore could hurt Jerome, he could definitely hurt DeShawn's folks. Wouldn't the police be protecting them?

But they hadn't protected Jerome.

DeShawn knew better than to believe for a second that the cops would care about a handful of black folks who lived in the hood.

He needed to check on his grandparents.

He needed to get out of here.

"Hey, baby, what you doing?"

Nina sounded drunk. Her voice was thick. He wanted to rant at her but the others were listening and watching. He didn't like this. Drinking in excess was bad.

"Jerome is dead," he muttered. "So are those men who brought us here."

She hugged herself around him. "I'm sorry about Jerome. He was a nice guy."

"Yeah, he was," DeShawn snapped. "And now he's dead because of your brother and guys like that." He stabbed a finger at the thugs in the other room.

"Look!" Nina pointed to the TV. "It's that cop lady." She beamed a bleary-eyed smile up at him. "She got in my brother's face today. I mean, she was fearless, Jose said. She is so perfect for what comes next."

DeShawn pulled away from her. "What's going on, Nina? I thought we were trying to escape your brother, not hang around to watch him kill our friends. He could hurt my grandparents!" Fear wrapped tighter and tighter around his chest. Why didn't she see?

"Shawney, listen to me." She took his face in her hands. "I told you running away wouldn't help. I'll never be free until Salvadore is dead. This is a war. We have to be strong. So many of his people are on our side. See." She waved to the guys in the other room. "And there are many more."

DeShawn shook his head. "I don't understand. What're you saying?"

"I'm saying Salvadore is going down and that cop lady is going to help us make it happen."

That was crazy talk. "That cop is not going to do anything for you! Listen to what you're saying, Nina! The only thing she'll do if she catches us is put us in jail for all the trouble we've caused."

"She will help us," Nina insisted. "She will do it to save *you*."

19

Mountain Brook, Friday, July 30, 10:30 a.m.

Did Detective Wells mention what this meeting was about?" Harper inquired.

Jess wondered how closely Harper and Wells's relationship mirrored hers and Burnett's. With the emotional balancing act between personal and professional, any sort of relationship, even friendship, was difficult. Did they play the same tug-of-war with boundaries? Were they perfect for each other but destined to be apart for one reason or another? Did their respective pasts and all the baggage—and exes—they'd acquired over the years keep them from moving forward?

No, that would be her and Dan.

He'd sent her a good-night text just before midnight. For about three seconds in his office she had sensed that he was jealous of the idea that she had contacted Wesley. Which made about as much sense as her being jealous of Annette.

God, they were screwed up.

Jerome Frazier and DeShawn Simmons had haunted her dreams when she'd finally gotten to sleep last night. She needed to find that kid. It was too late for his friend and she intended to see that Lopez paid for that somehow.

First thing this morning she and Harper had sat in on the search team commander's briefing on the nothing they had found despite their hard work and a rundown of the hotline tips, which were growing fewer and fewer with each passing day. The reward had prompted an initial rush but the response had slowed considerably now. Damn, but they needed a break.

She'd also accompanied Harper to the nine o'clock meeting with Burnett. Harper had gotten basically the same don't-do-that-again talk she'd been given last night.

"Wells said she had information about the Chandler case," Jess finally said in answer to Harper's question.

He nodded. "You mean the case that's not our case."

"Exactly," Jess confirmed. Their investigation, beyond the ongoing search, was at a standstill and it was driving her nuts. As much as she wanted to help DeShawn, there was nothing else she could do until Lopez made a move or a lead came their way.

Later today Darcy Chandler would be laid to rest. Afterward there was a celebration at her home for close friends and family. The grandmother had invited Jess. She needed to go. Mainly to watch all those dance moms, especially Dresher, and the husband. But also to take another look around that second-floor landing.

Lori breezed in through the entrance of the café. Jess waved and Lori hurried over to their table. She looked great. Rested. And, judging by the spark in her eyes, ready to get back to work—officially. And since both her personal physicians and Dr. Oden had released her, that was happening on Monday.

After the good-mornings were swapped, Lori asked, "Did you guys order?"

"Coffee." Jess lifted her cup. She'd had two already.

"I'm starving." Lori waved down a waiter.

Another Broken Egg was new to Jess but she was glad Lori had chosen this café. The atmosphere was relaxing and amazing smells were coming from the kitchen.

When they'd placed their orders, Jess couldn't take it anymore. "What have you learned?"

Lori had been keeping tabs on Corrine Dresher and her daughter Katrina. She had also looked into the accidental death of Michelle Butler.

"I've asked Sandra Butler, the mother, if she'll talk to you and she's agreed."

"You think there's something there?"

Lori lifted her shoulders and let them fall in a noncommittal shrug. "The accident report is as clean as a whistle. No one saw anything other than a woman and two girls walking along the street. Suddenly one *stumbled* into the street in front of an oncoming car. Three days later the little girl is dead and Katrina Dresher gets her spot on the team."

Silence settled while the waiter delivered Lori's coffee and refilled the empty cups on the table.

"I have to tell you, ladies," Harper said, "this cutthroat little girl dance team business is creepy."

Jess had to agree with him.

"I was a dancer when I was a kid," Lori piped up. "Not all the dancers and their moms are insane."

Harper chuckled and Jess was almost envious of the look that passed between the two. If Lori didn't watch out, she was going to find herself married to this man. Not that sharing a life with Harper would be a bad thing by any stretch of the imagination. But Lori was fiercely independent. Jess wondered if last week's near-death experience had her rethinking all that she believed about herself and life.

"What conclusions have you reached?" Jess was dying to hear all of it. Maybe something Lori discovered would help her find the missing piece of the Darcy Chandler puzzle. That would be a welcome respite from getting basically nowhere on the Simmons case.

"Fourteen years ago, both Corrine Dresher and Alexander Mayakovsky were dancers in the Hamburg Ballet, the most prestigious dance company in the world."

"Dresher was a ballerina?"

"A very good one," Lori confirmed. "She was like at the top of her game but something happened or changed and she disappeared from the limelight fourteen years ago. I'm thinking that based on the age of her child, she left her career because she was pregnant."

To belong to such a celebrated and elite dance company would require tremendous dedication and a grueling schedule. Having a child certainly wouldn't fit into that daily agenda. Why would Dresher give that up at such a pivotal time in her career? Had the pregnancy been planned?

"What about the Russian? Is there any possibility that he and Dresher were more than dance troupe friends? He and Chandler didn't hook up in New York until twelve years ago, two years after Dresher left Hamburg." The two decided to marry and came to Alabama and took over her grandmother's ritzy school. "If Dresher and he had an affair, Chandler may not have known."

"Not necessarily so," Lori countered. "Darcy Chandler was also a dancer in the Hamburg Ballet. She was an alternate. Part of the company but not one of the premier ballerinas. She spent her time there way in the background. Like a stand-in three times removed."

"It would be nice to know the dynamics of their relationships back then." Expecting the truth from Dresher or the Russian was wishful thinking, Jess figured. And finding members of their old dance troupe would take resources the department would not want to expend on a closed case.

"The point is," Lori offered, "the three knew each other back then, so Dresher and her daughter's appearance here last year was more like a reunion. Fourteen years ago Dresher disappeared. Chandler stayed way out of the limelight and then she returned to the US. She didn't fare much better with the New York City Ballet. Kind of like always a bridesmaid but never a bride. According to the few records I found she remained on staff as a sort of nobody until she moved home to Birmingham."

"Mayakovsky suffered one knee injury too many and he was out next," Harper interjected. "That was supposedly the reason for his move from Hamburg to New York where he became a training coach."

"Until he came here with Darcy," Jess summarized.

"There is no way all this can be coincidence."

Jess wholeheartedly agreed with Lori's assessment. The waiter arrived with breakfast. Jess could hardly contain herself until he'd gone away again. "So if Dresher and the Russian had a thing…and she shows up here fourteen years later with *his* daughter in tow…"

"That would certainly turn Darcy's world upside down if she discovered the truth," Lori surmised.

"Her grandmother said something changed about two weeks ago but Darcy wouldn't talk about it."

"I have a friend," Harper announced, "who owes me a favor."

Jess and Lori exchanged a look. "Go on," Jess urged.

"He can have a look at certain bank accounts and see if there have been mutual exchanges. Of course, none of what he discovers would be admissible in court."

"Do it, Sergeant."

"I'll make the call now."

He stepped away from the table. Lori watched him go. The yearning in her gaze was about as inconspicuous as a neon sign.

"If you're game," she offered, "I can see if Ms. Butler is available this morning."

"I don't know what we're going to be able to accomplish with all this," Jess admitted, "but I can't let it go." Darcy Chandler's shoes had been nagging at her for days. She needed to get back in that house. The idea that she was being buried today, the final event in her existence, with so many unanswered questions made Jess feel ill.

"So you and Harper got called on the carpet this morning," Lori prompted. "I'm missing all the drama."

Jess stared at her omelet and wished she could revive her appetite. She knew the food would be awesome. Everything on the table looked and smelled heavenly.

"We did," Jess confirmed. "Burnett will have my hide if I don't watch my p's and q's from now on. We have a big meeting on Monday morning to go over what SPU is about. He scheduled staggered staff meetings for the entire afternoon to ensure the whole department gets what we're here for." She stabbed at the mass of eggs and veggies on her plate with her fork. "I made a lot of folks angry but I accomplished the first phase of my goal."

Lori gave her a nod. "Then you did what you had to do." She grinned. "Harper told me what happened. He said you put that gangbanger in his place. Scared the hell out of him."

Jess laughed. "I tried."

"He also said you talked to your ex," Lori ventured. "Anything there I need to know about?"

Jess went for another laugh but it fell flat. "Just that he knows the world of gangs inside and out. I needed his help and he came through."

"Wow." Lori gave her a knowing look. "Does the chief know?"

"He does and it's kind of weird."

"Like watching him with Annette," Lori guessed.

"Exactly."

Harper returned to the table. "He needs three, maybe four hours." He draped his napkin in his lap and prepared to dig into his own omelet. "Then we'll know if this triangle has been exchanging more than heated words."

The money trail was frequently littered with bodies and loaded with motive.

Vestavia Hills, 12:55 p.m.

"Ms. Butler, I appreciate you seeing me." Jess sat on the edge of the sofa, wishing she didn't need to do this.

The woman had been through enough. Losing her daughter had devastated her as it would anyone. Eight months was not nearly enough distance from the tragedy to face the kind of questions Jess needed to ask.

Like the Simmonses' home, this one looked and felt more like a shrine to the little girl who was now gone than a home where people lived. Jess understood that it was the way this woman had survived. She had surrounded herself with memories. Whether or not she would be able someday to slowly sift out some of the past, Jess couldn't say. Some folks never recovered from losing a child. It was too devastating. It went against nature...against the cycle of life.

Sandra Butler was Jess's age and had once comanaged a Chevrolet dealership with her husband. But when Michelle was born, she had decided to become a full-time stay-at-home mom.

"I love talking about Michelle." She smiled, her hands twisting together. "People think it's too hard so they try to avoid bringing up the fact that I ever had a daughter." She shook her head. "I need to talk about her but they don't understand."

"I know what you mean," Jess offered. "They think they're helping you but they're really just helping themselves. It makes most people uncomfortable to talk about that kind of loss."

"I believe you're right." She smoothed her hands over her skirt, adjusting a nonexistent wrinkle. "You know, I tried so hard to get the police to investigate Corrine and her daughter, but they just wouldn't listen. I guess that's why I'm surprised you're here now."

This was the second time this week Jess had been

accused of being a little late. In reality, she had been too late in the Simmons case to save Jerome Frazier and the same was true with this one. There was no evidence that Michelle Butler's death was anything other than a tragic accident. Just as there had been none in Darcy Chandler's until her husband up and confessed for a crime they couldn't even prove had occurred.

"As we've been investigating Ms. Chandler's case," Jess disclosed carefully, "it, of course, came to our attention that this same dance studio had already suffered a tragic loss. I noted in your statement that you felt there should have been further investigation of the event that took your daughter's life."

"As I told your colleague"—she nodded to Lori— "Katrina is an absolute bully. She made all the girls miserable then and I'm sure she still does. I know she does. I still have lunch with some of the other mothers occasionally. When they can bear to be around me."

"When you say she's a bully," Jess asked, needing clarification, "do you mean physically aggressive or verbally abusive?"

"Both. I've seen her push the other girls during rehearsals. And the things she says." She shuddered. "Katrina would taunt Michelle with the most hurtful comments. She told her she was ugly and couldn't dance. The worst was how she threatened that when Michelle was out of the way she would be the star."

"Did no one attempt to stop this behavior?" Bullying was, like the federal deficit, out of control. No one seemed to be paying attention much less doing enough to stop it.

"Katrina was careful. We mothers rarely caught her being bad." She shook her head. "And you know what they tell us, try to let the children work it out themselves. I can't tell you how many teachers I've had say those words to me and to friends who've had children with bully problems. It's so frustrating."

"But there were complaints," Jess suggested.

"Yes. Several of us spoke to both Darcy and Alex. They promised to take care of it but no one ever did. Alex excused the girl every time. He was the one who insisted she should be on the competition team when the kid can't dance. She has no coordination skills and her posture is atrocious." She drew in a deep breath and let it go slowly. "It kills me to think that she took my Michelle's place."

Without doubt Katrina Dresher had hurt Michelle Butler in life, but there simply was no proof that she or her mother caused her death...or anyone else's. There were lots and lots of ill feelings. Lots of suspicions. Lots of unanswered questions. But no clear-cut motives and no tangible evidence.

"I knew those two were capable of most anything," Butler continued. "I warned Darcy that she would be sorry she'd let them into our group. But I'm not so sure she believed me until a few weeks ago."

Jess snapped to full attention. "What happened that might have made her change her mind?"

"I finally realized it was time to go through Michelle's clothes and toys. It's selfish to hang on to all that when others could benefit from them. Some things hadn't been touched. Like her backpack from school that day. My sister-in-law had collected all of Michelle's belongings from the hospital and school and stored them away in Michelle's room. I worked up the courage to open the backpack." Her eyes filled with emotion. "Touching the things she touched the last day of her life was like touching her. It took my breath away."

Jess moistened her lips and held on to her emotions. Next to her on the sofa she could feel the tension that stiffened Lori, too.

"I found this paper all folded up in one of those squares and triangles like kids will do when they send silly notes to each other. There were hearts drawn all around on the page. Each heart had a K in it. That's what Katrina did. Whenever she sent a note or drew a picture for anyone she would draw those damned hearts and put a K in each one." Her lips started to tremble and the tears won the battle she had been waging.

Jess waited until she had composed herself. "What was in the note, Ms. Butler?"

"One line." She dragged in a harsh breath. *"Dead ballerinas don't get to dance."*

A telling chill crept through Jess's bones. "Ms. Butler, did you show this note to Ms. Chandler?"

Butler nodded. "She asked to keep it so she could go to her husband and the authorities with it. I kept waiting to hear back from her but she never called. Then I heard...that she was dead. Everyone was saying it was an accident just like Michelle's. But I didn't believe it. I had almost talked myself into calling the police when I saw the news about Alex confessing." She shook her head. "I can't believe he would do that." She wrung her hands together more tightly. "I can't believe I couldn't find the courage to make the call. But after being told over and over that I was making something out of nothing, I guess I was afraid that people would start to believe the rumors that I was losing it. I think Corrine or her daughter or both killed my Michelle. If that makes me crazy, then I guess I'm crazy."

Sandra Butler showed them Michelle's room and a few photographs of the girls on the dance team. When she at last saw them to the door, Jess managed to maintain her cool until she was in Lori's Mustang and driving away.

"We have to find that note," Jess said in a rush, her heart pounding. There was something to this mother's story. Something evil and festering.

"Where to now?" Lori asked, sounding as breathless as Jess felt.

Jess scrambled through the contents of her bag for her phone. "The Chandler residence."

"But the memorial service is in less than an hour."

"I can probably still reach Dorothy Chandler at her own home to get permission."

"You're the boss."

Jess made a call to Dorothy Chandler. She needed to get inside Darcy's home. Now. This couldn't wait for better timing.

This couldn't wait for anything.

Cotton Avenue, 2:50 p.m.

It hadn't been necessary for Dorothy Chandler to rush over and unlock the mansion that had belonged to her granddaughter.

The caterers, florist, and musicians were there preparing for the celebration of Darcy's life after the memorial service. The whole downstairs was set up for an elegant gala. Beautifully framed photos of Darcy from childhood until her death were placed around each room. Trophies and awards held positions of honor. A three-piece orchestra was already playing a lovely melody in the entry hall.

Jess and Lori had threaded their way through the goings-on to get to the second-floor landing.

"Her shoes were there." Jess showed Lori the place. "Like this." She removed her own beige pumps and placed them just so. "Exactly like that."

"Considering where the body was found and this"— Lori gestured to the shoes—"it would be safe to assume she went over the railing here."

Jess agreed. "And the bruise Schrader discovered is the only part of what happened that gives any credence to the Russian's confession."

"But the rest of the autopsy report showed no signs of a struggle. So she didn't fight him. She just let him grab her and throw her over. She wasn't drugged, so why would she just let him do that?"

"Even then there would likely have been bruises on her arms." Jess studied the second-floor landing and hall that flowed in either direction, wide open. There was no way he could have sneaked up on her. No place to hide. "Obviously Corrine Dresher didn't pick her up and throw her over the railing."

She peered over the railing at the curving staircase and the cold, hard marble floor where the musicians had set up.

"Dresher's daughter wouldn't have been able to accomplish that feat either."

"Not likely." Jess thought about how she'd taken her shoes off to climb all those sets of stairs last evening. "But Darcy took her shoes off for a reason. Why?"

Jess turned to where her shoes sat and surveyed the

area. Floor, walls, and ceiling. There was nothing but the big elaborate chandelier that hung overhead.

"There's bookcases," Lori pointed out. "But they line the wall on the other side of the landing." She gauged the distance. "About eight feet from the railing."

The bookshelves were built-in and spanned the length of the upstairs hall, interrupted occasionally by a door or a window. A brass rail was mounted along the top for the library-style ladder that glided on that path. But the bookshelves and the ladder were permanent attachments.

Two chairs flanked a table that sat before a massive window at the end of the hall. "Even if she'd dragged one of those chairs down here and jumped of her own free will— hitting her leg on the handrail—who dragged the chair back to the table?"

"But there's no known motive for suicide," Lori reminded her.

"None." Annette Denton had said that Darcy Chandler loved her life. But what if something had threatened it? Something like Corrine Dresher showing up with Darcy's husband's love child?

Would she be so weak as to refuse to fight for what was hers? But then her grandmother had said that Darcy changed about two weeks before her death. About the time Sandra Butler gave her the note.

Jess wandered down to the big window. She moved around behind one of the lovely upholstered antique chairs and started to push it some fifteen feet to reach the railing where Darcy had fallen. The chair wasn't very heavy. Picking it up wouldn't have been a problem.

When she positioned the chair next to the shoes, Jess stepped back to see what having it there accomplished.

"Puts you closer to the top of the handrail," Lori pointed out.

"Uh-huh." Jess tapped her chin. But what else? Her gaze moved upward. The chair sat under the chandelier. She moved to where the chair stood, all the while studying the brilliant chandelier. She squinted. The light was really bright. Blindingly bright.

"I need a flashlight."

"I have one in my car," Lori offered. She started to go but then hesitated. "Don't move until I get back."

The only moving Jess did was to go over to the wall next to the top of the stairs and turn off the chandelier. She blinked to encourage her eyes to adjust to the natural lighting. The house faced east but even at this time of the afternoon daylight still poured in through the numerous and expansive windows.

"Why were you up here, Darcy? What made you go over that railing?"

Perfect balance, that was another thing Annette said about Darcy. Perfect balance and everything to live for.

Lori bounded up the stairs, flashlight in hand. "I was thinking"—she took a sec to catch her breath—"why was Darcy up here at that particular time? I mean, this is her house. Sure. But Dresher had just arrived with lunch. Darcy was on the phone with her husband. Was she looking for something?"

Jess shook her head but caught herself. "The only person we know for sure who was in the house looking for something at that time was Katrina. That's when she found the body. She came in the house looking for the other two girls' boas. They'd left them up here when they were playing earlier. I checked. There are two black boas in the den.

Second door on the left." Jess nodded toward the rear of the house. At that end of this upstairs hall there was a second, narrower staircase that led down to the kitchen.

The house was enormous.

Lori offered the flashlight. "What're we looking for?"

"I don't know, but you can't see anything when the chandelier is on; the dozens and dozens of little bulbs are blinding. That's why I need the flashlight. I want to inspect it a little more closely since it's the only thing in this spot. Maybe Darcy was changing a bulb."

Seemed a ridiculous idea since Jess had learned that a team of housekeepers came in once a week. Why wouldn't she hire out that kind of menial chore?

"Okay." Lori peered up at the light fixture. "What do you want me to do?"

Jess climbed up onto the seat of the chair.

"Be careful. You are way too close to that railing for comfort." Lori moved nearer, putting her body between the chair and the railing.

Jess hesitated a moment. "You know her death could have been the result of something as simple as changing a lightbulb except there was no chair or ladder involved."

"Doesn't make sense," Lori agreed.

Placing a hand on Lori's shoulder for balance, Jess directed the flashlight's beam onto the chandelier and searched one ornate arm after the other. Downstairs, the chatter of the caterers and the clatter of preparations reminded Jess that very soon the house would be full of friends and family come to share their memories of the woman who had lived and died here.

Wait. Jess moved the light's beam back over an arm on the lower tier. There was something fuzzy stuck there. As high as she stretched, she could not reach it. Her fingertips were maybe ten or twelve inches from the lowest tip of the elegant light fixture.

When she was back on solid ground, she turned to Lori. "I need a ladder."

Lori scratched her head. "Don't have one of those in my car."

After putting the chair back where it belonged and reclaiming her shoes, she and Lori went on an expedition. Somewhere on this massive estate there had to be a ladder. Their search ended in the detached garage. Several ladders to choose from, all aluminum and fairly lightweight except the largest one, which was an extension ladder. They didn't need one of those anyway.

"The six-footer will work best," Jess decided.

Lori helped her carry it inside and up the stairs, past the musicians who eyed them skeptically. Jess simply smiled and kept going.

With the ladder in place, Jess climbed up high enough to reach the chandelier. Lori held the ladder steady just in case.

Two, no three fuzzy little white things. Jess plucked one, then the others, and climbed back down to where Lori waited.

"What is it?"

Jess stared at the tufts of fuzz in her palm. Anticipation sent her pulse into a faster rhythm. She lifted her gaze to Lori's. "Turkey feathers. They're used to make feather boas."

"They're white," Lori said, her words scarcely a whisper, as realization obviously dawned on her as well.

Jess nodded. "Only one little girl was wearing the white boa this week."

20

Mayor's office, 4:00 p.m.

Mayor Joseph Pratt was one of the few members of Birmingham's upper crust who wouldn't be at the Darcy Chandler memorial celebration. Worked to Dan's advantage. He needed a moment of the man's time. Although the subject was Darcy Chandler, which made the timing rather ironic.

Since the mayor was a busy man and never wanted anyone to forget it, Dan didn't mind waiting for a bit. He paged through a magazine that touted the wonders of the Magic City. Birmingham had come a very long way in the last fifty years, but there was a good distance to go yet and Dan wanted to be a part of that journey.

Joseph Pratt was basically a good man, but his and Dan's visions for the city and the way law enforcement should be conducted didn't always mesh. Some days it was an uphill battle. Others, like today, reminded him of why he had worked so hard to reach the position he held.

Jess had called him not ten minutes ago. Her instincts about the shoes had been right all along. There was far more to the Darcy Chandler case than her husband tossing her over the railing.

Dan did not want to know how she had learned that both Darcy and Alexander had given Corrine Dresher large sums of money over the past eighteen months—since her arrival in Birmingham. There also appeared to be some evidence that these monetary gifts had been ongoing for years. Somehow Jess had possession of this no doubt illegally obtained information. Be that as it may, that knowledge, along with Sandra Butler's statement about the note to her daughter, not to mention the feathers found in the chandelier that were likely the same ones found in the victim's hand, compelled Dan to reopen the case.

The mayor wasn't going to like it. But he would get right with it because Dan was not backing off. Pratt had no problem with a speedy closure when there was no evidence of foul play. But that had changed now.

Jess might be a long way from nailing the perpetrator, but she had rock-solid reasonable cause for further investigation. Chief Black was on board and en route to help Jess with the operation they all hoped would close the file on this one once and for all.

"Chief, the mayor will see you now."

Dan stood. He fastened the middle button of his jacket and produced a smile for Pratt's secretary. "Thank you."

The mayor was scouring letters and signing next to the little yellow tabs that called out for his attention. "Have a seat, Dan. I'll be right with you. I just have to finish this so Martha can leave on time today."

Dan took the seat he always claimed when he visited

the mayor: the lavish leather wingback chair that gave him a view out the window just past the mayor's shoulder.

Pratt signed twice more, then closed the folder. He looked up, his gaze settling heavily on Dan. "Do we have a problem?"

"I wanted to stop by and give you a heads-up on a change in the status of an investigation."

Pratt sighed and removed his reading glasses. "I spent the better part of the last two days attempting to smooth things over with several high-level federal offices. Please tell me that your new deputy chief hasn't gotten into more trouble. I tell you, Dan, I have to wonder if hiring Ms. Harris was not a grave mistake."

Oh, that was perfect. "Actually," Dan said, "she's why I'm here."

"Good heavens, man. What has she done now? The whole city is up in arms over DeShawn Simmons's disappearance and the fact that *your* department has been able to do nothing about it. I can tell you right now, Dan, if that young man is found dead, he will be escalated to martyr status instantly, right alongside his poor friend. Between his case not getting the same treatment as those young ladies two weeks ago and the growing animosity between certain Latino and African American sections of the community, we are in for a hurricane of trouble."

Maintaining his cool proved easier than Dan had expected. "Jess and her team are coordinating that investigation with members from all over the department. She is doing all humanly possible to find that young man. Besides that, she has discovered evidence of foul play in the Darcy Chandler case. The investigation is officially reopened."

Pratt's eyebrows winged upward. "The husband confessed, for Pete's sake! Since when is a confession not enough proof for you?"

Dan stood. "Since that confession prevented the real murderer from being brought to justice. I wanted to let you know. Have a nice evening."

Since Pratt appeared speechless, which was rare, Dan headed for the door. He had one more stop to make before he caught up with Jess.

"You are aware of my personal feelings on the matter," Pratt said before Dan was out the door.

Dan considered just saying yes and leaving it at that, but there had been too much of exactly that in the past couple of years. He was done playing the political games.

"I am." He turned back to the man who held the highest position of power in the city of Birmingham. "I'm also aware that's likely why your daughter-in-law was whisked out of town rather than being available to offer any useful information she might have had to help with the Chandler investigation. I hope that wasn't the case. Interfering with a homicide investigation is a very serious offense."

The standoff lasted all of five seconds.

"Cynthia will be back in town tomorrow. If you have any questions for her, I'm certain she will be more than happy to assist in the investigation of the death of her friend."

Dan gave him a nod.

"You know," Pratt said, delaying him once more, "there is a storm coming. If Harris doesn't find that young man alive, there's very little chance we'll be able to stop it, and your deputy chief is going to be right in the middle of it since she appears to be the face of your department these days."

"I'm aware of the trouble brewing."

"She pushes too hard, Dan. Crosses too many lines. I hope this city can tolerate her brand of justice."

Dan held his gaze for a beat, then two. "So do I because I have a feeling that her brand of justice is going to be demanded by the citizens of Birmingham from now on."

"I suppose we'll see."

Dan left it at that. The old regime was crumbling. Pratt had better get used to it.

That was the thing about power. Too much changed a man. Joseph Pratt wasn't a bad man...just one determined to hang on to the power he had achieved.

The drive to Mountain Brook took thirty minutes instead of twenty since it was rush hour on a Friday afternoon. Everyone wanted out of the city. Annette had called and begged him to stop by when he left the office. She and Andrea had gotten through Darcy's memorial service and gone to the celebration at the Cotton Avenue house. But Annette just wasn't feeling up to staying, so she'd gone home almost immediately. Andrea had wanted to stay, so Annette was alone and needed someone to talk to.

He parked in her drive and made the journey up the walk to her door. When they were married, he had lived in this house with her and Andrea. It wasn't his home and at first he hadn't wanted to move in here. But Annette had pointed out that Andrea needed to feel like she hadn't lost her home as well as her father. So for Andrea's sake he had moved in. But this had never been a home to him. This had been Brandon Denton's home. It still was as far as Dan was concerned. Whether Denton opted to stay here or not.

Annette opened the door before he had a chance to knock. Her face was flushed from crying. That was the first thing he noted. The second was that she was wearing a robe.

"I'm so glad you came." She grabbed his hand and pulled him inside.

"I can't stay long," he warned as she closed the door. And locked it.

She turned to Dan, more tears crested on her lashes. "He says that since Andrea is in college we should sell the house. Downsize. He wants me to give up my home. I must have been out of my mind to take him back."

"You have an outstanding attorney." He knew this from experience. "If you want to keep the house, fight for it." Dan surveyed the soaring foyer. "Make sure that's what you really want. It's a big place to take care of alone."

She wrapped her arms around him. "Come sit with me. Would you like a glass of wine or a beer?"

He removed himself from her embrace. "I can't stay, Annette. I have to meet Jess and Detectives Wells and Harper. We have some issues to iron out on a case."

A frown worried her brow. "Can you come back after you're finished? I really need to talk to you." She hugged her arms around herself. "You know what I'm going through better than anyone. You always know the right course to take."

"I do know what you're going through, Annette. We've been there before. After your first divorce from Brandon. That's a place I can't revisit. I adore Andrea and I hope you and I can remain friends, but that's all we can be."

He'd done it. Said what needed to be said.

Tears welled in her eyes and he wanted to bang his head against the wall. He absolutely did not want to hurt her. But she was forcing the issue.

"It's Jess, isn't it?" She blinked back the tears. Resignation registered in her expression. "You still have feelings for her."

He plowed a hand through his hair and blew out a breath. Was it Jess? Not entirely. "You are a beautiful, intelligent woman, Annette. What we had for that short time was great. But it wasn't what either of us really wanted. We found that out pretty quickly." He laughed sadly. "And I genuinely appreciate our friendship now just as I did before we became a couple. This isn't about another woman; it's about facing the reality of who we are and what we really want. I think we both know this is not it."

She waved him off and shook her head, her eyes bright again. "You're right. I know this. But I also know it's her you really want. Maybe that's why I feel so afraid."

He frowned. "Why would you be afraid?"

"We've known each other a long time, Dan. You've always been there for me. Especially these past three or four years. Now it feels like I'm losing every part of you to her."

Well, there was a mouthful. "I don't know what to say."

She smiled, the expression a little sad. "You don't have to say anything. I'll get used to it and eventually I'll be okay with it. I should have realized the first time I saw you two together that you were off the market."

He laughed, sort of. "I'm not sure I was on the market, but Jess would definitely tell you that she has not made any major purchases, not even a lease."

"Either she's kidding herself or you're kidding yourself. It's inevitable, Dan. Mark my words."

He shrugged. "I don't know about that, but I do know

this. Twenty years ago I screwed up with Jess. The thing I've realized the past couple of weeks is that if it takes me twenty more, I will make it right. We may never be anything more than friends, but I'll do it right this time."

Annette hugged him and whispered, "She's a lucky woman."

Dan felt a smile tug at his lips. "No. I'm the lucky one."

21

Cotton Avenue, 5:35 p.m.

Everyone is in place, ma'am."

"Thank you, Sergeant." Jess was ready to get this show under way. "Chief Black arrived with the Russian?"

"He did."

"Good." That was a huge relief. She needed everyone here if this was going to work.

Dorothy Chandler had made it clear that she did not want the bastard anywhere near her family, but she had agreed considering what Jess had planned.

When all was said and done, Jess was pinning her hopes on another confession that might not come. If she could get the right players in place, maybe the truth would find its way to the surface—with the proper prodding.

It had taken some finagling but the cast was, it seemed, all here.

After one last appraisal of her staging on the second

floor, she turned to Harper. "A final walk-through, Sergeant, and we'll be ready."

"Yes, ma'am."

Downstairs the crowd was thinning. Dorothy Chandler had gone all out to bid farewell to her beloved granddaughter. The food, the flowers, the china and linens. Not to mention the crystal and silver. And, of course, the lovely little orchestra. Talk about going out in style. Even Jess was impressed, and this sort of gala didn't usually move her much.

As she crossed the parlor, her attention was drawn to Burnett, his mother on one side of him, his father on the other. Burnett fit in perfectly in this world. But then he'd been groomed for this his entire life. Which made Jess and him kind of like vinegar and water. They most likely wouldn't ever mix.

She would have to remind herself to tell him that his navy suit was her favorite. Brought out the color of his eyes. And something about the cut went above and beyond the call of duty to complement his tall, lean build.

Before she moved on, his gaze connected with hers and she gave him a nod. Not because he looked damned awesome, but because he had her back and that meant more to her than all the promotions and raises in the world.

Lori, Harper, and Jess converged next to the French doors at the rear of the house. Lori had made her way through the dining room and kitchen. Harper had threaded his way through the trail of those saying their good-byes in the entry hall.

"Andrea has taken the girls to the garden," Lori confirmed.

Jess nodded. "Good." She didn't want any of those

little girls accidently walking into the middle of what was about to happen. Officer Cook was in the garden as well to make sure none of those still lingering outside came back into the house.

"Let's do it."

Lori and Harper fanned out to take their positions.

Jess wandered. The closest of friends and members of the family were all that remained inside the mansion. Jess didn't know any of them except the dance moms and their daughters she had interviewed five days ago. The beige suit she wore wasn't her favorite but it fit in well enough, she supposed. Just this time yesterday she'd been butting heads with gangbangers.

How was a girl ever to know the right outfit to wear, much less the perfect shoes?

Jess had checked Darcy Chandler's closet that first day. The woman loved her shoes. Those shoes had told a story that Jess hadn't been able to ignore.

She wandered through the remaining folks gathered. There was the Russian, who had, by all accounts, loved his wife. He'd just had a problem with fidelity. But his wife had had enough.

Then she was dead.

Jess's gaze roamed the room until she found Corrine Dresher. Now there was the lady with the real motive. Her daughter may have been fathered by the Russian, who then left her to pursue Darcy. She had obviously decided to return after all this time to collect on her little growing dividend.

But why wait until now?

She appeared to have been receiving some sort of payment all along, so it wasn't necessarily about the money.

Then there was the child. Allegedly mean-spirited. Not
a very good dancer. The other girls probably made fun of
her. Had her and her mother's lives been difficult? Had
they come here with hatred in their hearts and vengeance
on their minds?

Often children merely acted out what they heard and
saw at home. *You are what you live.* If Corrine said ugly
things about the other little girls, Katrina likely adopted
that behavior.

With Darcy out of the way and Daddy getting a big
insurance settlement, perhaps they could finally be
together as a family. The one thing Corrine and Katrina
had never had.

But then the Russian had confessed to killing his wife.

Considering that Darcy and the Russian had no children of their own, being with Corrine and Katrina might
have been his only hope to have a family in the truest
sense of the word.

So why the sudden confession?

Jess checked her watch. It was time.

As if they had synchronized their watches, Andrea
hurried into the parlor from the front entry hall. She
walked straight up to Corrine Dresher. Jess didn't have to
be in earshot to know what she said. *Ms. Dresher, Katrina
went upstairs and refuses to come back down. No one's
supposed to be up there.*

Dresher was heading for the stairs before Andrea finished speaking.

Jess followed. Giving her a good head start.

Behind her, amid those still gathered, Chief Black
would be watching for his cue.

The musicians continued to play, the elegant tune

uplifting, though Jess couldn't place it to save her soul. Something by Mozart, she thought.

As she reached the upper part of the staircase, she saw Corrine standing in the upstairs hall, staring dumbfounded at the elements Jess had staged. A chair sat under the chandelier and a bright pink boa hung from its ornate arms.

"I haven't quite figured out how the boa got trapped in the chandelier," Jess explained.

Corrine's attention snapped to Jess as she took the final steps up onto the landing. "What is this?" she asked with admirable shock and maybe even a pinch of disgust.

"That's how Darcy Chandler fell over the railing." Jess gestured to the chair she had dragged over from the desk at the end of the hall. "A boa was trapped in the chandelier for some reason and she pulled the chair over to get it down." Jess shook her head. "I knew there had to be a reason she removed her shoes and set them aside. This was it."

"What're you talking about?" As indignant as Corrine sounded, the fear was beginning to show in her eyes.

"Her shoes." Jess slipped off her shoes and placed them just as Chandler had placed hers. "She put them there so she could climb up on the chair seat. The trouble is, whoever pushed her over the railing didn't notice her shoes."

"Someone pushed her?" Corrine asked, her voice noticeably high-pitched now. "I thought Alexander fought with her and that was how she fell."

Jess shook her head. "You saw him downstairs, didn't you?"

"I did." She adopted a look of shock and disgust. "And frankly I'm stunned the family allowed him to come after what he did."

"That's only because he recanted his confession." Jess shrugged. "Apparently he's innocent."

"I didn't hear anything about that." Corrine visibly braced. "It wasn't on the news."

Jess nodded. "It was. The five o'clock news. Only you were here, so you didn't see it."

"What you're saying makes no sense. Why would Darcy have been up on a chair? And why is that boa hanging there like that? What're you trying to prove?"

"Darcy died because of a boa like that." Jess gestured to the feathered accessory. "She was trying to get it down. Somehow it got hung up there. We found the feathers trapped on the chandelier from where it was pulled loose. The medical examiner found tiny pieces of those same feathers stuck to the fingers of Darcy's right hand. Like I said"—she indicated the chair and the boa again—"that's why she fell."

"So it was an accident," Corrine suggested, her tone and expression wary.

"It might have been except that whoever put the boa there was watching when Darcy climbed into that chair to rescue it."

"How could you possibly know that?"

"There were two people, by their own admission and based on eyewitness accounts, who were the last to see Darcy Chandler before she died. You, when you brought lunch for the girls, and then your daughter, Katrina, when she came inside and found her."

"What does that prove? How do you know Darcy fell off a chair? You're guessing," Corrine accused.

Jess touched her lower left leg. "The medical examiner also found a bruise where Darcy hit her leg on this railing as she fell over it. The only way for her to bruise her leg there was to fall from a position above floor level." She pointed to the chair. "So you see, the evidence speaks for itself. I know who set up the whole scenario. I just can't figure out how *you* could have put the chair back in place and not notice the shoes."

"What are you implying?" she demanded.

"Alexander told the police what you did, Corrine. That's why he's here. We know you pushed Darcy over that railing." That wasn't exactly true...the Russian hadn't admitted anything new just yet.

Corrine's defiant expression wilted into one of defeat. "I'd had it with her. When she dismissed Alexander from the studio, that was the last straw. She was so determined to hurt him and she was only hurting the girls. But I did not kill her. After I delivered lunch that day, she and I came back into the house and I followed her upstairs. We were arguing." She hugged her arms around herself. "We were always arguing. She was a bitch. I don't know how the boa got trapped in the chandelier. Perhaps when the girls were playing earlier that morning. They throw them around sometimes."

She fell silent for a long moment, her expression distant. "We were arguing and she climbed up on the chair to try and get the damned thing free. I said something, she shouted something back, and suddenly she was falling. I don't know if she turned the wrong way. Or just lost her balance. But she fell. I was in shock and afraid so I snatched down the boa and moved the chair. Then I rushed to check on her but she was dead. I don't even remember what I did then, but I know I left because when my daughter called I was already two or three miles away." Tears streamed down her cheeks. "It was an accident. A horrible, horrible accident."

Wow. Another confession. Too bad both the *confessors* screwed up so badly. First, the husband confesses, stating that he rushed away without calling for help for his beloved wife. Then Corrine confesses that she moved the chair and boa before going to see if Darcy survived her fall. Not that it wasn't possible for folks to go completely against human nature. It was.

The trouble was, the evidence—such as it was—didn't back up their stories.

"There's just one problem with that, Corrine."

Fear claimed her face. "I don't know what you mean."

"You see, the boa couldn't have been hanging here like this unless your daughter was here, too. I used a pink boa today, but the feathers found in the chandelier and in Darcy's hand were white. There is only one white boa, and Katrina was wearing it that day for being the best. She had it on when Andrea sent her inside to get the other two girls' boas." Jess traced her fingers along the soft fluffy thing hanging from the chandelier. "Katrina may very well have been tossing the boa and got it hung on the chandelier. But I wonder why she would have done that knowing the others were waiting on her to return so rehearsals could begin."

Corrine shook her head. "She didn't do this! I did. I did it! I pushed her. I'd had enough!"

"Except you had already driven away. The first time Katrina called your cell phone you were already far enough away that you got the call through a cell tower that doesn't service this area. We checked. She told you what she'd done. You turned around and rushed back.

Snatched down the boa and moved the chair back where it belonged, just like you said."

"No...no...you're wrong," Dresher argued.

"You told Katrina to tell Andrea she had found Ms. Darcy that way. Then you left again, only before you got out of that long, long driveway you called Alexander to tell him. Then you drove away and waited for the next call. Thirteen minutes later, a cell tower away from here, you got the second call from your daughter."

Dresher shook her head as tears streamed down her cheeks.

"That's the thing about cell phones," Jess explained. "They give a damned accurate log of where you've been and at what time. The same way we know that Alexander never left the Botanical Gardens that day. He was in shock." There was a remote possibility he could have made it from the gardens to the house and back again, but it was highly unlikely. Jess was banking on her theory.

"It was an accident," Corrine insisted. "Darcy was trying to get the boa down and Katrina was trying to help her!"

"You mean the way she was trying to help Michelle Butler when she gave her that little inconspicuous boost into oncoming traffic?"

Chief Black and the Russian appeared at the other end of the hall. Jess had never thought about how handy a second staircase could be until now.

"It's true," Alexander said, tears dampening his cheeks. "You told me what Katrina had done. Dear God, she's just a child. When I saw on the news that the case might be ruled a homicide, I knew I had to try to protect her."

"Your daughter?" Jess confirmed.

He nodded. "*My* daughter. The one I deserted. Darcy tried to tell me there was something wrong with Katrina but I wouldn't listen. Darcy wanted her away from the studio and the other girls. When I refused to listen, she exiled me as well."

"Tell them all of it, you bastard," Corrine roared.

"It's enough," Alexander said. "We will all pay for this. Darcy has already paid the most."

Now Jess was confused. "She's your daughter," Jess said to Corrine, "and his, right?"

Corrine shook her head. "Katrina is his and Darcy's daughter, but Darcy didn't want a child. I gave up everything," she said to Alexander, "to raise your child because the woman you were obsessed with didn't want her. I was certain one day you would come back to us but you didn't."

"You were compensated well for your sacrifice."

She scoffed. "Oh yes. I had it all. But I didn't have you and Katrina didn't have her father. She needed a firm hand. I couldn't control her once she grew old enough to go to school. I was constantly moving because of her behavior. Finally I decided to bring her back to you. Only Darcy still didn't want her. By then she didn't even want you. She wanted that other woman. How does that feel, Alex?"

When the two started screaming at each other, Jess held up her hands. She had heard enough. She looked to Black, who confirmed with a nod that he was ready as well.

"Ms. Dresher, you are under arrest," Jess said somberly. Two counts of accessory to murder and interfering with a criminal investigation. "You have the right to remain silent."

Chief Black echoed the same words as he rearrested Alexander.

By now Cook had already separated Katrina from Andrea and the other girls.

History had always shown that the hand that rocked the cradle ruled the world. But this time it was the hand that reached out from the cradle that possessed all the power.

In Jess's research she had discovered that experts often disagreed about why children committed murder. Katrina Dresher's acts of violence didn't appear to be the result of long-term abuse. Had she experienced horrors that were yet to be discovered? Travesties that warped her young mind? Or had she merely been born evil?

Some believed that evil was passed along in the genes, just like the penchant for stellar coordination or the lack thereof. Poor Katrina was like her biological mother. Though she had the balance, she just didn't have the precise coordination to be the best in a field that required that attribute above all other talents. Always in the background. Always second choice when it came to dance and even to being a daughter. Her real mother hadn't wanted her and her father had refused to choose her over his own selfish desires.

Exposing the true face of evil in Darcy Chandler's murder was done.

No one had expected that face to be a child's.

22

Downtown, 8:15 p.m.

Jess didn't care that it was hot as Hades in her car. She also didn't care that Burnett would probably be annoyed that she hadn't waited for him to finish with the press conference before leaving. But she was just too tired. Besides, she wanted to join Harper across town near Five Points West. He was interviewing a couple of former MS-13 members who had agreed to meet with him as long as their names were kept off the record. Officer Cook had gone with Harper. Maybe the guys who had come forward had information about Simmons or Nina.

She frowned at the piece of paper stuck beneath the wiper on her windshield. Jess leaned forward and squinted to get a better look. A parking ticket!

"No!" She jerked her door open and snatched up the ticket. "This is ridiculous!"

She glanced around as if expecting to see the culprit who'd left it scurrying away. Yes, she had parked in a no-parking zone, but it had been after six when she got here. She hadn't wanted to bother with the parking garage, and fifty news vehicles had already surrounded the BPD.

Did they all get tickets, too?

"Damn it!"

Her cell clanged at her from inside the car.

"Damn. Damn." Harper was waiting for her. What if something had gone wrong? And here she was, wasting time stewing over a dumb parking ticket.

She ducked inside and grabbed her phone. "Harris."

"Jess, it's Wesley."

Bumping her head, she cursed softly as she drew out of the oven the interior of her car had become. She and Wesley had talked yesterday. He'd given her a great deal of information about the Lopez family and what she could expect from Nina and her stepbrother, Salvadore. He'd even e-mailed her a lengthy file on the history of the family and their criminal activities.

Had he forgotten something?

"Jess?"

"Hey." She cleared her throat. "I was just leaving the office." At this hour she wasn't going to tell him she was on her way to an interview for her current case. They'd argued many times about her heavy work schedule.

"Me, too. I hope this isn't a bad time. I learned some interesting information about Nina Lopez and I felt you needed to know as quickly as possible."

Jess crumpled the ticket and threw it into her car. Her pulse rate picked up at the prospect of learning details that might help find DeShawn Simmons. "Now is fine. What've you got?"

"The word I'm hearing now is that Nina—"

Strong hands closed around her upper arms. She tried to twist away but she was jerked backward. Her phone flew from her hand and hit the pavement.

Jess elbowed her assailant and screamed at the top of her lungs.

Another hand closed over her mouth.

Shit! There were two of them.

She kicked. Elbowed. Bit at the hand covering her mouth as she was dragged backward. Her legs hit something metal. A vehicle.

She twisted and kicked as she was dragged into the dark van.

The door slammed.

The vehicle lunged forward, rocking her between her two assailants.

She struggled harder but there were two or more. Strong. Male.

She tried to see their faces in the dim light.

A bag went over her head.

She kicked harder. Hands grabbed her arms and legs and held them down. Another pressed over her mouth, pinched her nose.

She couldn't breathe...

23

Dan had answered the final questions thrown at him by the reporters. He and Chief Black as well as Mayor Pratt had parted ways. It was late and, as elated as everyone was to have solved the Chandler case, they were all dragging from the long day. It hadn't helped that several of the reporters had wanted updates on the DeShawn Simmons case and Dan had nothing concrete to give them except they were working on it.

The young man's face was plastered all over the city with pleas for information. The reward kept growing but the number of credible leads continued to shrink. No one who knew anything was talking. The fear of repercussions from MS-13 was far too strong.

He'd wanted to catch up with Jess but she'd already left her office and her cell went straight to voice mail. Knowing her, she was in that damned low-rent motel bathtub with a bottle of good wine by now. The two just didn't pair well. But he'd promised not to mention that anymore.

A smile tugged at his lips. What was he going to do with her? She was determined to kick ass and take names. The mayor and his powerful corporate and political cronies were unsettled by her tactics. Dan had to admit that he was damned unsettled with a few, like facing off with Salvadore Lopez on his home turf.

She'd promised to give due consideration to future dangerous maneuvers before acting, but Dan wasn't laying any wagers on her keeping that promise.

His cell vibrated against the desk. He picked it up and checked the screen, frowning at the unfamiliar number. Didn't the 310 area code belong to LA? "Burnett."

"Chief Burnett, Wesley Duvall here."

The muscles along Dan's spine tightened with a new kind of tension. Why in blazes would Jess's ex be calling him? He reached for calm. Something to do with the Simmons case probably. "Agent Duvall, what can I do for you?"

"I was just on the phone with Jess and I'm very concerned. We were in the middle of a conversation when I heard a slapping sound as if she threw her cell against something or dropped it on the ground. Three, maybe four seconds of shuffling feet and then I heard her scream. There was another slamming sound, then squealing tires. I haven't been able to get her back on the line. Perhaps there's another explanation for what I heard, but I felt compelled to follow up. Do you know where she is right now?"

The first trickles of fear seeped into Dan's veins. "Did she mention where she was before . . . you lost contact with her?" He put Duvall on speaker and moved to the contacts menu on his phone. Using the office landline on his desk, he called Harper's cell. "Hold on, Duvall. Let me check with—"

"Harper," echoed from the desk phone speaker.

"Sergeant Harper, is Chief Harris with you?"

"No, sir. She was supposed to be here twenty minutes ago. I guess she got held up. I tried her cell but there's no answer."

Dan's heart rate climbed. "How long ago did you speak with her?"

"Forty, forty-five minutes. She was on the way to her car."

"Contact me immediately if you hear from her," he said to the detective.

"Sir, is everything—"

The office door burst open and Gina Coleman rushed inside. "Dan, you need to come outside right now."

"I'll call you back," he said to Harper.

If Dan hadn't known Gina as well as he did, he might suspect the reporter wanted to set him up for a little one-on-one camera time, but he did know Gina and what he saw on her face and in her eyes right now mirrored the dread building in his chest.

"What's going on?" he demanded.

"Harris's car is parked on the street." She gestured vaguely to the wall behind him. "Driver's side door is open and the keys are in the ignition. Her cell phone is lying on the street." She moved forward a few more steps. She was trembling. "Her bag is in the car, Dan. She never goes anywhere without that damned bag."

"You hearing this, Duvall?" Dan rounded his desk and sprinted for the door.

"Indeed. I want to hear from you when you find her, Burnett."

Dan wasn't sure if he answered the man but the call ended.

"What do I do?" Gina shouted as she hurried down the corridor after him.

"Take me to her car."

As they rushed down the stairs, Dan put through another call to Harper and warned him that they had a situation. Harper would complete the interviews as quickly as possible since Jess would not want him to miss an opportunity to learn information on Simmons for anything.

When Dan reached Jess's Audi, Gina's cameraman stepped aside. "I've been guarding her stuff with my life," he vowed.

"We didn't touch anything," Gina assured Dan.

He stared at that damned bag of hers before carefully peeking inside. Her Glock was there. His heart crashed against his sternum. No way would she leave of her own free will without her weapon.

He made the call to dispatch that no cop ever wanted to make. "Officer down. First Avenue and Nineteenth."

Dan stood in the middle of the street and turned all the way around. He spotted the nearest security camera. The mayor'd had surveillance cameras installed around the downtown area four years ago. As if some techie had picked up on his thoughts, his cell vibrated with an incoming call from ION, the security company responsible for the city's surveillance system.

Sixty seconds later the video of Jess being abducted by two thugs in masks and driving a generic white Dodge van streamed to his cell phone. Sirens filled the night air, providing an eerie score to the images filling the screen as officers all over the city responded to the call.

Dan's chest seized as he watched Jess's futile but courageous fight to prevent those bastards from dragging her into that van.

Gina, still standing at his side and seeing the terrifying moments captured digitally, grabbed the sleeve of his jacket. "Oh my God," she murmured.

Dan stared at the screen as the scene played again and again. He forced himself to focus on the details of the vehicle and the assailants. The two men were just a little taller than Jess's five four. No way to tell their age with the masks in place. They wore black T-shirts with no discernible symbols or images and jeans and sneakers. He touched the screen and zoomed in to get a closer look at the forearm wrapped around Jess's waist. He could just make out the tattoo.

XIII

His heart squeezed with the reality of what he hadn't wanted to acknowledge. These were Lopez's goons. Ruthless killers. *If the boy is still alive...it's because they have a plan for him.* Jess had said that about DeShawn Simmons.

Dan prayed they had a plan for Jess beyond executing her.

Gina's voice dragged his attention from the screen. She stood in a pool of light, speaking in her reporter voice to the camera.

"If anyone has seen Deputy Chief Jess Harris, please call the number you see on your screen. Chief Harris is missing and believed to be in extreme danger. She was taken by two males driving a white Dodge van with no markings. Chief Harris risks her life each day to protect our community and now she needs our help."

He felt helpless even as police cruisers and unmarked cars jammed into the street from both directions.

When detectives and uniforms had surrounded him, the fear disappeared. He was the chief of police. He couldn't afford to be afraid. These men and women were waiting for his direction.

Deputy Chiefs Black and Hogan were at his side and within twenty minutes search teams had been organized and grid patterns established. Crime scene techs were going over Jess's car and personal belongings. Dan stepped aside and put in a call to Ted Allen.

"I want a meeting with Salvadore Lopez now."

Allen hedged. "I'm not sure I can make that happen, Chief. We're only just—"

"Make it happen," Dan ordered before stabbing the end call button.

"Chief!" Harper cut through the crowd.

Dan followed Harper farther away from the temporary command post that had been established on the street. Traffic in all directions around Linn Park had been diverted.

"The word on the street is"—Harper looked around to ensure no one was paying them any mind—"that Salvadore Lopez ordered this strike. Apparently he believes we have his sister, Nina. His second in command, Jose Munoz, says they will trade Chief Harris for Nina. We have until sunrise or she dies."

Dan struggled to contain the fury. "Do we have a fucking clue where this sister is?"

Harper moved his head side to side. "But we do have one thing."

"What the hell is that, Sergeant?"

A smile quirked one corner of the detective's mouth. "Salvadore Lopez."

24

9:30 p.m.

Jess held very still and listened.

She considered the time she had been in the vehicle: thirty minutes at the most. Music had blared from the radio the whole time. But not a radio station. A CD, she supposed. Her wrists and ankles had been secured with wide tape.

The two men had spoken in Spanish during the ride but they kept their voices too low for her to comprehend their conversation over the music. Her Spanish was pretty rusty but she would likely have picked up a word here and there if she had been able to hear.

Once they arrived at their destination they'd brought her into a building or house and shoved her into a corner. Wherever they were holding her it wasn't far from downtown.

Puffing out a breath, she wished they had removed the damned bag. She hated not being able to see. She thought of those moments before the first bastard had grabbed her. Why hadn't she been paying better attention? How had she allowed someone to sneak up on her like that? News vans had been parked all around Linn Park. Maybe that was the reason she'd ignored the one parked near her car. It damned sure hadn't driven up while she was talking to Wesley. Her abductors had been lying in wait.

The floor under her felt like wood. No carpet. Not smooth enough to be vinyl or cool enough to be tile. The place smelled of stale tobacco and tequila. She would recognize that smell anywhere. She'd had too many margaritas once. Back in her college days. Way, way too many. She'd puked for two days.

Whoever was holding her had gathered in another room. The low rumble of voices was distinguishable but, once again, not the words.

Judging how long she had been here was a bit more difficult. Fifteen or twenty minutes maybe. Dan would have found her car by now. And her weapon. God, and her bag and phone. Her phone was probably dead. It had hit the pavement hard.

There went two hundred bucks and that was if she was due an upgrade.

She tried to recall if she had gotten the insurance plan and whether it covered thug damage.

Hopefully Wesley hadn't thought she'd hung up on him. It was a shame he hadn't gotten to finish telling her about what he'd found on Nina Lopez.

If she didn't get out of here, the next life celebration she attended might be her own.

Working her hands and twisting her wrists as best she could, she hoped to loosen the tape. With her back to the wall and her hands behind her, maybe anyone watching her wouldn't notice. She couldn't discern any other presence in the room, but the bag over her head dulled her senses to a degree so she couldn't be sure.

Footsteps warned that someone was entering the room. She listened to the steps, estimated there were at least three persons approaching her position. She braced.

"So this is the famous Deputy Chief Jess Harris. Woo hoo."

The voice was female. Slight Hispanic accent.

"You have to stop this. This is crazy. This lady ain't done nothing but try to help us."

Male. Southern for sure.

"DeShawn?" Jess asked. "Is that you? Your grandparents have been worried sick."

"See there?" the man she suspected was DeShawn said. "We can't do this, Nina."

Nina Lopez. Well, well. "You should listen to him, Nina. Your brother is not happy either." Jess wished again that she knew what Wesley had been calling about. She could have used that right now.

"My brother is dead to me," Nina snarled.

Young people. They made Jess want to scream. "Well, he may be dead to you but he's very much alive and looking for you."

The bag was snatched off her head. Jess drew in a grateful breath.

"He's going to die at sunrise, *jefa*. And you're going to help us make that happen."

Jess looked from Nina to DeShawn and back. Both appeared to be unharmed. Nina looked ready for war. DeShawn, on the other hand, looked terrified.

"I already said what I had to say to your brother. I don't think he and I have anything left to talk about."

Nina flaunted a big smile. "You won't need to do no talking. You'll be too busy dying."

She turned and strutted away. Poor DeShawn. He hadn't had a chance against a sexy, streetwise girl like Nina. Her gangbanger friend followed her out of the room. DeShawn lingered near Jess.

"Are my grandparents okay?"

Jess nodded. "I sent them to stay with friends so Lopez couldn't get to them."

He swiped his hands over his face and shook his head. "I don't know what's happening. Everything is out of control."

Jess had a pretty good idea. "It's a power play. Nina wants what her brother has. It's a battle as old as time. Sibling rivalry."

DeShawn shook his head. "But she doesn't want any part of the gang life. That's why she left LA. She thought it would be different here."

"Sometimes people show us what they want us to see." Jess had a sneaking suspicion that DeShawn was beginning to understand that he was nothing more than a pawn in Nina's plans. He was the bait to lure the police into her game. He was the perfect ploy. A good, upstanding young man who would have the community in an uproar to ensure he received the same attention as the white girls had a couple weeks ago.

Worked like a charm.

He squatted down and searched Jess's face. "I don't know what to do. She's got five guys in there planning and plotting with her. There's three or four more outside. I don't have a weapon or a cell phone."

Jess managed a faint smile for the kid. "Listen to me, DeShawn. I'm a deputy chief with the Birmingham PD. My job is pretty important, so you have to believe me when I say that I know the business of police work, right?"

He hesitated a moment but then he nodded his agreement.

"That's right. I have my own unit with several detectives who do exactly what I tell them to do every day." Most of the time anyway.

He wrapped his arms around his knees and waited for whatever she had to say next.

"So when I tell you what you need to do, you can feel confident that I know what I'm talking about, right?"

He nodded again.

"Good." She leaned forward to put her face closer to his. "You don't worry about Nina or her friends or me. The first opportunity you get, you run."

His eyes widened in disbelief.

"Your grandparents are counting on you, DeShawn. You run as fast as you can, and don't you dare look back."

25

216 Aquarius Drive, 10:20 p.m.

Harper wound through the parking area until they reached the back of the meatpacking plant. He guided his SUV to the east perimeter of the property and shut off the engine. The lampposts were few and far between this far from the plant but Dan suspected the meager lighting and the seclusion were the reasons they'd been instructed to wait here.

This was the sort of business best conducted where no one would see.

"You're telling me," Dan asked, needing clarification now that he'd had time to get a grip on his composure if not his trepidation, "that Salvadore Lopez is going to show up here to *talk*? We have nothing to offer him," he reminded Harper. "We don't know where his sister is, but he wants to talk anyway?"

Dan just didn't see that happening. This could be a major waste of time they didn't have.

"That's what I'm telling you," Harper confirmed. "The two members of his clique I was interviewing when you called about Chief Harris conveyed a personal message from Lopez. He wants to work out this situation privately with *you*."

"Are these the same people who told you Lopez had taken her and we had until sunup to produce his sister?"

"That was the word from the folks blowing up their phones during the interview."

Dan surveyed the deserted lot a third time, or maybe it was the fourth. "Pardon the hell out of me if I opt not to trust Lopez's friends. Did he confirm Chief Harris is safe? Did he provide proof of life?" Damn it, they were wasting time here. Jess was counting on him and he was sitting in this damned SUV waiting for Lopez and some member of his posse to show up and, as likely as not, start a shoot-out. "The whole thing could have been staged."

What were the chances that they could have this tête-à-tête without weapons being drawn?

"Lopez is supposed to explain everything when he arrives. It's not an optimal situation, sir, but I didn't see that we had any other choice."

"And where exactly is our backup, Sergeant?" Dan felt ready to explode. He needed to do more than talk.

Tension thickened in the air for a beat. He was angry and sick with worry and damned terrified—all this he was taking out on Harper.

"We don't have any, sir. That was the deal breaker for this meet."

Dan laughed. He didn't mean to, but this was just too much and, frankly, if he hadn't laughed he might have just lost it. He railed at Jess all the time for taking risks like this and here he was following that same pattern. He had known damn well they didn't have any backup before he asked. "I think Harris has rubbed off on you, Harper."

"That could be the case, sir, but I have reason to believe this lead is on the level."

Dan checked his weapon, then reholstered it. "You did the right thing. If Lopez had contacted me, I would have come alone if necessary." *Whatever it takes to get her back.*

Harper glanced at Dan. "The man, Hector, who set this up is related to Jorge Debarros."

"Christina's father?" The thirteen-year-old had been missing for six years and Jess had waltzed into town and four days later solved the case. The remains discovered in the basement of the home of the couple who'd abducted Andrea a little over two weeks ago were those of Debarros's daughter, Christina. He and his family had suffered all those years, wondering and worrying. Jess's relentlessness had allowed them to finally give their little girl a proper burial.

"When Jorge saw the first newscast about Chief Harris's disappearance," Harper went on, "he called his brother Hector, who's tight with Lopez. Hector and another of his clique were meeting with me at the time. They both appeared a little edgy when they got the news. Hector called his boss and Lopez asked for this meet."

Dan checked the time. Jess had been missing for approximately two hours. A volatile combination of fear and fury churned in his gut. "Are we early or are they running behind?" If Lopez wanted this meet so badly, where the hell was he?

As if to emphasize his thought, the digital clock on the dash blinked to 10:35.

Had they been here only fifteen minutes? It felt like an hour and yet that fifteen minutes was fifteen too many to have squandered.

Harper checked his cell. "They just turned into the parking lot."

Headlights came around the corner of the building and pointed in their direction. Dan cleared his mind, sharpening and narrowing his focus to the here and now. What happened next was critical to how this meeting would shake down and to finding Jess alive.

The Cadillac Seville parked in front of Harper's SUV, leaving getaway room between the two front bumpers. When the lights had extinguished, the front doors opened and two men got out. They moved to the strip of pavement between the two vehicles and waited, hands held out to their sides in a voluntary stance of submission.

"The one on your right is Hector Debarros. I'm sure you recognize the other guy as Lopez." Harper looked to Dan. "Ready, sir?"

"Let's get this done."

Braced for any sudden moves from their guests, they emerged from the SUV. When they reached the front of the vehicle, the man Hector spoke up. "Where are your weapons?"

Both Dan and Harper opened their jackets to show their holstered weapons.

"Where is Deputy Chief Harris?" Dan demanded. He had no desire to make small talk. Getting to the point was the only item on his agenda.

"I had nothing to do with taking your cop," Lopez

boasted. "My sister, Nina, is attempting a takeover. Her followers took your cop. There isn't much time if you want her back in one piece."

"Why are your own people saying otherwise?" Harper challenged.

"Nina has started a war," Hector explained when Lopez looked away as if too ashamed or overwhelmed with emotion to say the rest. "She's been collecting allies for weeks behind Salvadore's back. A war is coming—"

Lopez held up a hand when Hector would have said more. "She ordered the execution of four of my people when she killed the Negro Jerome Frazier. That was her work, not mine. It's your job to stop her. That's all you need to know."

Dan saw how this was shaping up. Lopez had a little uprising on his hands. He couldn't exactly kill little sister without rubbing Daddy the wrong way. So he wanted the BPD to do it.

"We're supposed to take your word for who killed whom?" Dan laughed. "I don't think so. We don't do family counseling. Maybe you can talk to your priest about your family issues."

Fury hardening his face, Lopez stepped forward.

Dan braced for battle. Next to him, Harper did the same.

"Don't do it for me," Lopez said to Dan, his posture as cocky as his tone, "do it for your cop. Nina will kill her and spread the word that it was me who ordered the hit and brought the five-oh down on our people. She wants a war. She wants to win, and the only way to do that is for me to die. You kill me and she takes over. That part might not matter to you, Chief of Police Burnett, but it means everything to your lady cop."

"Where is she?"

"I can tell you where to find her." He studied Dan a moment. "But I warn you, Chief of Police Burnett, choose your most trusted men. Not all of them care if your lady cop survives."

Saturday, July 31, midnight

Jess snapped to attention after dozing off and took stock of her surroundings as best she could in the dark. They'd turned off the one lamp in the room. There were other lights on in the house that filtered this way but not enough to make much difference.

The partying continued in the kitchen and dining room or whatever lay beyond the wall she leaned against. The music was loud enough that the wall vibrated. Definitely of the rap variety, with Spanish lyrics. She decided this was a small living room. There was a couch and an old box television set but it either didn't work or had been left turned off.

No air-conditioning. It was stifling hot. Her wrists ached from twisting the tape back and forth, trying to wiggle out of it. Beneath the tape her skin was raw. She didn't try to loosen her ankle restraints. One of the drunken goons checked on her from time to time. Which-

ever one popped in seemed to enjoy staring at her legs.
It was best not to have him notice she'd tried to escape.
When she got her hands loose, she would take care of the
tape around her ankles. She would be loose already if not
for her captor having gotten tape happy.

She hadn't seen DeShawn again. She hoped he had
taken her advice.

Nina Lopez had spun him a tale as sad as Cinderella's
woe-begotten saga and he had swallowed it hook, line,
and sinker.

From the signals Jess picked up when she and DeShawn
talked, he was feeling a little disillusioned and frustrated.
If Nina was picking up the same signals, it might be a
little too late to turn his situation around.

For his and his grandparents' sakes, Jess hoped not.

The laughter in the next room suddenly drowned out
the music.

Maybe they'd all get shit-faced and pass out. How the
hell had screwups like this managed to pull off kidnapping a deputy chief not a hundred feet from headquarters?

Maybe the problem was that Jess had been too distracted. Or maybe it was just dumb luck.

DeShawn walked into the room. Jess sat up a little
straighter. He glanced over his shoulder several times as
he approached her. Maybe he was coming around to her
way of thinking.

He squatted next to her. "I thought about what you said."

"Good. You need to get away from these people,
DeShawn." She gave him a smile. "I'm proud of you for
making the right decision."

He glanced over his shoulder again, then pulled a knife
from under his shirt. "But I can't go without you."

Damn. "Leave me the knife and go." She looked him straight in the eyes. "This is not the time or the place to try to be a hero. Go."

"No way, lady." He sliced the tape on her ankles.

Jess scooted forward and let him do the same to the tape around her wrists. Then he gave the knife to her. "Come on."

He ushered her out of the room and into a small, dark entry hall. "They're all out back right now," he whispered.

He'd just flipped the dead bolt when the overhead light came on.

"What the fuck?" a gruff male voice demanded.

A shotgun racked directly behind Jess. She flinched, then froze.

Apparently DeShawn did not understand that when the sound echoed right behind you, it was best not to move.

He turned around and got in the face of whoever was wielding the shotgun. "You gonna shoot me now?" he demanded. "I think you better ask Nina about that."

While DeShawn ranted at the guy, Jess tucked the knife, a six-inch fixed blade as best she could estimate, into the waistband of her skirt and tugged her jacket down over it.

"Bring her to Nina," the guy said.

His voice sounded vaguely familiar.

DeShawn took Jess by the arm and turned her around.

Jose Munoz, Lopez's second in command.

Jess lifted her eyebrows at him. "I've seen what your friends do to traitors. I guess you're not worried about losing your head."

"You won't be around to see, so what do you care?" he taunted. To DeShawn, he growled, "Bring her to Nina now."

Munoz backed up for DeShawn and Jess to walk past him.

DeShawn led her through the room where she had been held and into the well-lit kitchen. Four other men and Nina were draped on counters and relaxed in chairs. Looked as if the tequila was doing its job.

Too bad Munoz was still as sober as a judge. He was no doubt the only reason this ragtag crew had gotten this far.

The music stopped abruptly. The silence was deafening after the hours of booming and thumping. The kitchen was longer and wider than the room where Jess had been restrained. There were numerous windows besides the one over the sink. None were covered, which struck her as odd. Either the tequila had stolen their inhibitions or the whole lot was just more stupid than she had thought.

Unless they were in the middle of nowhere, which Jess doubted, and Nina was supremely confident that her brother wouldn't find them, she was definitely not the brightest bulb in the light show.

Nina jumped off the counter and slinked over to where Jess and DeShawn stood. Unlike Munoz, she was as drunk as a skunk.

"What's going on, Shawney?" She curled up against him. "You weren't being a bad boy, were you?" Her words were slurred.

"We need to let her go," he said. "What we're doing is wrong."

Nina held out her hand to the man closest to her. He placed a black semiautomatic handgun in her palm. She waved it at Jess, then at DeShawn. "I give the orders around here." She twirled around, giving them her back. "You see that tattoo, cop lady?"

Jess spotted the butterfly on her shoulder.

"You see it?" Nina screamed.

"I see it," Jess answered. "It's a nice pink-and-blue butterfly."

"My mother stole me away from my father"—Nina turned around once more—"when I was just a baby. She hid me from him for sixteen years. When I was thirteen, she had the butterfly with the number thirteen in its wings inked on my shoulder to show I had escaped the life." She laughed, swayed some more. "But she didn't understand. The *life* is in my genes. My father is Leonardo Lopez. This"—she waved her arms wide—"is my destiny."

"What about your brother?" Jess countered. "Isn't the life in his genes, too?"

Everyone in the room laughed. One by one Nina shot them a fierce glare. "He doesn't understand that it's my turn now. I'm"—she poked herself in the chest—"the new *jefa* of this clique. Since he refused to move over, he has to die." She smiled at Jess. "And you and Shawney are going to help me make that happen."

"Stop it, Nina," DeShawn demanded. "You're talking crazy talk."

"Get on your knees," she said to Jess.

"You should listen to him, Nina," Jess suggested. "He's the only real friend you have."

Munoz shoved Jess downward, onto her knees.

Nina pointed the weapon at Jess, who held her breath and tried not to shake, but the quaking had started deep inside her. She really wished she had peed when she had the chance. It was so embarrassing when victims lost control at a time like this. It would be her luck that smart-mouthed Dr. Schrader would be the one called to the scene. That would really suck.

"No." DeShawn stepped in front of Jess. "I won't let you do this. Maybe you ain't got the sense to see what's going down, but I do. These people are using you to overthrow your brother. They'll do the same thing to you."

As much as Jess didn't want her brains scattered all over this beat-up linoleum floor, she wished the kid would get out of the way before he got himself killed.

"He's right, Nina. Your pal Munoz there is double-crossing you." Jess had no idea if that was true or not but the suggestion might buy her some time.

"What's she talking about?" Nina demanded of the man now standing next to her.

"She's fucking with your head, Nina. Just shoot her and get it over with."

While they argued, with DeShawn right in the middle, Jess slipped the knife from beneath her jacket and hid it in her right hand with the blade resting against the back of her wrist.

DeShawn got in Munoz's face. "Why should she listen to you? She's my girlfriend."

Munoz grabbed him by the throat and forced him to his knees next to Jess. "But she's my woman," he snarled. "She listens to me."

Nina shot him in the head. The sound exploded in the room. Blood and brain matter spurted. Munoz collapsed to the floor in front of Jess and DeShawn.

DeShawn screamed and scrambled away from the body as the crimson pool beneath Munoz's head spread wider and wider.

Jess knew better than to move. Luckily the floor wasn't level, so the blood flowed in the other direction.

"I don't belong to no man," Nina screamed at the dead man. "And I do what I want."

The other four in the room had backed away from her. Maybe they'd all make a run for it.

"Put the gun down, Nina."

DeShawn was on his feet and trying to talk to her again. Damn it. Why didn't he get the hell out of here? You couldn't tell the younger generation a thing! Not even one who had been raised to respect his elders.

Likewise, Nina wasn't listening to DeShawn. She was staring at Jess. As if in slow motion, she trained the handgun on Jess's face once more. Whether it was the alcohol or mental illness or just plain old evil, anticipation danced in her dark eyes. She was looking forward to this.

"Good-bye, cop lady."

Jess flung herself to the left. The weapon fired. Hit the floor.

More gunfire erupted. Glass shattered.

Nina screamed. Her followers were yelling and running for cover.

The gunfire was coming from outside. Not wide sweeps. Precise, tight shots.

Cops.

DeShawn was trying to get Nina to listen to him. Jess scrambled up on all fours and rammed into his legs. He went down.

Nina hit the floor next, screaming in agony.

DeShawn tried to move toward her. Jess held him still. "Don't move until it's clear."

"She's hit," he argued. "I need to help her."

"You can't help her if you're dead." There were more gunshots outside.

DeShawn relented and stayed on the floor with Jess.

"Police! Put your weapons down and your hands up!"

Doors were kicked inward. Bodies in full SWAT garb swarmed into the room.

Nina was sobbing, but DeShawn made no move to comfort her now.

He had learned a hard lesson.

The best part was he'd lived through it.

Howard Johnson Inn, 5:30 a.m.

"You don't need to come in," Jess assured him.

Dan shut off the engine. "You're kidding, right?"

She didn't want to argue. Too tired. Using the last of her strength, she dragged her bag from the floorboard and reached for the door handle, but Dan was already there with the door open.

Before she could fathom his intent, he scooped her out of the seat and into his arms.

"Dan!" she protested.

"I'm not letting you walk across this parking lot in bare feet."

Her shoes hadn't been found. Damn it. She had liked those ivory-colored pumps. Now she'd have to find something else to wear with this suit. Damn it.

Right now, though, she just didn't care. She relaxed in Dan's arms and savored the smell of his skin. God, she loved the way he smelled.

When they reached her door, she dug around in her bag until she found her key.

In the room he settled her on the bed.

"I'll start you a bath."

"Thanks." Too bad she didn't have any wine. Wine would be good right now.

The water started to run in the bathroom and the sound soothed her. She leaned into the comforter and closed her eyes for just a second. A smile tugged at her lips as she thought of how happy Mr. and Mrs. Simmons had been to see their grandson.

Dan had promised them he would see to it that no charges were filed against DeShawn as long as he agreed to counseling.

Jess was glad. DeShawn had made a mistake. He'd fallen in love with the wrong girl.

Nina's injury hadn't been life threatening. Jess imagined that before she got out of prison she might wish it had been.

God, she was so tired.

She'd wrapped up two cases in one week.

It wasn't her usual closure rate but it was a good start.

Next week would be better.

27

Sunday, August 1, 7:00 p.m.

Jess should never have allowed Dan to talk her into this.

Dan. She glanced at the man driving. When they were off duty and she wasn't mad at him, using his first name was automatic. Instinct.

Funny how those little habits just sort of crept up on a person.

He'd been so sweet yesterday morning. She'd fallen asleep five minutes after they got to her place. He'd covered her up and settled in the chair in her room and gotten some shut-eye himself. He'd stayed with her all morning. Brought breakfast from the Waffle House down the street and run a fresh bath for her before leaving.

He'd left without even a kiss.

On some level she had appreciated his sensitivity but then...she'd wondered. Were he and Annette growing closer? Finally Jess had let it go and just decided to enjoy the weekend.

"Did you and Wells see anything you liked today?"

"She can't make up her mind if she wants a condo or a house." Jess pulled down the sun visor and checked her reflection in the lighted mirror for the third time. They were almost *there*.

Maybe she should have bought something new to wear. But this old sleeveless A-line had two things going for it. The pale turquoise color was her favorite, and the cummerbund-like pleated waistline that flowed down into a form-hugging skirt hit just the right spot three inches above her knees. She'd had the thing at least ten years.

She flipped up the visor. Why in the world had she agreed to have dinner with his parents?

Didn't matter. It was too late for second thoughts now.

"What about you?" he prodded. "Nothing you toured struck your fancy?"

Ten houses and six condos. She and Lori had spent the entire day with a Realtor who understood Jess could not live on the same street with her sister. That was simply impossible.

She also could not live anywhere near Dan's neighborhood. Or his parents'. Or Annette Denton's.

The price had to be as low as possible and well…that was it, she supposed. She had no other requirements.

"They were all in my price range. My preferred neighborhoods. But nothing that made me want to make an offer that probably wouldn't be accepted." Most sellers hated when contingencies were added to an offer. But, in her case, there was no choice. Her ability to purchase hinged on selling the house in Stafford.

"You'll know it when you see it." He slowed for the turn into his parents' drive.

Jess cringed. How would she get through the next two hours without doing or saying something she would regret? Really, it didn't matter what she said or did. Katherine would make something of it.

"Tell me again why we're doing this." Her pulse rate had escalated considerably since he put the Mercedes in park.

"Because"—he turned to Jess and smiled patiently as the interior light faded—"the Chandlers are dear friends of my mother and she wants to show her gratitude to you for not giving up on finding the truth."

Jess exhaled a big breath, wishing the tension could be so easily expelled. "She could have gone the Hallmark route. I love those cute little cards." God, she did not want to do this. Dan got out and walked around to her side of the vehicle. She considered making a run for it when he opened the door.

"The deputy chief," Dan said as he waited for her to unfasten her seat belt and climb out of the car, "who allegedly told Salvadore Lopez that she didn't care whether she took him dead or alive is afraid of my little old mother? Come on now."

Jess unfastened the seat belt and did what she had to do. When she was on the ground and the door was closed, blocking her escape back into the vehicle, she eyed Daniel Burnett with blatant speculation. "Remind me to remind Harper that he isn't allowed to talk out of school. And your mother is far scarier than any gangbanger I have ever encountered."

Dan laughed good-naturedly. "How is that possible, Jess?"

She harrumphed as he guided her with his hand at the

small of her back toward the front door. "That's easy. With a gangbanger you know where you stand. He wants to kill you before you can kill him. With your mother"— she shot him a sideways glance—"you never know."

Dan senior greeted them at the door. Katherine waited in the formal living room with a bottle of wine already uncorked. Surprisingly, the house smelled of fried chicken. Had to be something else. Katherine Burnett would never in a million years fry a chicken in her high-end gourmet kitchen.

Stemmed glasses filled with a crisp chardonnay Dan senior had selected just for the occasion were passed around.

Jess resisted the impulse to drink hers down and demand a refill.

Katherine lifted hers. "Thank you, Jess, for helping my friends find the truth in the midst of this horrible tragedy."

Both Daniels echoed a hear, hear.

A broad smile flashed across Katherine's wrinkle-free face. *Figure that one out.*

"To you, Jess," she offered, "for having the relentless instincts of a coonhound."

Oh, yes, she was going to need a lot more wine.

When glasses had clinked and all had sipped their wine, Katherine grabbed Jess by the arm. "Let's eat, dear. I've prepared a meal that will remind you of the good old days when you and Lily were just kids."

Jess snagged the bottle of wine with her free hand before allowing the woman to usher her toward the kitchen. "You don't say?"

"Fried chicken," Katherine touted. "Buttery mashed potatoes, green beans, and turnip greens. Dan senior even made corn bread."

Jess propped a smile in place. "That's just...incredible."

Whatever the menu said about Katherine's opinion of Jess's lower-middle-class roots, the food was quite tasty. Jess actually hadn't had fried chicken like that since she was a kid. She would, however, go to her grave believing that Katherine had hired someone to prepare the chicken and deliver it to her kitchen.

In the end it hadn't really mattered. Three, four, maybe five glasses of wine later and Jess was in a calm and happy place, filled with fried chicken and mashed potatoes.

10:08 p.m.

Jess liked watching the stars go by as Dan drove through the darkness. No matter how long she'd been away, she never forgot the way it felt to rush through the night with him. In high school he'd had a convertible Thunderbird. Between the promise of the night and the sultry summer breeze it had felt like they could do anything.

How in the world had the two of them ended up together during their high school years? He had been Mr. Popular. Captain of the football team. President of his class at the city's ritziest private school. She had been no one with a capital N-O at public school on the low-rent side of town.

They'd literally bumped into each other at Birmingham's Central Library. Her books and papers had gone every which way. He had apologized profusely while attempting to gather her things into a manageable armload. She had been totally and completely mesmerized. She hadn't been able to take her eyes off his face.

She'd seen him around at various hangouts of course. But not up close.

From that moment she had been completely, utterly in love with him. And he had loved her relentlessly. They had been inseparable.

But that was then and this was now.

She studied his profile, the dim glow from the dash giving her just enough illumination to see the details that had captured her heart so totally all those years ago. That strong, square jaw. The straight nose and full lips. More than just classically handsome, he was pretty damned hot. Had been at seventeen and he still was. It was so unfair that men aged so well while women...grew frumpier and crinkly.

Jess turned her attention forward and laughed. Once she started she couldn't stop. It was just too incredibly hilarious.

When she finally had to catch her breath and swipe her eyes, Dan demanded, "What's so funny?"

"Your mother." The giggles started again. A whole minute was required to regain control. "She compared me to a coonhound." Jess giggled some more. "But at least she didn't call me fat." She dissolved into hysterical laughter. There was just no stopping it.

Dan joined her, his deep, smooth laughter filling the space around her, making her feel warm and safe.

Before Jess had composed herself, he'd taken an unexpected turn and was heading in the opposite direction. "Where're we going?"

"I'm taking you to a special place."

That he said this with such mystery aroused her curiosity. "What special place? You know I don't like surprises."

She hated surprises. She'd had a few too many in her life. But the feel-good factor of the wine and the solving of two cases had made her agreeable. Actually it could very well turn out to be three cases, since the Michelle Butler case had been reopened.

"I think you'll like this surprise."

Jess sat up straighter and surveyed the landscape. When he took the exit for Thirty-First Street and meandered around to Thirty-Third, she gasped. "You wouldn't!"

He flashed a grin. "You dare me?"

She dropped back against her seat, still stunned that he would even consider it. "I double-dog dare you."

True to his word he drove straight into the parking area for Sloss Furnaces. "We could be arrested," she warned.

"Not if we don't get caught."

With all the public tours and television hype around Sloss Furnaces, one of Birmingham's oldest and most famous historic landmarks, it was a bit more complicated to enter these days. The old iron blast furnaces once used for turning iron ore into steel served as an open-air museum, but the rusting industrial park was best known for its numerous and infamous accounts of hauntings.

Dan easily found a way onto the property. The old smokestacks and slag buckets were a sight to see in the daytime. At night it was the platform atop Furnace One that had always drawn them. They climbed the ladderlike stairs and settled in their favorite old spot.

"Oh my God," she murmured as she stared at the city from their perch. Emotion swelled in her chest and she fought the tears that threatened. "I used to stare at those tall buildings and all those lights and wonder how Birmingham could be so big when it felt so small and confining to me.

When a train would go by and we were up here all alone and away from everything, the sound just sort of went through me. Made me wish I could jump aboard and go with it."

He was watching her. She shivered. He'd always been able to do that to her.

As if he feared the breeze that had suddenly kicked up had made her shiver, he shouldered out of his jacket and wrapped it around her. His arm lingered on her shoulders and she couldn't help leaning into him.

"Your top priority was to get away," he agreed. "I'm glad you're back. What you did this week was why I became a cop. You didn't let the absence of evidence or the unclear motives deter you. You refused to give up. We're lucky to have you on our team."

She pressed her lips together to stop their trembling. When she could speak without her voice quavering, she responded to his generous compliment. "I just never could quit picking at anything that didn't feel right to me," she confessed. "But I feel like there's a lot more to do. This gang business is out of hand."

"That story isn't over yet."

Jess looked up at him. "Has something else happened?" Salvadore Lopez was in federal custody but refused to talk, while his sister was giving up all she knew on him and her father.

Dan shook his head. "Unrest is brewing in the community. Families like DeShawn Simmons's and Jerome Frazier's are sick of the gangs taking over their neighborhoods and the cops seeming to turn their heads the other way. I think we're in for a war."

She didn't doubt it. "People are weary of waiting to be rescued."

"People are tired of a lot of things, but maybe there's more we can do about the rescue part."

That made her smile. "You're a good guy, Daniel Burnett. Rescuing is what you do best."

He'd rescued her after her fall at the bureau. That was for sure.

For a long time they just stood there, enjoying the present and remembering the past. How he remembered so much about the crazy things they did she would never understand. Maybe he remembered more because he had been here all this time...*home*...where they'd made all those memories.

They climbed down the rusty old ladder slowly and found their way back to the parking lot. The traffic on the nearby interstate overpass hummed and vibrated the air as they climbed into his Mercedes.

"You know that buying this vehicle means you're turning into your parents," she pointed out. "And that house, too." She turned in her seat to face him. "Both scream *Katherine, Katherine!*"

"I bought this vehicle because it's big and roomy." He pressed a button and his seat moved back farther from the steering wheel. He pressed another button and it moved forward once more. "It's comfortable and I just liked it. My mother had nothing to do with it."

He turned to her then, as if waiting for her rebuttal. In the faint light drifting in from the streetlamps she could see he was looking for her approval. His jaw was shadowed with a long day's beard growth. She still wore his jacket, so the white shirt was a stark contrast to his skin...his thick black hair and that face. The one that had haunted her dreams for more than two decades. No matter how far she ran or how hard she tried to forget.

"Push that first button again," she whispered, her body weak with need.

His seat powered back until it reached maximum distance from the steering wheel.

She moistened her lips and gave him another order. "Take off your belt and unfasten your trousers."

The ache of need that claimed his face undid her a little more. The hiss of leather sliding through the silk loops lit a fire deep inside her. She kicked off her pumps and climbed across the console, careful of the still-healing injury on his side from last week's encounter with the Player. He scooted her dress up her thighs and she reached down and felt for him.

He growled with desire when his fingers found her bare bottom. "Do you always go out to dinner without wearing panties?"

"Shut up. I need to do laundry. I didn't have any clean that wouldn't show under this dress." She made a desperate sound as her fingers wrapped around him and guided him to the right spot. Then she eased downward, all thought ceasing as the explosion of sensations filled her mind and body.

He caressed her bottom while she moved in that natural rhythm that had them both rushing toward climax. She ripped open his shirt so she could touch him. The place where the knife had dug in terrifyingly deep... his chest... his face. She wanted to touch all of him and she did not want to close her eyes. She watched. Watched as he unraveled. Watched until passion caught them both in that final incredible burst of pleasure. He pulled her mouth down to his and he kissed her like he had never kissed her before... like this might be the last time he would have that opportunity.

And then he held her there until they had both stopped gasping for breath. Afterward he whispered the sweetest words to her. "I'm taking you home and I'm keeping you at least for the night."

Every part of her still throbbed with pleasure. His taste had melted in her mouth like the chocolate she loved so. If she could smell nothing for the rest of her life except his skin, that would be enough. Right now, this minute, if she died, she would die more physically satisfied than she had ever been in her entire life.

"What if I don't want to go to your house?" She licked his jaw just to taste him again.

"What's wrong with my house?" He groaned as she wiggled her bottom.

"That's your chief of police house. I'd rather go to my place."

He laughed. "This is my chief of police car and that didn't stop you from seducing me."

She threw her head back and laughed. "I so did not seduce you. You brought me here and gave me your jacket and looked at me the way you looked at me..." She sighed. "And I was besotted and lost my mind for a few minutes."

He was the one laughing now. The way the sound vibrated in his chest made her breasts tingle. "Okay." He reached up and traced her cheek with his fingertips. "We'll go wherever you want."

"Good answer." She climbed back across the console, pulling her dress beneath her bottom as she went.

The silence felt good as he drove. She sat with her legs curled under her and her face pointed at him so she could just look. His shirt was ripped open. His trousers hastily fastened. The fancy Mercedes smelled of hot sex. She smiled. The night hadn't turned out so bad after all.

"If you don't stop looking at me that way," he threatened, "we're going to be making another stop before we get to your place."

She laughed and faced forward. What she needed was a distraction from him. Dragging her bag into her lap, she scraped around the bottom for her cell phone. Inevitably that was where it always ended up.

There shouldn't be any missed calls, but she had an app for checking local news.

"What the hell?"

Her head snapped up at Dan's comment and she saw the flashing lights up ahead.

There were cop cars and fire and rescue...all over the parking lot of the Howard Johnson's she called home.

She grabbed her shoes and yanked them on, then reached for the door latch.

"Stay in the car until I see what's going on," Dan ordered.

"Like hell." She wrenched open the door and bailed out. His jacket floated off her shoulders and landed on the seat.

She reached the official crime scene perimeter before he did. When she glanced back, Dan had tucked his shirt-tail in and pulled on his jacket to try to camouflage the fact that most of the buttons on his shirt were missing.

"What's going on here, Officer?" Jess flashed her credentials.

"A couple of the rooms were vandalized. A lot of gunfire but no one was injured. Just a couple of scared residents." He lifted the yellow tape for her to cross under it. "I heard one of the detectives say it was gang related."

The officer suddenly snapped to a higher state of attention as Burnett appeared behind her and showed his ID.

Jess's instincts were screaming. She hurried through the side entrance she always used and past the swimming pool. Cops were swarming around her room and the ones on either side of it.

The cell phone she was still holding vibrated in her hand.

Harper calling.

"Harris."

"Chief, we have a problem. Where are you?"

She spotted him beyond the open door of her room. "Coming up on your position now, Sergeant."

He looked up and nodded. "I see you."

Burnett beat her to the door but allowed her to enter first.

Her room had been torn apart. Her clothes...all of her stuff...was scattered around the room in pieces. The walls were filled with line after line of bullet holes. Anything breakable was shattered.

"It was MS-13, ma'am," Harper said as she stalled beside him.

"I see that, Sergeant." Her full attention remained on the wall above her bed where a warning had been left in what appeared to be spray paint.

The RAGE has started.

She slowly turned around, studying the Roman numerals that marked this work as that of MS-13.

Burnett was talking to a crime scene tech and Captain Allen. The crime scene folks had gotten here in a hurry. GTF as well.

Jess focused on the warning written in big red letters.

"Do you know if that means something, Sergeant?" She pointed to the word *rage*.

He nodded, his face grim. "Yes, ma'am. It's a video game set in a postapocalyptic world where the players have to shoot to kill, and survival in the new world is about kill or be killed because civilization as we know it is over. A lot of gangbangers talk about the end of the world and a total takeover. They thrive on the anger—the rage. That's how they keep their members motivated."

"And right now some of them are pretty pissed off at me," she suggested.

"Looks that way."

As if a robocall had gone out to the entire department, Harper, Burnett, and Allen all reached for their cell phones. Jess suddenly felt hers vibrate. Lori calling.

"Harris."

"Jess, have you seen the news?"

"I haven't." From the looks of her demolished television set, she wouldn't be seeing it anytime soon. "What's going on?"

"That house on Center Street where Lopez's crew was hanging out just exploded. A group calling themselves the Black Brotherhood has claimed responsibility. I'm reading you the breaking news scroll right off the screen," Lori explained. "According to Channel Six and Gina Coleman, an anonymous source reported that this is just the beginning. The day of reckoning is at hand."

Jess pressed her hand to her stomach and stared at the warning over her wrecked bed. "Whoever is behind this just left me a message at the HoJo's."

Now where was she going to stay? More importantly,

how many lives would be lost if this situation got further out of control?

"Jess, you can stay at my place."

There was nothing salvageable here; that was for sure. Everything was destroyed.

"Jess, are you there?"

Lori's voice dragged Jess's attention back to the phone. "Yeah. I'm here. But I have to go and figure this out." She ended the call and surveyed her place again.

Even her shoes had been spray-painted or ripped apart.

Burnett moved to her side. She almost laughed at herself. Less than five minutes at a crime scene and she was already calling him Burnett.

"If there's anything you want to take with you, grab it. I need to get you someplace safe until this is over."

She felt reasonably confident there would be no safe place for anyone until this was over.

"Jess?"

She froze as her brain assessed and identified the voice. That was impossible. She turned around, certain she was mistaken. *He couldn't be here.*

Supervisory Special Agent Wesley Duvall stood just inside the door of her wrecked motel room. Dressed in a stylish charcoal suit, white shirt, and navy tie, and even at this hour there was not a jet-black hair out of place.

He gave her a nod. "I have to hand it to you, Jess. When you decide to shake things up, you don't hold back."

"Wesley." Jess smiled as best she could, considering Burnett was standing beside her, glaring at her ex-husband and she was...stunned. "What're you doing here?"

He closed the distance between them and gave her a firm hug. He held on to her when he drew back as if he needed to look her over thoroughly. "It sounded to me as if you were in trouble and I came to give you a hand."

Speaking of hands, Burnett's hand thrust between them. "Daniel Burnett, chief of police."

Wesley released Jess to shake the other man's hand. "We spoke yesterday. I appreciate the heads-up that Jess was safe and sound."

This was truly . . . unexpected.

Wesley turned back to her and flashed a warm smile. "I am so pleased to see you. *We* have a lot of catching up to do."

Jess wasn't sure if that was an invitation or a warning, but right now she needed a new home and at least six hours of sleep.

"Well." She looked from Wesley to Dan and back. "It's been a long day. I'm certain I'll see both of you tomorrow."

Before either man could summon a proper response, Jess walked away. She didn't know how far she would get before one or both rushed after her, but it felt good to be the one doing the walking.

She needed a ride to Lori's for the night. Her Audi was still at the lab. Tomorrow was Monday and time to get back to work. A hurricane was brewing in her hometown and she was, it seemed, right in the eye of it.

Wouldn't be the first time she'd been surrounded by trouble. She doubted it would be the last.

The truly strange part was that she'd just lost basically everything she owned, yet somehow she felt as if she were finally home.

Right on cue she was promptly flanked on either side by six feet of walking, talking testosterone. Perhaps this aspect of the evening was the really strange part. The two most relevant men from her past were abruptly right here, beside her.

One she had alternately loved and hated for half a life-time...the other she had married.

"We should get you moved to a new hotel," Dan suggested from his position on her right.

"Don't you have a safe house?" Wesley countered from her left. "Until this situation is properly assessed, she needs protection."

Jess shook her head. What she needed was for Sergeant Harper to get her out of here.

As if she'd telegraphed the thought, he appeared. "Ready to go, ma'am? Detective Wells called to say you needed a ride to her place."

"Absolutely, Sergeant." Jess looked from one over-protective high-ranking male to the other. "Good night, gentlemen."

Whatever happened tomorrow, one thing was absolutely certain. It would be undeniably interesting and immensely complicated.

The story of her life.

Messages written in blood.
A murder scene straight out of a
Charles Manson playbook. Only one
special agent can get to the bottom of
Birmingham's latest nightmare...

Please turn this page
for a preview of

Rage

Five Points, 7:35 a.m.

Hello Jess.

The appearance of those two words on the screen of her cell phone should not have stolen her breath or weakened her knees, but they managed to do both in the space of a single heartbeat, forcing her to wilt down onto the toilet seat.

Jess Harris shoved a handful of damp hair behind her ear, then hugged her knees to her chest. It wasn't really the words that had her crouched on the toilet seat of the cramped bathroom. It was the identity of the sender.

Tormenter.

Eric Spears...the *Player.*

Jess curled her fingers into her sweaty palm to stop their trembling. She pressed her fist to her lips and fought the trepidation howling inside her. *Answer him!* This might be the last time he reached out to her if she didn't do something.

She touched the text box on the screen and prepared to enter a response. Before she tapped a single letter another bubble of words appeared.

I watched you on the news last night. Your ex has impeccable timing. I can't wait to see who wins this round.

Pulse fluttering wildly with an infusion of anger, she considered telling Spears that, as he was no doubt aware, his current location could be tracked via this connection and that she intended to promptly inform the bureau.

But that would be a lie. Worse, he would recognize the lie. Spears knew her far too well.

Using the pad of her thumb she tapped one letter at a time until she'd filled the text box with the message she wanted to send the sociopath who had murdered dozens of women, maybe a hell of a lot more, in his sadistic career as a serial torturer-murderer. Jess smiled as she reread the words she hoped would prompt his need to grow ever closer to her.

One thing's for sure, it won't be you. I'm the one who got away, Spears. Guess that makes you a loser and a coward.

After hitting send, she reveled in the idea that her words would burrow under his skin and fester like boils until he just had to claw at the itch. Eric Spears's malignant narcissistic side wouldn't deal well with failure. Not only did he not like to lose, he hated the idea of being wrong about anything or anyone. He'd made several mistakes of late. Skating so very close to getting caught was one of them. Allowing Jess to live was another.

Whatever it took, she would get him.

Her cell clanged that old-fashioned tone, announcing an incoming call. She jumped. Nearly dropped the damned thing. Spears wouldn't dare...

Harper calling appeared on the screen, banishing the stream of conversation between her and Spears.

"Jess, you are truly pathetic." She swallowed back the lump of undeniable fear that had risen into her throat and forced herself to breathe normally. "Harris."

"We have a homicide, Chief. Shady Creek Drive off Columbiana Road."

Jess dropped her feet to the floor and banished thoughts of Spears. "How many victims, Sergeant?"

"Just one...but..."

The silence that filled the air for several endless seconds had Jess's pulse revving with the surge of adrenaline charging through her veins.

"It's bad, Chief. Really bad. It's the wife of one of our own. Lieutenant Lawrence Grayson's wife, Gabrielle."

Oh damn. "Crimes Against Persons isn't working this one?" No need to start the week off like the last one, in a pissing contest with Deputy Chief Harold Black, bless his ornery heart. Today's staff meeting was supposed to clarify some ground rules and cement the team spirit to ensure better cohesion as they moved forward. That meeting likely wouldn't happen now. Couldn't be helped. Justice was the last thing the dead should have to wait for.

"I got the call since the first officers on the scene felt the murder might be connected to the Lopez situation," Sergeant Chet Harper explained. "The wife was decapitated and there's a message including some of the buzz words from this weekend's hit on your place."

"Jesus Christ." Jess scrubbed at her eyes with her free hand. Images from the destruction that had been her room at the Howard Johnson Inn flickered through her mind. They had to get a handle on this escalating gang situation.

It was turning into a blood bath and resurrecting the ugly memories of the city's violent, racially unjust past.

The MS-13 clique operating in Birmingham, once lorded over by Salvadore Lopez, was at war with a faction that had split off to follow his younger sister, Nina. The sister was currently in custody for kidnapping Jess, among other charges. Salvadore had gone into protective custody with the promise of rolling over on his infamous father, Leonardo. The elder Lopez was the messiah-like leader of the West Coast's rampant and ruthless MS-13 activities. Every three-letter agency in the country wanted him to go down, and now they had their chance.

Squaring her shoulders, Jess began the process of tuning out her personal frustrations with the whole damned Lopez family and the regret for the loss of life—particularly an innocent life—that would only get in the way. "Is Captain Allen on the scene?" Allen headed up Birmingham PD's Gang Task Force. His insights would be invaluable if a gang connection was substantiated.

"En route as we speak."

"I'll be there shortly, Sergeant. You know what to do."

Jess ended the call as she pushed to her feet and headed for the door. She caught her reflection in the mirror over the pedestal sink and paused mid-stride. Her damp hair would just have to dry on its own. She shoved her phone into her robe pocket so she could pile her blond locks into a manageable mass that was annoyingly curly when wet and snapped a claw clip in place. Makeup she could take care of en route. A flick of mascara and a dab of lip gloss would do.

She silently repeated the mantra she'd clung to for the past thirty-six hours or so. *I'll be okay.* It would take more than being kidnapped by some ditzy, power-hungry teeny-bopper and having her place and her things destroyed to knock Jess off her game.

The tone that accompanied an incoming text had her rummaging for her cell.

I'm deeply wounded, Jess. I thought by now you would miss me as much as I miss you. See you soon.

"The sooner, the better," she grumbled. Jess Harris was not afraid of anything. Except maybe the possibility of failing to get Spears before he added more victims to his heinous résumé.

With renewed purpose she deleted the conversation and emerged from the bathroom to find Lori, on her cell, probably getting the news about the murder. Jess grabbed the one suit that had survived last night's kill-the-deputy-chief's-stuff episode and ripped it free of the dry cleaner's plastic. She'd failed to pick it up from the dry cleaner on Friday, which was the only reason it had been spared from the carnage.

Since her Audi had been at the lab for processing related to her abduction—and still was, damn it—the car and this one suit were about all that remained of the belongings she'd rolled into Birmingham with. Well, except for the dress and the turquoise pumps she'd been wearing last night. The pumps would just have to do until she had time to shop.

"You need a cup of coffee to go?" Lori asked as she headed for the kitchen with her own mug. Her Five Points studio was one big room with a small bath and closet carved out of the already-tight floor space. Any level of privacy was basically impossible.

"That'd be great." Jess stepped into her pumps while

she picked through the bag of undergarments, cosmetics, and necessities she'd purchased at Walmart late last night. Living out of a plastic bag was no fun, and though Lori insisted she was happy to have her as a guest, Jess was anxious to get a place of her own. She liked Lori a lot, and was proud to have the detective on her team, but staying on Lori's couch was going to get old, fast. Maybe it had something to do with being in her forties and set in her ways, but having alone time felt immensely important, especially when she hadn't had any in about forty-eight hours. She needed her space. Along with a new wardrobe and almost everything else a woman required to operate on a day-to-day basis.

Unfortunately, all of that would have to wait.

She had a homicide to get to.

Shady Creek Drive, 8:30 a.m.

"Whoa." Lori surveyed the crowd gathered as she turned off Columbiana Road. "This is going to be complicated and"—she blew out a big breath—"messy."

News vans cluttered the intersection of Columbiana and Shady Creek. Birmingham Police Department cruisers lined the street on either side of where they needed to turn. This tragedy had befallen one of their own and a show of strength was expected. The gesture was heartfelt, but there was no place for crowds at a homicide scene. At least not until after complete scene documentation and thorough evidence collection. The potential for contamination and/or loss was far too great with every warm body that entered a crime scene.

"Do you know Lieutenant Grayson?" His name sounded familiar but Jess couldn't recall meeting him. She'd been introduced to so many of Birmingham's finest since her arrival scarcely three weeks ago that she couldn't say for sure whether she'd met him or not.

"I've seen him around but I don't really know him." Lori powered down her window and showed her badge to the uniform controlling access to the block. When he'd waved her through, she went on, "Grayson is with Field Operations, South Precinct."

Still didn't click for Jess.

"What kind of reputation does he have?" As wrong as it seemed, close family members were always the prime suspects in a case like this until evidence and alibis proved otherwise. Lawrence, aka Larry, Grayson was a cop, so the fundamental steps in a homicide investigation would be no surprise to him.

"A good one as far as I know. I've heard his name a few times when accommodations were handed out." She glanced at Jess. "If you're asking me if he would kill his wife, I don't know him that well, Chief."

"I guess that's something we'll need to learn." They were on duty now. Jess was the deputy chief of SPU, Special Problems Unit, and Lori Wells was one of her detectives. Their ability to be friends and step back from those rolls as needed fascinated Jess. After nearly two decades doing investigative work, this was her first time to have friends, in the true sense of the word, on the job. She'd certainly never been the houseguest of a coworker.

Maybe an old dog could learn a new trick.

The houses along Shady Creek were modest *Brady Bunch*–style ranches and split-levels, circa the seventies;

it was a typical blue-collar neighborhood. Good folks who were forever stuck on the low end of middle class while being overworked and underpaid.

Crime scene tape circled the yard, using trees and shrubs for support and announcing that bad things had happened to those who called this address home. Outside that gruesome yellow line a host of cops had surrounded an emotionally distraught man and were struggling to get him into the passenger seat of a sedan.

"That must be him." He looked vaguely familiar, but Jess still couldn't say for sure if she'd met him.

"Yeah. Damn." Lori shook her head. "Looks like he's lost it."

Jess grimaced at the emotionally charged scene. "Who wouldn't?" She steeled herself in preparation for what was to come. No matter how experienced the investigator, when murder hit this close to home—a fellow cop—it was difficult to take in stride.

"You see any sign of the coroner's wagon?" Between the cruisers and all the other vehicles crowding the street, not to mention what looked like a brigade of cops and no shortage of neighbors, it was difficult to see beyond the driveway.

Lori guided her Mustang as far to one side as possible considering the middle of the street was about all that was left in the way of unoccupied pavement and shut off the engine. "It's the van right behind that Camry riding my bumper."

Jess craned her neck to see. There appeared to be a male passenger but, with the sun glinting on the other side of the windshield, she couldn't see the driver. Opting to jerk to a stop in the middle of the street, whoever was at the wheel of the van didn't seem to care if more of a bottleneck was created.

Jess climbed out of the low-slung Mustang. Instantly the heat crushed around her. The humid air was as thick as molasses. Last night's storm had ensured a sweltering morning and that little or no viable evidence would be found outside the home.

With one more glance behind her, she checked to see if the ME had climbed out of the van yet. She probably wouldn't be lucky enough to get Schrader again. For all she knew Dr. Harlan Schrader could be on his way to the job offer at the Mayo Clinic by now. They'd worked a case together last week and not having to go through that awkward *first time* business again so soon would be nice.

The driver's side door of the van opened and a female emerged. Shoulder-length brown hair, pale complexion. No one Jess had met so far, that she recalled anyway. The woman wore a lavender wrap dress with matching strappy stilettoes. Her sophisticated—scratch that—arrogant body language confirmed they had not met. Jess was one hundred percent certain she would remember that cocky stride, not to mention the haughty tilt of the woman's chin.

"This should be interesting," Lori murmured as she moved up to the front of the Mustang, where Jess waited.

"What's that?" At the scene perimeter, Jess showed her badge to the uniform.

"That's the associate coroner, Dr. Sylvia Baron. She's the lieutenant's ex-wife." Lori ducked under the crime scene tape and Jess followed. "She's a little pushy. No one likes getting stuck on a case with her."

Pushy or not, sounded like a conflict of interest to Jess.

An older man had gotten out on the passenger side of

the van and joined the woman's purposeful movement toward the house as Jess and Lori made their way up the sidewalk. He looked vaguely familiar. Sixty maybe. Tall. Broad-shouldered. Blond and tanned. All he needed was a diamond stud in one ear and he'd have the whole Harrison Ford thing going on.

At the front door she and Lori stopped long enough to drag on shoe covers and gloves. "Who's the man with her?"

"That's Dr. Leeds."

That was Martin Leeds, the Jefferson County chief coroner? Jess really had to find some time to get to know the various chains of command in Birmingham. She was woefully uninformed. In her own defense, she'd held the position for only two weeks and she'd been embroiled in murder and mayhem all fourteen or so of those days. Well, maybe she'd had a small break here and there. The unbidden memory of steamy, stolen hours spent between the sheets with Daniel Burnett the weekend before last had butterflies taking flight in her belly.

Those frantic and breathless minutes in his fancy Mercedes just last night wouldn't exactly be dismissed any time soon either. Particularly since he was her boss.

"I don't want that bitch anywhere near my wife!"

Jess's attention snapped back to the street as Lieutenant Grayson's angrily shouted words reverberated in the impossibly thick air. Those closest to Grayson were trying to calm him, but he was having no part of it.

Jess decided that an introduction to Leeds and the former Mrs. Grayson could wait until they were inside and had surveyed the crime scene. The situation outside was a ticking bomb and it wasn't going to get any calmer until Lieutenant Grayson had been removed from the scene.

The man's wife had been murdered. The ability to think clearly or to reason was long gone.

Inside the house the atmosphere was somber and *cold*. Jess shivered. It was a sweltering dog day in August here in Alabama but she was wishing she had a sweater just now. Her nose twitched. Even the frosty temperature couldn't completely conceal the distinct odor of coagulated blood hanging in the air as if she'd stepped into a meat locker rather than a home where a family lived.

Techs were already on-site documenting the scene and gathering evidence. Jess's first step and top priority was to find the motive, in part based on what she observed here this morning. Had the wife been murdered during the commission of a robbery? Were drugs, money, or both the reason she was dead? There was always a slim chance the killing was a random act of violence. Slim because this was the home of a cop and the neighborhood was not exactly a prime target location for thieves. These weren't rich folks with a treasure trove of readily sellable goods for the taking.

In Jess's experience, when a cop or a cop's family was the target the motive was often vengeance. There was always jealousy, of course, if one or the other had a problem with fidelity. Whatever evidence Jess discovered here, final assessments and conclusions could not be reached until all witnesses or persons with knowledge were found and interviewed. Every hour that passed before all those steps happened lessened the likelihood of success in solving the case.

Harper spotted their arrival and made his way through the main living area and into the foyer. "Chief, the body's this way."

"Detective Wells"—Jess hesitated before following

Harper—"why don't you find the officers whose duty it is to protect the scene and explain how that concept works." She surveyed the number of warm bodies milling around inside the house and shook her head. "I want anyone who's not a witness or who doesn't belong to the Crime Scene Unit or the coroner's office out of here *now*."

"Yes, ma'am."

Lori headed in the opposite direction as Harper led Jess through the kitchen and down a few steps to a large room at the rear of the house. Jess stalled in the entryway of the room and gave herself a few moments to absorb the details of the scene.

There was so much blood.

Words were scrawled in blood around the walls.

Pig. Whore. Kill the bitch. Kill the pigs, One by one.

The chilly air seemed to freeze in Jess's lungs as she stared at the other word written in large, sweeping strokes.

Rage.

She blinked away the images from her motel room that attempted to transpose themselves over those currently burning her retinas. Shaking off the eerie sensation of déjà vu, she visually inventoried the rest of the room.

A massive flat panel television hung over the stacked-stone fireplace. A local morning talk show filled the screen but the sound had been muted. Beefy, well-worn leather sofas stood like sentinels on either side of the fireplace waiting for the family to gather. Windows, blinds tightly closed, spanned the walls. The only natural light breaching the space was from the broken sliding door, its two panels of glass lying in pieces on the tile floor. Beyond the broken door, a wood privacy fence surrounded the backyard and swimming pool.

Jess shivered again. "What's going on with the air-conditioning, Sergeant?"

"The thermostat was adjusted as low as it would go," he explained. "It's about sixty-two degrees in here."

"Seems our killer took the time to think things through before taking his leave." And he or she obviously knew a little something about skewing attempts at determining time of death. Just another reason to hate all those *CSI* shows.

"I believe the murder was carried out right here," Harper said as they moved across the room. "The child, a six-month-old boy, was left in his crib in a bedroom. Nothing in the house, as far as we can tell, was disturbed beyond the damaged patio doors. The standard grab-and-run items like laptops and jewelry are still here."

"Where's the child now?" Jess hoped he wasn't out there amid the chaos on the street. Grayson was in no condition to care for himself, much less a child.

"The lieutenant's partner, Sergeant Jack Riley, called his wife and she took the baby home with her as soon as a paramedic confirmed the child was unharmed."

After fishing for her glasses, Jess shoved them into place and moved closer to study the placement of the body. Dressed in a yellow spaghetti-strapped nightgown, the victim lay supine on the tile floor, a pool of coagulated blood around her, her head severed from her body but left right next to the stump of her neck. Tissue was torn in a jagged manner as if the perp had had a hard time getting started with a sawtooth-type tool. Multiple stab wounds along the torso had dotted the pale yellow gown with ugly rusty spots. Her arms were outstretched at her sides, crucifixion style. Legs were straight and together.

Across the victim's forehead, written in what appeared to be her own blood, were the words *PIG WHORE*.

Jess stepped nearer and eased into a crouch. She pointed to the victim's upper arms. "Looks like our killer had a good grip on her at some point." There was bruising on the chest, just above her breasts. Jess passed a gloved hand over the area. "He held her down while he committed this final atrocity. Judging by the bruise pattern I'd say he was right-handed."

Harper nodded. "I counted ten stabs to her torso. All postmortem, like the beheading. Didn't see any indication she had been sexually assaulted."

"I agree, Sergeant." The coroner's office would check for sexual assault, that was SOP. As for the rest, there wasn't nearly enough blood for the visible damage to have been inflicted while her heart was still beating. No arterial spray from the decapitation. A little castoff from the saw, but that was about it, other than the blood that gravity drained out of the body. In fact, seemed as if the killer waited until livor mortis was well under way before bothering to play psycho surgeon.

Harper pointed to the victim's hands. "No defensive wounds on her hands or forearms to indicate she fought her attacker. No ligature marks to indicate she was restrained."

Very strange. Lividity indicated she had been in this position since her death or very quickly thereafter. But why here and like this? Had the victim been watching television when her attacker crashed into the room? Had she fallen asleep on the sofa? Or did she hear the breaking glass and come to check it out? How had he disabled her?

"Could be damage to the back of the head," Jess suggested. There didn't appear to be any to the temple areas or the forehead.

"I don't see any blood matted in her hair close to the skull." Harper pointed to the long hair fanned around her head.

That was true. Jess rubbed at the wrinkle furrowing her brow with the back of a gloved hand. "Once he'd killed her, what distracted him for so long before he did the rest?" She glanced around the room. Had someone come to the door and interrupted his work? Had the baby started crying and thrown him off balance? The latter wasn't likely, since the baby was still alive.

"Reminds me of the Manson murders," Harper said. "I watched a documentary the other night. The anniversary is coming up this weekend."

Jess had noted that similarity, too, but she wasn't about to say it out loud. Not with so many ears around. All they needed was the media bringing that kind of connection into this. She scrutinized the tile floor around the victim. Not a single footprint. The perp had been exceptionally careful. "No blood anywhere else in the house?"

"Nothing we've found so far. Looks like someone showered recently in the hall bath. The shower floor is damp and so's the rug in front of it. There's a faint smell of shampoo, gardenias."

Surprised, Jess said, "The shampoo should be logged into evidence. We need to be sure the techs check the drain as well. What about a towel?"

Harper grunted a negative sound. "Not in the bathroom or laundry room. If the perp was the one who took the shower, he took the towel with him. Already took care of the rest."

Jess lifted the victim's arm. "We have full rigor. She's been dead nine or ten hours anyway. Maybe longer."

The manner of the decapitation was primitive. As if the perpetrator hadn't been able to get the job done on his first attempt, he'd started over a couple of times, mutilating tissue and making one heck of a mess. "No murder or mutilation weapon lying around?"

"No, ma'am. Whatever the perp used, he took that with him as well."

With no weapon and no ready signs the perp had been careless, the odds of nailing him were stacked against them. "Who discovered the body?"

"Johnny Trenton," Harper said. "The pool guy."

Jess made a face. "They have a pool guy?" She'd noticed the pool out back, but this wasn't exactly the kind of neighborhood where one expected to encounter a cabana boy.

"He arrived at six this morning, as scheduled, to clean the pool. He has a key to the garage and the door that leads out of the garage into the backyard." Harper gestured to the patio and sparkling pool beyond the broken sliding door. "He made the nine-one-one call. Says he didn't come inside for fear of stepping in the blood or otherwise damaging the scene. Since it was obvious Mrs. Grayson was dead, he figured there was nothing he could do anyway."

"He didn't come in the house to check on the child or the husband?" If he knew the family, he had to know there was a kid and a husband.

"He says the place was as quiet as a tomb when he arrived, so he assumed anyone else in the house was dead, too."

More likely he hadn't wanted to risk suspicion by entering the scene and leaving behind a footprint or fingerprint. "Where is this pool guy?"

"In the dining room. I didn't see any blood on him and his hair definitely doesn't smell like gardenias."

"Well, that certainly rules him out," Jess mused.

Harper cast a somber look at the victim and shook his head. "I don't think he did this, Chief. This involved some serious rage and a good chunk of time. Trenton doesn't seem like the type to invest that much emotion, if you know what I mean."

"Have him transported downtown. I'd like to question him in a more formal setting." Being driven downtown in the back of a police cruiser should have him eager to cooperate if he knew anything at all. And Jess did understand what Harper meant. Like a crop of choking crabgrass the I-don't-care-about-my-neighbors attitude had taken root among Southern folks, too. No one wanted to get involved anymore.

She pushed to her feet and walked to the now useless slider and stared across the yard. The lawn was thick and lush. No sign of mud, which meant no footprints out here either. Only the tops of neighboring homes were visible above the fence but one, at the farthest end of the yard, was a two-story like the Grayson home. A pair of side-by-side windows overlooked the Graysons' backyard.

"Have the neighbors been canvassed?" Jess strained to see any movement beyond the windows across the way. Anyone looking out those windows at just the right time would have had a clear view of the murder.

"Yes, ma'am." Harper pointed to the house with the windows that had captured Jess's attention. "We checked that one first. Looks abandoned. Yard's all grown up. The utility meter has been pulled. No answer and no vehicle in the drive."

"Damn." She turned her attention back to the victim, Gabrielle Grayson. Dark hair and olive skin. Thirty or thirty-two. "Latino?" she asked Harper.

"Mrs. Grayson was born in this country but her parents moved here from Spain. Lieutenant Grayson's partner told me she was a nurse until her son was born and she opted to become a full-time mother."

"We need to know if she has any connections whatsoever to the gang world." This was the fifth decapitation Jess had encountered in the last week. The other four ritual killings had been carried out by members of the MS-13 against those they deemed traitors. The major difference was those decapitations had been accomplished while the victims were still alive. This one looked wrong. The words scrawled on the walls were unfocused. The whole scene, including the possibility the perp had showered, was way off when compared to an MS-13 assassination scene.

"There's no connection that we know of, ma'am."

Another of those aggravating frowns tugged across her brow. "Where is Captain Allen? I thought he was en route."

Harper looked away and cleared his throat. "He… ah…dropped by. Took a quick look and said he'd let us know if he heard any rumblings about this. He knows Grayson. Said the lieutenant and his partner have been helping out with GTF but neither has been involved on a level that would ignite something like this. He doesn't think there's a connection."

"He couldn't hang around until I arrived?" Jess understood the guy had it in for her since she'd barged her way into the Lopez case and stolen the big takedown Allen had had planned, but this was a homicide for Christ's sake. A cop's wife.

Jess took a breath, brought her voice down an octave or two. "Stay on Allen, Sergeant, and find out from Grayson's division chief if he's worked a case, past or present, within the division that may have landed him on someone's hate list."

"Yes, ma'am."

Jess was as sure as anyone could be that this murder didn't have anything to do with the MS-13. It was way too neat and there were too many discrepancies. But she couldn't rule out that possibility just yet any more than Allen could. "We also need cause of death ASAP," she said, more to herself than to the detective next to her. "The media will have a field day with this. We need something to give them before they start making up stuff."

In the past forty-eight hours a Lopez hangout had been blown up and three clashes in the streets of downtown Birmingham had barely been defused without bloodshed. A couple of fires had been started in abandoned houses. No matter that the Lopez clique was falling apart all on its own, there were some in the community who were looking for an excuse to take matters into their own hands. The murder of a cop's wife—the mother of a small child—would fuel that fire into a raging inferno.

"There was another clash in Druid Hills just before daylight," Harper mentioned. "Another house burned after being hit by Molotov cocktails, but no one was injured."

Damn. Druid Hills was the neighborhood where this war had started. Jess had lived there for a while as a kid. Not much had changed in all this time. Harper's news just confirmed what she already knew. They needed damage control on this one. "What the devil is taking Leeds and his colleague so long?"

She hated waiting. Worse, Jess's attention settled on the victim; she hated for this woman to lie here like this any longer than necessary. She hoped Grayson and his ex hadn't gotten into a war outside.

"I'll check on that," Harper offered.

"Do that, Sergeant, and make sure—"

"If you'll get out of the way," a haughty female voice announced, "we'll try to make up the time we lost due to BPD's incompetence at securing the scene and preventing the flash mob outside."

Jess turned and came face-to-face with the tall brunette in the lavender dress who appeared determined to live up to her reputation of being pushy. *Sylvia Baron.*

"Somebody adjust that damned thermostat," she shouted at no one in particular. "Are we trying to turn this vic into a Popsicle or what?"

"I'll take care of that," Harper said as he made himself scarce.

Jess thrust out her hand. "I'm Deputy Chief Harris. I'll be investigating this case."

"Dr. Sylvia Baron, associate coroner and medical examiner. This is Dr. Martin Leeds, Jefferson County's chief coroner. As I said, if you will get out of the way, we'll attend to our responsibility in this matter."

As true as it was that the coroner had jurisdiction over the body, Jess was king of the hill when it came to the scene. "Dr. Baron, I'm certain this is an awkward and perhaps difficult time for you. Be that as it may, considering your ties to the victim's husband, I have strong reservations about your ability to maintain objectivity under the circumstances. Your being here obviously represents a conflict of interest."

Baron didn't look surprised that Jess had already heard about who she was. In fact, the ME laughed. "Like I care about your reservations. Now step aside or I'll call Chief Burnett and have you removed from this case."

A bad, bad feeling struck Jess. Was this woman another of Burnett's fancy private-school cronies? Or maybe Sylvia Baron was a former lover or another ex-wife? The man had at least two exes Jess hadn't met. Either way, she wasn't running this investigation. Jess was.

Big breath. Stay calm. She stepped around the body and moved closer to Baron. "I think that's a very good idea. Calling Chief Burnett, I mean." Jess kept her smile in place as she reached into her bag and retrieved her phone, then offered it to the other woman. "Why don't you use my phone? Burnett's at the top of my contact list."

The woman matched Jess's fake smile with one of her own. "No need." She whipped out her iPhone and made the call with scarcely more than a swipe and a tap. "He's at the top of mine as well."

**Don't miss the first electrifying
Faces of Evil novel!**

Please turn this page for an
excerpt from

Obsession

Birmingham, Alabama
Wednesday, July 14, 1:03 p.m.

Special Agent Jess Harris's career was in the toilet along with the breakfast she'd wolfed down and then lost in a truck stop bathroom the other side of Nashville.

God, this wasn't supposed to happen.

Jess couldn't breathe. She told herself to either get out of the car or power down a window, but her body refused to obey a single, simple command.

The scorching ninety-five degrees baking the city's asphalt and concrete had invaded the interior of the car about two seconds after she parked and shut off the engine. That appeared to be of little consequence to whatever reason she still possessed considering that ten minutes later her fingers were still locked around the steering wheel as if the final hours of her two-day drive had triggered the onset of rigor mortis.

She was *home*. Two weeks' worth of long overdue

leave was at her disposal. Her mail was on hold at the post office back in Stafford, Virginia, where absolutely no one would miss her. Still, she hesitated in taking the next step. Changing her mind and driving away was out of the question, no matter how desperately she wanted to do exactly that.

Her word was all she had left at this point. The sheer enormity of her current circumstances should have her laughing hysterically, but the muscles of her throat had constricted in equal parts disbelief and terror.

Screw this up and there's nothing left.

With a deep breath for courage, she relaxed her death grip, grabbed her bag, and climbed out. A horn honked a warning and she flattened against the dusty fender of her decade-old Audi. Cars and trucks whizzed by, determined to make the Eighteenth Street and First Avenue intersection before the traffic light changed. Exhaust fumes lingered in the humid air, mingling with the heat and the noise of downtown.

She barely recognized the heart of Birmingham. Renovated shops from a bygone era and newer, gleaming buildings stood side by side, their facades softened by carefully placed trees and shrubbery. An elegant park complete with a spectacular fountain welcomed strolling shoppers and relaxing picnickers. Great strides had been taken to transform the gritty streets of the city once recognized as the infamous center of the civil rights movement to a genteel version of a proud Southern town.

What the hell was she doing here?

For twenty-two years she had worked harder than a prized pupil of Henry Higgins himself to alter her speech patterns and to swipe the last damned trace of the South from her voice. A master's degree in psychology from Boston College and seventeen years of relentless dedication to build an admirable career distinguished her résumé.

And for what? To come running back with her tail tucked between her legs and her head hanging low enough to the ground to smell the ugly truth.

Nothing had changed.

All the spritzing fountains and meticulously manicured storefronts couldn't hide the fact that this was still Birmingham—the place she'd put in her rearview mirror at eighteen—and the four-hundred-dollar red suit and matching high heels she wore would not conceal her plunge from grace.

He had called and she had promised to come and have a look at his case. It was the first time he'd asked her for anything since they parted ways after college. That he extended any sort of invitation astonished her and provided a much needed self-esteem boost. No one from her hometown had a clue about her current career debacle or the disaster zone that was her personal life. If she had her way, they would never know. The million-dollar question, however, remained: What did she do after this?

The wind from a passing car flapped her skirt around her legs, reminding her that this curbside parking slot was not exactly the place to conduct a cerebral overview of *This Is Your Life*.

Game face in place, her shoulders squared with determination, she strode to the Birmingham Police Department's main entrance. Another bout of hesitation slowed her but she kicked it aside, opened the door, and presented a smile for the security guard. "Good morning."

"Good morning to you, too, ma'am," said the guard, Elroy Carter according to the name tag pinned to his shirt. "I'll need your ID. You can place your bag here." He indicated the table next to him.

Jess handed over her official credentials and placed her bag as directed for inspection. Since she'd stopped bothering with earrings years ago and the gold band she still wore for reasons that continued to escape her didn't set off any alarms except in her head, she walked through the metal detector and waited on the other side for her bag.

"Enjoy your visit to the Magic City, Agent Harris." Another broad smile brightened the big man's face.

Probably retired Birmingham PD, undeniably Southern through and through. He obviously took pride in his work, past and present, and likely carried a wallet full of photos of his grandchildren. The only trait that wouldn't be readily discernible by way of a passing inspection was whether he was an Auburn or an Alabama fan. By September that, too, would be as clear as the rich color of his brown eyes. In Alabama, college football season turned even the closest of friends into fierce rivals.

"Thank you, Mr. Carter."

Extending a please, welcome, and thank you remained a stalwart Southern tradition. On the etiquette scale, the idea of passing a stranger without at least smiling ranked right below blasphemy. Keeping up with your neighbor's or coworker's business wasn't viewed as meddling. Not at all. It was the right thing to do. Concern was, of course, the motive.

Jess would give it twenty-four hours max before speculation about her business became the subject of water-cooler talk. Then the sympathetic glances would begin. Along with the reassuring smiles and the total pretense that everything was fine.

Fine. Fine. Fine.

As much as she wanted to avoid her dirty laundry being aired, the odds of complete circumvention fell along the lines of being hit by falling satellite debris twice in the same day. Once the news hit the AP there would be no stopping or even slowing the media frenzy.

Her life was a mess. She doubted any aspect of her existence would ever be *fine* again. But that was irrelevant at the moment. She was here to advise on a case—one that wouldn't wait for her to gather up the pieces of her life or for her to lick her wounds.

Jess set those worries aside, steeled herself, and headed for the bank of elevators that would take her to the fourth floor. *To him.*

None of the faces she encountered looked familiar. Not the guard who'd processed her in or either of his colleagues monitoring the lobby and not the woman who joined her in the elevator car to make the trip to Birmingham Police Department's administrative offices.

Once the doors glided closed, the woman attempted a covert inspection, taking note of Jess's Mary Jane pumps with their four-inch heels, the swath of skin separating the hem of her pencil skirt from the tops of her knees and the leather bag that had been her gift to herself on her fortieth birthday. When eye contact inevitably happened, a faint smile flashed, a superficial pleasantry intended to disguise the sizing-up of competition. *If she only knew.*

The car bumped to a stop. The other woman exited first and strolled down the long corridor on the right. Jess's destination waited straight ahead. The office of the chief of police. At the door she conducted a final inventory of her appearance in the glass, straightened her belted jacket, and plucked a blond hair from her lapel. She looked ... the same. Didn't she? Her hand fell to her side.

Did she look like a failure? Like the woman who had just provided a heinous killer with a get-out-of-jail-free card and who'd lost her husband to geography?

Deep breath. She reached for the door sporting the name Daniel T. Burnett and passed the point of no return.

"Good afternoon, Agent Harris." The young woman, Tara Morgan according to the nameplate on her desk, smiled. "Welcome to Birmingham."

Since Jess hadn't introduced herself, she assumed that the chief had ensured his office personnel would recognize his anticipated visitor. "Thank you. I'm here to see Chief Burnett."

"Yes, ma'am. If you'd like to have a seat, I'll let the chief know you've arrived."

At last, Tara politely left off. Jess was late by twelve minutes, most of which had been spent fortifying her resolve and gathering her composure to face the final buffeting winds of the emotional hurricane that had descended upon her life. The receptionist offered water or a soft drink. Jess declined. Getting anything, even water, past the massive lump lodged firmly in her throat was unlikely. Keeping it down, an unmitigated no-go.

Jess used the intervening time to evaluate the changes Birmingham's newest chief had made since taking over the office of top cop. From the marble-floored entry to the classic beige carpet and walls, the tranquil lobby looked less like the anteroom to the chief of police and more like the waiting area of a prestigious surgeon's office. Though she hadn't been in this office since career day back in high school, the decorating and furnishings were far too fresh to have seen more than a couple years' wear.

Law enforcement and political journals rested in a crisp stack atop the table flanked by two plush, upholstered chairs. The fabric resembled a European tapestry and carried the distinct flavor of his mother's taste. It wasn't enough she'd influenced the decorating scheme of the palatial homes belonging to select members of Birmingham's elite simply by hosting a grand soiree and inviting the city's who's who list. Katherine Burnett set the gold standard for keeping up with the Joneses.

Jess wondered if the fine citizens of Birmingham approved of such wasteful use of their tax dollars. Knowing Katherine, she had paid for the renovation herself and spelled it all out on the front page of the lifestyle section of the *Birmingham News*.

Just another example of how nothing changed around here. Ever. Jess deposited her bag into a chair and stretched her travel-cramped muscles. Eight grueling hours on the road on Tuesday and four this morning had taken its toll. She was exhausted. A flight would have provided far more efficient transportation, but she preferred to have her car while she was here. Made the potential for escape much more feasible.

Actually she'd needed time to think.

"You made it."

Whether it was the sound of his voice or the idea that he looked better now, in spite of current circumstances, than he had on Christmas Eve ten years ago, she suddenly felt very fragile and unquestionably old. His dark hair was still thick without even a hint of gray. The elegant navy suit he wore brought out the blue in his eyes. But it was his face, leaner than before but no less handsome, that conveyed the most damage to her brittle psyche.

The weight of the past seventy-two hours crashed down on her in one big knee-weakening wallop. The floor shifted beneath her feet and the urge to run into his strong arms or to simply burst into tears made a fleeting but powerful appearance.

But she wasn't that kid anymore. And they...they were little more than strangers.

She managed a stiff nod. "I did."

Funny how they both avoided calling each other by name. Not funny at all was the idea that five seconds in his presence had the two little words she'd uttered sounding as Southern as the day she'd hit the road after high school graduation.

She cleared her throat. "And I'm ready to get to work. First, I'd like some time to review the files."

"Of course." He offered his hand, then drew it back and gestured awkwardly as if belatedly realizing that touching was not a good idea. "Shall we go to my office?"

"Absolutely." She draped her bag over her shoulder and moved toward him, each step a supreme test of her self-control. Things that hadn't been said and should have battled with the numerous other troubles clashing in her head for priority. *This wasn't the time.*

"Coming all this way to help us figure this out means a great deal to me."

Still skirting her name. Jess pushed aside the confusion or frustration, maybe both, and the weariness and matched his stride as he led the way. "I can't make any promises but I'll do what I can."

He hadn't given her many details over the phone; that he had called at all was proof enough of the gravity of the situation.

He introduced her to his personal secretary, then ushered her into his office and closed the door. Like the lobby, his spacious office smacked of Katherine's touch. Jess placed her bag on the floor next to a chair at the small conference table and surveyed the four case files waiting in grim formation for her inspection. Clipped to the front of each jacket was a photo of a missing girl.

This was why she had come all this way. However much his call gratified her ego, piecing together this puzzle was her ultimate goal. She leaned forward to study the attractive faces. Four young women in the space of two and a half weeks had disappeared, the latest just three days ago. No common threads other than age, no suggestion of foul play, not a hint of evidence left behind. Macy York, Callie Fanning, Reanne Parsons, and Andrea Denton had simply vanished.

"These two are Jefferson County residents." He tapped the first and second photos; Macy and Callie were both blondes. "This one's Tuscaloosa." Reanne, a redhead. "The latest is from Mountain Brook, my jurisdiction." The fourth girl, Andrea, was a brunette and his attention idled there an extra moment or two.

Jess lowered into a chair. She opened the files, one by one, and reviewed the meager contents. Interviews with family and friends. Photos and reports from the scenes. All but one of the missing, Reanne, were college students.

"No contact with the families? No sightings?"

She looked up, the need to assess his facial expressions as he answered a force of habit. His full attention rested on the files for a time before settling on her. The weight of the public service position he held had scored lines at the corners of his eyes and mouth. Lines that hadn't been there ten years ago. Funny how those same sorts of lines just made her look old, but on him they lent an air of distinction.

He shook his head in response to her question.

"No credit card or cell phone trails?" she went on. "No good-bye or suicide notes? No ransom demands?"

"Nothing."

With a fluidity and ease that spoke of confidence as well as physical strength and fitness, he propped one hip on the edge of the table and studied her, those familiar blue eyes searching hers as blatantly as she had assessed his seconds ago. "Sheriff Roy Griggs—you may remember him—and Chief Bruce Patterson in Tuscaloosa are doing all they can, but there's nowhere to go. The bureau won't budge on the issue of age of consent. All four of these girls are nineteen or over, and with the lack of evidence to indicate foul play there's nothing to investigate, in their opinion. File the report, add the photos to the various databases, and wait. That's what they can do."

According to the law, the bureau was correct. Unless there was evidence of foul play or vulnerability to a crime, there was no action the bureau or any law enforcement agency could take. He knew this, but his cop instincts or his emotions, she hadn't concluded which yet, wouldn't let it go at that. And she did remember Griggs. He had served as Jefferson County sheriff for the past three decades.

"But you think there's a connection that suggests this is not only criminal but perhaps serial." This wasn't a question. He'd told her as much on the phone, but she needed to hear his conclusion again and to see what his face and eyes had to show about his words.

His call, just hearing his voice, had resurrected memories and feelings she'd thought long dead and buried. They hadn't spoken since the summer after college graduation until ten years ago, when they bumped into each other at the Publix in Hoover. Of all the grocery stores in the Birmingham area how they'd ended up at the same one on the first holiday she'd spent with her family in years still befuddled her. He had been newly divorced from his second wife. Jess had been celebrating a promotion. A volatile combination when merged with the holiday mania and the nostalgia of their explosive history. The last-minute dessert she had hoped to grab at the market before dinner with her sister's family had never made it to the table.

Jess hadn't heard from him since. Not that she could fault his after-frantic-sex lack of propriety; she'd made no attempt at contact either. There had been no random shopping ventures since on her rare visits to Birmingham.

"There has to be a connection." He surveyed the happy, carefree faces in the photos again. "Same age group. All attractive. Smart. No records, criminal or otherwise. Their entire futures—bright futures—ahead of them. And no one in their circle of family or friends saw a disappearing act coming." He tapped the fourth girl's photo. "I know Andrea Denton personally. There's no way she would just vanish like this. No way."

Two things registered distinctly as he made this passionate declaration. One, he wasn't wearing a wedding band. Two, he didn't just know number four personally. He knew her intimately on some level.

"Someone took her," he insisted. "Someone took them

all." His expression softened a fraction. "I know your profiling reputation. If anyone can help us find these girls, it's you."

A genuine smile tugged at the frown Jess had been wearing most waking hours for days now. She had absolutely nothing to smile about but somehow the compliment coming from him roused the reaction. "That might be a bit of a stretch, Chief." Sitting here with him staring down at her so intently felt entirely too familiar...too personal. She stood, leveling the playing field. "And even the best can't create something out of nothing and, unfortunately, that's exactly what you appear to have so far."

"All I'm asking is that you try. These girls"—he gestured to the files—"deserve whatever we can do."

He'd get no argument from her there. "You know the statistics." If they had in fact been abducted, the chances of finding one or more alive at this stage were minimal at best. The only good thing she could see was that they didn't have a body. *Yet.*

"I do." He dipped his head in a weary, somber move, emphasizing the grave tone of his voice.

Eventually she would learn the part he was leaving out. No one wanted to admit there was nothing to be done when anyone went missing, particularly a child or young adult. But this urgency and unwavering insistence that foul play was involved went beyond basic human compassion and the desire to get the job done. She could feel his anxiety and worry vibrating with escalating intensity.

"Will your counterparts cooperate?" Kicking a hornet's nest when it came to jurisdiction would compound her already complicated situation. That she could do without. Once the news hit the public domain, there would be trouble enough.

"They'll cooperate. You have my word."

Jess had known Daniel Burnett her whole life. He believed there was more here than met the eye in these seemingly random disappearances. Unless emotion was somehow slanting his assessment, his instincts rarely missed the mark. More than twenty years ago he had known she was going to part ways with him well before she had recognized that unexpected path herself, and he had known she was his for the taking that cold, blustery evening in that damned Publix. She would lay odds on his instincts every time.

She just hadn't ever been able to count on him when it came to choosing her over his own personal and career goals. As ancient as that history was, the hole it left in her heart had never completely healed. Even knowing that hard truth, she held her breath, waiting for what came next.

"I need your help, Jess."

Jess. The smooth, deep nuances of his voice whispered over her skin and just like that it was ten years ago all over again.

Only this time, she would make certain they didn't end up in bed together.

THE DISH

Where authors give you the inside scoop!

♥ ♥ ♥ ♥ ♥ ♥ ♥ ♥ ♥ ♥ ♥ ♥ ♥ ♥ ♥ ♥

From the desk of Hope Ramsay

Dear Reader,

I have three brothers and no sisters. So when I was young, I read a lot of "boy" books—mostly having to do with space travel. When I reached the ripe age of thirteen, my aunt decided I needed to have my horizons broadened. She put three "girly" books in my hand: *Pride and Prejudice*, *Jane Eyre*, and *Little Women*. Need I say more?

I was hooked the moment I read the immortal line: "It is a truth universally acknowledged, that a single man in possession of a good fortune must be in want of a wife."

Holy moly, I had no idea what I was missing!

So it's not surprising that I turned to these favorite books when I decided to write a series featuring members of the Last Chance Book Club.

In the first book in this series, LAST CHANCE BOOK CLUB, the ladies of the club decide to read *Pride and Prejudice*. And before long some of them are finding some interesting similarities between the book and their lives.

In the beginning of my story, the hero and heroine dislike each other intensely. Like Darcy, Savannah White has come to Last Chance from the big city. She's there to renovate the old run-down theater. Dash Randall, like Lizzy Bennett, isn't at all pleased with this new arrival in town. Dash thinks Savannah is a stuck-up snob. And she thinks he's a no-account good ol' boy. My hero is the one with the snarky sense of humor, and my heroine the one with the preconceived notions that will have to soften. Even though my plot and setting are wildly different from Austen's, the underlying theme of pride and prejudice is what makes the love story of Dash and Savannah so much fun. I've also included a few other Austen-inspired complications, like a minister who is looking for a wife, a whole passel of matchmaking matrons, and a street dance that's surprisingly like the Netherfield Ball.

I had such a fun time writing this story. It allowed me to connect in a much deeper way with one of my old favorites. I'm sure Jane Austen fans will enjoy searching for the Easter eggs I've sprinkled through the book. But even if you aren't an Austen fan, you're still going to love this story about a couple who discover the hidden depths of character in each other as they grow from enemies to friends to lovers.

Hope Ramsay

♥ ♥ ♥ ♥ ♥ ♥ ♥ ♥ ♥ ♥ ♥ ♥ ♥ ♥ ♥

From the desk of Debra Webb

Dear Reader,

I am so thrilled to be sharing the Faces of Evil adventure with you! This series has lived for several years in my heart. I can't tell you how pleased I am to be working with the fabulous folks at Forever to bring these stories to you.

I grew up in Alabama with deep roots in Birmingham. While my husband served in the army, we traveled far and wide, but Alabama was still home and we were most happy to return. Many years would pass before I realized that Alabama was not only home for me but also a place with a rich past and a vibrant present perfect for the setting of suspense stories. I zeroed in on Birmingham, where much of Alabama's most volatile and notorious history has taken place. Being no stranger to the city, it was easy to settle in and have my characters experiencing all sorts of dilemmas in the Magic City.

Birmingham also holds a special place in my heart for its renowned Children's Hospital and incredible doctors. When my first child was born she was in serious trouble and in need of immediate surgery—a surgery that was her only hope for survival and at the same time a procedure she was unlikely to survive. The quick thinking of my small-town doctor, Dr. Louis Letson, got her straightaway to Birmingham in the hands of a revered pediatric surgeon. Dr. Letson's decisive action and the unparalleled skill of the folks at Birmingham's Children's Hospital saved my daughter's life. Eight weeks later the tiny girl who changed our lives proved to one and all that she had come into this world to live. And thirty-six years later she is still living life with immense passion. As you can see, Birmingham really is the Magic City!

Please watch for all twelve installments of the Faces of Evil series featuring Jess Harris and Dan Burnett and their journey through a maze of evils to find the love and happiness they both deserve.

Best,

Debra Webb

Find out more about Forever Romance!

Visit us at
www.hachettebookgroup.com/publishing_forever.aspx

Find us on Facebook
http://www.facebook.com/ForeverRomance

Follow us on Twitter
http://twitter.com/ForeverRomance

NEW AND UPCOMING TITLES

Each month we feature our new titles
and reader favorites.

CONTESTS AND GIVEAWAYS

We give away galleys, autographed copies,
and all kinds of exclusive items.

AUTHOR INFO

You'll find bios, articles, and links to personal websites
for all your favorite authors—and so much more.

GET SOCIAL

Connect with your favorite authors, editors, and
other Forever fans, and share what's important to you.

THE BUZZ

Sign up for our monthly romance newsletter,
and be the first to read all about it.

VISIT US ONLINE AT

WWW.HACHETTEBOOKGROUP.COM

FEATURES:

**OPENBOOK BROWSE AND
SEARCH EXCERPTS**

•

AUDIOBOOK EXCERPTS AND PODCASTS

•

AUTHOR ARTICLES AND INTERVIEWS

•

**BESTSELLER AND PUBLISHING
GROUP NEWS**

•

SIGN UP FOR E-NEWSLETTERS

•

**AUTHOR APPEARANCES AND TOUR
INFORMATION**

•

SOCIAL MEDIA FEEDS AND WIDGETS

•

DOWNLOAD FREE APPS

BOOKMARK HACHETTE BOOK GROUP
@ WWW.HACHETTEBOOKGROUP.COM